Beyond all Measure

Center Point
Large Print

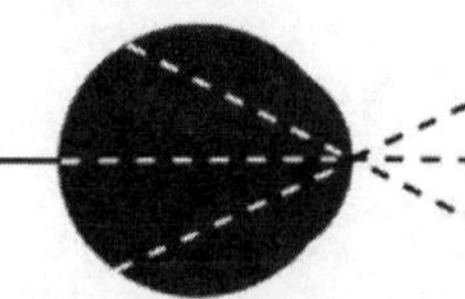

This Large Print Book carries the
Seal of Approval of N.A.V.H.

Beyond all Measure

DOROTHY LOVE

CENTER POINT LARGE PRINT
THORNDIKE, MAINE

This Center Point Large Print edition
is published in the year 2011 by arrangement with
Thomas Nelson Publishers.

The text of this Large Print edition is unabridged.
In other aspects, this book may vary
from the original edition.
Printed in the United States of America
on permanent paper.
Set in 16-point Times New Roman type.

ISBN: 978-1-61173-103-3

Library of Congress Cataloging-in-Publication Data

Love, Dorothy, 1949–
Beyond all measure : a Hickory Ridge romance / Dorothy Love.
p. cm.
ISBN 978-1-61173-103-3 (library binding : alk. paper)
1. Tennessee—Fiction. 2. Large type books. I. Title.
PS3562.O8387B49 2011b
813′.54—dc22

2011009196

For the brave and faithful women of the South,
past and present—heroines all

He Whose heart is kind beyond all measure
Gives unto each day what He deems best—
Lovingly, its part of pain and pleasure,
Mingling toil with peace and rest.

Carolina Sandell Berg,

"Day by Day" (c. 1865)

One

Hickory Ridge, Tennessee
June 1871

Holding tightly to her worn travel satchel, Ada Wentworth stepped through a cloud of billowing steam and scanned the rain-slicked railway platform, looking for the woman who had promised to meet her. Smartly-dressed travelers folded their black umbrellas and pushed through a knot of farm wives, mill workers, and station peddlers hawking candy and magazines. A line of buggies and wagons waited in the heat, the placid horses swishing their tails against a cloud of flies. A group of schoolboys jostled Ada roughly as they passed, their languid, high-pitched accents falling strangely on her ear.

She pulled her handkerchief from her cuff and blotted her face, her gaze traveling from one person to the next. People aplenty, but no red-haired woman carrying a white parasol.

She skirted a mound of baggage and wound her way toward the agent's office, trying to quell her growing apprehension. She'd known Hickory Ridge wouldn't be anything like New England, but this bustling village rimmed with fog-shrouded mountains was unlike any place she'd ever been.

Outside the station agent's office, she paused to get her bearings. A steady stream of travelers flowed around her like water around a stone. She swallowed the hard lump forming in her throat. What on earth had she done?

"Purty little town, Hickory Ridge, ain't it?" The salesman who had slept away the entire morning's journey leaning against her shoulder grinned at her, exposing a mouthful of rotted and tobacco-stained teeth. "Hotter'n blazes, though. Rain didn't do a bit of good if you ask me."

Ada moved farther down the platform and brushed the cinders from her traveling dress. The salesman followed, his battered sample case banging against his knee. He tipped his hat, a brown felt bowler that had seen better days. "Name's Cyrus McNeal, ma'am. From the Southern Medicinal Supply Company. Any type of curative, preventative, or tonic you may require, I'm yer man."

Opening his case, he produced two small brown vials. "Would you like some free samples? One's fer yer stummick ailments, and t'other calms yer nerves."

"Thank you. No."

"Suit yerself. There's more'n two hours before my train to Nashville. I figger to have me a good hot meal at Miss Hattie's. You care to join me?"

The station agent, a lanky man with a thick walrus mustache and graying hair parted in the middle, made his way to her side. “Is this here feller botherin’ you, Miss?”

The salesman dropped his samples into his pocket. “I was just leaving.”

Ada nodded to the agent as the salesman disappeared into the crowd. “Thank you. That tiresome man made a nuisance of himself all the way from Knoxville.”

He gestured toward the far end of the platform. “That your trunk?”

“Yes.” She suppressed a long sigh. Twenty-six years old, and all her worldly possessions fit into one moldering trunk. Given half a chance, the auctioneer would have taken it too. As it was, she had nothing, not even a proper mourning dress. But mourning clothes were of no consequence here at the edge of the livable world.

The agent wiped his forehead with a wrinkled blue handkerchief. “Is someone supposed to meet you?”

“Miss Hannah Fields. She wrote that she’d carry a white parasol so I could recognize her. I don’t suppose you know her.”

“Hickory Ridge is growin’ these days, but I pretty much know everybody around here. Miss Hannah should be along directly. That is, if Old Starch and Vinegar hasn’t thought up somethin’ else for her to do.”

“Starch and vinegar?”

“Mrs. Willis. The woman Miss Hannah works

for. Folks call her Starch and Vinegar, but not to her face, o' course." He grinned. "No ma'am. Not to her face."

A piercing whistle sounded. The engine heaved, belching smoke and cinders, and lumbered down the tracks. Another shower of sparks rained down. Ada brushed the ashes off her skirt. Now she regretted having worn her best dress for travel, but she needed this job desperately. First impressions were important.

Her stomach rumbled. Although there had been plenty of good food aboard the train, it had come at a price. Mindful of her swiftly dwindling resources, Ada had made do with bowls of lukewarm soup and cups of bitter hot chocolate as the train lumbered southward, taking her farther away from all that was familiar. She couldn't remember when she'd last enjoyed a full, hot meal. Hungry and dazed with summer heat, she swayed on her feet.

"Careful, ma'am!" The agent took her arm and led her to a wooden bench on the shady side of the platform. "You just sit tight, and I'll get you some water."

Ada sank heavily onto the bench. Last evening, as Miss Fields's letter had instructed, she had sent a wire giving the woman her arrival time. Where in blazes *was* she? Ada blotted her face again and fought a wave of panic. Suppose the offer of employment had been withdrawn? It had taken most of her cash just to make the long trip to Hickory Ridge. There wasn't nearly enough for a return ticket.

Not that returning home was an option. Ada's heart squeezed with sadness. She tucked away her handkerchief and blinked back sudden tears.

The agent returned with a glass of water, and she drank it gratefully.

"Better?" he asked.

"Yes. Much better. Thank you."

He consulted his pocket watch. "I should get back to the office. You're welcome to wait inside if you've a mind to, but the truth is, it's cooler out here. I'm sure Miss Hannah will be along before too much longer."

He went back inside. Restless with nerves, Ada rose and walked to the far end of the platform, which afforded a better view of the town. The streets rang with the clatter of horses' hooves, the rattle of harnesses, and the faint tinkling of shopdoor bells. Along one side of the street stood the mercantile, and next to it a bank with gold lettering on the windows. Farther down was a newspaper office and a dentist's office. A haberdashery, a barbershop, and a bookshop occupied the opposite side of the street, next to the Hickory Ridge Inn. Behind the newspaper office sat the Verandah Hotel for Ladies, a faded blue building with drooping shutters and a weathered sign that hung unevenly from a rusty chain. In the distance, the tree-clad mountains stood like sentinels against the rain-washed sky.

Of course Hickory Ridge can't compete with Chattanooga or Knoxville, Hannah had written, *but for a small town we're quite progressive.*

Ada watched two women in old-fashioned poke bonnets emerge from the mercantile, their arms laden with packages. A progressive town was precisely what she needed to secure her future. Not that she planned to stay forever in Hickory Ridge. But the employment notice in the *Boston Herald* had seemed the perfect solution to her immediate dilemma. A chance to start over in a town where no one knew the first thing about her while she set her plan in motion.

It had seemed simple enough. Now she was much less certain that she'd made the right decision. It was one thing to make a plan and quite another to put it into action.

A buckboard rattled down the street and came to a stop near the elevated platform. The driver, a man in rough clothes, boots, and a wide-brimmed hat, smiled up at her. Backlit by the sun, he appeared muscular and broad shouldered. "Miss Wentworth? Ada Wentworth?"

"Yes."

"I'm Wyatt Caldwell. I'm here to drive you out to Miss Lillian's place."

"But I thought Miss Fields was coming for me."

He smiled, crinkling the lines around his eyes.

"Yes ma'am, that was the plan." He scanned the now-deserted platform. "I assume that trunk is yours?"

"Yes." Ada took a deep breath to steady her nerves. Where was Hannah Fields? Had Old Starch and Vinegar dismissed her without any warning? Another wave of anxiety rippled through her. If that happened to *her,* where would she go? Her resources were nearly depleted. Letters to her mother's Southern cousins had gone unanswered, leaving her with few options apart from the clattering, stifling textile mills of Lowell, Massachusetts —or, even worse, a life as a mail-order bride, brought west to cook and clean and bear children for a man she'd never met.

Her escort, his face shadowed by a battered Stetson, jumped lightly to the ground. Shoving aside a stack of wooden planks and a couple of gleaming saw blades, he hoisted Ada's trunk into the back of the wagon.

"Ma'am, are you ready? Miss Lillian's place is a good seven miles down this road. We ought to get going."

Ada sized him up. He appeared trustworthy, but experience had shown her that people weren't always what they seemed. "Thank you, but I'll wait for Miss Fields."

"Then you're going to be waiting for quite a while. Hannah Fields up and left town last night without so much as a by-your-leave." He smiled. "I'm afraid you're stuck with me."

He offered his hand to help her onto the buckboard seat and climbed up beside her. "I apologize for the undignified conveyance. I didn't know until an hour ago that you were expected today. There wasn't time to fetch my rig." He handed her a parasol and a bundle wrapped in a red-checked tea towel. "I brought you some of Miss Hattie's fried chicken. I figured you'd be hungry."

"Thank you. I am famished!" Leaving the parasol on the seat between them, Ada unwrapped the chicken, bit into a drumstick, and chewed with relish.

Her Boston aunt, rest her soul, would be horrified at such undignified behavior. She could almost hear Kate's chiding voice. *"That's why you've never made a suitable match, Ada. You're too forthright. Too lacking in the feminine graces."*

Well, she had made a perfect match once, but now she was alone in the world. She would do as she pleased. As the buckboard gathered speed, she devoured the second piece of chicken, polished the apple on the sleeve of her jacket, and took a bite, enjoying the satisfying and decidedly unladylike crunch.

"You *are* hungry!" Wyatt said. "Hollow all the way to your toes."

Ada blushed and then chided herself for caring what he thought.

"That's all right," he added. "I like a woman with an appetite."

Ada took another bite.

"So, you came out here from Boston." His friendly demeanor seemed to have cooled a little. Not surprising in a Southern town, so soon after the war—and from his voice, Mr. Caldwell was obviously a Southerner.

Oh well. She lifted her chin a little. She could only hope to do her job and eventually win over the townsfolk.

They passed the ladies' hotel. Two white-haired women sat on the porch. Wyatt nodded to them and touched the brim of his hat as they passed. The buckboard rattled onto a narrow rutted road that led upward into the foothills.

"Yes, Boston." Ada wiped apple juice from the corner of her mouth. "The land of steady habits, as they say."

He nodded. "Miss Lillian will appreciate that. She's a stickler for order."

She took another crunchy bite.

"Your letter said you were born there?"

"Yes. I lived there off and on for most of my life." A wave of bitter recrimination and regret nearly brought her to tears. Determined not to dwell on the life that was lost to her, she concentrated on the play of sunlight in the rain puddles beside the road and on the soothing sound of his voice as he pointed out clumps of wild honeysuckle, their pale blossoms shimmering like ghosts.

"You're sure a long way from home," he observed. "Hannah placed the ad in the *Boston Herald* as a last resort. She was surprised to actually receive an application from so far away."

Ada chewed slowly. "My father and my aunt died in March, and I need to make a new start. This position as lady's companion to Mrs. Willis seemed suitable." She turned toward him, her skirts rustling against the rough wood of the seat. "Tell me, Mr. Caldwell, do you know anything about the rest of the household staff? The cook and so on?"

"The—" He threw back his head and laughed. The horse snorted as if he, too, found her words amusing.

Something snapped inside her. "Stop this wagon!"

"Beg your pardon?"

"I said stop this wagon, Mr. Caldwell, or so help me, I will jump."

"Oh, I'm sorry." He surveyed the empty road. "The closest outhouse is down the road a ways, at the Spencer place. But the woods are—"

"I am not in need of the out—the ladies' facilities."

"Then what—"

"I have no intention of spending the next several hours, or however long this dreadful journey takes, riding next to a man who laughs at me."

"You're right. I apologize."

"Too late." She stood and braced herself against the movement of the buckboard.

"Whoa!" He pulled on the reins. The horse stopped and tossed his head, rattling the harness. "Just how do you intend on getting out to Mrs. Willis's place, if I may ask?"

"I'll walk."

"All that way?"

Without another word she dangled her legs over the side of the wagon and dropped to the ground, wincing as her feet made contact with the dirt road. Squaring her shoulders, she marched ahead of the wagon.

Wyatt slowed the buckboard and studied her as she set out along the road, her feathered traveling hat perilously askew, her arms swinging. A prettier woman he'd never seen, but she sure was prickly.

Miss Ada Wentworth had the fairest skin he'd ever laid eyes on. Dark-brown hair that lay in shiny waves beneath her hat. Wide gray eyes fringed with thick, dark lashes. A generous mouth that would be even lovelier if she'd smile more. But, as she was in mourning, he really couldn't fault her for that. She was wrapped in a neat package, he couldn't help noticing—small and compact, with hills and valleys in all the proper locations.

He guided the buckboard around a deep rut in the road, reining in the horse to avoid getting ahead of Ada. She was nearly perfect, from his point of view—if only she weren't a Boston blue blood. He'd checked out her references and discovered that she was from an old New England family. A family with connections and power.

A family that represented everything he detested.

She slipped and then regained her footing. He fought the urge to scoop her up and set her back into the buckboard. She might be a Yankee born and bred, and she was acting tough as nails, but she couldn't mask the hurt and vulnerability beneath her brave facade.

He flicked the reins and pulled up alongside her. "I didn't mean to offend you, ma'am. Honestly. It was your question about the staff and the cook that hit my funny bone."

She kept her eyes on the ribbon of road in front of them. She'd begun to limp and was trying hard not to show it. Wyatt glanced at the delicate spooled heels of her thin leather shoes. He didn't know the first thing about ladies' footwear, but any fool could see that those shoes were meant for city streets, not seven-mile hikes over a rutted country road.

"You sure don't sound like a regular Bostonian." He raised his voice to be heard over the creaking of the wagon wheels. "I kinda like the way you talk, if you don't mind my saying so."

Ada walked on.

"Miss Wentworth?"

She stopped, arms akimbo, and stared up at him. "What is it, Mr. Caldwell?"

"My lumber mill is just over that next hill. It will be embarrassing if I have to drive past there with a pretty woman walking alongside the wagon. My men won't ever let me live that down. I sure would be obliged if you'd reconsider and come on back up here. I promise to be on my best behavior."

Two

Ada shaded her eyes with one hand. Already a painful blister had formed on one toe. Undoubtedly, she'd need a salt soak and a camphor patch tonight. But she wasn't about to let this infuriating Southerner get the best of her, no matter how charming his smile. "Why should I care what they think?"

"I guess you're right. Never mind." He flicked the reins and urged the horse onward.

Ada's toe was on fire. She could feel blood oozing into her stocking. Her blouse was drenched in sweat, and a thick layer of dust coated the hem of her skirt. Maybe she would ride with him now, at least until he made her angry again.

She hurried alongside the wagon. "Very well. I'll ride with you."

He looked down at her. "I'm sorry. Did you say something?"

She ground her teeth. "You're enjoying this, aren't you?"

A wide grin split his tanned face. “Maybe.”

He jumped down, ran around the buckboard, and lifted her onto the seat. Settling himself beside her again, he snapped the reins, and the horse set off at a brisk trot. “Do you mind if I ask you a question?”

She rested her throbbing foot and retrieved the parasol he had brought. “What is it?”

“You’re from Boston, but there’s more than a trace of the South in your speech. I’m wondering why.”

“I spent a lot of time with my mother’s family in New Orleans when I was growing up. Their accent rubbed off on me—much to my father’s chagrin.”

“What did he have against New Orleans? It’s a great city. And Louisiana gumbo makes one fine meal.”

Ada shook her head. There was no explaining Cornelius Wentworth. She’d never understood him.

“Guess it’s none of my business,” he said. “I was just making conversation, trying to make you feel at home.”

She brushed away sudden tears. “Boston is home.”

“I know exactly how you feel.” Wyatt guided the wagon around another rut in the road. Above the jingle of the harness, he said, “Myself, I was born and raised on a cattle ranch west of Fort Worth. As far as I’m concerned, Texas is the best patch of earth ever created. But after the war, I was needed here. I started a lumber business that’s doing real well.”

"Miss Fields said as much in her letter. She said the entire town has grown since the war ended."

"Folks say we might be headed for some bad times in Tennessee, but for now, Hickory Ridge is doing all right. Still, I'm going to sell the mill one of these days and buy myself a piece of Texas. Build up the best herd of longhorns in the state." He glanced at her. "Do you know anything about cattle, Miss Wentworth?"

She sighed. Creation, but this man was a talker! "I'm afraid not."

"Longhorns are a cross between the stock the Spanish explorers left behind and the English stock folks brought down from the north and the east," he began, obviously relishing the chance to enlighten her. "They're one of the toughest breeds there is, which makes 'em ideal for the trail. They have an instinct for finding food and shelter in bad weather, and the cows produce offspring for a good long time."

Even though she hadn't completely forgiven him for making fun of her and for ignoring her question about the Willis household, Ada couldn't help smiling at his boyish enthusiasm for all things bovine.

Wyatt went on. "Now that the war is over, the demand for cattle on the northern ranches oughta go sky high. A man with a healthy herd will do right well for himself." He grinned. "But that's all in the future, of course. My mama always said to bloom where you're planted, and for the present, I'm planted right here in Hickory Ridge."

Ada nodded. It felt strangely intimate to see this stranger's enthusiasm and know his plans for his future. What would he think of her own plans?

The buckboard passed through a stand of hickory trees so thick that it momentarily blotted out the sun. Moisture dripped onto the thick moss below. Bees droned in the sedge beside the road. As they emerged again into the patchy sunlight, Ada felt parched inside and out. Already she regretted her decision to move south. She missed the sight of the ships in Boston Harbor and the cool morning mist rising off the river. Here, she felt caged, the forest hemming her in.

The feeling had crept upon her three days into her journey, when the rails turned westward and then south, revealing the remnants of the brutal war that back in Boston had seemed so remote it might as well have happened on another continent. From the sooty windows of the train, she'd glimpsed once-prosperous farms now ravaged and burned to the ground, denuded forests, broken breastworks rotting in the sun. Here and there lay rows of grass-covered mounds—obviously the graves of fallen soldiers. An aching sadness seemed to lie over the land, intensifying her own sense of loss.

Wyatt cleared his throat. "I'd best fill you in on Aunt Lillian before we get there."

"*Aunt* Lillian?"

"By marriage. I took over her affairs a few years ago."

Her anger flared again. "Then *you're* my employer?"

"Technically. I put money into her account and she takes it out. It makes her feel that she still has some control over things."

She stuck out her bottom lip and blew her sticky curls upward. "For the love of Pete! You might have said so, Mr. Caldwell."

"Please call me Wyatt. And don't go getting your feathers all ruffled. I was coming to it."

"My feathers aren't ruffled. I simply prefer to be apprised of all the facts."

"Fair enough. Aunt Lillian married my daddy's brother when she was just a slip of a girl. They came here from North Carolina and bought a farm. A few years after Uncle Pete died, she sold the farm and married Doc Willis. After he died, she took care of that big house and the gardens all by herself, even through the war, but then she broke her hip. Since then—well, she has good days and bad days. But I reckon Hannah told you all about that."

Ada looked at him with grudging respect. There weren't many men who would defer their own dreams and take on the responsibility for an aged woman who wasn't even his blood kin. "I'm sure she appreciates your looking after her."

He nodded. "She took care of me off and on, when my mama was sick and my daddy was away tending his cattle. I spent quite a bit of time with her. The year I lived with her, right after my mother passed on, she sent me to school, taught me some manners." He sent her a rueful smile. "I was pretty hard to handle, but she never gave up on me. I can't turn my back on her now."

"Of course not."

"Hannah . . . Miss Fields . . . was the latest in a series of companions," he continued. "It's only fair to warn you that Aunt Lillian can be a handful sometimes. She resents needing help and takes her frustration out on whoever is around. It's more than some people can take."

She felt him studying her, gauging her reaction. What did it matter? It was too late to change her mind.

"We knew that Hannah planned to leave sometime soon," he went on. "We weren't expecting it quite *this* soon." He shook his head. "I don't know what gets into folks that makes 'em turn tail and run at the most inopportune time. But that's beside the point now."

"Miss Fields wrote that your aunt is seventy-nine."

"Thereabouts. She's been known to fudge the numbers in both directions, according to her purposes. A couple of years back, the newspaper offered a prize in exchange for a story about the oldest citizen in the county. Aunt Lillian admitted to her true age then and won a year's subscription to the *Gazette*. Otherwise, she usually shaves off a couple of years. She's a corker, all right."

The last of the clouds had dissipated. The sun beat down with merciless intensity. Ada unfurled the parasol and rested the thin wooden shaft against her shoulder.

"Aunt Lillian enjoys having someone read to her in the mornings and again before bed. She says it helps her sleep, but she's not above taking a bit of brandy to speed things along." He glanced at Ada. "She's at the age where she has so few pleasures left I can't deny her the comfort of an occasional sip. I hope you don't object."

"It isn't my place to object."

"When the weather's nice she likes to sit outside in the garden. She takes tea at four in the afternoon. Supper at six, bed by eight. You'll have the evenings for your own pursuits."

Ada stared out at the passing landscape. What pursuits awaited her in a small town in the foothills of the Appalachian Mountains? Back home, before everything collapsed, her life had been filled with dinners and concerts, skating parties, and lectures at the public library. Now all that seemed like a dream, like something that had happened to someone else.

She shook her head, a gentle warning to herself to stop dwelling on the past. *Think about your plans. You'll have time in the evenings to get things started.*

They approached a white clapboard church, its steeple piercing the sky. A few wild rosebushes struggled to bloom in the patchy graveyard connected to the church property by a winding brick walkway; a handful of pale pink blossoms littered the ground. A few mottled tombstones dotted the plot, but most graves were marked with simple wooden crosses, several of which listed to the side as if blown about by a strong wind.

"The church is Aunt Lillian's second home," Wyatt told Ada. "Preaching at eleven every Sunday morning, and the ladies' quilting circle on Wednesdays." He grinned. "Although from what I hear, the quilting circle is as much about gossip as sewing."

The wagon continued along the road. Wyatt pointed out the homes of his neighbors dotting the valley and showed her the stands of timber that belonged to his company. At a sharp bend in the road, he pulled into the yard of a sawmill bustling with activity.

Wagonloads of timber lined up before long wooden sheds, waiting their turn at the circular saws. A small army of workers moved about the vast lumberyard, unloading the logs and placing them on a conveyor belt powered by a small steam engine. Two men in sweat-stained shirts shoveled coal into the engine's firebox, sending a plume of steam into the air.

"We just received a big order from Chicago."

Wyatt raised his voice above the whine of the saws and the crack of newly sawn boards being loaded onto waiting wagons. "Ten thousand board feet for a new mercantile they're putting up." He pointed to a house situated on a rise behind the sheds. "That's mine. I built it a couple of years ago."

Constructed of overlapping rows of white-washed planks, the house boasted a wide porch that wrapped around three sides, and a steeply-pitched tin roof. Tall, lace-curtained windows on either side of the door afforded views of the mill and the forest. Beside the door, flowers bloomed in a riot of colors. A pair of rocking chairs occupied one end of the porch.

It was a fine house, beautifully constructed and well tended—a house meant for a family. Ada imagined smiling faces around a candlelit supper table, winter evenings before a merry fire, the murmurs of sleepy children at evening prayers. That had been her dream once, and it had almost come true. Now that dream had been supplanted by one less emotionally satisfying but infinitely more practical.

She sighed. Mrs. Wyatt Caldwell, if there was one, was a lucky woman indeed.

A man in a beat-up felt hat and brown pants wiped the sawdust from his face and trotted over to the buckboard. Ada took his measure: rough hewn and compact, with a sun-browned face and kind hazel eyes that regarded her calmly from beneath his hat brim.

Wyatt said, "Miss Wentworth, this is my foreman, Sage Whiting. Sage and I served together in the war."

The foreman tipped his hat. "Ma'am."

He turned to his boss. "The oak and hickory are looking real good, but that pine . . . well, there's too many knots in it. Might not be good for nothin' 'cept kindling."

"Mill it out anyway, Sage. Scooter Johnson said something about wanting to build his missus some new furniture. Maybe he'll buy it."

"All right." The foreman nodded. "You oughta talk to Nate Chastain at the bookshop too. He may need more shelves for that trainload of books he got in last week. We could let him have the pine pretty cheap, since we wouldn't have to ship it."

"Good idea," Wyatt said. "I'll mention it to him."

Ada shifted on the hard wagon seat and tried to stem her rising impatience. Her backside had gone numb. Her blistered toe pulsed painfully in her tight shoe. The shade from the parasol couldn't mitigate the infernal heat that sat on her head like an anvil. Perspiration trickled down the back of her neck and into the limp collar of her dress. And all this man could think about was timber.

At last, he picked up the reins. "I need to get Miss Wentworth settled at Aunt Lillian's, but I'll be back to pay the men by the end of the day."

Mr. Whiting waved his arm toward the wagon-loads of timber. "We've got plenty to do. Nobody's going anywhere till quitting time."

Catching Ada's eye, he again touched his index finger to the brim of his hat. "Pleasure meeting you, ma'am. I hope you'll like Hickory Ridge."

Three

Wyatt glanced at his passenger. Despite the heat, she sat up straight, one hand grasping the handle of the parasol, the other resting in her lap. He could tell that the long journey, coupled with the heat and her ill-advised hike along the road, had worn her out. He felt a stab of sympathy for her and regret that his words had caused her to take offense.

"It won't be too much longer, Miss Wentworth. We'll get you settled and cooled off. Aunt Lillian usually has lemonade waiting on days like this."

He hoped the prospect of lemonade would coax a smile out of her, but she merely nodded and blotted her face with a frilly handkerchief that in his opinion had seen better days. He spoke to the horse, and the buckboard rolled down the road. A bit farther on, he indicated the turnoff to a twisting dirt road that was nearly obscured beneath a tangle of vines and undergrowth. "That's the road to Two Creeks. You'd best avoid it."

"It does look rather rugged."

"That isn't the problem. Two Creeks is a colored settlement. Things have gotten a little wild down there since emancipation."

"How so?" She tucked her handkerchief back into her cuff.

"Some of them are a mite too fond of their whisky. Gambling and cockfights and spirits are a volatile mix." Mercy, it was hot! He pulled a red bandanna from his pocket and mopped his face. "Still, there are some fine families down there. The Dawsons work for me. Josiah's my wheelwright. His daughter Libby does Aunt Lillian's laundry. You'll meet her when she comes to pick it up."

"Then how will I avoid them?"

"Isn't exactly what I meant. You know about the Klan, of course."

"Only from a few conversations with my father. He abhorred their secrecy and their hatred."

"Most folks around here feel the same. The Klan organized here in Tennessee a few years back and, I am sorry to say, we've had some trouble with them."

He paused. How much should he tell her? Too much information and she was apt to hightail it all the way back to Boston. On the other hand, her safety might depend on knowing just what she was up against. At last he said, "They don't like it when whites and blacks get too friendly—and it's hard to tell what they're going to decide is too friendly. Last year they hanged a black man for looking too long at a white woman."

Her lovely gray eyes went wide. "But that's criminal! Surely the authorities saw to it that they were punished."

"They tried. The legislature passed a law against their shenanigans some time back, but the Klansmen hide behind masks and robes when they go out. They meet behind closed doors. They protect each other. It's hard to bring them to justice."

He watched her expression change from distaste to fear and back again. Now he wished he'd saved this bit of information until she'd settled in. "I've frightened you, and I didn't mean to. You'll be fine so long as you stay away from Two Creeks and don't fraternize with the coloreds."

She waved away a cloud of gnats hovering about her head. "The whole thing seems so—"

"Uncivilized," he finished. "In some ways, the violence has gotten worse since the war ended. We don't have wild gangs terrorizing citizens on the roads anymore, but there were a lot of hard feelings around here between secessionists and the unionists, and those feelings didn't go away after Appomattox. The two camps still blame each other, and both groups blamed the Freedmen's Bureau, even after it closed down."

They passed an ox-drawn wagon loaded with lumber heading toward town. Wyatt nodded to the driver and went on. "I don't want you to have a poor opinion of Hickory Ridge. There are such problems everywhere these days."

"Apparently so. On the train this morning, I was reading about that terrible blood feud in Texas."

"Lee and Peacock. Everybody's talking about that one. They say Peacock was unarmed and on his way to the outhouse wearing nothing but his long drawers when Lee's men gunned him—" Heat rushed to his face. *Tarnation!* The woman was already frightened. Now he'd embarrassed her. "Pardon my language. I didn't mean to be indelicate."

She frowned. "How much longer, Mr. Caldwell?"

"Wyatt." He smiled, hoping to lighten her mood. "Not much farther."

She folded her arms across her chest. "That's what you said when we left your mill."

He snapped the reins, and the horse sped up.

The wagon gathered speed as they descended a hill. Presently, his aunt's house came into view. Bordered on either side by tall stands of trees, flowering hedges, and meandering rose gardens, it was an older, larger version of his own. He'd driven up this road a thousand times, and his first glimpse of the house and the river beyond always gave him a sense of belonging. He hoped Ada Wentworth would come to feel the same way.

He halted the buckboard. A young boy ran barefoot into the road and grabbed the reins. "Hey,

Mr. Wyatt. Guess what? Me and Toby McCall caught six trout this morning. They was bitin' faster than we could get our lines in the water."

"Good for you!" He jumped lightly to the ground and turned to help Ada down. He lifted her, his hands around her waist. Mercy, but the woman felt good in his arms. Smelled good too, like warm skin and some kind of exotic flower.

He set her down and turned back to the boy. "Robbie, this is Miss Wentworth. She's going to be staying here now, looking after Miss Lillian. Miss Ada, this is Robbie Whiting, Sage's boy. He helps out with the chores around here, so feel free to ask if there's anything you need."

"Hello, Robbie." Ada straightened her hat and smiled at the boy. "Six trout! You're quite a fisherman for one so young."

"I'm not young. I'm going on eleven!" Robbie flushed and added shyly, "Ma'am."

Wyatt hoisted Ada's trunk onto his shoulder. He couldn't help noticing that the clasp was loose and that it felt half empty. The poor girl must be worse off than he thought. He handed her the travel satchel. "Let's get these into the house."

He ruffled the boy's hair. "Look after the horse and wagon, will you, Rob?"

"Yes sir. Hey, Wyatt. Do you reckon Miss Ada would fry up those fish we caught? I've got 'em in a bucket on the back porch."

"Not tonight. She's had a long trip. Take those

fish on home to your mama. She'll fry 'em for you."

"No, she won't. She can't stand gutting them."

Wyatt laughed. "I suppose gutting fish is a man's job."

He opened the door and carried Ada's trunk into the hallway. "Aunt Lil? We're home!"

"There's no need to shout, Wyatt. I'm right here."

Ada straightened her hat and smoothed her skirt as a frail woman with piercing blue eyes and a cloud of white hair rolled her wheelchair into the entry hall. The woman set the brake and stared up at Ada. "You're the one Hannah cajoled into coming here."

"I'm Ada Wentworth." She peeled off her damp lace gloves and extended her hand. "I'm very pleased to meet you."

Ignoring Ada's proffered hand, the old woman said, "We'll see if you're still pleased a week from now."

"Now, Aunt Lillian," Wyatt said, "there's no need for that kind of talk."

"Well, I don't see why you insist on my having yet another keeper. It's a big waste of money if you ask me." She peered at Ada. "So. You've come all this way from Boston, Massachusetts."

"Yes." Ada twisted her gloves into a tight ball. Where was the rest of the staff?

"Why?"

"I needed a job. I wanted to see another part of the country."

"You came to the middle of nowhere for a change of scenery?" Lillian shook her head. "I smell a rat."

"Lillian," Wyatt said sharply. "Miss Wentworth is tired. I doubt she feels like submitting to the Inquisition."

"I'm trying to figure out why a Yankee girl would want to settle in Hickory Ridge, that's all. It seems to me she'd rather have stayed among her own kind."

Ada lifted her chin. "It's true that I was born in Boston, but my mother came from one of the oldest families in New Orleans. The Robillards."

Lillian's fine white brows went up. "Well, if that don't take the rag right off the bush! How in the world did a nice Southern girl wind up married to a Boston Yankee?"

Ada's nerves, already wound tight as piano wire, snapped. "My father won her in a poker game."

Lillian gaped at her.

Wyatt's deep laughter filled the vestibule. "You had that one coming, Aunt Lil."

"I have every right to know who's sleeping under my roof, Wyatt Caldwell, and don't call me Lil. You make me sound like a dance-hall girl."

"You'd have made a fine one in your day," he teased.

"Oh, for heaven's sake. I don't know why I

put up with your foolishness." She glared at Ada. "Well, don't just stand there. Make yourself useful and bring us some lemonade. It's on the sideboard in the kitchen. Wyatt, take her things up to Hannah's old room."

"Yes ma'am." Wyatt winked at Ada. "The kitchen's that way, through the dining room and to your right."

The kitchen? Heavenly days, was she expected to cook and serve meals too?

"The cook doesn't—"

"Cook?" Lillian frowned. "I don't know what Hannah told you, but this isn't some fancy plantation house, girl. There's no one here but me."

Ada fled the room, her thoughts racing. She didn't know the first thing about cooking. She hadn't realized that all of the irascible old woman's care would fall to her. What else had the Fields woman neglected to mention?

In the kitchen she found three glasses and poured lemonade from a cut-glass pitcher. Fighting a sudden bout of dizziness, she rummaged through the cabinets for a tray and set the glasses on it. Beads of sweat popped onto her forehead. Her hands shook. Wyatt Caldwell's warning about Two Creeks and the Ku Klux Klan had taken her completely by surprise. Hannah Fields had described Hickory Ridge as a peaceful and close-knit town. Ada had never dreamed it would be so full of violence and secrets.

Tears threatened to overwhelm her, but she blinked them away. She picked up the heavy tray and started down the hallway, trying to ignore the worsening pain in her blistered toe.

"Miss Wentworth!" The old woman's voice was as sharp and startling as a rifle report. Ada looked up, and the toe of her shoe caught the edge of the wool carpet. She stumbled, splashing lemonade onto her skirt, the carpet, and the watered-silk wallpaper. The pitcher and glasses thudded onto the heavy carpet and rolled beneath the dining-room table.

Instantly Wyatt was on the floor beside her. "Are you all right?"

"I'm so sorry!" She flapped her hands uselessly at her skirt, the sticky carpet, and the wayward glasses. "What a mess."

"It isn't that bad." He retrieved the pitcher and the glasses. "Nothing is broken."

"Wyatt!" Lillian called. "Where in the devil has that Yankee gotten to?"

"We're coming, Aunt Lil!"

Wyatt drew Ada to her feet and led her back to the kitchen, where he refilled the glasses and placed them on the tray. "Go ahead and take it in."

"But the carpet!"

"I'll take care of it. Go on. No, wait!" He found a towel and blotted her skirt, then dabbed at her cheeks. He smiled down at her, and she really looked at him for the first time. A shock of thick dark hair brushed the collar of his denim work shirt. A straight nose. A full mouth that turned up at the corners. But it was the unusual color of his eyes that held her attention. They were the deepest blue she'd ever seen. The color of the sea in shadow. Boston blue, her mother would have said.

"There," he murmured. "That's better."

She went still. There was no denying that Wyatt Caldwell was a most attractive man. And he was looking at her with such frank interest that she felt her face grow warm. "I'd better go."

She carried the tray to the parlor where the older woman sat with a quilting bag in her lap. Without looking up, Lillian said, "It took you long enough."

Ada set a glass of lemonade on the table beside Lillian's chair. At last the woman shifted her gaze. "Good heavens! What in the Sam Hill happened to your dress?"

"Just a little accident," Wyatt said smoothly, coming into the parlor. "It's already taken care of."

Ada sent him a grateful look. Wyatt drained his glass. "I'd love to stay and chat, but it's Friday, and the men are waiting for their pay."

"Go on." His aunt waved him away. "If I need anything, Miss Wentworth here will see to it. That's what you're paying her for."

"Please call me Ada."

With a curt nod, Lillian went back to her needlework.

Wyatt kissed his aunt's cheek. "I'll be back on

Sunday morning to drive you to church."

"Don't be late. I hate having everybody watch me walk down the aisle."

Ada followed him back to the entrance hall. "Thank you for meeting my train, Mr. Caldwell. And for"—she glanced toward the parlor, where Lillian was still bent over her work—"everything."

"You're welcome. Don't take her words to heart. Beneath all that bluster, she's the kindest of souls."

Ada nodded, hoping her doubt didn't show.

"I hope you'll be happy here," Wyatt said. "It can't be easy, starting out all alone."

The prospect of true happiness seemed dim, but Ada said, "I'm sure I will be, when I've made some friends. Perhaps your wife will come to tea some afternoon?"

He smiled and crossed his arms across his chest. "Well done!"

"I beg your pardon?"

"Your invitation to tea. A subtle way to ask whether I'm married."

Ada blushed to the roots of her hair. She had honestly assumed that a man as handsome and successful as Wyatt Caldwell would have a wife, but now she could see that her question looked as if she were fishing for information . . . as if she were interested in him anyway. Well, any woman still capable of breathing oxygen *would* be, but getting involved with him was just one more luxury she could not afford. "But your gardens, the flowers . . . they're lovely. I assumed—"

"That's Aunt Lil's doing. She thought the place needed a woman's touch and planted them when the house was built. I'm so busy I hardly have time to tend them." He retrieved his hat from the hall tree.

"There is no Mrs. Caldwell?" She was stunned at how happy she felt at that prospect. But then she reminded herself why she'd come here.

"Nope." He jammed his well-worn Stetson onto his head and opened the door. "I'll see you Sunday."

Wyatt crossed the yard to the buckboard. Ada returned to the parlor. Lillian hunched her shoulders, concentrating on a quilt square as if Ada weren't there. Through the tall windows, Ada watched a wren flitting in and out of an apple tree in the orchard. The clock in the parlor whirred and chimed. She cleared her throat. "Mr. Caldwell said that you take tea at four in the afternoon. Would you like me to make some?"

Lillian looked up from her work. "I don't think so. You'd probably burn the house down trying to boil water."

"Mrs. Willis, I'm very sorry about—"

"Don't think for a minute that I'm fooled about that 'accident'—I know that Wyatt covered up for your clumsiness just now. He's too softhearted with everybody. Spoils his men silly when what is needed is discipline."

Ada clenched her fists. Why did this woman have to be so unpleasant? "If there's nothing you need, I'd like to go up to my room. It has been a long day, and I'm a bit the worse for wear."

"Supper at six. Hannah left bread and butter and half a ham. See if you can serve a meal without destroying the kitchen in the process." She went back to her work. Her needle clicked against her thimble. "Your room is at the top of the stairs, the first one on the left."

Ada hurried up the stairs. The room was barely large enough for a bed, a cheval glass, a washstand, and a small wardrobe, but the tall windows afforded a view of the garden and the distant mountain peaks cloaked in summer green. She opened the window and inhaled the scent of roses. The lace curtains flapped softly in the warm wind.

She removed her shoe, rolled off her stocking, and examined her injured toe. As she suspected, the blister had burst; blood and yellow fluid were forming a crust on her thin stocking. She stripped down to her chemise, poured water into the blue and white porcelain basin sitting on the washstand, and unwrapped a bar of lavender-scented soap. She bathed, running the washcloth over her hot skin and the back of her knees. Then, sitting on the edge of the narrow bed, she rested her foot in the cool, soapy water and gingerly washed it clean. She took a bottle of camphor from her trunk and dabbed some onto her toe, wincing when the smelly liquid touched her skin. She sighed. Why had she been so stupid? Now she'd have to hobble around as she went about her chores—all because of the stubborn streak that had always gotten her into trouble. She unpinned her hair, turned back the pale blue coverlet, and sank gratefully onto the bed.

It seemed that only moments had passed before Ada heard a furious pounding on the wall and Lillian's strident voice echoing in the stairwell.

"Ada! Ada Wentworth!"

"Coming!" Ada rose with a start and pulled on her dress, her fingers clumsy at the buttons.

She ran down the stairs, her unbound hair flying, bare feet skimming the treads, and rounded the corner, only to find Lillian sitting calmly by the open window, watching a couple of hummingbirds at the feeder in the magnolia tree.

"Are you all right, Mrs. Willis?"

"It's a quarter past six. I wondered whether you'd died in your bed."

"I fell asleep. I'm sorry. I'll see to dinner right away."

Lillian waved one mottled hand. "I'm not hungry. Come and sit for a moment. The garden is lovely this time of day."

Ada breathed a relieved sigh at the change in the old woman's attitude. She perched on the horsehair settee, tucked her throbbing foot under her, and looked out. Late afternoon shadows lay across the garden. A slight breeze stirred the roses and the magnolia blossoms, releasing a heady perfume into the cooling air.

Lillian inhaled and closed her eyes. "Magnolias remind me of my youth. My first husband always said I bewitched him with moonlight and magnolias." She laughed softly. "He was a corker, that one."

She turned her watery gaze on Ada and said abruptly, "Have you ever been in love, girl?"

The question was so unexpected that Ada spoke before thinking. "Once. But my father disapproved, and my intended broke our engagement."

"That must have been difficult for you."

Difficult didn't begin to describe the anguish of betrayal at the hands of the two men she'd loved and trusted. The pain of it had seeped into her skin and lodged in her bones, becoming as much a part of her as her own breath. Her heart was still numb with bitterness. "I never forgave my father. I couldn't understand why he wanted to deprive me of the happiness I might have had."

"Surely he wanted only what was best for you." Lillian gazed out at the lengthening shadows. "Just as our heavenly Father does."

Ada watched as the evening clouds gathered above the mountains, forming a billowing canopy of apricot and blue. How could a heavenly Father think it was best for her to lose the one man she was meant to love and to lose her mother just when she most needed a woman's guidance? Aunt Kate had tried her best to fill that void, but it wasn't the same.

Standing in the raw March wind as her father's coffin was lowered into the cold earth, Ada had tried to make peace with her losses, but she still had no idea how to go about it. There was no reason for anything, as far as she could tell. Things happened the way they happened, and all anyone could do was to keep moving forward by whatever means necessary.

Lillian grasped the windowsill and turned her wheelchair around. "It's still a heavy burden on your heart."

Ada shrugged.

"I know it isn't easy," Lillian said, her voice gentle. "But when somebody needs your forgiveness, think about the One who forgives you. When you forgive those who have wronged you and let go of your grief and bitterness, your heart will heal."

It sounded simple, this letting go, but so far she had been unable to accomplish it. Every thought of Edward, and her father, accomplices in the theft of her future, left her feeling angry and resentful.

Lillian turned back to the window. "I'm hungry now."

Ada went to the kitchen and filled a tray with the food Hannah Fields had left. Lillian lit the lamp, filling the room with lambent light. Outside, the whip-poor-wills and cicadas sang. A squadron of fireflies buzzed in the bushes, lighting up the garden.

Lillian ate with obvious relish and finally pushed her empty plate away. "That was good. Now fetch my Bible, and let's hear a few verses before I nod off."

Ada opened the Bible to the place marked with a silk tassel. "Ecclesiastes?"

"My favorite, along with Proverbs and the Psalms."

Ada began reading. "To every thing there is a season, and a purpose to everything under heaven . . ."

She had read but a few verses when Lillian's eyes began to droop. Ada closed the Bible and stood. "Mrs. Willis, shall I help you get ready for bed?"

"I can manage." Lillian yawned. "Clear the dishes and be sure the doors are locked. Wyatt and that wild child of Sage's come and go with never a thought to my safety. Last week Rob brought a bucket of blackberries, which I did appreciate, but then he ran home and left the back door standing wide open. It's a wonder I wasn't murdered."

Ada looked up in alarm. "Your nephew told me about the Klan."

"The Klan," Lillian spat. "I wasn't talking about that bunch of ignorant cowards. Hickory Ridge is on the rail lines going every whichaway. You never know who might come blowing in here on the train." She released the brake on her wheelchair and started down the hall. "Good night, girl."

Ada washed the dishes, wiped the sideboard, and checked the doors. Upstairs, she undressed and slid between the sheets, intending to read for a while, but her conversation with Lillian, so freighted with loss and regret, had left her feeling too restless to concentrate. She turned her face to the window and looked up at the summer sky, listening to the old house pop and creak, settling for the night.

She was sorry for having shared so much of her past with a stranger. Sorry that she had come here at all. But it was too late now.

There was no going back.

Four

Bright orange flames licked at her face and hair, searing her skin. Thick black smoke billowed above her, filling her lungs and stealing her breath. The stench of burning flesh overwhelmed her senses. A chorus of screams and the frantic ringing of a distant fire bell filled her ears.

Ada cried out and sat up, her heart pounding. Her nightdress was bunched about her waist and drenched in sweat. Outside her window, birdsong and the faint pealing of church bells echoed through the valley. She lay back on the bed and waited for the too-familiar nightmare to dissipate.

She shaded her eyes from the brilliant sunlight piercing the lace curtains and released a small moan. Yesterday with Lillian had proved a pure trial that began at breakfast and lasted most of the day.

The old woman had insisted on having her morning tea and toast outdoors. It took Ada half an hour to prepare a tray and settle Lillian beneath the shade of the towering magnolia. Ten minutes later, Lillian declared the morning too hot for all but Satan himself and demanded to be taken back indoors. Then she kept Ada running all morning bringing her quilting supplies, her spectacles, her footstool. At noon, Ada struggled to prepare the potato soup Lillian requested, only to be told it was too peppery. An afternoon nap had been a full production requiring the positioning of a mosquito net, the raising and lowering of windows to catch the right amount of breeze, and finally the fetching of a glass of fresh water from the pump in the kitchen.

The downstairs pendulum clock chimed the hour. Ada groaned. Wyatt Caldwell would be here soon to drive his aunt to church. She rose, poured water into the basin, and checked her reflection in the cheval glass beside the door. *Creation!* Her fevered dream had left her looking as limp and pale as a plucked chicken. She pinched some color into her cheeks, donned a dove-gray silk dress, and went downstairs, the vestiges of her nightmare still clinging like cobwebs in the corners of her mind.

Lillian appeared in the hallway, a frown creasing her forehead. Determined to remain pleasant, Ada summoned a smile. “Did you sleep well?”

"Not so's you'd notice it. The ham you fixed for supper was too salty. I practically died of thirst in the night."

Ada silently counted to ten. "I'm sorry, but the meat has been cured. There isn't much I can do to take the salt out of it."

"Hannah managed."

"Then we must write to her at once and find out her secret."

"Not likely. She's probably halfway to Argentina by now—the little redheaded ingrate."

"What happened?" Ada opened the curtains, letting in the morning light. "I understood that Miss Fields was to meet my train, but Mr. Caldwell said she had left unexpectedly."

"Unexpected to him maybe. Not to me. She wasn't about to go to her aunt's in Missouri, not after she met that drummer from Denver. I watched her making eyes at him every time he passed through town." Lillian fixed Ada with a stare. "Traveling salesmen are no good. She'll be sorry soon enough."

"Perhaps." Hannah Fields had thrown caution to the wind and grabbed onto a chance for happiness. Ada admired the woman's courage. She glanced at the clock. "We've time for breakfast before your nephew arrives. What would you like?"

"Not ham—I'll tell you that much. And just to be clear, you will be coming with us this morning."

"Oh, no thank you. That's very thoughtful, but—"

But I don't know how to talk to the one who denied me the only man I ever loved, let my father fall into financial ruin, and forced me into servitude to a difficult old woman living in the middle of nowhere.

"I'm not giving you a choice, Ada. Hannah always went with me. I expect no less from you."

"But your nephew will be there, in case you need anything."

"Everybody needs the Lord, girl, even you. I'm finished with this discussion. Now, I'll have biscuits and a fried egg. Don't leave the yolk runny. I hate runny yolks."

Ada spun on her heel and headed for the kitchen. She set the skillet on the stove and broke an egg into it.

"Oh! Oh! Oh!" Lillian's voice echoed down the hallway.

Ada hurried down the hall to the open doorway of Lillian's bedroom. "What's the matter? Are you all right?"

"No, Miss Wentworth, I am not all right." She handed Ada a leghorn straw hat with a ragged hole in the brim. "My best summer hat, and it's ruined. What am I to do? I can't go to church without a proper hat. What will people think?"

Ada poked a finger through the coin-sized hole. "What about another hat? Shall I look in your wardrobe?"

"Certainly not. I don't want you pawing through

my things! Besides, this hat goes with my dress. I can well imagine what Bea Goldston will say if I show up in the wrong hat. She's the meanest woman in Hickory Ridge."

Ada blinked. There was someone in town meaner than Lillian Willis? Heaven help them all. Then, to her surprise, she heard herself say, "I can fix it."

Lillian sniffed like a child at the end of a tantrum. "Really?"

"After I've finished making your breakfast, I'll see what I can do."

"Forget breakfast." Lillian flapped one hand in dismissal. "I'm not hungry anyway."

"Surely you'd like a bite of something before church."

Lillian glared at her.

"All right then." Ada took the hat upstairs and retrieved a wooden box from the bottom of her trunk. Even after so many years, her eyes welled at the sight of it. Scratched and worn with age, it was the only tangible reminder of her mother.

Ada opened it, releasing the faint scent of cedar and lavender, and ran her fingers along the edges of the box. She smoothed the petals of a single silk rose her mother had bought in Paris, feeling a connection across time and space. Though Elizabeth never opened the hat shop she often dreamed about, fashionable Boston ladies had found their way to the Wentworths' home, where her mother crafted hats of her own design or copied from the latest European styles.

Ada took out her scissors and snipped away the ragged edges of the hole in Lillian's hat. She found a length of yellow ribbon and a pearl-tipped hatpin and quickly looped the ribbon around the pin to form a flower with the pearl at its center. She added a bit of lace around the brim to make the repair less obvious. Then she gave the hat a gentle brushing and took it back to Lillian.

The old woman's face lit up, making her seem younger than her years. "Oh! Oh my! How positively beautiful!" She flapped both hands. "Quick! Help me put it on."

Relieved at having finally done something that met with Lillian's approval, Ada pinned the hat to Lillian's fine hair and handed her the silver-backed mirror from the dressing table.

Lillian turned her head, admiring her reflection. "Why, Ada, I had no idea you were so clever. Wherever did you learn such a skill?"

Before Ada could respond, Lillian caught her hand. "You must forgive my behavior yesterday. I'm sure it must be difficult for you, without any parents to rely on. I'm sorry you've lost them both."

Ada felt tears burn her eyes. Lillian's sympathy was harder to endure than her constant demands. "So am I," she managed. "If there's nothing else you need—"

"Actually"—Lillian smiled at her reflection—"I find that I am quite hungry after all."

Ada returned to the kitchen to make breakfast. She filled a tray, and the two women ate in the parlor beneath an open window. Between bites, Lillian described the women in her church quilting circle.

"There's Bea Goldston, of course. Thinks she has to run everything. I suppose we can't blame her. The town hired her to teach school three years ago, and she's accustomed to being in charge."

Ada spread her biscuit with marmalade. "It must be difficult to keep a room full of rowdy children in line. Is there a Mr. Goldston?"

Lillian laughed. "Oh my lands, no. When you meet her you'll see why." She took a bite of her poached egg. "Mariah Whiting, on the other hand, is the sweetest little thing you'd ever hope to meet."

"Whiting? Isn't he the foreman at the mill?"

"Sage, yes. He and Wyatt served together in the war. Sage and Mariah make a fine pair. They dote on their boy."

"Robbie seems to idolize your nephew."

"When Robbie was just a baby, Sage regaled him with stories of Wyatt's exploits during the war." She reached for the marmalade. "The Texas Brigade was quite famous. General Lee favored them most highly."

Ada sipped her tea. "Did Mr. Caldwell serve with the general?"

Lillian was quiet for so long, Ada thought the older woman had drifted off to sleep. But finally

Lillian said, “Perhaps he should tell you about that himself.” She brushed crumbs from her fingers. “He should be here any minute.”

Ada cleared the table and went back to her room to find her own hat, a gray silk toque adorned with a single curved peacock feather. She sighed. Her restless night had left her gritty-eyed and exhausted. She wasn’t in the mood to sit all morning in a hot, crowded church surrounded by people she didn’t know—people who had no use for a Boston Yankee. But she couldn’t afford to incur Lillian’s wrath either. She needed this job until she could save enough to move on.

“Ada?” Lillian called. “Hurry up! Here comes Wyatt!”

Wyatt looked up as Ada descended the staircase carrying a prayer book and her Sunday hat. He couldn’t help noticing her paleness and the faint circles beneath her extraordinary eyes. Her plain gray dress was clean and pressed, but the somber color made her seem older than her years. If he had his way about it, she’d be wearing something with plenty of ruffles and lace. In pink, maybe, or sky blue.

“Good morning.” He inclined his head. “How have you and Lil been getting on?”

His aunt tottered to the doorway. “Are you gossiping about me, Wyatt Caldwell?”

“Of course not.” He bent to kiss her cheek.

"You're looking fine this morning. New hat?"

"After a fashion. Ada repaired a hole in the brim. I told you I was wise to hire her."

He couldn't stop the laugh that started deep in his chest. "Oh, yes. And you were eagerly anticipating her arrival, eh?"

"Don't make fun of me."

"I can't help it, given the conniption fit you threw when I told you she was coming. Now that she's made you a new hat to show off, all of a sudden the whole thing was your idea."

"She can't cook worth a plugged nickel."

He glanced at Ada, hoping she wasn't offended. "Aunt Lil, that's impolite."

"But it's true," Ada said. "I'm not much use in the kitchen. I said as much in my letter to Miss Fields."

Lillian frowned. "Are we going to stand here jawing all morning, or are we going to church?"

Wyatt's heart kicked in his chest as Ada stopped before the hallway mirror and deftly tucked her hair into a neat knot. He was fascinated at the graceful way she lifted her arms to secure her hat with its pins, with the way her dress hugged her curves.

"There." She retrieved Lillian's Bible and picked up her prayer book. "All set."

"It's about time," Lillian said.

Ada smiled then, lighting up the room. Wyatt felt suddenly shy, like a callow youth discovering women for the first time.

He and Ada each offered an arm to Lillian.

They moved slowly along the porch and crossed the yard to the buggy. Wyatt helped Lillian and Ada onto the seat. He settled himself beside them and flicked the reins. "Sorry it's a bit crowded, but the buggy's more comfortable than the buckboard, and it'll keep the sun off your face."

They set off, his knee bumping hers as the buggy rolled down the road. In the distance a train whistle sounded.

"That'll be the ten o'clock bound for Nashville," he told Ada. "It doesn't stop here on Sundays, but I sure do like the sound of it." He pointed to his left. "You can just about see the trestle through that stand of trees."

"How many trains come through here?" Ada asked.

"Ten a week. Not bad for a little town." He couldn't keep the pride out of his voice. His mill was one of the reasons Hickory Ridge was on the move. "The way Hickory Ridge is growing, it won't be little for long."

"Too crowded, that's what it is," Lillian grumbled. "There was a time when I knew every family who lived here. Now when I go shopping, all I see is a passel of strangers." She waved her hand. "When I was a girl you could get anything you needed, from nails to molasses, at the mercantile. Now we've got those fancy stores selling lace and writing paper and such. Who needs all that highfalutin' stuff is what I'd like to know."

"Progress isn't all bad," Wyatt said. "I, for one,

am glad to have the bookshop right here in town instead of having to go forty miles to Knoxville for the latest Mark Twain." He slowed the buggy for a curve in the road. In the distance, the church steeple protruded above the trees. He glanced at Ada, who had seemed preoccupied during most of the trip. "Miss Wentworth, have you by any chance read *Innocents Abroad*?"

Her sudden smile touched his heart. "Yes. My father sent me to Europe with my Aunt Kate the summer I turned eighteen. I enjoyed Mr. Twain's articles about some of the places we visited."

"I've always wanted to see Europe. Maybe you'll give me an account of your travels and save me the trip."

"I'm afraid I couldn't do it jus—oh, we're here."

Wyatt drove the buggy into the shaded lot beside the church and set the brake. He helped Lillian and Ada from the rig and tipped his Stetson. "Enjoy the sermon, ladies."

Five

Ada looked around the bustling churchyard. Young couples, older folks, and nearly-grown youths chatted quietly, awaiting the start of the service while the younger children chased one another and played hide-and-seek among the buckboards and buggies lined up beneath the trees.

Spotting his mill foreman arriving with his family, Wyatt touched one finger to the brim of his Stetson. "Excuse me, ladies. I need a word with Sage."

"Oh, Wyatt." Lillian frowned. "Talking business on the Lord's Day?"

He grinned. "I'll see you later."

He loped across the yard, dodging a group of noisy children tossing a ball. Lillian tucked her Bible under her arm. "Here comes Queen Bea," she murmured to Ada. "The schoolteacher I told you about."

Miss Goldston was much younger than Ada had imagined. She was tall and angular, her features too uneven to be conventionally beautiful, but the thick, dark hair tumbling over her shoulders and her regal bearing certainly commanded attention. A handsome woman, Ada's father would have said. The teacher glanced over at Lillian and Ada, smiled, and nodded.

"She seems nice enough," Ada remarked.

"She's nice when it suits her." Lillian swatted at a bee buzzing around their heads. "But mark my words—Bea and her friend Betsy Terwilliger would rather create a scandal than eat." She leaned closer to Ada. "I know it isn't right to gossip, but you're new here and it must be said: Bea Goldston is mean as a snake. She takes pleasure in stirring up trouble for no good reason."

Ada fanned her face with her prayer book. "There must be some reason for her bitterness."

"Well, she was born on the wrong side of the

blanket, and she took a lot of ridicule when she was a girl because of it—even got into fights, I've heard. There were rumors that her daddy was a big bug around here." Lillian lowered her voice. "A married man. It's still a mystery. But that's no cause to be mean to people. Then she shows up here every week, pious as a nun and smiling like she's everybody's friend."

Ada watched Miss Goldston mingle with the other churchgoers. A couple of burly boys rushed past the schoolteacher, trampling the hem of her skirt. Both arms shot out and stopped the two boys in their tracks. One of them tried to slip from her grasp. She hauled him around so hard that his feet practically dangled above the ground.

Ada shook her head. The woman was strong as an ox. Still, there was no sense making up her mind about her before they'd even met.

"That's the sheriff over there." Lillian nodded to a lanky, craggy-faced man who had stopped to talk to the boys. "Eli lost his wife a couple of years back." She pulled a lace handkerchief from her sleeve and dabbed her forehead. "Lawsa, it's hot."

"Shall we go inside?"

"Let's wait. The preacher hasn't showed up yet, and there's no sense in roasting for any longer than—Jacob Hargrove, watch where you're going."

A couple of young men raced past, jostling them. One of them turned and called, "Sorry, Mrs. Willis."

Lillian frowned at the boys' good-natured teasing.

"Since his mother passed, that boy's gone a little wild. Wyatt gave him a job, thinking that might settle him some, but he didn't last more than a few weeks."

Ada knew just how the boy felt. She hoped he still had an adult to turn to.

Jacob detached himself from a group of boys and ambled over to a pretty blond girl in a bright blue calico dress standing apart from the others.

"That's Sabrina Gilman, the banker's daughter," Lillian supplied. "Her folks go to that fancy church in town, but Sabrina comes here to see Jacob." She made a *tsk-tsk* sound. "Young love. Too bad it's doomed."

"How so?"

"Sabrina's daddy is one of the richest men in Hickory Ridge. It isn't likely he'll allow his only daughter to settle on a poor farmer. No doubt he has other suitors in mind."

Ada felt a hot surge of anger toward the meddling banker. Why couldn't fathers get out of the way and let love take its course?

A buckboard rattled into the yard and found its place among the other wagons. A woman in a yellow bonnet climbed down and waved to Lillian before hurrying across the yard to greet a woman dressed in mourning clothes. The widow stood apart from the others, cooling her face with a dull black fan. A single reddish-blond curl had escaped the limp lace brim of the black bonnet she wore tightly tied beneath her chin.

"Carrie Daly lost her husband at Shiloh, went into mourning, and never came out." Lillian shook her head. "It's a pity—she's still a young woman. Lives with her brother, Henry Bell. He works with Wyatt down at the mill. Come on. Let me introduce you. That way you'll know everyone when our quilting circle meets next week."

"Quilting circle? I . . . I hadn't really planned on—"

"Nonsense. What would you do with yourself every Wednesday afternoon while I'm down here?"

Ada had the sense of being drawn into an ever-tightening web from which there was no escape. The prospect of becoming part of Hickory Ridge society, even for a short time, made her feel exposed and vulnerable.

"We make quilts for everyone," Lillian went on. "New brides, war orphans, the missionaries overseas. And we make all the costumes for the church's Christmas pageant every year. The whole town turns out for that."

She started across the yard. Ada couldn't get over how much Lillian knew about everyone. Now she was sorrier than ever that she'd told the older woman about her broken engagement. How soon would it be before *her* life was an open book too?

Midway across the yard, Lillian stopped. "Well, Ada, are you coming?"

Ada gathered her skirts and followed. But

before Lillian could make the introductions, the rosy-cheeked woman in the yellow bonnet clutched Ada's arm. "I know who you are! My husband met you on Friday. I'm Mariah Whiting."

"Ada? I'm Carrie," said the widow. "Hannah Fields told us all about you. She said you seemed very pleasant from the tone of your letters."

"That was kind of her. I'll try to live up to her good opinion."

"Oh, we have no doubt you will!" Mariah spied Lillian's hat and went stock still, one hand over her heart. "Lillian, is that a new hat?"

"Do you like it?" Lillian turned her head from side to side.

"I adore it. I know it didn't come from Norah's. If you wouldn't mind, would you say where you bought it?"

"Ada made it. Or rather, she remodeled it."

Mariah peered more closely. "Of course, I recognize it now. But truly, it looks even better than new."

She turned to Ada. "Could you possibly make one for me? Not an exact duplicate, of course, but something similar, with some of that ribbon trim? This old spoon bonnet is ten years old and bedraggled as a wet hen. I'd love something stylish to wear for the harvest festival."

Ada hesitated. She hadn't counted on starting her millinery business so soon. And until she received her first pay from Lillian, she was down to her last few dollars, not enough to purchase supplies. She glanced at Lillian. The older woman hadn't uttered a word, but Ada could feel disapproval coming off her in waves. She felt a lurch of fear in her chest. What if Lillian got angry enough to dismiss her?

"Perhaps later on," she told the foreman's wife. "I've only just arrived."

"But the festival isn't until October," Mariah persisted. "There's plenty of time." She opened her bag and pressed a couple of bills into Ada's hand. "I'll pay in advance. Please say you'll do it. We've had so few luxuries since the war."

Lillian frowned. "Ada works for *me,* Mariah. She doesn't have time for such distractions." The church bells rang. "The reverend is here. Let's go in."

Ada looked around for Wyatt, but he was nowhere in sight. She tucked the bills into her bag and followed Lillian and the others across the dusty yard. As they reached the open doorway, Mariah looped her arm through Ada's. "Don't pay Lillian any mind. She just doesn't want to share you with anybody."

Mariah joined her husband and son in a pew near the door. Lillian made her way to the front and motioned for Ada to join her. The young pastor took his place behind the carved wooden lectern and, after the opening hymn, announced his text for the morning: the parable of the talents from the book of Luke.

Lillian nodded off during the reading, her hands clutching her hymnal, her head listing to one side. Listening to the story of the man who had given his servants ten pounds to invest in his absence, Ada wondered whether the message was somehow meant for her. She thought of the money Mariah Whiting had given her. Could she use it to seed the new start she so desperately needed? But how could she use her talent at all without Lillian's blessing?

She glanced at the older woman. In repose, Lillian looked positively ancient, so fragile that she might at any moment meet her Maker. Ada fanned her face and tried to quell the jumpiness in her stomach. What would happen to her once Lillian passed on?

The last hymn had ended some minutes ago, the final sweet notes drifting and dissipating into the still morning. Now the only sound was the occasional birdsong and the low buzz of insects skittering across the shimmering river. Wyatt shed his shirt, shoes, and socks. Leaving them in a heap on the riverbank, he rolled the legs of his trousers and waded out to his favorite spot, a large, flat rock in the middle of the stream. He stretched out and closed his eyes, the dappled sunlight warming his face.

This was the highlight of his week, when the frantic pace at the mill stopped and a man could be alone with nature to sort out his thoughts. He rubbed one hand across his face. Since last Friday, too many of his thoughts had been centered on a certain young Bostonian with soft gray eyes and a stubborn streak a mile wide. He found himself thinking of her at the oddest times, imagining her making tea for Lillian or gathering flowers in the garden. He wondered what she'd look like dressed in a riding skirt and a Stetson, cantering with him across a rolling Texas grassland.

A fish flopped in the river, and Wyatt opened one eye. A ridiculous thought, Ada Wentworth in Texas. She was a city girl, accustomed to fancy stores, theaters, libraries, and such. Ranch life was a whole other world.

He heard a rustling in the bushes beside the river and sat up. "Hello?"

Ada emerged, and he would have been hard-pressed to say which of them was more surprised. She turned her head, obviously embarrassed, and he was suddenly aware of his bare torso.

"Wade on in," he said. "The water's nice and cool this morning."

"I'm sorry. I shouldn't have been spying on you."

"That's all right." He couldn't help grinning. "You're the prettiest spy I've ever seen, if you don't mind my saying so."

Ada spun away, her cheeks blazing. "I'll wait for you in front of the church."

"Don't go." He jammed his hat onto his head and splashed across the water to the bank.

"We should go back. Your aunt will be wondering where we are."

"She knows where to find me." He slipped his shirt on, retrieved his boots, and sat down on a fallen log to pull them on, trying to think of some way to hold on to her company a little longer. "There's a pretty little waterfall just upstream there. I'd love for you to see it. It isn't far."

"I shouldn't." She kept her eyes trained on the river. "We shouldn't even be here. You know how some people love to talk."

He sighed and buttoned his shirt. "I suppose you're right. Another time, then."

They started back along the path. "I didn't see you during church," Ada said.

"I'm afraid the Almighty and I parted ways back in '64, at Cold Harbor." He paused and looked past her shoulder to the shimmering green mountains in the distance.

Ada nodded. "I read about it in the *Herald*."

"It was worse than any newspaper account could ever convey. We trapped seven thousand Federals in a ravine, and ten minutes later they were all dead. The crossfire was the worst I'd ever seen. Smoke so thick you couldn't see your hand before your face." He shook his head. "I felt bad for the poor devils. Of course, it wasn't just the Federals. Our side took heavy losses too."

"I can't imagine it."

"It was hell on earth," he said. "General Lee could barely stand it."

She nodded. "Father supported the Union, of course,

but even he was stunned by what happened at Cold Harbor. It was his opinion that Grant should have relented sooner and saved his soldiers' lives."

"Cold Harbor's the only mistake Grant ever owned up to. Not that it made any difference."

"Were you wounded?"

He shrugged. "Broken bones, some lacerations. Took a bullet to the shoulder."

"But you're all right now."

"For the most part." He absently rubbed his shoulder. The physical wounds were never the worst part of war. "The strange thing was that when I was first hit, it didn't even hurt. All I felt was surprise. And then I saw my blood pumping into the dirt and I started blacking out. Sage was right next to me. He was hurt too, but he dragged me to cover."

"It's a miracle you survived."

"I don't believe in miracles. It was the luck of the draw, that's all." He wiped his brow. "That was the day I realized that as much as people want to believe in some divine plan, there isn't one. Everything that happens, for good or evil, is just a matter of chance."

"I feel that way too." She looked into his eyes, and he saw the sympathy in her calm gray gaze. "I'm glad you survived, however it was accomplished."

He nodded.

"Your aunt said I should ask you about your exploits during the war."

"There's nothing much more to tell." He bent to pick up a smooth stone, enjoying the warm weight of it in his hand. "I never thought it was a fight we could win, even after General Lee won at Chancellorsville. But I couldn't stand by while my friends—boys I'd known all my life—went off to fight." He skipped the stone across the river. "I enlisted more out of loyalty to them than to the idea of dissolving the Union. I'm no statesman, but I just didn't see how the South could survive as a separate nation. We're mostly farmers and planters down here. We've never had the industries the North enjoyed."

"You risked your life for them."

They continued along the path. "I'm nothing if not loyal to my friends, Ada. You'll find that out about me as time goes on."

"Kapow! Bam! Yiyiyiyiyi!" Robbie Whiting and his friends appeared on the hill above them, playing cowboys and Indians. Robbie's Sunday shirt had come untucked and was streaked with dirt. His hair, so carefully combed for the church service, was falling into his eyes. When he saw Ada and Wyatt standing below him, he waved, clutched his heart, and spiraled to the ground.

The old longing for a family, a son of his own, tugged at Wyatt. "That boy has more imagination than any ten men I know."

"You're his hero."

"He's young. Easily impressed."

"But the Texas Brigade is famous!" He heard the admiration in her voice. "Even the Boston papers carried stories about their bravery at Gettysburg and Chickamauga. General Lee himself took note of it."

"He appreciated us, all right, but it went both ways. Any one of us would have charged hell itself for that old man." He swallowed the hard knot in his throat. He hadn't been at Appomattox on that quiet April morning when the end came, but he'd since read General Order Number 9, the general's simple, affectionate, heartfelt farewell to his army. Six years later, the memory of it still had the power to move him. He cleared his throat. "When Lee died last year, it was like losing my own father."

They climbed the embankment, Ada in the lead. As they reached the top, her foot slipped. She stopped suddenly, and he trampled her dress, leaving behind a large muddy bootprint.

"Oh!" She lifted her hem to assess the damage.

"Forgive me. I should have been paying better attention." Feeling like an utter fool, he bent to brush away the dirt, but Ada stopped him.

"It's too wet. Brushing will only make it worse."

She pushed a strand of hair back under her hat, but it came loose again and she left it. "I shouldn't have distracted you with so many questions about the war. I didn't intend to bring up such painful memories."

"It's all right. It's in the past now."

They arrived back at the church just in time to see a middle-aged man in a blue suit mount up and ride away.

"I'm sure he's smarting from Lillian's tongue-lashing," Ada told him. "She cornered him after church this morning, incensed that he's behind on his promise to fix her porch."

Wyatt sighed. "I should do it myself, but things at the mill have been so busy I haven't had time. Only last week we got a contract to supply lumber for a new hotel in Philadelphia." He paused. Usually he didn't tell anyone about his business. There were some in Hickory Ridge who didn't like the fact that many of his best customers came from up North. He admitted it—he wanted to impress her.

"That's wonderful!" she said. "Congratulations."

Ada waved to Lillian and the Whitings. Wyatt followed her along the winding path and into the churchyard, admiring the gentle sway of her skirt and the pert angle of her hat.

"Wyatt Caldwell! A word . . ."

He groaned inwardly, Bea Goldston was hurrying toward them, her face alight, but her smile faded when she spotted Ada. She scanned Ada's muddy skirt, messy hair, and flushed face. "Well, well, if it isn't our little visitor from Massachusetts. Miss . . . Wentworth, isn't it?" She narrowed her eyes. "And looking all pink-faced too! I'm afraid our Southern heat must not agree with you. Or is there some other reason you're looking so flustered?"

The color in Ada's cheeks deepened, and Wyatt felt his own face heat up. "Now look here, Bea. There's no call for you to—"

"There you are, Miss Wentworth!" Sage and Mariah Whiting appeared at her side. "Thanks for fetching Wyatt for me," Sage said. "Did you find him tending the graves out back like I said?"

Before Ada could reply, Wyatt sent her a pointed look and said smoothly, "She had to look a little farther than that, but she did find me. Is something wrong?"

"Nothing wrong. Just a question about that shipment going out tomorrow."

Mariah laid a hand on her husband's arm. "Can it wait? Robbie and I are ready to go."

"Me too," Lillian said. "This heat is about to take the starch right out of me."

"Well, then, ladies . . ." Wyatt offered an arm to Lillian and Ada. They brushed past Bea Goldston—who was looking a bit pink and flustered herself—and headed for the buggy.

Six

Ada sorted through her supplies: scissors, thimbles, tailor's chalk, a tape measure so old the numbers had all but worn away. In the bottom of the wooden chest, nestled in folds of soft muslin, lay her mother's silk flower, some spools of thread, a few pieces of matted felt, and several bits of creased and faded ribbon. Taking in her meager assets, she felt tears pooling in her eyes.

Even with the money from Mariah Whiting, there wasn't nearly enough to begin the millinery business she'd planned. And where were her customers to come from anyway?

She'd been crazy to come here. Crazy and naive. Most of the women in Hickory Ridge were farm women who needed sturdy poke bonnets instead of frilly confections of feathers and lace. If Wyatt's prediction was true and hard times were on the way, nobody would have money for such frivolous purchases. She was trapped, without enough money to go or to stay. After setting aside a few dollars for her future, the money Wyatt was paying her for looking after Lillian was barely enough to keep her in soap, stockings, and hairpins. And even though Lillian might overlook Ada's making a hat for Mariah, she would surely object to anything that diverted attention from her own needs.

Recalling her father's failed financial schemes, Ada felt something close to panic. She didn't want to repeat his mistakes. Fresh anger at him for leaving her without money or a husband built inside her chest.

Her gaze fell on a small woolen skating cap in robin's egg blue nestled in the bottom of the box. She lifted it and held it to her face. *Oh, Mother, I don't know what to do.*

Her throat tightened at the memory of the cold winter's day when her mother had made the cap. The pond behind the house had frozen solid. Icicles adorned the eaves of the porch overlooking the snowy lawn. In the bare branches of the trees, a few jays fluttered and scolded.

"Mother? Must I finish this book? I am bored senseless."

Twelve-year-old Ada set down her book and stared longingly at the glittering pond and the gaggle of noisy children sledding down Patriot's Hill.

Elizabeth sat up in her bed, her thin face rosy in the glow of the fire that danced in the grate. "What has your father assigned you this week?"

Ada wrinkled her nose. "Emerson's *Essays*—so stuffy. If Father insists that I read, why can't I at least read something interesting? Dickens, for instance, or that autobiography of Frederick Douglass that Father has been reading." Her eyes shone with mischief. "Or Mrs. Wetherell's novel! Pansy Ashmore brought a copy to school, and she and Elise Summers and I read it while we were supposed to be resting. We got all the way to the chapter where Ellen is about to get married before Miss Trimble found us out."

Elizabeth smiled. "*The Wide, Wide World* is an entertaining story, but it was not meant for children."

"I'm not a child. I'm almost thirteen."

"Come here, darling."

Ada crawled onto the bed with her mother, who drew her close and smoothed her hair. "My sweet daughter. When I'm no longer here to tell you so, promise you will remember how much I love you."

Ada snuggled closer. "I promise." She had long since given up the pretense that her mother would get well. For almost two years, she had watched as Elizabeth grew weaker, finally abandoning her beloved sitting room with its view of the river in favor of her upstairs bedroom.

Elizabeth planted a kiss on Ada's head. "If you'll help me with Mrs. Peabody's hat, I'll finish knitting your cap, and tomorrow you may go skating on the pond. But you mustn't tell your father."

"I won't!" Delighted to be sharing a secret with her mother, Ada hurried to the wooden cabinet where the white felt hat had been left to dry. Elizabeth opened her wooden chest and extracted a stiff brush, a needle and thread, and three delicate ostrich feathers. She showed Ada how to brush the felt to raise the nap, how to bind the feathers together with a bit of ribbon and attach them to the brim of the hat with stitches so fine they almost disappeared.

"It's beautiful, Mama. May I try it on? Just for a moment?"

Elizabeth laughed. "Just for a moment."

Ada donned the hat and preened before the mirror. "Mrs. Peabody will adore it!"

"Let's hope so. She's promised to pay handsomely for it." Worry tinged her mother's voice. "I'm setting aside my hat money for you, Ada. One day it may be your only inheritance."

Ada's heart sped up. Was that what her parents' arguments were about?

"Now," Elizabeth said briskly, "put Mrs. Peabody's hat in that hatbox in the clothes press. Then bring my knitting needles, and I'll finish your skating hat."

The next day Ada invited Pansy for lunch and they spent the afternoon skating on the frozen pond. Ada held out her arms and twirled on the ice. She and Pansy joined hands and glided back and forth, laughing and gossiping about school and boys and the new Latin teacher, recently arrived from New York. When darkness fell, they removed their skates and trudged up the snowy hill. Leaving their heavy cloaks and damp stockings drying on the porch, they went inside for hot chocolate and tiny sandwiches the cook had left for them.

After Pansy had gone home, Ada climbed the curving staircase to her mother's room. Elizabeth sat in her chair by the window, the lamps still unlit, an unopened book on her lap.

"There you are, darling." Elizabeth coughed into her handkerchief until she was nearly breathless, but finally she managed a wan smile. "Did you have fun?"

"It was the best day, Mama. Thank you."

Elizabeth nodded. "I watched you all afternoon. I'm proud of you, Ada."

"Well, I'm glad of that, even if I don't know why. I'm not musical like Elise. I'm not tall and beautiful like Pansy."

"You don't look like Pansy, it's true, but you are beautiful in your own way."

"Father says I'm too stubborn and too outspoken. So does Aunt Kate."

"You're strong and smart and opinionated. Those aren't bad traits to own in a world run by men." Elizabeth's voice caught.

"What is it, Mama? Did something happen?"

"Your father—" She shook her head. "Never mind. I'm very tired now. I want to rest."

It wasn't until many years later that Ada learned just how angry Cornelius had been that day, his pride wounded at the discovery that his wife was earning her own money. Ada was stunned. Somebody had to! The stack of bills on his desk grew higher and higher, and he grew angrier and more withdrawn.

That had been the beginning of her alienation from her father.

The parlor door slammed, and Ada heard the rhythmic sound of Lillian's wheelchair rolling across the wood floor. She went downstairs to find Lillian sitting by the open window, watching a wren build a nest in the eaves of the porch. The sweet scents of early summer drifted on the breeze.

"There you are, Ada," she said without turning her head. "I don't have much of an appetite. Get yourself something to eat and then fetch my needlework bag. Wyatt will be here soon to take us down to the church for quilting circle."

"You should eat something. How about a biscuit and some jam? Or a poached egg?"

Lillian turned from the window. "Don't boss me, girl. I reckon I know when I need to eat, and right now I am stuffed to the gills from that farmer's breakfast you laid on."

"I made what you requested."

"My eyes are bigger than my stomach. And never mind your own lunch. Here comes Wyatt."

Remembering the few minutes they'd spent together on the river, Ada felt her pulse jump. Her face warmed at the memory of his direct gaze holding hers, the brush of his fingers against her hand. The way her heart had lifted when he defended her against Bea Goldston's insinuating words.

Wyatt rode into the yard and slid from the saddle. He took off his Stetson and wiped his brow with his shirtsleeve. Even the stains on his hat and his dusty work jeans couldn't detract from his lean good looks. Ada sighed. Surely God had made Wyatt Caldwell to prove just what he was capable of. But it didn't really matter. Sooner or later, he'd be off to Texas and she would be . . . where? All her worries crowded in.

"Ada?" Lillian rose unsteadily to her feet. "Where's my hat . . . and my quilting bag?"

Ada retrieved Lillian's things and climbed the stairs to get her own hat and her sketchbook.

Despite Lillian's certain opposition to her future plans, Ada was eager to share her hat sketches with the mill foreman's wife. The sooner she could earn some money with her hatmaking, the better.

Downstairs, the door opened, and Wyatt's voice filled the entry hall. "Aunt Lil? Ada? Are you ladies about ready?"

"Coming!" Ada hurried down the staircase.

Wyatt flashed a smile that stole her breath. "There you are."

She smiled back. "We're ready to go."

They helped Lillian down the porch steps and into the yard. Wyatt had harnessed Lillian's mottled gray horse to the rig that waited under the trees. He helped Ada and Lillian into it and handed Ada the reins. "Have you ever driven one of these before?"

She shook her head. "Never. I don't know the first thing about it."

"Well, lucky for you, old Smoky here knows everything. Just flick the reins when you want him to go, and pull back a little and say 'whoa' when you want him to stop."

She gaped at him. For the love of Pete! She couldn't even make soup or dust the parlor to Lil's liking. She'd barely mastered the kitchen water pump and the cookstove. What if she wrecked this contraption and killed them both?

Wyatt's grin only made her angrier. "Surely you don't expect me to—"

"I'm sorry, but I have to get back to the mill.

Two of our sawyers failed to show up this morning. We're racing to get the rest of the lumber ready for shipping on Friday's train."

Lillian glared at her nephew. "Wyatt Caldwell, for once I agree with Ada. Have you lost your mind, turning this girl loose with a horse and buggy? Have you no concern for my safety? I might as well try to drive myself, even if I can't see where I'm going."

"You'll be fine, Aunt Lil. Smoky knows the way to the church. Besides, you can coach Ada if need be." He patted the horse's sleek flank. "I'll be back around six to unhitch him and give him his feed."

"Mr. Caldwell." Ada folded her arms across her chest and swallowed her disappointment. She'd begun to think Wyatt Caldwell was different from other men, more in tune with her sensibilities. But apparently she'd misjudged him. It wouldn't be the first time she'd been wrong about someone. "I understood that my duties were to serve as companion to your aunt. There is nothing in my list of duties about driving this thing."

"I'm adding it to the list."

"What if I refuse?" She stared at him, her insides churning. Wasn't this just like a man? The minute you thought you understood the rules, they up and changed them.

He regarded her solemnly. "You won't refuse, Ada."

"And how are you so certain of this?"

"Because you care for Lillian, and you wouldn't allow her to drive alone."

He was right. Already, she had developed a grudging concern for the older woman. What made her so angry was that Wyatt saw it and was using it to his advantage. She huffed out an exasperated breath.

"I am sorry for surprising you this way, but something tells me you'll do just fine." He tipped his Stetson. "I'll see you ladies after work."

Lillian sighed and pulled on her lace gloves. "Might as well plan on staying for supper then."

"Yep," he drawled, a gleam of mischief lighting his eyes, "might as well."

He swung effortlessly into the saddle, then cantered his horse across the yard and onto the road, churning up a cloud of dust behind him.

"Well?" Lillian tucked her skirts beneath her. "Are we going, or are you planning to sit here all day mooning over my nephew?"

"Mooning? Over him? Absolutely not." Ada picked up the reins and yelled, "Get up!"

Smoky snorted and shook his head. The buggy jostled across the yard and rolled down the lane. Soon the horse settled into a comfortable trot. Far ahead of them, Wyatt's horse moved smartly down the road. As the buggy neared a sharp bend, horse and rider disappeared into the trees. Ada released a pent-up sigh.

Lillian dabbed her forehead with a lace handkerchief. "I can't imagine what I was thinking, agreeing to the hiring of yet another young woman after what happened with Hannah Fields."

"You needn't worry." Ada glanced at the older woman. "I promise not to abscond with a traveling salesman."

"People in love do strange things, especially when the love they feel is not reciprocated."

"Surely Miss Fields wouldn't have gone away with someone for whom she had no tender feelings."

The rig rolled past wide, green fields and thick sedges bending in the breeze. Far above, a hawk turned in slow circles, casting a shadow onto the grass.

"It wasn't the drummer that she loved."

Understanding dawned. Ada's stomach dropped. "Mr. Caldwell?"

"It isn't as if he tries to attract attention. People are just naturally drawn to him."

Ada recalled Wyatt's easy conversation with his mill foreman, his gentle ways with Lillian, his quiet confidence. There *was* something about him that made people want to be near him.

"He's always been that way," Lillian said, "from the time he was a boy. My house was the most popular place in town whenever Wyatt Caldwell arrived for a visit. People showed up just to find out what he'd do next." She laughed. "One time—he must have been eleven or twelve—he and his best friend Billy Rondo made a raft out of an old piano crate and headed down the river like Lewis and Clark. That escapade very nearly stopped my heart."

Ada smiled, imaging an intrepid young Wyatt, lanky and blue-eyed, setting off on an adventure.

"It was to be expected, I suppose," Lillian said, her conversation looping back to Hannah Fields. "A young and handsome bachelor with his own business would be a catch anywhere, but especially in a town like Hickory Ridge. We lost so many men to the war."

"Wyatt told me about Cold Harbor."

"Did he? That's a surprise. He rarely talks about the war to anyone."

They passed the road to Two Creeks. Lillian said, "I hope he warned you about going down to the colored settlement."

Ada nodded, remembering what Wyatt had said about the Klan. The mere mention of it made her stomach tight with apprehension. She had no intention of ever setting foot in Two Creeks.

Smoky *clop-clopped* past the lumber mill. The yard teemed with men removing bark from newly felled trees and loading them onto wagons. The steam-powered saws screamed, and the crack of axes echoed through the trees. In a small paddock behind the office, Wyatt's horse stood placidly cropping grass.

Ada drove on. She was curious to know what

had happened between Wyatt and Hannah Fields but stifled the question that could spoil Lillian's good mood. As they drove into the churchyard, Ada saw a couple of rigs and a buckboard tethered to the hitching post.

"Whoa." Ada tugged the reins. The horse halted and swished his tail. Ada sent Lillian a triumphant grin. "We made it!"

"Naturally." Lillian gathered her quilting bag. "Help me down. My knees have gone stiff as a washboard."

Ada helped Lillian out, then reached inside the buggy for her sketchbook.

A small, neat figure appeared in the church doorway. "Ada! Lillian!"

Lillian squinted through her thick spectacles and waved. "Hello, Mariah!"

Mariah ran out to greet them, her cheeks rosy, her brown eyes bright with anticipation. "Ada, you can't imagine how excited I am about my new hat. I've brought my *Godey's* book, but I see you've brought some ideas of your own." She nodded toward Ada's sketchbook.

Lillian frowned. "My lands. Is that all you can think about?"

"I'm sorry, Lillian." Mariah offered Lillian her arm and they started into the church. "I can't help it."

"First things first. We must finish that quilt for the orphanage this afternoon."

"Of course. You're right." Mariah winked at Ada. "But it's been so long since I've had anything fashionable to wear. I'm dying for something new for the fall festival."

They entered the church and walked past the rows of polished wood pews to a room off a narrow hallway. Carrie Daly was already seated at the quilt frame. The brightly colored fabric scraps spilling from the basket at her feet made her simple black mourning dress look even more somber. Sunlight poured through the open windows and spilled across the scrubbed pine floor. A light breeze drifted in, bringing with it the smell of honeysuckle.

Lillian took a chair on the opposite side of the quilt frame and motioned Ada to join her. She took needles and thimbles from her bag and passed one set to Ada. "Do you know how to quilt?"

"I learned a little, helping my mother with her hats. We quilted riding bonnets for the mother of one of my school friends."

Just then the door opened and Bea Goldston strode into the room. "Sorry I'm late, ladies, I had to—" Spying Ada, she stopped short. "Miss Wentworth, I certainly didn't expect you here today."

Lillian's needle plied the colorful fabric. "In case it has escaped your notice, Bea," she said without missing a stitch, "this is a church. Everyone is welcome."

"Yes, of course"—Bea's smile didn't come close

to reaching her eyes—"for Sunday preaching and such. But the quilting circle . . . it's different, isn't it? I thought it was just for our little group. But never mind." She turned to Lillian, her gray skirts whispering on the pine floor. "I heard that Wyatt is frightfully busy at the mill these days. If it's a matter of transportation, Lillian, I'll be happy to drive out and get—"

"Ada and I can manage. Sit down, Bea, if you're of a mind to help us finish this quilt."

Bea took a seat, and they all set to work. When Bea, Carrie, and Lillian were busy threading their needles, Mariah smiled at Ada and pantomimed trying on a hat. Ada smiled back, tapping down her apprehension. Was it possible to earn a living making hats?

And if not, what other choice was there?

Wyatt reined in his horse, dismounted, and tossed the reins to Robbie Whiting. "Give Cherokee some water, will you, son, and take her out to the paddock."

"Sure thing, Mr. Wyatt." The boy grinned and fished a half-eaten apple from his pocket. "I saved this for Cherokee."

"I'm sure she'll appreciate it."

Boy and horse disappeared around the corner. Wyatt checked on his sawyers, then went inside and tossed his hat onto a chair piled high with papers and books and the last three issues of *Harper's* magazine. He was grateful that the mill was doing so well but regretted that it left him little time for the pleasure of reading.

The map marking the location of his timberlands had fallen down, and he tacked it back into place. He drank a dipper of cool water from the bucket beside the door and glanced at the stack of order forms, shipping invoices, receipts, and canceled checks Sage had placed on his desk that morning. He raised the window shade and settled into his chair, waiting for Lillian's buggy to roll past. He felt a pang of regret. He shouldn't have expected Ada to drive the buggy today. He didn't blame her for being angry with him.

He didn't know quite what to make of Ada Wentworth. She tried so hard to appear strong and independent, yet underneath her bravado he sensed a sad resignation that was both heartbreaking and intriguing. And she was such a pretty little thing. He couldn't stop thinking of the warm fragrance of her skin and the way her soft curves had pressed against him when he lifted her in and out of the wagon.

He hadn't been so attracted to a woman in a very long time. Unlike Hannah and Bea, who had signaled their interest in him in none-too-subtle ways, Ada was a woman of refinement. The kind of woman who could be an intellectual equal and still retain the gentler qualities so long missing from his world of ranchers, soldiers, and mill workers.

He'd definitely felt a spark between them. He was sure she felt it too. A lazy grin began somewhere deep in his gut and migrated to his face.

The rig came into view, Lillian's gentle horse behaving as Wyatt had expected. Both Ada and Lillian sat up straight, their hats perched neatly on their heads. Lillian seemed to be smiling, and for that Wyatt was grateful. His aunt had tolerated Hannah Fields's ministrations, but Wyatt could not recall seeing Lillian smile even once during the younger woman's stay.

He sighed. Perhaps Lillian had sensed Hannah's unrequited attraction to him. It still embarrassed him to recall the evening in February when Hannah appeared at his door unannounced, a picnic basket over her arm. Exhausted from meetings in town and a long afternoon at the mill, he'd been looking forward to a plate of scrambled eggs and some quiet time with a new book. But with the temperature dropping fast and a light snow falling, he couldn't turn her away.

The decision to invite her inside proved to be a mistake. After plying him with warm bowls of chicken pot pie and cherry crumb cake, Hannah boldly announced that she was in love with him and intended to marry him. He was flattered and sorry for the girl and deeply relieved when she left town with that fellow from Denver.

Oh, Hannah was pretty enough, with a peachy complexion and red hair that fell in thick ringlets down her back. But never once had he felt about her the way he was feeling about Ada Wentworth. Which didn't make one iota of sense, considering the way he usually felt about Yanks. It wasn't just because of the war. It went way past politics and fighting. It was personal. But somehow when it came to Ada Wentworth, it didn't seem to matter quite so much.

When the buggy was out of sight, Wyatt found his leather work gloves and went out to the cavernous shed to help Sage and the others. He cocked an ear. One of the saws was making that funny noise again. He couldn't afford to have it malfunction when they were so swamped. He made a mental note to check it out.

Sage hurried over with a question about the Friday shipment. One of the sawyers, a young man from Alabama, was right behind him, asking Wyatt for a day off. Robbie Whiting tore around the corner to ask whether he could ride Cherokee.

Wyatt responded in turn to each of them, but his thoughts were still of Ada. Pulling on the gloves, he helped load the finished lumber onto the wagons, feeling a deep sense of loneliness that just wouldn't go away. He sensed in Ada that same sense of isolation, a holding back, as if she didn't trust him.

He took off his hat and wiped the sweat from his brow. Given his distrust of Yanks, maybe that evened the score.

Seven

Ada set aside her thimble and closed her eyes. Her fingers were sore from the constant pressure of the needle, and her insides were a jumble of nerves. Now that the quilt was finished, Mariah would expect to talk about her hat, and Lillian was sure to disapprove. The older woman had been quiet during the afternoon. Whether she was preoccupied or just feeling poorly, Ada couldn't tell.

Mariah got to her feet. From a small cupboard on the far wall, she took out glasses and plates and opened her woven basket to retrieve jars of lemonade and a platter of cookies. Carrie and Bea removed the quilt from the frame and carefully folded it for delivery to the orphanage.

"I can't stay." Bea tossed her hair and picked up her sewing bag. "I must prepare for tomorrow's school-board meeting." She sent Ada a withering glance. "Some of us have important work to do."

Mariah flipped the pages of her fashion magazine. "Good-bye, Bea."

When she departed, Mariah set the magazine aside. "I know we're supposed to love everybody, but it's difficult to have any charitable feelings toward someone as cantankerous as Bea." She patted the empty chair next to hers. "Ada, come and look at these hats. And don't give Bea Goldston another thought."

She handed Ada the *Godey's Lady's Book*, opened to a page featuring the latest styles in hats. "I like this one. Can you make one like it for me?"

Ada studied the drawing of a pale yellow postilion-styled hat with a cinnamon brown brim and matching brown pompoms on each side. The crown was encircled with three rows of cinnamon velvet. "It's simple enough to make," she said, "but I'd want to trim it with a color other than brown. Green satin, perhaps, or an ostrich feather."

"Perfect! How about green satin *and* ostrich plumes?"

"I can do that. It's easy to change the trimmings to match whatever dress you want to wear." Ada flipped through the magazine and tried to shake off her lingering irritation toward the schoolteacher. "For instance, this hat has a buckle trim."

"I like feathers better. When can you start?" Mariah laughed at her own excitement, and Carrie smiled. Despite Bea's sour comments and Lillian's disapproving frown, Ada felt, for the first time in a long while, the sweetness of belonging.

Mariah flipped through the book until she found a drawing of a round, crowned hat with a wide brim, decorated with flowers and feathers. "I like this one too."

Ada considered Mariah's small form, her warm brown eyes, heart-shaped face, and thick copper curls. "I could make that hat for you as well, but before you decide, would you take a look at my sketchbook?"

Mariah took the book and turned the pages, exclaiming over Ada's sketches of feathered bonnets, satin toques, and small flat hats in leghorn straw decorated with pleating, flowers, netting, and beads.

Ada pointed to the sketch she'd made with Mariah in mind—a small toque fashioned of the finest straw, trimmed with chocolate brown velvet and blond lace, and set off with tiny green-feather ferns surrounding a single rust-colored flower. "This is a copy of a hat my mother bought in Paris one year. It's still very much in fashion, and it's perfect for you."

Mariah pored over the sketch. Even Carrie seemed momentarily interested. Her eyes lingered on the page before she left her chair to stare out the window. Ada's heart broke for her.

"I adore it!" Mariah said. "How much will you charge?"

Ada stole a glance at Lillian. She could ill afford to anger the old woman, but she had to think of her own future. The sooner she could bring in some paying customers and get her business started, the better. Lillian stared out the window, feigning disinterest, but Ada could tell the older woman was taking in every word.

"Another two dollars should cover it." Taking into account the cost of her supplies and the number of hours it would take to make the pattern, shape the hat, and attach the trimmings, she would not make a cent on this hat, but perhaps it would serve as a good advertisement of her skills.

She opened her bag and took out her mother's worn tape measure. "I'll need your size, and I'll have to buy supplies. I don't have any milliner's gauze or any wiring. I'll need some new trimmings as well. Those will have to be ordered."

"How long will that take?" Mariah stood still while Ada took her measurement.

"A few weeks perhaps."

"But it will be finished by October? The harvest festival is the biggest event in town."

"Surely by October," Ada assured her. "I'll let you know as soon as my materials arrive."

"Wonderful!" Mariah consulted the small watch suspended on a chain around her neck. "Now, I must run. If I hurry, I can deliver our quilt before suppertime."

She said her good-byes and left the church. Carrie swept up the cookie crumbs, gathered their glasses, and went outside to wash them at the water pump. Leaving Lillian ensconced by the window, Ada followed Carrie outside.

"Need some help?" She primed the pump and lifted the handle. A thin stream of water trickled out. "These old pump handles are so heavy, aren't they?"

Carrie nodded and concentrated on swirling clean water through the glasses.

"It sure is hot, isn't it?" Ada blotted her forehead. "Is it always this warm here so early in the summer?"

Carrie shrugged.

"I heard your husband died at Shiloh," Ada said quietly. "I can only imagine how that must feel."

Carrie's hands stilled. Water ran over them and into the trough. "Everyone said I'd get over it, but I don't want to."

Ada nodded. For years she'd felt the same way about her mother. "I realize that losing one's parents isn't the same thing as losing a husband, but I—"

"I didn't *lose* Frank," Carrie said with surprising fierceness. "Why do people say that—as if I carelessly misplaced him somewhere? It's so stupid! He was *taken* from me, and in the end, what did it matter anyway?" She brushed away tears. "If I stop thinking about Frank, if I stop mourning him, then he's gone forever."

"Carrie." Ada took the glasses from Carrie's hands and set them aside. "We've only just met, and I hope you won't think I am speaking out of turn, but here's something I've learned. Our grief, however profound, doesn't keep our loved ones alive."

"Then what does?"

"Honoring them with our own lives." She grasped Carrie's hands. "You're still a young woman.

There is much that you can do to bring honor to your husband's memory."

Wordlessly, Carrie finished washing the glasses and started back inside.

"I saw the way you looked at my sketches," Ada said. "Please let me make a new hat for you. I won't charge you anything."

Carrie paused without looking back. "Miss Wentworth, I know you mean well, but please . . . leave me alone."

Stung by Carrie's rejection, Ada lingered for a moment before following her inside. Lillian had fallen asleep in her chair, her head lolled to one side, her hat with its yellow flower trim askew.

"Lillian?" Ada shook the old woman's shoulder. "Time to go."

Lillian jerked awake, blinking. "What time is it?"

"Almost five, I would think."

"Now why did you let me fall asleep? We'll be late making supper for Wyatt."

Carrie finished putting the clean glasses away and picked up her quilting bag. "Don't worry, Lillian. This morning Henry told me that Sage and Wyatt are planning to work an extra hour today to get the milling done."

Lillian got to her feet and straightened her hat. "Is that a fact? Why didn't Wyatt say so?"

"It doesn't matter," Ada said. "Now we'll have plenty of time to make supper."

They went out to the churchyard. Carrie

climbed onto her buckboard and started home. Ada looked up. The sun had disappeared behind thick clouds, threatening rain. In the distance, thunder rumbled. Ada settled Lillian on the seat, unwound the reins from the hitching post, and climbed into the buggy.

"Get up there, Smoky." She was surprised how quickly she was growing accustomed to driving. They turned out of the churchyard, and another flick of the reins had the gray horse trotting toward home.

"I enjoyed the quilting circle," Ada said. "I'm glad you invited me."

Lillian sat stiffly, her hands folded on her lap, her face stony. She seemed acutely interested in Smoky's hindquarters.

Ada sighed. "I'm sorry if you're upset with me about the hat."

"My nephew hired a lady's companion, not a milliner."

"I won't neglect my responsibilities to you."

"For what Wyatt is paying you, I should have your undivided attention."

Heavenly days! Had Lillian gone shopping lately? Had she no idea of the cost of even the barest of necessities? Seven dollars a month might sound like a lot, but it would go all too quickly.

"You will have my full attention whenever you need me. But in the evenings—"

"I don't want to talk about it anymore. You'll do

what you want to do no matter what I say. But—"

A sudden gust of wind stirred the dust on the road. Lillian clamped one hand on her hat and looked up. "I don't like the looks of that sky. We may be in for a blow."

Ada urged Smoky into a faster trot. They passed the lumber mill. Men scurried about, covering the equipment with tarps and driving the loaded wagons into the long sheds.

"Should we stop here?" Ada glanced at the sky with growing apprehension. Thick black clouds boiled up, obscuring the mountaintops.

"I want to go home. If you'll stop dawdling, we can make it before the rain hits."

Ada pushed the horse as fast as she dared. Just as the house came into view, the sky opened. Lightning arced across the darkened sky. Rain pelted their faces.

"Drive into the barn!" Lillian yelled.

Ada flicked the reins once more and Smoky obeyed, coming to a halt at the barn door. Ada jumped down, and her shoes sank into mud that was rapidly becoming as thick as cake batter. She lifted the bar, heaved open the door, and led the horse inside, past hay bales, rakes, pitchforks, and a heap of dusty harnesses. The smell of hay and manure filled her nose.

"Wait here," Ada told Lillian. "I'll fetch your rain cape and umbrella."

"I'm all right. Or I will be as soon as I get out of

these wet clothes. I feel like a drowned rat. Help me down."

Ada wrapped one arm around Lillian's waist and led her across the mire. By the time they reached the porch, they were soaked to the skin, and Lillian was pale and shivering. They took off their muddy shoes and went inside.

"Do you need help changing your clothes?" Ada sat on the bottom stair and peeled off her clammy stockings.

"I can manage." Lillian waved her away. "You should get out of your things, too, before you catch a cold."

"I'll change as soon as I put the teakettle on."

"Forget tea. My feet are wet and cold as a wagon tire. A day like this calls for spirits." Lillian gestured toward the sideboard. "Pour us a brandy, girl—purely for medicinal purposes, of course. Then we've got to get supper started."

Half an hour later, dressed in dry clothes and warmed by the brandy, Ada spread her wet clothes on the porch rail beneath the overhang and went to the kitchen to start supper. Lillian snuggled into a blue dressing gown and sat in her wheelchair near the cookstove, directing Ada as she mixed the dough for biscuits and sliced apples for dumplings. While the biscuits baked, Ada set the table and started a pot of coffee.

Wyatt arrived a short time later and went straight to the barn to see after Smoky, then opened the front door and stepped into the parlor.

"Take that rain gear off, Wyatt Caldwell!" his aunt called. "Don't you drip water on my floor."

"No ma'am, I won't."

He stepped into the kitchen holding a wrinkled wad of soggy white linen, a smile teasing the corner of his mouth, his eyes full of merriment. "Did one of you ladies lose your unmentionables?"

Ada stopped dead still, a laden platter in each hand. Her cheeks flamed. "I . . . I put it out to dry."

"Must have blown off the porch. I didn't want it to get muddy." He pulled a chair close to the cookstove and carefully spread her soggy chemise over it. "There. It'll be dry in no time."

Ada watched his hands smoothing the thin fabric. He smiled a slow smile that made her insides go soft, seeming not to notice her acute discomfort. He seated his aunt and took his place between the two women. "Something sure smells good."

"Shall we pray?" Lillian peered at her nephew, her gold-rimmed spectacles flashing in the lamplight.

Considering what he had told her at the river, Ada wondered if he would object to praying. But he enveloped Ada's hand in a warm and gentle grip as he asked the Lord to bless the house, the food, and the company. He thanked God for the rain and asked his blessing on the mill and his workers. "Amen and pass the biscuits."

Ada picked up her fork and studied Wyatt beneath lowered lashes. Despite her earlier irritation over having to drive the buggy, she felt something sparking between them, a connection, an energy that was both exhilarating and unsettling.

"Ada?" He smiled at her across the candlelit table. "I have to go into town on Friday to oversee a shipment and talk to some people at the bank. I thought you and Aunt Lil might like to come along. She hasn't been to town in quite a while, and you haven't really had a chance to see the place."

"Thank you. I'd like that."

The rain had stopped. Outside the kitchen window, water dripped from the eaves into the rain barrel beside the door. He nodded and concentrated on his meal.

Ada found herself studying the planes of his face, the way his eyes shone with pleasure when he tucked into the apple dumplings she'd made. She quickly dropped her gaze. It would be much too easy to fall in love with Wyatt Caldwell, to trust her future to someone else. She knew better than that now. It was safer to rely upon herself.

Besides, Wyatt had dreams of his own. When Lillian was gone, they'd go their separate ways. As appealing as Wyatt Caldwell was, giving her heart to him didn't make a lick of sense.

Even if she decided that he was worthy of her trust, why start something they couldn't finish?

Eight

The next morning, while Lillian slept, Ada sat at the kitchen table making a hat pattern. Bright sunshine slanted across the whitewashed table, painting the kitchen in a golden glow. Outside the open window, a cardinal took up his morning song, *pretty-pretty-pretty*.

Earlier Libby Dawson, the young colored girl from Two Creeks, had come to collect the week's laundry. After Libby bundled their sheets, chemises, and dressing gowns onto the wagon, Ada gave the girl a scrap of ribbon. Libby pinned the ribbon into her hair and climbed, agile as a gazelle, onto her buckboard. It seemed to Ada that the girl sat a bit straighter as she drove away.

"Miss Ada!"

Ada dropped her scissors and spun around. "Robbie Whiting! You scared the life out of me!"

The boy stood before her holding a tin bucket. "I knocked on the door, but I guess you didn't hear me."

"Well, you mustn't walk into people's houses uninvited. I'm certain that your mother has taught you better manners than that."

"Yes ma'am, but Miss Lillian don't care. She knows me. I come here all the time." He handed her the bucket. "I brought you some blackberries. There's tons of them down by the river. I could bring you some every day if you want."

"That's very thoughtful of you, but I'm not sure Miss Lillian and I could eat so many berries every day."

"You could make blackberry cobbler. Mr. Wyatt, he likes it a lot. I guess it's just about his favorite dessert in the whole world."

Ada smiled. "I'll keep that in mind."

Robbie leaned over the table. "Whatcha doing?"

"Making a pattern for your mother's new hat."

"Yeah, Mama's been talking about that hat ever since you got here. She told Pa she needs a new dress to go with it."

He was such an appealing child that Ada couldn't resist ruffling his hair.

He grinned up at her. "Guess what I found down by the river."

He dug through his pockets for a white, coin-sized object and set it on the table between them. "It's a real mouse skull, and there's hardly any of it missing."

"That's quite a find."

"Yes ma'am. And guess what else?" He produced a ridged, triangular stone and slid it across the table. "It's a genuine Indian arrowhead. You can keep it if you want."

"That's very nice of you, but I couldn't take such a valuable treasure."

"Oh, I've got buckets of 'em. Mr. Wyatt says

it's prob'ly from the Cherokees. They lived around here in prehistoric times."

Ada smiled. The child's concept of time was more than a little skewed; Wyatt had mentioned that most of the Cherokees had been moved west only fifty years before. "Well, if you're sure, I'd be delighted to have it." She set it on the windowsill.

"My mama says Miss Hannah told her that your ma and pa are dead. Are they?"

"I'm afraid so." Ada smoothed the hat pattern and swallowed a pang of grief.

"How come?"

"My mother died of a disease called consumption when I was not much older than you are now."

Robbie nodded soberly. "Tuberculosis. It's a disease of the lungs."

"That's right. How did you know?"

"Sophie at the orphanage told me. I play with her when Mama and I go there. Her mama died of tuberculosis when Sophie was not even two years old." He stuffed the mouse skull back into his pocket. "Her daddy might be dead. Or alive. We're not for sure. He ran away when Sophie was born because she's partly white and partly colored."

"I see."

"That's why nobody wants to play with her. But I like her. She's smart. And she's pretty too. Like a drawin' in a storybook."

"I'm sure she appreciates having a good friend like you."

He shrugged. “What happened to your pa? Did he get tuberculosis too?”

“You know, Robbie, it’s such a beautiful day, I don’t think I want to talk about sad things.”

“No ma’am.” To her complete surprise, Robbie wrapped his arms around her waist and pressed his cheek against her apron. He smelled of sunshine, river water, and sun-warmed blackberries. Ada’s eyes filled.

“I’m sorry about your ma and pa. And I’m sorry I made you sad.”

It was easy to see why Wyatt set such store by this boy. He was a treasure. She held him by the shoulders and smiled into his bright blue eyes. “You are a wonderful boy, Robbie Whiting, and I can never be sad when you’re around.”

He smiled, and she swallowed the lump in her throat. “I’d better get back to work before Miss Lillian wakes up wanting her breakfast.”

“Yes ma’am.”

“Thank you for the blackberries. I’m sure we’ll enjoy them.”

“You should make a cobbler. Because it’s Mr.—”

“Yes, I know. Mr. Caldwell’s favorite.”

He headed for the door. “Pa says Mr. Wyatt is taking you to town tomorrow.”

“My goodness, you don’t miss a thing, do you?”

“Mama says little pitchers have big ears.”

“Indeed.” She made a shooing motion. “Run along now. I have work to do.”

She settled herself at the table just as Lillian appeared, still dazed from sleep, her hair sticking up, stockings bunched at her ankles. She propelled her wheelchair to the table and set the brake.

"Did you sleep well?" Ada started clearing away her work. "What would you like to eat?"

"Hardly slept at all, if you want the truth of it. It's one of the aggravations of getting old." Spying the berries she said, "Robbie's been here."

"Yes. Would you like some berries?"

Lillian nodded. "And a biscuit, if there are any left."

Ada bustled about, filling a plate. "Are you sure you won't have some bacon? A poached egg? This doesn't seem like much food."

Lillian buttered her biscuit. "Another hazard of being almost eighty. Appetite comes and goes." She picked up her spoon. "Mostly it goes."

Ada felt an unexpected surge of affection for the older woman. Lillian had managed to hold on to her faith despite her private sorrows and to face up to the inevitable indignities of old age—even as she complained about them.

She waved Ada into a chair. "Sit. Keep me company. I hate eating alone."

Ada sat. Lillian ate the berries with obvious relish. "Nothing as good as fresh picked berries. You should make a cobbler."

Ada rose to clear the table. "That seems to be the consensus around here."

"Come walk with me in the garden." Lillian struggled to her feet. "Before it gets too hot."

Ada glanced out at the sun-filled garden. Nothing stirred. It was already too hot, but she found her hat and Lillian's, and they went through the back door into the garden. Roses and hollyhocks bloomed in profusion next to bright-orange daylilies and a row of shrubs covered with a cascade of white blooms.

Lillian stretched out a hand to caress the delicate flowers. "The bridal veil is blooming. I carried a bouquet of these when I married the doctor." She picked a cluster of the creamy-white blooms. "People said we were a perfect couple. But I'll tell you something, Ada, the only ones who really know what goes on in a marriage are the two people who are in it."

Ada knew this to be true. People had thought Elizabeth and Cornelius Wentworth's union was perfect too. No one knew about Cornelius's jealousy of his wife's talents, the disparaging remarks he made about the work that meant so much to her, or of their worsening financial situation as, one after the other, her father's ventures failed. Ada was never allowed to talk about any of it. In her social circle, scandal was still far worse than death.

Lillian and Ada walked farther into the garden. Lillian was in an expansive mood, and Ada let her talk. "I'm not saying the doctor was a bad man. You ask anybody, they'll tell you he did a lot of good in this town. But he was an indifferent husband." Lillian pinched a couple of spent blooms from a rosebush and gathered a bouquet of daylilies. "I suppose he used up his tenderness on his patients, and there wasn't much left for me. Even when he was alive I lived in a kind of empty stillness." She regarded Ada with the saddest expression in her watery blue eyes. "Many a day there was only God to fill it."

Ada felt sorry for her. To be trapped in a loveless marriage would be far worse than living alone. To distract Lillian from her memories, Ada asked questions about the various plants in the garden. Leaning on Ada's arm, Lillian pointed out the pale pink heirloom roses that had been growing in the same spot for almost a hundred years. It seemed that every plant had a story, and Lillian relished recounting each one.

The morning was nearly gone by the time they went inside. The clock chimed. Lillian set her bouquet on the sideboard and cocked her head like a small bird, listening. "Noontime," she said. "The doctor will be here any minute. I must get his meal ready. He doesn't like to be kept waiting."

Ada placed a hand on the old woman's shoulder. "Miss Lillian, the doctor has passed on. Remember?"

"What?" Lillian blinked. "What are you talking about?"

"Just now," Ada said gently. "You said your husband was coming home."

"I said no such thing! What nonsense." Lillian burst into tears. "You just wait till I tell Wyatt that you're telling lies on me. He'll send you packing soon enough."

Ada blew out a long breath. Why had no one warned her that Lillian was unstable? Wishing she'd accepted the calming elixir from the salesman on the train, she poured a glass of water and handed it to Lillian. "Please don't cry. It was a misunderstanding, that's all."

"I'm not crazy!" Lillian's hand trembled as she brought the glass to her lips.

"I know that. You're tired, and you've had too much sun. Why don't I freshen your bed and let you rest for a while. Would you like me to read to you until you fall asleep?"

"You *can't* read to me because somebody stole my Bible!"

Perhaps it was better to humor the older woman than to argue. Ada took Lillian's arm. "Who do you suppose took it?"

"How should I know? People steal from me all the time. Maybe you took it, Yankee girl. Yankees steal everything that isn't nailed down."

They went down the hall to Lillian's bedroom. Ada straightened the bed and opened the window and helped Lillian to bed. "There, that's better. And look, there's your Bible on the dresser. Whoever stole it must have thought better of it and brought it back."

She seated herself in the rocking chair beside the bed and read aloud from Psalms until the older woman fell asleep and began snoring softly. Outside the open window, a dove cooed, a mournful sound that brought her nearly to tears. What a pickle she was in! She could learn to cook and drive the rig. She could put up with Lillian's unpredictable moods. But looking after someone with a mental condition was more than she could handle.

Every day in this house brought another unwelcome revelation. Why hadn't Wyatt told her about this? Despite his charm, she was tempted to pack up her bags and light out for parts unknown, money or no. It would serve him right.

Nine

Wyatt arrived early the next morning dressed for town in a dark suit and a pearl-gray Stetson. Ada watched him from the window as he climbed down from his rig and headed for the house, whistling a loud tune, slightly off-key. Despite yesterday's disconcerting episode, she found herself smiling. She checked her reflection in the hallway mirror and opened the door. "Come in. We're not quite ready."

"That's unusual." Wyatt stepped into the hall.

"Aunt Lil complains about the busyness in town these days, but she looks forward to going all the same."

"We had a difficult day yesterday, Mr. Caldwell." Briefly, Ada described Lillian's confusion and her accusations.

Wyatt nodded. "She has these spells from time to time. There's a tonic for when she gets all worked up. Didn't Hannah mention it in her letters?"

"She certainly didn't. Your aunt scared me out of a year's growth. I had no idea what to do."

"I'm sorry. I'll show you where we keep it." He went to the kitchen and took a brown glass vial from the cupboard. "The directions are on the label.But she won't take any medicine voluntarily. Hannah usually put it in her cocoa."

He returned the bottle to the cupboard. "How does she seem this morning?"

"I haven't had the heart to disturb her."

"Let's get her up and dressed. I have a meeting at the bank at eleven."

"I'll see what's keeping her."

Ada knocked on Lillian's door. When there was no answer she called loudly, "Miss Lillian?"

"What's the trouble?" Wyatt loomed in the hallway.

"She won't answer me."

He opened the door. "Aunt Lil? Can't you hear us talking to—"

The bed was empty. One pale tiny foot protruded from beneath the bed. Wyatt bent down and lifted the corner of the bed skirt. "Lillian Caldwell Willis, what in heaven's name are you doing under there?"

"What does it look like? I'm hiding!"

He dropped to his knees and stuck his head under the bed. "Hiding? From what?"

"Ghosts! I saw them last night riding up the road. They came back to steal my Bible again, but I fooled 'em. I have it right here."

Ada's stomach clenched. Was the nighttime visit a warning from the Klansmen that she was unwelcome here?

For a split second, Wyatt's gaze flickered as if he harbored similar thoughts, but he sent Ada a reassuring smile. "It was probably just the wind, blowing against the curtains."

"I know what I saw," Lillian insisted, her voice muffled.

"Don't you want to go shopping at the mercantile?"

"I most certainly do not. It's too crowded, and they never have half the things I want anyway. Tell Hannah to bring me some of that French milled soap. The one that smells like lemons."

"Aunt Lil," Wyatt said patiently, "Hannah lives in Denver now. You know that. Now come on out from under there before I'm forced to drag you out."

She crawled out on all fours, her nightgown black with dust, her hair standing up in little white wisps.

Wyatt helped her into her chair. "If you don't want to go with us, I'll send Libby Dawson to stay with you. I saw her on the way in. She's just down the road at the Spencer place delivering laundry."

Ada touched Wyatt's sleeve. "It's all right. I can see the town another time."

"No need to cancel our plans. Libby is used to staying with her. Lil likes her." He motioned Ada into the hallway and lowered his voice. "She started having these spells a couple of years back. There's nothing we can do about it." He glanced into Lil's bedroom. "I'm sorry you weren't informed of it before you arrived."

"Apparently quite a lot was kept from me." Now that the crisis was past, Ada felt her anger building. "For instance, I had no idea that this part of the country was overrun with scofflaws and ruffians. No idea that I'd be required to cook and keep house, not to mention having to handle a horse and buggy. Not that I can't master it—"

"You did just fine the other day, from what I was able to see."

"That isn't the point. You should have prepared me."

"I relied on Hannah to give you the particulars. That was my mistake. I apologize."

She sighed. "What else should I know?"

Wyatt's deep blue gaze held hers. "That I am grateful to you for the concern you've shown my aunt in the short time you've been here. She was practically glowing at supper the other night."

Ada blew out a noisy breath. Mercy, but he was exasperating. It was impossible to stay mad at him. She stood rooted to the spot, her gaze locked on his, afraid to move and break the spell. At last Wyatt stepped back and cleared his throat. "Shall we go?"

Ada glanced toward Lillian's room. "She'll be all right until Libby arrives? What if Libby can't come?"

"Once Aunt Lil takes her medicine, she sleeps for a long while. But if Libby can't come, we'll go to town another day."

He went to the kitchen, measured a dose of the tonic into a glass of milk, and coaxed his aunt into drinking it. Then he helped her to the bed. "Go to sleep, sweetheart. Everything's all right."

Ada collected her hat and gloves, her handbag, and her parasol. When she peeked into the room again, Wyatt was sitting in the chair with a book propped on his knees, and Lillian was fast asleep.

A moment later Ada and Wyatt crossed the yard to the rig. He helped her onto the seat and they drove away, a renewed sense of ease blossoming between them. They stopped at the Spencers' to speak to the Dawson girl and headed for town.

Ada unfurled her parasol. "Your aunt says this is

the hottest June in Hickory Ridge in a long while."

"It's a scorcher, all right. But it isn't as hot as Texas can be this time of year. One summer, I must have been seventeen or so, we had a bad drought. It was a hundred and ten in the shade for weeks on end. Grass dried up. The cattle dropped dead. We lost almost two hundred head before the rain came."

Ada shuddered, imagining an endless arid landscape littered with bloated, rotting carcasses. How could he bear it?

"It's one of the hazards of ranching." Wyatt took out his handkerchief and wiped his face. "But it's not always that way. You have to take the good with the bad—like most anything else in life, I reckon."

She adjusted the angle of her parasol. "Of course, in Boston, it's the winters that can be hard to take. There's hardly anything more miserable than January in Massachusetts."

He nodded. "That's the honest truth."

She looked up at him from beneath her parasol. "I didn't realize you'd ever been to Boston."

His expression went hard. "I was there once. Before the war."

Ada was overcome with curiosity. What had brought him to Boston in the dead of winter? Not a pleasure trip, surely. What did he think of her hometown? Had he ridden past the pretty brick houses on Acorn Street? Braved the cold to walk in the park beside the river? But one look at his stony expression told her that Boston was the last thing he wanted to talk about.

They rounded a bend. Far ahead of them, a wagon laden with lumber headed toward town. Maybe it was better to find a safer topic of conversation. "How did you come to be in the lumber business?" she asked. "I can't think of what it has in common with ranching."

"A friend of the family owned a little mill in east Texas. Harvesting pine mostly. One summer I had a falling out with my daddy and left ranching for a good long while. Mr. Trask put me to work—taught me everything I know. After the war, I figured the demand for lumber would go sky high." He shrugged. "Can't raise longhorns around here, but there's plenty of good timber. Starting a lumber business just seemed like the logical thing to do."

"What about your father? Did you patch up your differences?"

"We did. He's a good man." Wyatt smiled. "He's got some big plans for when I get back home."

Ada felt a rush of envy that sat like a stone in her stomach. If only she had reconciled with her father. If only she had a home to go back to and someone waiting for her there.

Wyatt rested his hand on his knee, the reins loose in his fingers. "Sage tells me that Mariah can hardly talk about anything but her new hat."

"After going without everything for so long, I suppose anything new is appreciated." She fanned her face. "It's hard to imagine the hardships women here have survived. I feel so sorry for Carrie Daly."

He nodded soberly. "Carrie's been through a lot. But if she wasn't so busy looking after her brother Henry, she might find love again. I know for a fact there's one or two good men in town who would love to court Carrie."

When they reached the mill, Wyatt sent Robbie Whiting to find the wheelwright Josiah Dawson. "Tell him Libby is out at Aunt Lillian's until we get back from town this afternoon."

"Sure thing, Lieutenant!" Robbie sprinted down the road, his bare feet sending up little puffs of dust.

Wyatt flicked the reins, and the horse broke into an easy trot.

Ada smiled. "He called you 'lieutenant.' Was that your rank in the brigade?"

"It was. But don't be too impressed. General Hood always said that the most dangerous thing in the army is a lieutenant with a map."

Ada laughed and gave herself over to the beauty of summer in the valley. Though the morning was hot, a breeze drifted across the meadow, bringing with it the scents of grass and wild honeysuckle. In the distance, dense forests gave way to blue-green mountains that stretched toward a clear azure sky.

They passed a couple of farmhouses and the

church. The rig clattered across a wooden bridge spanning the river and jostled over the railroad trestle. Soon the train station came into view. Travelers milled about on the platform among a jumble of trunks and wooden crates. A young peddler moved through the crowd hawking his wares.

Wyatt drew up beside the agent's office. "I need to check on my shipment going out this afternoon. I won't be long."

Ada sat beneath her parasol, content to watch the activity unfolding around her. Down the street, a steady stream of customers came and went from the bank and the general store. The smells of cinnamon and yeast emanated from the bakery on the corner. In front of it, a group of little boys played mumblety-peg, the blades of their knives flashing in the sun. Their giddy, carefree laughter rose above the noise of the train station. Ada laughed with them, sharing their joy.

Wyatt returned with a sheaf of papers that he tucked into a leather pouch. Taking out his pocket watch, he said, "It's still early. Would you like a tour of the town?"

"Yes, I'd love that."

They drove down the main street past the shops and the post office and the Verandah Hotel for Ladies, then turned west onto a macadam road shaded by hickory trees. On either side of the road, new houses were going up; the smell of paint and new lumber filled the air. Carpenters, brick masons, and painters swarmed over several houses in various states of completion. On one side of the street sat a long, low building with many windows and a red front door. A flagpole sat in the middle of a grassy yard that sloped away from the back of the building into the trees.

"That's our new school." Wyatt halted the rig. "We opened it only three years ago, and already we're expecting fifty students this fall. Bea will have her hands full."

"That seems like a lot of students for one teacher."

He nodded. "The school board hired a second teacher this spring, a gentleman from Virginia. This fall he'll take the older students and serve as headmaster. Bea will have the younger ones."

She gazed at the neat, welcoming building. "It isn't at all what I expected."

He urged the horse onward. "Perhaps you pictured a log cabin."

She blushed. "You're right. I did."

"Sorry to disappoint you. But the days of Davy Crockett are long past in Hickory Ridge."

She smiled. "I'm only now realizing how much I have to learn about your town."

"It's your town too—for now, at least." His smile brought an unexpected reaction—a warm tightening inside. She felt her face grow warm. What was the matter with her? She had no business at all feeling this way about Wyatt Caldwell. She concentrated on the sound of the horse's hooves on the road and on the passing scenery.

They passed a redbrick church and, next to it, a smaller building enclosed by a white picket fence. Under the watchful eye of a woman in a dark green dress, groups of children played tag in the dusty yard. A little boy, perhaps three or four, bounced a ball against the side of the building. On the stone steps, a young girl in a tattered yellow dress sat alone, a curtain of glossy black hair hiding her face.

"Orphanage," Wyatt said. "First opened back in the fifties, after several children were orphaned in a flash flood. We added on to it after the war handed us even more young folks with no kin to take them in." He nodded toward the girl on the steps. "Mrs. Lowell does the best she can for them, but I always feel bad for Sophie over there."

Sophie. The child Robbie had told her about seemed utterly lost, the very picture of dejection.

Ada's heart twisted. She knew just how those children felt. Abandoned. Afraid. And in Sophie's case, friendless, except for Robbie Whiting. She found it hard to look away. Surely something could be done to ease that child's loneliness.

They came to a small grassy park with a white gingerbread-trimmed gazebo and a merry-go-round. "This is where we have the Founders Day picnic every Fourth of July."

He pulled the rig to a stop, tethered the horse, and helped her out. They walked along a meandering footpath paralleling the river and came at last to the gazebo. There they sat with their backs to the road, the forest in front of them.

"I loved coming to Founders Day when I was boy and staying here with Aunt Lil," Wyatt said. "One year when I was about ten or eleven, an acrobatic group performed, and I decided that's what I'd be when I grew up."

He laughed then. Ada wished she'd known Wyatt Caldwell when they were both young and everything seemed possible. He went on. "Since the war ended, we still have a concert and games for the children, but Founders Day has turned political. There's always some kind of a dustup between the diehard rebs and the unionists."

"I'm surprised there *are* any unionists this far south."

"This part of the state was heavily divided—and feelings still run strong on both sides. It's as if folks have forgotten Appomattox ever happened. I keep my distance."

Ada nodded. "I suppose old hatreds die hard whatever the cause. In Boston—"

He got to his feet. "Let's go. I don't want to be late for my meeting."

Without waiting for her, he turned and headed back to the rig.

Stunned at his abruptness, Ada hurried after him. "Mr. Caldwell, did I say something wrong?"

He shook his head, handed her into the rig, and clicked his tongue to the horse.

When they passed the orphanage, Ada looked for Sophie. But recess was over; the children were marching back inside. She stole a glance at Wyatt. He seemed disinclined toward conversation, lost in his war memories perhaps. What had she said to upset him?

All the joy had gone out of her day. Ada sat quietly until he parked the rig in front of the bank.

"I shouldn't be more than an hour." He retrieved his leather pouch. "Why don't you look around, do your shopping, and when I'm finished we'll eat at Miss Hattie's." At last, he smiled again. "She makes the best fried chicken this side of Fort Worth."

Ada nodded, relieved at his change of mood. "That sounds good."

He headed into the bank. Ada slipped her bag over her arm and set off down the main street, grateful for the opportunity to explore the town on her own. She found the post office and mailed her letter and supply list to the ancient Horace Biddle in Boston, hoping his memory of her mother would induce him to extend the credit she needed. At the mercantile, she purchased a length ofribbon for Mariah's hat and another packet of needles. She stared longingly at a display of stockings. She needed a new pair to replace her old, holey ones, but she didn't dare spend the money. It might be months, a year even, before she could afford even the basic necessities. She'd never before realized how taxing it was to live in fear of running out of cash. She thought of her father. Had he felt this same sense of hopelessness?

Outside Norah's Fine Frocks, she stopped to admire a sky-blue silk dress displayed in one window. Another window showcased fringed parasols and embroidered shawls. A hand-lettered sign urged customers to look for the latest styles in the *Hickory Ridge Gazette*.

Ada remembered an evening with her father when they had discussed his most recent undertaking, an investment in the future manufacture of horseless carriages. When she ventured her opinion—that people would never give up their reliable horse-drawn conveyances for something new, unproven, and possibly dangerous—he'd simply laughed and patted her hand. "You'll see, Ada. Never underestimate the public's appetite for the latest thing!"

The latest thing. Her father's investment had failed to pay off, but perhaps his advice could help her now. With a final glance into the shop window, Ada headed for the newspaper office.

Ten

The bell above the door jingled as Ada entered the small cluttered newspaper office. Sunlight filtered through a single window facing the street and illuminated several full pages of newsprint preserved behind glass. The air was thick with the smells of coffee and ink. Behind the desk sat a young, freckle-faced woman in a faded blue calico dress, a pair of gold spectacles perched on the tip of her nose. A thick braid of dark hair lay across one shoulder. She chewed her bottom lip as she pounded away on a typewriting machine, oblivious to Ada's presence. Through an open doorway Ada saw an older man setting type and a couple of young boys surrounded by stacks of newspapers.

"Begging your pardon!" Ada called at last.

The woman looked up and peered at Ada through her glasses. "Hello! May I help you?"

"Yes. I'd like to speak to the person in charge of taking advertisements."

"That would be me." The woman rose and drew Ada to a chair beside her desk, speaking in staccato sentences that matched the cadence of her typewriter. "I'm in charge of adverts. Also, reporting, editing, and circulation." She grasped Ada's hand and pumped it. "Patience Greer. Everyone calls me Patsy."

"Ada Wentworth."

"I figured as much. Bea Goldston was in here last week and mentioned you'd arrived. I take it you want to place an ad?"

"Yes." Ada fingered the clasp of her coin purse. "If it isn't too expensive."

"Do you have the copy?"

Ada frowned. "Pardon?"

"Have you written down what you want the ad to say?"

"The idea just came to me, and I haven't had time to give it much thought."

Inserting a clean sheet of paper into her typewriter, Patsy said, "Talk to me."

"I'm starting a millinery business. I have one customer so far. I hope to get more by advertising."

Tap-tap-tap went the keys.

"My hats will be of the finest materials and in the latest styles, like the ones from Europe."

"Woo!" Patsy looked up and grinned. "Fancy hats. Might be a good name for your business."

"I *have* thought about that. It's to be called Wentworth's, after my mother."

"That's real sweet. But just so you know, the undertaker one stop down the rail line is named Wentworth. He does most of the burying for folks around here." Patsy leaned across the dusty desk. "The way I see it, women buy hats when they're in a good mood. Or when they're in a bad mood and need something to make them feel better. Thinking about the undertaker might put a damper on things."

"I suppose you're right." Ada swallowed her disappointment. She had so wanted to keep her mother's name alive.

"So, what are we left with here? 'Fancy Hats,' 'Hats by Ada,' 'Hats of Distinction'?" Patsy leaned back in her chair. "Now that I think about it, you don't want to get too highfalutin' with the ladies around here. They appreciate nice things, but they're practical too. I think 'Hats by Ada' may be the way to go."

Ada felt a headache building behind her eyes. "If you think that's best."

"I do. How can folks get ahold of you?"

"I . . . I'm not sure. The post office, I suppose."

Patsy nodded. "That'll work. You can ship your hats from the railway office. Our station agent is very reliable."

"Excellent." Ada hadn't anticipated having to make so many decisions so quickly. "I'm grateful for your help."

"It's what I'm here for." Patsy lifted the paper carriage. "Hold on a minute while I check for mistakes." She patted her typewriting machine, a tall black box embellished with a painting of pink roses. "This newfangled contraption makes my work more efficient, but the problem is that you can't see what you've typed without lifting up the carriage."

She scanned her work. "I'll get this typeset, maybe add a drawing of a hat to catch people's eyes. I'd recommend running it the week after next in my special Founders Day edition. All the local merchants run specials for that week, and more folks buy the paper so they won't miss out on anything."

"I'm sure you know best." Ada opened her

coin purse, praying she had enough to cover the cost. Besides the ad, there was one more essential purchase she needed to make. "How much?"

"My usual rate is a dollar a month, payable in advance. But since you're a new customer, why don't you wait until I get the ad ready? You can come by and take a look before we run it. If you like it, you can pay me then."

"That will be fine."

Patsy nodded. "You might want to set up a charge account at the mercantile. That way you can get supplies when you need them and pay the bill at the end of the month. Jasper Pruitt is the one you need to talk to."

Ada left the newspaper office and returned to the mercantile. A few farmers and mill workers filled the aisles, buying everything from molasses to chicken wire. In the back, beneath a high, dusty window, a group of women pored over bolts of yellow flannel and brightly printed calico. A young man who had not been there earlier in the day sat on a wooden stool, adding up a long column of figures.

"Pardon me." Ada set her bag on the counter. "Are you Mr. Pruitt?"

He looked up and blinked. "No ma'am. I'm his clerk. Hold on a minute. I'll get him."

He disappeared into the back and came back with a gray-haired, bushy-bearded man dressed in denim pants and a stained white apron. "This here's Mr. Pruitt."

He left to help another customer.

Ada offered her hand. "Good morning. I'm Ada Went—"

"I know who you are." The storekeeper's eyes were small and round. Pig's eyes. He shuffled a sheaf of papers lying on the counter. Half of his index finger was missing. The stub quivered when he spoke as if it were somehow connected to his voice box.

"Yes, well, I want to open a charge account, please. For my new business."

"You want me to let you buy on credit?"

"Yes. Miss Greer at the paper said—"

"You buy from me, you'll pay cash."

"But I don't understand. I can pay my bills. I have a position, working for Wyatt Caldwell. Looking after his aunt."

"I know all about that, but it don't change my mind one iota. Plain and simple: I don't give credit to the likes of you." He let go a spurt of tobacco juice that narrowly missed her face before landing in a copper spittoon by the door. "You Yankees think we've forgot how things was down here during the occupation? You think now the war's over we can let bygones be bygones, let the Nigras take over everything?"

Ada stiffened. "It's true that I am a Yankee, but you, sir, are the most offensive boor I have ever had the misfortune to meet!"

"A bore, am I? Mebbe so, but my customers

don't come here for the entertainin' conversation." He turned and walked out.

Ada stared after him, torn between anger and laughter. Heavenly days, what an ignoramus!

"I hate him," said a voice at her elbow. She turned to find a familiar-looking youth packing up his purchases.

The boy's shaggy hair was falling into his eyes. His knobby wrists poked from the frayed sleeves of his work shirt. Something about him evoked her sympathy.

"You're Jacob Hargrove, aren't you?"

He looked up in surprise. "Yes ma'am. Do I know you?"

"I'm Ada Wentworth. I saw you at church last Sunday. Mrs. Willis told me about your mother."

"It's awful hard, being without her."

"I know it is. My mother died when I was thirteen."

Jacob nodded. "Ma might have lived longer if we could've got the tonics she needed to build up her blood, but Mr. Pruitt cut off Pa's credit just when we needed it most."

"That's terrible."

"He's a terrible man." Jacob hoisted his box onto his shoulder. "I should be going. Pa's waiting for these nails."

They went outside. Jacob set the box in his wagon and climbed up.

"I saw your girl, Sabrina," Ada said. "At church. She's very pretty."

"Yes'm, she sure is." Jacob blushed to the roots of his hair. "I'm thinking of marryin' her one day when I can take care of her proper."

He looked so vulnerable and so full of hope that Ada felt moved to encourage him. "I imagine a girl like that expects a lot from her beau."

"Ma'am?"

"She'll want someone steady, with a good future ahead of him. Someone she can depend on. A man who doesn't quit when a job proves difficult."

He looked sheepish. "You mean the mill."

"I'll bet Mr. Caldwell would take you back if you asked."

"Maybe I will, if Pa and me ever get caught up. On the farm, there's always something that needs doing. Plus, in winter, I got my trap lines up at the riverhead. For catching foxes and muskrats mostly, sometimes a mink. I sell the fur." He flicked the reins. " 'Bye, ma'am. And don't worry none about what Mr. Pruitt said. He don't like nobody who's not from around here."

He started down the road. Ada waved after him, then crossed the street to the bookshop. At the sound of the bell, a gray, yellow-eyed cat blinked awake and jumped up to wind itself around her ankles.

The shop owner, a middle-aged man with side whiskers and gold-rimmed spectacles, sauntered to the counter, his pipe in his hand. "That's India," he said, smiling. "I hope you like cats."

"I love cats." Ada bent to stroke India. "I had a Persian when I was growing up. Her name was Athena. She lived to be almost seventeen."

"I'll remember that next time this one has a litter." The man puffed on his pipe, and a thin stream of smoke curled toward the ceiling. "I'm Nathaniel Chastain, but everyone calls me Nate. Welcome to my shop."

She extended her hand across the polished pine counter. "Ada Wentworth."

"Pleased to make your acquaintance. Was there anything in particular that you're wanting?"

"Many years ago my mother had a book, *The Hatmaker's Manual*. It was published around 1830, I think. I realize that's a long time ago, but I was wondering if you might have a copy. I'm beginning a millinery business, and I need to refresh my memory on certain points of construction."

Nate puffed on his pipe and shook his head. "That far back, it's probably long out of print, but I seem to recall a similar book that came in a couple of years ago." He set his pipe down, opened a thick sheaf of papers bound with a leather thong, and ran his finger down the pages. "Yes, here we are. I ordered it for Norah over at the dress shop, but then she changed her mind. I'm sure it's still around here somewhere." He smiled. "Not a lot of call for hatmaking books in these parts."

"Splendid. I'll take it."

"Might take me a few minutes to locate it,

though." Nate indicated the jumble of books spilling from every shelf, nook, and cranny. Books were piled on the partner's desk at the rear of the shop and stacked knee-high beneath the windows overlooking the street. "Take your time and look around. I'll see if I can scare it up."

While he searched for the book, Ada browsed the shelves, reading random passages from new works and old favorites. Holding the pages to her nose, she breathed in the smells of paper and ink. Of all the things she'd given up for auction to settle her father's debts, she felt most keenly the loss of his vast library.

"That's a good one." Wyatt stepped up behind her. "I love the part where Becky Sharp finally gets her due."

Ada jumped. She'd been so engrossed in one of Thackeray's rambling sentences, its cascade of dependent clauses falling one after the other,that she hadn't heard the shop door open. She smiled up at him, relieved that his sunny mood had returned.

"You've read *Vanity Fair*?" She set the volume on the shelf.

Amusement glinted in his eyes. "You seem surprised."

"No! Well, yes, actually. The fortunes of a conniving social climber hardly seems a subject that would interest you."

He raised his eyebrows. "Maybe you need to know me a little better before you decide what interests me." He flipped through a book and set it back on the shelf. "What do you think of Mr. Thackeray's novel?"

"Not much. Father insisted that I read it as an object lesson on the consequences of gossip and manipulation." She picked up another book and examined its gold-embossed cover. Would she ever be able to afford such luxuries again?

"I'd say Thackeray did a fair job of getting that point across, and quite elegantly in places."

She ran her fingers over a row of leather-bound books. "He's good at clever turns of phrase, but I don't much care for his low opinion of the fairer sex."

"Oh?"

"Surely you remember that he compares women to the beasts of the field, incapable of recognizing their own power. It's quite insulting really."

Wyatt grinned. "He ought not to have said that. But he also wonders whether realizing one's desires in the world actually increases happiness. It's an interesting question."

"Personally, I'd prefer contentment. Happiness is fleeting." She thought of her old life in Boston. Of the promises Edward had made and broken. "One's fortunes can change overnight and take happiness along with it."

"True enough, I reckon. Still, you should give the book another—"

"Found it!" Nate Chastain materialized from

the chaos of his shelves brandishing a small red book. "I knew I had it here somewhere."

Ada handed him a wrinkled bill, and he turned away to make change.

Wyatt said, "You're not taking *Vanity Fair*?"

"Not today. I bought millinery supplies this morning and placed a notice in the paper. Hats by Ada."

He frowned and pushed his Stetson to the back of his head. "Pardon me?"

Her stomach dropped. She hadn't meant to tell him so soon. In her excitement at having taken a step toward implementing her plan, it had slipped out. But there was no going back now. And besides, he had big plans for his own future. Surely he'd understand hers. "I'm going to build a business making hats. Eventually I want to move back east and make my living that way."

"Is that a fact?" He passed one hand across his chin.

Ada hurried on. "Mariah Whiting is my only customer for now. But I'll need many more, and everybody in town reads the *Gazette*." She glanced at him nervously. "You did promise I'd have the evenings for my own pursuits."

"I assumed you'd spend your free time like most ladies do, playing the piano or reading or writing letters to your friends."

"I'm afraid my piano playing never progressed much beyond the beginner stage." Thanks to her father, she no longer *had* friends back east, but that was irrelevant now.

He leaned against a table piled high with dusty books. "It never crossed my mind that you'd spend your time checking invoices or writing out bills or worrying about shipments and supply orders. Running a business, even a small one, takes a lot more time than you think."

Her pulse raced. Surely he wasn't going to stop her before she even got started. It wasn't fair. "But you know I'm making a hat for Mariah."

"And it's a fine thing, making a hat for a friend. But this is not the time to begin a commercial enterprise. Not when I need you to look after Lillian."

"My work won't interfere with my taking care of her. I understand my responsibilities to her and I—"

"Here's your change." Nate returned and dropped the coins into her hand.

Wyatt took *Vanity Fair* from the shelf and handed it to Nate. "I'll take this one. For the lady."

"That isn't necessary." Ada tried to hide her disappointment. "I'd rather wait until I can buy it myself."

"Miss Wentworth," Wyatt said, his opposition to her fledgling business apparently forgotten, "please let me do something for you, as a friend who happens to share your appreciation for books."

She started to protest further, but Nate intervened. "Miss? In all my years of running this shop

I have never known Wyatt here to buy books for any lady exceptin' Miss Lillian. If I were you, I'd take advantage of this rare moment of generosity."

Wyatt handed the bookshop owner a couple of bills. Nate wrapped the books, tied the package with string, and handed it to Ada. "I hope you enjoy them."

They left the shop. Ada turned on her heel and headed for the rig. Wyatt caught up with her. "Miss Hattie's place is the other direction. Behind the bakery."

"I don't care. I find that suddenly I'm not very hungry. And we should get back and check on Lillian. That *is* my job, after all."

"Wait just a minute." He took her arm and turned her around. "Are you mad at me because I squelched your hat business or because of the book? Don't folks from Boston know how to accept a gift?"

"Of course we do! But I asked you not to buy it, and you went against my wishes anyway."

His blue eyes darkened. "I see. I'm sorry for my clumsy efforts at friendship. It won't happen again."

His apology pierced her defenses. But still . . . She swallowed. "A true friend would want me to succeed."

"The one thing I can't abide is deceit. Maybe I'd have been more amenable to the idea if you'd been honest with me from the beginning."

She clutched the books tightly to her chest. "The way you were honest with me about Lillian's condition? About the absence of any other staff to help me?"

"I told you how that happened, and I've apologized. It was not *my* intention to hide the truth."

His accusation was like a dash of cold water to the face. The fact that she might have deserved it made things worse.

Wyatt held out both palms in a "don't shoot" manner. "Let's call a truce for now and go eat. I'm hungry."

"Well, I'm not. Not anymore. I'd rather go home."

"You can go if you don't mind walking. I'm going to Hattie's for the fried chicken I've been looking forward to all week."

"Fine." Ada strode to the rig to retrieve her parasol. The sun had reached its zenith, and the long walk back to Lillian's would be brutal. No doubt her feet would be a mass of blisters after the seven-mile walk. Already she regretted her impulsive decision, but she couldn't give in now without looking like a weakling. She tossed her purchases into the rig, snapped open the parasol, and started walking.

Eleven

Wyatt watched her go, his feelings a mixture of desire and frustration. Ada Wentworth was the most exciting and exasperating woman he'd ever met. And the truth was, after only a week of her acquaintance, what he felt for her was more complicated than mere friendship. Her words about leaving Hickory Ridge had taken him aback. He wanted her to stay, and not only because of Lillian. He watched her striding past the mercantile. Clearly this was not the time to say so.

He was sorry that his sour mood this morning had spoiled her visit to the park. He was usually better at leaving the past where it belonged. But Ada, despite her charm, was still a daily reminder of all that he had lost at the hands of the Yanks. He watched her toss her packages into the rig and take up her parasol. He genuinely regretted dashing her hopes for a business of her own, but with the mill running night and day to keep up with demand, he had to rely on her for Lillian's care.

Still, he had no intention of letting her walk all the way home. He'd let her walk a little way, vent some of her anger, and then go after her. His stomach rumbled, and he cast a sad eye toward Miss Hattie's. No fried chicken for him today.

"Mr. Caldwell!" The postmaster hurried over,

his steps ringing on the wooden boardwalk. "Miss Stanhope at the telegraph office is looking for you. You just received a wire. She says it's important."

"Thanks. I'll go get it."

Wyatt jogged across the street to the office, retrieved his telegram, and tore it open.

"Bad news, Mr. Caldwell?" Mary Stanhope's assistant, a thin girl with short yellow hair and sun-browned skin, fanned her face and gulped water from a canning jar. In the back, Miss Stanhope sat hunched over her desk as the teletype chattered, spitting out another message.

"It's excellent news, actually. Do you have a pencil? I need to send a reply."

The girl rummaged through the desk and produced a stub of a pencil. Wyatt scribbled his reply and slid it across the counter. "Ask Miss Stanhope to send this right away, will you?"

He left the office smiling. The telegram confirming yet another order meant that there would be enough work to keep his crew busy harvesting timber through the fall. Once it was too cold to work outdoors, the entire operation would shift to the heated sheds, where the sawyers would turn the raw timber into finished lumber. Normally, Sage Whiting was the first person he wanted to tell when good news happened. But today, despite their disagreement, he wanted to celebrate with Ada.

He quickened his steps. She must have reached the train station by now, maybe even the railroad trestle. He jumped into his rig and headed out of town just as the afternoon train from Memphis arrived, spilling passengers and their belongings onto the platform. At the far end of the street, a couple of his men mounted their empty wagons, preparing to return to the mill after delivering today's shipment. Wyatt didn't stop to talk. He needed to find Ada. To make things right.

He drove through town looking for a small, determined woman in a dark-blue dress, carrying a parasol and a big chip on her shoulder. He crossed the trestle and then the bridge, but there was no sign of Ada.

Fear twisted his gut. He wished now he'd told her the whole truth about the Klan, but he hadn't wanted to frighten her. It was true that they saved most of their vitriol for the coloreds, but their hatred ran deep enough to include foreigners and Yankees. For the most rabid among them, the simple fact that Ada was from Boston would be enough to mark her as a target. Everyone in town knew there was a Yankee woman in their midst.

A worrisome thought assailed him. Had Lillian's "ghost" actually been someone riding past the house in the middle of the night—a veiled threat to him and to Ada? Why hadn't he considered this before letting Ada set out on her own?

He urged Cherokee into a gallop, and the rig

bounced over the uneven road. He called Ada's name, scanning the woods at the side of the road. By the time he reached the church, his heart was racing. It has been less than an hour since she'd stormed away. She couldn't have gone this far. Not in those flimsy shoes of hers.

The horse was lathered and panting in the heat. Wyatt led the mare to the pump and filled the trough with water. While she drank, Wyatt splashed his face with water and sat on the ground, his head in his hands.

Ada was missing. And he was to blame.

He climbed back into the rig. At the mill, he saw that most of his drays had returned from the rail station and were lined up near the loading sheds. The horses had been unhitched and were quietly cropping grass. In the side yard, Josiah Dawson was at work repairing a wagon wheel. Wyatt urged the horse toward Lillian's.

Nearing the house, he saw two figures in the front porch swing and his heart jerked. Relief flooded his veins like a shot of whisky, followed immediately by a spurt of anger. He tethered the horse and crossed the yard. Ada and Libby Dawson rose from the swing.

Libby bobbed her head. "Miss Lillian still sleepin' like a baby, Mr. Wyatt. That tonic gentled her right down."

He took a couple of coins from his pocket and pressed them into the girl's hand. "I appreciate your coming, Libby. Tell your mama I'm obliged for letting you stay here today."

"She don't mind. You pay real good." Libby tucked the money into her skirt pocket. "'Bye, Miss Ada. Thank you for the story."

"You're welcome, Libby. Anytime." Ada closed the book she'd been reading and set it on the swing.

Wyatt waited until the girl had started down the road. Then he grabbed Ada's shoulders and brought his face within inches of hers. "Of all the harebrained, reckless, stubborn things to do, Ada. I've told you—the divide around here runs deep. Some folks can't stand the sight of a Yankee, and there are a few who would take advantage of any woman walking along the road alone. Don't you realize that something terrible could have happened if you'd met up with the wrong people?"

She jerked free and stared up at him, her eyes blazing. "If you were so concerned for my welfare, why did you suggest that I walk?"

"I had no intention of letting you get very far. You were angry and needed to cool off. And then you just . . . vanished."

"You said I'd be all right if I stayed out of Two Creeks. Now it seems I can't go anywhere. Although you weren't all that concerned when you made me drive Lillian to church for the quilting circle."

"It isn't that far to the church." He struggled

to hold on to his patience. "I rode out just ahead of you and kept an eye out until you passed the mill." He paused. "How'd you get back here today, anyway?"

"Mr. Whiting was returning from the rail station, and I asked him to drive me home. So you see, you needn't have worried. I can take care of myself."

"Ah. That's right, I forgot. Ada Wentworth doesn't need anyone."

"Well, I *want* to be independent, but you've quashed that notion, haven't you?" She wiped away angry tears.

Wyatt took her elbow and guided her away from Lillian's open window, across the porch, and into the fragrant shade of the magnolia tree. "I'm sorry that I've upset you so. But I've already explained my position. I need you to look after Lil. That was the agreement you made. Now you want to change it."

"I have no intention of neglecting my responsibilities to her, but I must plan for the day when she . . . after she's . . ."

"I realize she's lived many more years than are allotted to most folks. When Lillian goes to meet her Lord, you'll get an additional three months' salary, as we originally agreed. I won't turn you out on the street. That's a promise."

"People break promises all the time."

The look on her face, so full of hurt and vulnerability, nearly broke his heart. "I don't.

You'll be welcome to stay on here at the house until you find another situation."

"Another *situation?* Is this to be my life, then? Always a servant in someone else's house, dependent upon their whims, with never a place to call home?" Tears streamed down her face. "What kind of life is that?"

"I'm not asking you never to start your business," he soothed. "Only to wait until you can devote full time to it."

She pointed to Lillian's open window. "She has slept all day. I could have made three patterns by now, or trimmed a hat, or taken care of paperwork, and she'd never know. Do you know what I think? You just can't abide the fact that I have a mind of my own."

His patience snapped. "If you find the terms of your employment so onerous, perhaps you'd rather resign." He saw the pure panic in her eyes before she spun away from him. He caught her arm and turned her around. "Forgive me. I didn't mean that. I want you to stay."

"It didn't seem that way at the park earlier today. One minute we were having a pleasant talk and the next, you—"

"It didn't have a thing to do with you. I spoke too abruptly, and I regret it."

She nodded. "And I regret that you don't approve of my plans. But I must provide for my future. There's no one else to do it." She folded her arms across her chest. “And it seems there is no room for compromise.”

He let out an exasperated sigh. The woman was stubborn as a yearling on the end of a lasso. “We can stand here all day and not solve anything. I need to get back to the mill and pay my men.” He went to the rig and retrieved her parcels. “Here’s your hatmaking book. I’ll hold on to Mr. Thackeray’s novel.”

He touched his finger to the brim of his Stetson, turned the rig, and headed down the road.

Watching him go, Ada felt the blood rush to her cheeks. Despite his refusal to acknowledge her point of view, it was poor manners to have turned away his gift. Already she regretted their argument. She sat on the swing and set it in motion with the toe of her shoe. A cooling breeze drifted across the porch, releasing the faint scent of magnolias and setting the roses to nodding on their stems. Her eyes burned. The confrontation with Wyatt had left her feeling drained and deeply confused.

Despite her best intentions, she was beginning to have feelings for this man. A part of her longed for his companionship, even his affection. And yet she craved the peace of mind that would be hers when she no longer had to count every coin and fret over the smallest of purchases, when she would be beholden to no one. If she succeeded, she would be safe.

Even so, when Wyatt looked into her eyes, she'd almost been able to imagine a life with him by her side. She closed her eyes and willed the image away. It was far too soon—and too dangerous—to be thinking this way. Better to focus on her plan and not risk her heart.

She watched the lengthening afternoon shadows settling over the mountains like an indigo shawl and tried to convince herself that being on her own was the right choice.

Undoubtedly it was. But at what price?

Twelve

Three days of steady rain had turned the road to a sea of mud and left the house dank and smelling slightly of mold, but Independence Day dawned sunny and hot. On the morning of the Founders Day celebration, Ada woke with swollen eyes and a throbbing headache, a result of the relentless heat and her recurring nightmare. Images of a raging fire and its grisly aftermath played in her head as she prepared a blackberry cobbler for the communal dinner on the grounds.

Ada bent to check the oven. The flames leapt and flickered. The wood hissed and popped as it burned. A small, gray mound of ashes settled to the bottom of the stove. She began to shake. Her eyes welled with fresh tears.

"What's the matter?" Lillian paused in rolling out the pie crust to frown at Ada. "Surely this recipe isn't that hard."

Ada didn't bother refuting the old woman's words. Lillian had been in a foul mood ever since the rain began; arguing with her would serve no purpose and only put them both in a contentious mood. Despite the aftereffects of her nightmare, Ada was determined to enjoy her first holiday in Hickory Ridge.

She didn't expect to see Wyatt at today's festivities, a prospect that left her feeling both disappointed and relieved. They had spoken only briefly since the day she left him in town. She missed his smile and the languid musicality of his speech. She didn't miss his insistence that she put her plans on hold.

"You didn't put in the lemon juice!" Lillian angled her wheelchair closer to the table and pointed to the bowl of sugared blackberries.

"I'm just getting to it." Ada added lemon juice, poured the mixture into the baking dish, and laid the rolled dough gently over the top.

While the cobbler baked, she helped Lillian get dressed and then changed into her own dress, an old one of deep green that complemented the color of her eyes. She coiled her hair into a simple knot at the base of her neck and donned the small hat she'd worn for traveling. It wasn't really a summer hat, but it was the best one she had. It would have to do.

Mariah and Sage Whiting arrived to drive them into town. Ada gathered their things and took Lillian's arm. They picked their way across the muddy yard to the wagon, where Sage settled Lillian and Ada on the seat behind Mariah.

"Where's Robbie this morning?" Ada set the pan of cobbler at her feet.

"He spent the night with Toby McCall in town." Mariah handed Ada a light quilt. "Best cover your dresses so they won't get muddy. Those boys have been inseparable since the McCalls moved here last spring. I'm not so sure Toby is the right kind of friend for Rob, though." She frowned. "He seems wild. And more worldly than our boy."

"We can't protect him from everything," Sage said. "We've given him the right upbringing." He patted Mariah's hand, a gesture so sweet and intimate that it made Ada's heart hurt. "He'll make the right choices."

When they neared the church, they were joined on the muddy road by the preacher in his black rig and a couple of other families headed for town. As the wagon wheels creaked, churning up blobs of rust-colored mud, the women called out greetings. The men traded jokes about the condition of the road and made plans for afternoon games of horseshoes and darts.

By the time they arrived, the park was already packed with people, wagons, and horses. The musicians arrived and began setting up their chairs in the gazebo. Men rushed about in their rubber boots, setting up long tables for the dozens of pies, cakes, and covered dishes that appeared like magic to fill every available space. In a relatively dry spot near the road, Jacob Hargrove and his friends were setting the stakes for games of horseshoes. A group of girls, Sabrina Gilman among them, sat on thick blankets nearby, their pretty summer frocks spread out around them like flower petals. Jacob looked up as Ada passed and nodded. She waved, hoping that the banker's daughter wouldn't break the heart of such an earnest young man.

Sage went off to find his friends, and Lillian joined a group of older women at a table beneath the trees. After adding their offerings to the array of food, Ada and Mariah made their way to the gazebo and spread a blanket in the shade to await the concert.

Mariah spotted Robbie and his friend Toby and called him over. Already, Robbie's white shirt was speckled with dirt, and his shoes were caked with mud. He grinned at his mother. "What is it, Mama? Hey, Miss Ada."

"Hello, Robbie."

"I want you boys to go help your daddy with those tables." Mariah dug her fan out of her bag and snapped it open.

"But Toby and them are getting up a rock-throwing competition. Whoever throws a rock farthest down the river wins a brand-new silver whistle. It's wonderful, Mama. I want it really bad."

Mariah eyed him sharply. "We are not going to argue about this, son. Go help your daddy and then find some other way to have fun, or you can wait all day in the wagon. Do I make myself clear?"

"Yes ma'am."

"Now excuse yourself to Miss Ada and run along."

More people arrived for the celebration. Patsy Greer from the *Gazette* drove up with her father, followed by several of Wyatt's sawyers and their families. Nate Chastain appeared and made a beeline for Carrie Daly, who sat apart from the others, watching the children from the orphanage playing a game of tag.

Jasper Pruitt arrived from the mercantile. He joked with the other men as he set a huge jar of pickles on the table, his contribution to the meal.

"For mercy's sake, would you look at Jasper Pruitt? He looks like he tumbled into a hog pen." Mariah nodded toward the tables, where the very muddy owner of the mercantile stood. "Not his fault, of course," she added. "I can't remember the last time the road was this bad. But I couldn't miss the chance to catch up with everyone." She patted Ada's hand. "I don't suppose your supplies have arrived yet."

"No, but don't worry. Mr. Biddle is very reliable."

"I hope so. I'm counting the days until I can arrive at the harvest festival in a brand-new hat." Mariah's brown eyes shone. She sipped her lemonade. "Any more orders yet?"

The question reminded Ada of her unresolved disagreement with Wyatt. Every memory of their last conversation left her feeling regretful and unsettled. But that wasn't something she wanted to share, even with Mariah. "Not yet. But my notice will appear in this week's *Gazette*."

Just then Robbie rushed over, leading the young girl from the orphanage.

"Miss Ada, this is Sophie. The one I told you about, remember? She's almost eleven, same as me."

"I do remember." Ada looked into the face of the most beautiful child she had ever seen. The girl's coffee-with-cream skin was flawless. Her wide-set eyes were somewhere between green and gray, her long straight hair the blue-black of a raven's wing. Sophie wore an ill-fitting gingham pinafore that left her ankles exposed, but she carried herself with the natural grace of a princess.

"Hello, Sophie. I'm Ada Wentworth. Robbie tells me you are one of the smartest people he knows."

The girl raised one shoulder in an elegant little shrug. "Mrs. Lowell thinks I'm stupid."

"Sophie's got more brains than anybody," Robbie said loyally. "She knows the times tables better than me. And she tells the best stories you ever heard."

"I love stories!" Ada said. "When I was a girl at school, my friends and I read stories all the time, even when we were supposed to be resting."

"Ain't no resting time at the orphan house," Sophie declared. "Everybody but me goes to school, and after my lessons with Mrs. Lowell, I got my chores, then supper, then prayers, then bed."

Ada's heart broke. Sophie's potential was being wasted because of the mixed blood in her veins. In New Orleans, Ada had known others like her who had found acceptance in society. In another place, Sophie might be able to overcome the circumstances of her birth. In Hickory Ridge, it seemed she didn't stand a chance.

"Miss Ada, will you play tag with us?" Robbie tugged on Ada's hand. "Over there in the grass by the merry-go-round, there's hardly any mud at all."

"Robbie," said his mother, "don't bother Miss Ada."

"Well, what am I supposed to do, Mama? You told me not to play with Toby and them. I'm not having any fun at all. Might as well go home and do my arithmetic."

Ada laughed and got to her feet. "All right. One game, and then I want to visit with your mother."

"Last one there is a rotten egg!" Robbie took off, Sophie at his heels. With a backward glance at Mariah, Ada hiked her skirts and followed them across the wet ground to join the other children.

While the orphanage mistress watched from the sidelines, Ada, her hat askew, chased the squealing children around the old trees and along the path that led to the river. She let the youngest ones narrowly escape being tagged just to hear their delighted laughter. Robbie and Sophie circled and swooped past her, calling out to her, daring her to catch them. When at last she tagged them, the three collapsed onto the damp grass near the merry-go-round.

"That was fun!" Sophie said.

"It was all right." Robbie absently plucked a blade of grass and glanced longingly toward the opposite river bank where Toby and several other boys were tossing rocks and yelling at each other. "But I still want that silver whistle."

Just then a handbell clanged. Sophie scrambled to her feet. "That's Mrs. Lowell callin' us. I got to go before I gets in trouble."

Ada looked up. "Good-bye, Sophie. I hope to see you again. Perhaps we'll trade stories."

"Maybe." The girl looked at Ada with an expression that was half hope, half resignation—as if even the smallest of pleasures was too much to wish for. Then she left to join the others.

Robbie watched her go. "I sure wish Mr. Wyatt was here. He'd talk Mama into letting me play on the river. He can talk her into anything."

Ada smiled. "Mr. Caldwell can be very persuasive."

"What does persuasive mean?"

"Convincing."

"Oh. How come he didn't come to the celebration? Pa said he's working at the mill all day. On a holiday!"

"Sometimes holidays can make grownups feel sad. This one reminds Mr. Caldwell of friends he lost in the war."

"Yeah. Like Billy Rondo. Billy Rondo was Mr. Wyatt's best friend in the whole world, until he grew up and met my pa. Now my pa is his best friend. But I bet he still misses Billy Rondo."

"I'm sure he does. Miss Lillian told me about the time Mr. Caldwell and his friend Billy built a raft and went exploring on the river."

Robbie's eyes went wide. "By themselves?"

"I believe so." Ada smiled. "That must have been exciting."

Just then, she saw Wyatt striding across the park toward them. He met her eye, and the thunderous expression on his face set off warning bells in her head. "Would you excuse me, Robbie? Here he comes now."

Thirteen

Wyatt stopped in front of Ada, a wrinkled copy of the *Gazette* in his hand. "I thought we had reached an understanding."

Ada's mouth went dry. Clearly he was angry enough to send her packing without a moment's regret. She waited, her heart kicking.

His eyes blazed. "I thought we'd agreed you wouldn't pursue this hatmaking scheme so long as you're looking after Aunt Lil . . . and now this!"

He pointed to the ad. As promised, Patsy Greer had added a drawing of a feathered hat to the ad copy beneath "Hats by Ada."

Seeing her hopes spelled out in print made them seem possible and gave her courage. She crossed her arms and tucked her hands under them. "It isn't a *scheme,* Mr. Caldwell; it's a legitimate business venture. Believe me, I know the difference. Furthermore, we didn't *agree* on anything. You laid down the law and left, assuming I'd bow to your wishes."

He sighed. "I don't wish to pull rank here, Ada, but—"

"Yes, I know. I work for you. I couldn't cancel it this week even if I'd wanted to. You might have noticed that the roads are a mess. Libby Dawson didn't show up for the soiled laundry, which means I had to do the washing and dry it all indoors. And I am sorry to say that your aunt had another of her spells the day before yesterday." She pushed up her sleeve to reveal four purple bruises and a cross-hatching of long red scratches on the underside of her wrist. "She mistook me for an intruder and fought like a wildcat."

Concern softened the hard planes of his face. "I'm sorry. Is she all right now?"

"She's fine. Visiting with some of her friends over there by the food tables. She hasn't been neglected, I assure you."

The musicians began warming up. Ada felt empty, defeated. "You have me at a disadvantage, Mr. Caldwell. I need this job."

He nodded, his lips tightening. "Then act like it."

She wanted to scream at the injustice of it all, to convince him somehow of the utter impossibility of her situation. But creating a scene would only make them both angrier. She forced herself to speak calmly. "I will cancel the ad as soon as possible. For now, I'd like to enjoy the concert. If you have no objection."

The muscle in his jaw jumped. "No. No objection at all."

She turned on her heel, retraced her steps, and took her place on the blanket beside Mariah.

The musicians began with Stephen Foster tunes that soon had the audience clapping and singing along. As the music segued into "Dixie" and the "Bonnie Blue Flag," former Rebel soldiers, many of them near tears, stood and removed their hats. Dressed in tattered gray uniforms, they looked older than their years, but their grief and pride were palpable.

But not everyone in the crowd felt the same. A knot of unionists standing near the gazebo began a loud chorus of jeers, drowning out the last notes of the song. Someone yelled a string of curse words. Someone else threw a punch, and the melee was on.

Despite her anger and frustration, Ada couldn't help seeking Wyatt in the crowd. He remained where she'd left him, his worn Stetson in his hand, his sea-blue gaze locked on hers. She understood the pain that he was feeling in this moment, the worry that the divisiveness of the war might never heal. She returned his gaze, feeling something fleeting and precious pass between them. She regretted their argument. She hated knowing that he was disappointed in her.

The sheriff, his face red from the heat, waded into the fracas and separated the men. Some retreated to the far side of the park; others gathered their families and started for home. The concert continued with classical pieces that reminded Ada of home, her father, and that last painful evening in his crimson and gilt study, listening to Edward dispassionately dismantling her future. Coupled with her impasse with Wyatt, the memory was too much. To her complete horror, she began to sob, her shoulders heaving.

"Ada?" Mariah leaned toward her until their foreheads were touching. "Are you all right?"

"You must excuse me, I—"

"Come with me." Mariah led her through the crowd and along the footpath to a secluded spot beneath the trees. "Now, what's the matter?"

Ada pulled her handkerchief from her sleeve and blotted her face. "That song, the Mozart piece, was m-my fiancé's favorite. I thought I was past caring for him, but—"

"The song brings back all those old feelings."

Ada nodded. "I have no one to blame but myself." She dabbed at her eyes. "I am hopelessly naive and a terrible judge of character. Why couldn't I see his true nature? Surely there were clues, if only I hadn't been too stupid to see them."

"Don't be so hard on yourself," Mariah said. "Love is often blind. But isn't it better to know the truth than to harbor false hope?"

"I suppose. But I can't help wondering whether things would have been different if my father had stayed out of it. He convinced Edward to break our engagement. He *paid* Edward a lot of money to trample on my dreams."

"Oh, Ada. Are you certain of this?"

She nodded. "I overheard Father talking to Aunt Kate about it."

"I'm sure that was a hard thing to accept."

Ada dabbed her eyes, picturing that last evening with Edward in the parlor of her father's house—the falling snow, the fire snapping and crackling in the grate. Edward standing before the mantel, resplendent in his ship captain's uniform, his beard turning to burnished gold in the firelight, his deep voice resonant as he shattered her dreams.

"Ada?" Mariah placed a gentle hand on her arm. "Are you all right?"

Ada took a deep breath and nodded. "The night Edward called off our wedding, he promised me—he swore a solemn oath—that one day he would explain everything. For a while I held on to that. I thought that if I only understood the *why* of it, I could accept it. But of course he broke that promise too. I wrote to him twice after my father died, but I haven't heard a word."

"Did you ask your father about it?"

"I wanted to. But at first I was too angry. And then he died suddenly."

"That's too bad. Was it his heart?"

"That would have been a mercy." Fresh tears welled in her eyes. "A gaslight exploded in the theater. There was a flash fire. Father and my aunt were in our box in the balcony and couldn't get out before the whole building collapsed." She braided her fingers together. "Ten others were lost as well."

Mariah took her hand. "I had no idea!"

"I was supposed to go too, but I was angry

with Father and Aunt Kate. She disapproved of everything I did and took his side in every argument. That night I refused to leave the house. We fought about it. And then I never saw them again."

"You poor thing. I am sorry."

"And now I'll never know why he convinced Edward to abandon me. I can't forgive either of them."

Mariah's brown eyes filled. "You believe your father's interference ruined your life. But suppose he saw in your Edward the things you couldn't see—things that would have brought you even greater pain had you married."

Ada shrugged and smoothed the pleats in her skirt.

"What if, in sending your fiancé away, your father carved out a new and better path for you? One that will lead to greater happiness than you might have had with Edward? Isn't that possible?"

"I don't know. I never thought of it that way."

"Think of our heavenly Father," Mariah urged. "Sometimes we don't understand his ways, and yet if we are faithful in following the path he sets for us, we find more joy than we ever could have imagined."

Ada sighed. She wasn't sure she believed that, but Mariah's quiet smile soothed her heart. She envied Mariah the pure certainty of her faith.

She wadded her handkerchief into a tight sodden ball. "I want to believe that life won't always be so difficult and lonely, but every day is the same. Watching out for Lillian and keeping the house tidy is exhausting. Scrimping and saving for my future is a struggle. It's hard to see how anything will change."

"I know." Mariah's voice was gentle. "But I'm confident that in God's time you will find a man worthy of your affections." She smiled. "I saw you talking with Wyatt Caldwell earlier."

"He's angry with me because of my advertisement in the *Gazette*. He insists that I cancel it and forbids me to pursue my millinery business as long as I am employed as Lillian's companion." Ada sniffed. "It isn't fair."

Mariah shook her head in sympathy. "He can certainly seem intractable sometimes, but you can look all over Tennessee and never find a man with a kinder heart. When my daughter drowned, Sage got roaring drunk and stayed that way for a week. It was the only time he ever touched spirits. He was inconsolable. I was scared that I'd lost him too."

"I didn't realize you'd lost a child. That must have been unbearable."

Mariah nodded, her brown eyes luminous with unshed tears. "Wyatt stayed by our side day and night until Sage came to his senses. Somehow a funeral was arranged and all our bills were paid. When Sage went back to the mill, Wyatt never said a word about any of it. To this day, he still hasn't."

Mariah smiled and took Ada's arm. "It's nearly

noon. We should help the others set the food out. Are you all right now?"

"I'm fine. And mortified. I don't usually give in to my tears."

"Founders Day is always emotional around here." Mariah linked her arm through Ada's and they returned to the park. "Give Wyatt some time. He's a fair-minded man. He'll come around."

Wyatt leaned against the wheel of the buckboard and watched Ada and Mariah emerge from the trees. He was sure Ada had told her friend about their dustup this morning. Women were like that—able to tell each other the most embarrassing or troubling things and be fairly certain of a sympathetic response. He could tell from the set of Ada's shoulders that she was unhappy, and he wished he'd been more diplomatic in his dealings with her. But being around her evoked old resentments, and sometimes they took over.

Of course it wasn't her fault that she happened to be from the same town as Reginald Cabot. Until she arrived, he hadn't let himself think about that double-dealing cheat—the sorriest excuse for a man that Wyatt had ever met. The one who had cost the Caldwells a hundred acres of prime ranchland and, for a while, their sterling reputation among their fellow ranchers.

He couldn't forget the day Cabot arrived at the Caldwell place with a proposal to channel water from the river to the ranches in the area. The man came prepared with a bunch of fancy charts and tables showing how much water could be diverted, how many more head of cattle each acre would support, how much profit each rancher could expect once the system was in place. He approached Wyatt's father first. As the owner of the largest ranch in the region, Jake Caldwell was the key to convincing his neighbors to support the plan.

Dad was no fool. He'd been around long enough to know that in drought years the river turned to sludge and, channels or no, a certain percentage of cattle would die. That was a fact any Texas rancher had to accept. But Cabot had a ready answer. He promised to build a reservoir to collect water during rainy spells and release it during dry ones. All that was needed was a financial investment to make it all a reality.

Finally, his objections overcome, Dad wrote a check and convinced three of his neighbors to invest as well.

But the channel was never dug, the reservoir never built. And Wyatt's father was labeled a fast-talking swindler, even though he lost more money than any of them.

Wyatt was furious, not only for the loss of the land, but for the sullying of the Caldwell name. He wanted to hire a detective to find the elusive Yankee con man and bring him back south for a healthy dose of Texas justice. But his father wanted to let it go. He was getting older; he wanted to live out his life in peace. He sold off some land to repay his neighbors every penny.

That wasn't enough for Wyatt. Still determined to bring Cabot to justice, he traveled to Boston and hired an expensive Massachusetts lawyer to recover Jake's investment. But he soon learned that one set of laws existed for the rich and powerful and another for everybody else. Cabot's family name and connections kept him from having to pay for his crime. The injustice of it all still rankled.

What hurt Wyatt more than the loss of the money was the loss of land that was part of his history and his heritage. Even now, thinking of it, he felt a sharp hunger for the land. When the day came to leave Hickory Ridge and return home, he intended to buy back every last acre of it.

He scanned the park. Beneath the trees, Ada was busy setting out plates and opening baskets of food. His stomach rumbled. The food would be outstanding, a far cry from the hurried meals he made for himself after a long day at the mill. But he didn't feel much like eating. Despite the bad memories Ada's presence stirred in him, his feelings for her were growing like weeds and he wasn't sure he liked it.

The sudden burst of her bright laughter filtered through the trees and lodged in his heart. He wanted more of that sweet laughter. More of her.

And yet . . .

He knew it was downright ignorant to tar an entire group of people with the same broad brush. He was aware that Ada Wentworth had nothing to do with Reginald Cabot. But the fact remained that she was a Boston Yankee who had been less than completely honest with him.

And he wasn't sure he could get past that.

Fourteen

Ada helped the other women prepare the food for serving. Bea Goldston arrived in time to set out stacks of plates and jars of lemonade. She bustled about in her purple dress and mud-spattered boots, turning her schoolteacher's eyes on the knots of shrieking children with a look that would have petrified stone. Ada hid a smile. Never had countenance and occupation seemed more perfectly matched.

Bea finished her task and strolled over to Ada. "Good morning, Miss Wentworth!"

Ada looked up, so startled at Bea's cordial greeting that she nearly dropped a pan of blueberry buckle.

"Miss Goldston . . . hello . . ."

"How are you? Enjoying your first Founders Day in Hickory Ridge?"

"I am." Ada made room on the table for Bea's pan. "How are things at school?"

Bea smiled. "Busy. The school board approved my new curriculum for next term, and we're making plans to welcome a new teacher soon."

"So I heard."

Across the table, Mariah was gaping at Bea as if she'd suddenly sprouted an extra head.

"I should have stayed home today to write out my new lessons," Bea continued. "But a woman in my position has to do her part for the community." She looked around. "Anything else I can do to help?"

Mariah rearranged a couple of pans to make room on the table for a bowl of peaches. "I believe Mrs. Lowell could use some help. Those children have been running around like wild Indians, eyeing the sweets all morning. The younger ones are getting tired by now."

"Say no more!" Bea took off across the park, her ruffled skirt belling out behind her.

"Mercy sakes," Mariah murmured. "Wonder what's gotten into Bea? She actually seems human today."

"A welcome change." Ada shaded her eyes and looked across the meadow to the spot where the orphans were seated in perfectly straight rows. Mrs. Lowell stood in front of them, undoubtedly reminding them of their manners and of how lucky they were to be attending such a glorious celebration.

A bell clanged, and the townsfolk surged toward the tables. The mayor read a short declaration of remembrance for the war dead, and the minister of the church in town made his way forward to bless the food.

Ada bowed her head, but her gaze roamed over the assembled crowd. Where was Wyatt now? Had he shown up solely to chastise her for the newspaper ad?

". . . and bless this food to the nourishment of our bodies through Jesus Christ our Lord," the minister intoned.

"Amen," the crowd murmured before everyone made a mad dash for plates and forks. Ada filled her plate and helped Lillian with hers. They joined a group that included Patsy Greer from the newspaper and her father and quickly grew to include Norah Dudley, the dress-shop proprietress, and Hattie Hanson, the restaurant owner. Mariah and Sage spread their blanket and settled down next to Lillian. Then Carrie Daly arrived with a stocky, sandy-haired man, whom she introduced to Ada as her brother, Henry Bell.

"Ma'am." Henry nodded to Ada and plopped down on the blanket his sister had spread, his cheerful demeanor contrasting sharply with his sister's pale sadness. "Heard about you from Carrie and from Wyatt down at the mill. I hope you like it here in Hickory Ridge."

She smiled at his enthusiasm. "It's a nice town."

"We like it. Don't we, Carrie?"

Just then, a couple of men called to him and he

got to his feet. "Excuse me. I plumb forgot that I promised to help Charlie with his wagon."

"Don't forget to eat," Carrie said.

He grinned at his sister. "Not likely." He nodded to Ada again and hurried off.

Over the next hour, Ada nibbled at her food and listened to snippets of conversations going on around her. Mr. Greer and Sage discussed the changes taking place in Tennessee since the new governor had taken office. Patsy marveled at the news of a huge cattle drive that had just set out for Abilene. Her father and Hattie argued about whether President Grant had packed the Supreme Court to get his way on an important constitutional issue. The mention of the Union general who was now the U.S. president got everyone's attention.

"I remember the day the Federals first got here," Mr. Greer said. "I stood at my front winder and watched that bunch cut through this holler like a hot knife through butter. People my age, we couldn't hardly stand it, being overrun by Yankees. But some of the young girls didn't mind it too much." He glanced at his daughter. "They was one of 'em, a bushy-bearded captain from Ohio or somewheres like that, sweet on my Patsy."

"No, he wasn't," Patsy said. "Captain Franklin found out that we owned the *Gazette*, and he didn't want any bad publicity for the Union army." She tossed her dark braid over her shoulder.

"Unfortunately, it had nothing to do with me and my feminine wiles."

"Not that you would have courted a Yankee for a single minute," Norah Dudley said. "Honestly, what self-respecting girl would associate with the likes of him? Yankees are all thieves and liars, down to the very last one of—"

Mariah gaped at the dressmaker and reached across the blanket to grasp Ada's hand. Norah stopped talking and dropped her gaze. The group fell silent. All eyes turned to Ada.

Heat suffused her face. She set down her plate. "Just as all Southerners are ill-mannered and ignorant?"

Hattie, her eyes downcast, fiddled with her napkin. Patsy shaded her eyes and watched the horseshoe match going on across the way. The awkward silence went on until Mr. Greer said, "I reckon you got 'er dead to rights, there." He got to his feet. "Sage? Care to join me for horseshoes?"

The men headed off. Norah hurried to gather her things. "I must go."

Ada, her appetite gone, busied herself stacking the empty plates.

"Don't take Norah's words to heart," Mariah said when the shop owner had gone. "She didn't mean it. She wasn't thinking."

Ada nodded, sick with anger and with the certain knowledge that people here would never forgive her for her background. Even if she stayed in Hickory Ridge for a hundred years, there would always be the secretive Klan, watching and waiting, and people like Norah and Jasper Pruitt, nursing their hatred for Northerners.

She looked out across the park. Near the rows of wagons and buckboards lining the road, Wyatt was talking to Sage and Henry Bell.

As much as she hated deceiving him, she would have to go on with her plan. It was her ticket back to the world she knew and understood.

Wyatt leaned against the wagon wheel, his legs stretched out in front of him, his hat shading his eyes from the late afternoon sunlight streaming through the trees. The tantalizing smells of food had finally overcome his bad mood, and he had overindulged in fried chicken, watermelon, and a double serving of blackberry cobbler. He would have recognized Lillian's recipe anywhere—warm, sugary berries mixed with just the right amounts of butter and lemon, bubbling beneath a flaky brown crust.

He imagined Ada's delicate hands mixing and rolling out the dough, the faint blush on her cheeks as she bent over the hot cookstove. He'd thought about seeking her out to compliment her on the cobbler, but now she was marching back to the tables carrying a stack of plates with the urgency of a battlefield officer. He could tell from the angle of her chin that she was still upset. Maybe it was better to let her be.

He checked his watch and felt a stab of guilt. He'd planned to catch up on things at the mill today. There were letters to answer, the payroll to figure. And he needed to compose a wire to the hotel owner in North Carolina who had inquired about buying some oak. But the day was nearly gone, and there was something working at the back of his mind, a vague feeling that he couldn't quite place. He shifted his position and watched the children enjoying the celebration.

A performer from a traveling show wandered among the crowd juggling oranges, rubber balls, and rolls of ribbon, unspooling them in myriad colors that caught the light. Sophie from the orphanage jumped to catch two lengths of pale blue ribbon and offered one to Ada. Ada draped her arm loosely about the girl's shoulders, and the two of them walked across the meadow laughing and chatting as if they'd been friends forever.

Wyatt's heart seized. Ada's tender way with the child filled him with longing and reminded him of how alone he was. Even when he was surrounded by his workers, a deep inner loneliness remained. He had been part of this community for years, but in some ways he was still a solitary man.

He didn't like feeling this way. He wished he'd never come to the celebration at all, and he couldn't explain why he had. After years of avoiding Founders Day, with all its reminders of strife and loss, it was as if some greater force had brought him and held him here.

What he needed was a long walk in the woods. Solitude always cleared his head. Put things in proper perspective.

He got to his feet and headed off into the trees.

Fifteen

Ada had just sent Sophie off to play on the merry-go-round when she heard a fierce commotion behind her. Turning around, she saw a crowd running toward the river.

Urgent voices echoed through the trees. "Help! Somebody! Help!" Ada followed them to a place where a sodden Toby McCall and a couple of other boys stood, frantically pointing downstream. "You got to save them!" Toby yelled. "Their raft came apart and they fell in!"

"Who?" A panicked Mariah grabbed the boy by the shoulder. "Toby! Who fell in?"

"Jacob! An' Robbie. We tried to pull 'em out, but the current's too strong."

Mariah kicked off her shoes and jumped into the water. Immediately, she was dragged under. Ada scanned the roiling river. Bits of lumber, broken tree branches, and masses of waterlogged leaves swirled in the coffee-colored water. Then, far downstream, she saw a dark head break the surface. She took off her shoes and raced along the bank, her feet sinking into the soft earth. Tears blurred her vision as she looked around for a sturdy branch, a piece of rope, anything to get them out. Mariah had already lost one child to drowning. She couldn't lose Robbie too.

Just ahead of Ada, a man hurtled through the trees and arced into the river. Ada saw only a flash of dark hair in the sunlight as he hit the water, but it was enough. *Wyatt.*

Seconds later, Sage and the doctor arrived with ropes. Sage dove in after Wyatt, and the two men fought the raging current toward the person in the water. Ada stood frozen, barely able to draw breath. She sent up a fervent prayer for their safety.

Sage gave a shout, and Dr. Spencer tossed the rope. Moments later, they hauled a lanky body to shore. *Jacob! But where was Robbie? And Mariah?*

The doctor's wife bent over Jacob, murmuring words of comfort. The young man coughed and spat a mouthful of brown water. "I'm all right," he rasped. "Get Robbie."

A moment later, Sage hauled Mariah from the river. She clawed at his shirt, her eyes wild. "Let me go! I have to find our son!"

"We'll find him!" Sage shook her hard. "It won't help him if I have to worry about you too. Stay put, Mariah."

He dove back into the water. For several tense

minutes, the crowd waited silently on the bank, watching the angry current. At last Wyatt surfaced and yelled, “Over here!” and Sage swam frantically toward them.

“Robbie!” Mariah screamed.

The boy lay face up, wedged between the remnants of his log raft and a downed tree. Water swirled around his head, threatening to drag him down. Wyatt dove again and again, trying to free the heavy logs, while Sage kept his son’s head above the water. At last, Wyatt gave a mighty shove, and the raft broke free. Holding Robbie between them, the two men grabbed the ropes and swam for shore.

The doctor, Mr. Greer, and a couple of farm boys pulled them onto the bank. Mariah rushed to her son. Ada sank to her knees, trembling with fright and relief. Dr. Spencer dispersed the crowd and bent over Robbie. The boy was pale. His lips had turned blue, and he shivered despite the warm July afternoon. Someone brought a blanket. Another handed the doctor his medical bag.

“How are you doing, boy?” The doctor gently moved Robbie’s arms and legs, checking for broken bones.

“C-c-cold,” Robbie’s teeth chattered. But his gaze was steady as he sought his mother’s. “I’m sorry, Mama. I sh-should have s-stayed away from the river like you said.”

One leg of his trousers had been torn away,

revealing a deep gash in his knee. His arms and hands were covered with angry red scrapes. A huge bruise was forming near his temple.

Dr. Spencer cleaned and dressed Robbie's wounds before turning his attention to Wyatt.

"He seems to be all right," Mrs. Spencer, who had been tending to Wyatt, reported to her husband. "He has a deep wound in his shoulder and a bump on the back of his head."

The doctor bent over Wyatt. "How's your belly? Any nausea?"

"Some, but it might be from swallowing river water and too much blackberry cobbler. Not to mention the three pieces of stale cake I had for breakfast."

Dr. Spencer grinned. "Double vision?"

"A little at first. But I'm all right now."

The doctor cleaned the gash in Wyatt's shoulder and frowned. "This needs stitching up, my friend. It might hurt quite a lot. Can you stand it?"

"Will it hurt less than a bullet wound?"

"Considerably less, I should think." He rummaged in his medical bag for a needle.

Ada cringed as the doctor began sewing the wound. Watching Wyatt as he struggled in the water and lay there in pain had awakened new emotions in her. What if Mariah was right and God had a plan? What if she *were* destined to find someone to love?

Someone like Wyatt.

She retrieved her shoes and walked some distance away to pull them on, still thinking about her conversation with Mariah. Near the gazebo, a small crowd had settled in to await darkness and the start of the fireworks display. Others, their spirits dampened by the afternoon's events, were packing up their wagons and buckboards and making for home.

In the weary aftermath of the day's excitement, Ada found herself thinking about her father. Who was Cornelius Wentworth? The brash, reckless businessman or a lonely, brokenhearted father who had no inkling of how to relate to his grief-stricken daughter?

All those years she'd thought that he failed her. Perhaps he had. But she had failed him too.

"Miss Wentworth?"

Ada jumped. She hadn't heard anyone approaching. She got to her feet.

"I'm getting ready to call it a day," Patsy Greer said, "and I was wondering if you checked your ad in the *Gazette*. If you're pleased with the way it turned out."

"Very pleased." Now was the time to cancel the ad, as Wyatt expected. But the words wouldn't come. Norah Dudley had reminded her that she wasn't completely welcome here, that she needed to think about where she might go next and what she would do. Perhaps if the ad ran for just another week or two, she'd get a few more orders and, from then on, word of mouth might be all the advertising she would need. "If you'll wait a moment, I'll pay you."

"No hurry. We can settle up on your next trip to town. Daddy is completely worn out from all the excitement." She glanced toward the bank, where the doctor still worked on Wyatt. "I was planning to run a story about Founders Day on the front page next week, but this rescue will knock the founders clear over to page three. I just wish I had an illustrator around. A picture of Mr. Caldwell and Mr. Whiting bringing Robbie out sure would add some drama."

"I think we've had enough drama, don't you?" Bea Goldston stepped from the shadows and turned to a startled Ada. "I heard Robbie Whiting telling his mother that it was you who told him to build a raft. What's the matter with you? Couldn't you see how high the river is? Didn't you know he could get himself killed?"

"I didn't tell him to build a raft." Ada fought to control her anger. "Not that it's any of your business."

"Everything that happens in Hickory Ridge is my business." Bea's earlier friendliness had disappeared. "You have been nothing but trouble ever since you got here. And now, thanks to you, Wyatt Caldwell is hurt."

The look on the schoolteacher's face was open, revealing. Ada's heart jolted. *She loves him.*

"I talked to Mr. Caldwell not fifteen minutes ago, to get a quote for my newspaper piece," Patsy said. "He's making jokes about the whole thing."

"Wyatt makes jokes about everything, no matter how dire," Bea said. "That's just the kind of man he is." She pointed a finger at Ada. "If he dies from this, Ada Wentworth, I will never speak to you again."

Ada returned the schoolteacher's hard stare. "I'll try to bear it."

Patsy laughed out loud. "Good gravy, Bea. Nobody is going to die."

Bea's eyes flashed. "How do you know? Remember that girl from Chattanooga who broke her leg getting out of her carriage? Everybody said *she'd* be fine, but she died of pneumonia. From lying in bed too long."

"Somehow I can't picture Wyatt Caldwell languishing in bed long enough to ruin his lungs," Patsy said.

"Fine, make fun of me. But I know what I'm talking about."

Bea strode away, and Patsy shook her head. "Mercy sakes, what a pistol. Well, I'm off. I'll see you later."

Patsy left to collect her father, and Ada returned to the little group on the river. Mariah huddled with Robbie beneath the blanket and sipped tea someone had provided. Wyatt was sitting up, resting his back against a tree. Lillian sat on a quilt beside him, holding his hand. Jacob Hargrove, apparently none the worse for his ordeal, had left.

The doctor closed his medical bag and nodded to Ada. "Wyatt will be good as new after a couple of days' rest. The question before the court at this moment is where said rest shall transpire. He wants to go home, but I'd prefer he stay with someone who can look in on him overnight. A blow to the head can often be much more serious than a flesh wound."

"He'll stay at Lillian's, of course," Ada said automatically.

"Lillian is all for it, but he's resisting."

Ada strode over to Wyatt and dropped onto the grass. "You need looking after. You will stay with us. I won't hear another word about it."

"I appreciate the offer, but to tell you the truth, I'll rest better in my own bed."

"The bed in your room *is* your own bed, Wyatt!" Lillian said. "I haven't changed a thing since the day you moved out. You're just being contrary for its own sake."

"It'll make more work for Ada." He probed the swollen knot on his head and winced. "Besides, somebody has to drive my rig back."

"I can do it," Ada heard herself say.

Wyatt looked up at her, admiration in his eyes. "Cherokee is more spirited than old Smoky. Sometimes she's hard to handle. She'd rather be ridden than pull a buggy." He grinned. "I think it hurts her pride. I'd better ride along with you."

"That's settled," the doctor said. "Let's see about getting you all home."

Sage helped Mariah and Robbie to their feet. "I'll get our things and bring the wagon out here. I won't be long."

He soon returned, the wagon creaking and rocking over the uneven ground. He helped Mariah and Robbie, then Lillian, onto the wagon and turned for home.

Wyatt and Ada took a shortcut through a stand of trees to the road where Cherokee waited. Wyatt started to lift the harness, but Ada stopped him. "It won't do to pull those stitches out. Tell me what to do. I can handle it."

"Yes ma'am. I reckon you can do just about anything you put your mind to." He stood by, talking her through the process of hitching Cherokee to the rig. When it was done, Ada helped him climb in and then went around to the other side. She flicked the reins. The rig jolted as the mare trotted onto the road.

Wyatt fell asleep almost as soon as they left town, jostling awkwardly in his seat. Ada followed behind Sage's wagon. She turned her face to the burst of light in the trees and watched the setting sun rim the high clouds with gold. On the seat beside her, Wyatt stirred. Sunlight played over his face.

What a strange and unsettling day it had been, a

day with many more questions than answers. She needed some time to sort it all out.

By the time they reached Lillian's house, dusk was falling; fireflies blinked in the rosebushes, and the whip-poor-will called from the branches of the magnolia tree.

Sage helped Wyatt into the house and up the stairs to his childhood room. When the lamps were lit and the kettle was on the stove, Ada walked Sage out to the porch.

"I'm sorry for telling Robbie about Wyatt's boyhood rafting adventure, and I'm sorry for whatever influence it might have had over what happened today. I didn't mean any harm."

"I know." He nodded. "I should be going. I need to get my family home."

Ada watched him turn the wagon onto the road. How easy it was to cause harm when none was meant. She hoped Mariah would forgive her. She went inside, settled Lillian in her bed, and opened the window. "Would you like me to read to you?"

"Not tonight. My head hurts something awful." Lillian yawned. "See about Wyatt."

Ada climbed the stairs and knocked softly on Wyatt's door.

"Come on in."

She had never before set foot in this room. It was larger than her own, with a commanding view of the road and the distant river. The window was open to the last rays of light turning to silver on the water's dark surface. A pair of nesting doves cooed softly from the treetops.

Wyatt had lit the lamp and piled the pillows behind his back. He was sitting up, thumbing through one of the many volumes from a bookcase beneath the window. Atop the bookcase sat a glass jar filled with arrowheads, a porcelain horse, a broken slingshot, and assorted rocks and fossils —remnants of his boyhood.

It felt strange, too intimate, being in this room with him. Nerves skittered along her arms. Ada retreated to the doorway. "How do you feel? Would you like me to change the bed linens?"

He marked his place with his finger and smiled up at her. "Truthfully? I feel ridiculous. I barely got a scratch. I should be home, looking over my accounts. I was hoping to get caught up today." He grinned. "And these sheets are fine."

She leaned against the doorjamb. "I didn't expect to see you today."

"I hadn't planned to go to the picnic, but I got word I had telegrams waiting and I went into town to retrieve them."

And then you saw my ad in the Gazette. "Good news, I hope."

"Afraid not. One of my orders is on hold for a while. Waiting on the legislature to appropriate the money." He set his book aside. "I was on my way back to the mill when I ran into a couple of my workers heading to the park. We got to talking, and before I knew it that good food was calling my name. By the time I ate half of your blackberry cobbler, the afternoon was almost over."

She smiled. "How do you know it was mine?"

"Nobody uses lemon juice and butter quite the way Lillian does."

"I'm glad you were there today, regardless of the reason. Sage couldn't have pulled Robbie out by himself. The current was too strong."

She glanced around the room. "Is there anything you need? Some tea? Something to eat?"

"I'm not hungry." He cocked his ear to the soft night sounds coming through the window. "I'm usually so busy at the mill that I fail to notice how very long these summer evenings are."

It was the perfect opening to prove her point: that the long evenings afforded plenty of time to handle her millinery business without jeopardizing Lillian's well-being. But to bring the subject up would be to remind him of her promise to cancel her ad. She felt another sharp stab of guilt at keeping a secret from him, but her future was at stake.

Wyatt shifted on the bed and propped another pillow behind his injured shoulder. "So how *do* you spend these long evenings, Ada?" He smiled. "Since you're not much for the piano and such."

"When I traveled abroad, I kept journals of the places we visited and the interesting people we met. Sometimes I reread them in the evenings while Lillian sleeps. They remind me of happier times."

"I've always had a hankering to see the world, but somehow I think it's a trip better shared than undertaken alone."

"My aunt chaperoned me, and I enjoyed it. Except for the times she introduced me to certain young men of her acquaintance—sons of her old friends in London."

He grinned. "Tried to marry you off, did she?"

Ada blushed. "Something like that."

In the flickering lamplight, his gaze sought hers. "I'm pleased that she didn't succeed."

She met his gaze. A strange trembling began in her midsection and spread all the way to her toes. "If you're sure there's nothing you need," she said quickly, "perhaps I should say goodnight."

He nodded. "Goodnight, Ada."

Wyatt waited until he heard Ada's door close. He undressed and slid beneath the covers. The linens smelled a little musty now, but he could still recall his first long summer with Lillian, the way they'd smelled like sunshine and lavender. He couldn't remember precisely the last time he'd slept beneath this roof. Was it after his years at the university or the summer before he went off to war?

He was surprised and pleased that his aunt had kept all his books and treasures just as he'd left them. For a while, the war had stolen his spirit as surely as Cabot stole his father's money. During the worst of the fighting, when he came so close to dying, he had doubted that any part of his old life could remain.

He'd lost his faith then. Lost his belief that there was a purpose to anything.

He thought of that brutal dawn at Cold Harbor when Sage had dragged him to safety. The luck of the draw, he'd told Ada. But now, after today's events, things looked different somehow. Was it possible that he'd been wrong—that life wasn't so random after all, that God had a purpose in sparing him? Maybe he was meant to save Sage's only son from drowning. To build the mill that was reviving Hickory Ridge. And to find Ada.

He extinguished the lamp and lay listening to the night birds rustling in the trees. He hadn't been looking for a woman. Especially not a Boston Yankee accustomed to finery and big-city entertainments. Who had traveled abroad, for goodness' sake.

But then he saw Ada. Finding her standing on the railway platform that morning had been like finding a perfect string of pearls lying in the middle of the road. He couldn't believe that no one had claimed her. It was ironic that in fulfilling his duty to Lillian in a place he'd never really wanted to be, he'd found the woman who, despite their differences, he could come to love.

Sixteen

Creation! Surely there must be an easier way to beat this blasted heat. Ada pushed her sleeves up to her elbows, grasped the smooth wooden handle of the ice pick, and attacked the block of ice the deliveryman had brought. Shards of ice flew about the kitchen, lodging in her hair and on her forearms before melting into instant rivulets that dripped off her forehead and elbows. The blisters on her palms, the result of yesterday's floor scrubbing, oozed and burned.

"Ada?" Lillian called. "What's taking so long? Where in blazes is my ice water?"

"Coming!" Casting about the kitchen for a more efficient implement, she took up the meat cleaver and managed to hack off a chunk. She crushed it with a few more blows from the ice pick, filled a couple of glasses, and took them to the parlor.

Standing near the open window, Ada took a long, cooling sip and peered out. Waves of August heat shimmered above the browning grass. Nothing moved. Even the songbirds had gone silent.

Lillian drained her glass and handed it to Ada. "You'd better finish getting supper ready. Wyatt will be here any minute."

A shiver of expectation raced through her. Since

the accident on the river, she found herself thinking of Wyatt Caldwell at the oddest times. She imagined him riding the ridge scouting timber or working alongside his men, his shirtsleeves rolled to the elbow, or sitting on his front porch at the end of the day as the last of the light filtered through the sun-shot trees. She wondered if he ever felt lonely watching his men head off to their homes and families.

She shook her head. No use in wondering. They were on different paths.

"Everything's almost ready." She took their empty glasses to the kitchen, put the ice back into the icebox, and opened the oven door to check on the cobbler. It was torture, heating up the cookstove for so long on the hottest day of the summer, but blackberry season was almost over, according to Robbie Whiting, and Ada wanted to make something special for Wyatt.

Hoofbeats drummed along the road. She untied her apron and hastily tucked the tendrils of hair that had escaped their pins, then returned to the parlor just in time to see Wyatt stride in. He leaned over and kissed Lillian's cheek, then glanced up at Ada. He snapped his fingers. "I almost forgot—I have a delivery for you from town. I'll be right back."

She chewed her bottom lip as she waited. Maybe there was at last some word from Edward. The long-awaited explanation that would allow her to put her troubled heart to rest. To forget about the past with all its pain and regret.

But she didn't really believe there would be a letter. It had been too long.

Wyatt reappeared carrying a large box.

"My supplies from Mr. Biddle!" Ada opened the box and rummaged through the contents, running her fingers over the smooth hat block and the squares of milliner's gauze and netting. A bill fluttered to the floor. Too afraid to look at the enormous amount she undoubtedly owed, she tucked it into her pocket. "I had almost given up on these. I need them for Mariah's hat."

"You should have had it sooner," Wyatt said. "The rail agent asked whether I could deliver it. I took it over to my office a couple of days ago and forgot it was there."

"Well, I, for one, will be happy when that hat is done," Lillian said. "It's all Mariah can talk about. You'd think she'd never seen a hat before. Now, put that box aside and let's eat."

Wyatt tucked into his meal, obviously relishing the green beans and warm cornbread slathered with butter. When his plate was empty, Ada rose to serve the cobbler.

"I don't want any," Lillian said. "When it gets this hot, the berries aren't as juicy."

"I never pass up a chance for blackberry cobbler." Wyatt drained his glass. "We can eat it on the porch. Might be cooler out there."

"Go ahead." His aunt waved him away. "See how long it takes before the mosquitoes carry you off."

"Why so cranky, Aunt Lil? You're not your usual sweet self tonight."

Her usual sweet self? *Oh mercy*. Ada almost laughed out loud as she ducked into the kitchen. The hotter the weather, the worse Lillian's mood became. More than once this week, Ada had felt her patience withering in the wake of the older woman's constant complaints. As if Ada had the power to change the thermometer.

Lillian's reedy voice carried easily from the dining room. "You'd be cranky too, Wyatt Caldwell, if you spent all day stuck in this oven of a house."

Ada heard Wyatt's chair scrape as he pushed back from the table. "We could go swimming," he said. "River's down again, and the current's not too strong. We could go right now. It isn't that far, and there's still an hour or so before it gets dark."

Ada hurried out of the hot kitchen and handed him a bowl of cobbler. He sent her a lopsided grin and dug in. "This is very good. You don't know what you're missing, Aunt Lil. So, how about it, Ada? Shall we go for a swim?"

She studied his face. "You're suggesting that we go swimming in our street clothes? I certainly don't have a bathing costume."

"I can think of another option." His blue eyes glinted with mischief. "But it isn't exactly acceptable in mixed company."

Ada blushed, and Lillian waved one hand in the air. "What foolishness!"

"At least we can take a walk." Wyatt licked his spoon clean. "It's bound to be cooler down by the river, and there's enough breeze to keep the mosquitoes away. What do you say, Auntie? We'll go slow. You'll enjoy it."

"I'm too tired," Lillian said. "Besides, my hollyhocks need watering, and I have two more Christmas pageant costumes to sew. You two go on if you're a mind to."

He considered this for a few moments. "All right. If you're sure. We won't be gone long. Ready, Ada?"

The voice of reason whispered in her ear. *Falling in love will break your heart.* "The dishes," she murmured.

"They'll be here when we get back."

He lit the lamps and set a glass and a pitcher of water on the table in the parlor next to Lillian's chair. "We'll be right back, Aunt Lil. Stay put, all right?"

She picked up her needle. "You'd better quit fussing over me and go on, if you're going. Sun's almost down."

Wyatt and Ada crossed the yard and followed the well-worn path through Lillian's summer garden and down to the river. The sun rode low in the trees. Long shadows dappled the grass. The water shimmered like hammered gold.

"I love the river this time of day," he said. They picked their way along the bank, stepping over roots embedded in the ground and the flotsam and jetsam that littered the shore in the wake of a recent storm. A faint breeze stirred the trees and cooled their faces. Fireflies danced about their knees. "I reckon it's nothing special to someone used to having a whole ocean to look at, but it sure does soothe my troubled soul."

Ada gazed out at the placid river. "Problems at the mill?"

"Not at all. It's you that's troubling me, Ada, and I don't know what to do about it."

"Me?" She looked up. "Is my work unsatisfactory?"

"On the contrary." He took her hands and turned them over, palms up. "I noticed at supper—you've got blisters."

"Yesterday Lillian decided the kitchen floor needed a good, old-fashioned hands-and-knees scrubbing. I tried to convince her it was clean enough, but the more I talked, the more agitated she became. In the end it was easier just to do it than to keep arguing with her."

He pushed his Stetson to the back of his head. "I'm sorry for that. I never intended for you to work as a housemaid. I only wanted somebody to help her with the things she can no longer do for herself. Promise me the next time she gets such a notion in her head, you'll send for Libby Dawson.

She's a good worker, and the Dawsons can use the money."

"All right. But you know Lillian. When she decides she wants something, she doesn't like to wait."

"Me either." He paused. "I'm not very good at things like this. I'm not sure just what to say."

She stilled and lifted her gaze. Her eyes locked on his. He trailed one finger along the curve of her cheek and cupped his hand at the back of her neck.

Oh mercy! Wyatt Caldwell was about to kiss her.

And I want him to.

She released a trembling breath as the truth settled into her heart. Plain and simple, it was far too late to stop her feelings for him. And whatever the consequences for her millinery business, she could no longer deceive him about it. He deserved better.

"Mr. Caldwell—Wyatt? There's something I need to tell—"

"Shhh!" He held her close, one arm about her shoulders. "Did you hear something?"

From the direction of the house, she heard a muted shout.

"That's Lillian." Wyatt released her, and they took off at a dead run, racing over the slippery bank and along the path to the house.

Lillian met them on the front porch, brandishing

a lantern and a broom. She was shaking, her eyes wide and teary.

"Aunt Lil! What's the matter? Sit down." Wyatt tried to help her to the porch swing but Lillian stood firm, her tiny feet planted wide apart.

"An intruder, that's what!" she told him. "I saw him plain as day."

"Who was it?" Wyatt looked around. "Maybe you dozed off and—"

"I did *not* doze off. After I watered my hollyhocks I came in, and I was sitting there sewing, and all of a sudden a head appeared at the window."

"I see." Wyatt sent Ada a worried look. They ushered Lillian inside.

"You don't believe me," Lillian said. "But I know what I saw. By the time I got the broom and the lantern, he was headed toward Two Creeks."

Wyatt took the lantern from Lillian and headed for the door. "I'll look around outside."

Ada put her arm around Lillian's shoulder. "Come on. I'll make some tea. It'll calm your nerves. Wyatt will find whoever is out there."

Lillian followed Ada to the kitchen and sat at the table while the kettle heated. Ada cleared their supper dishes and put them into the dishpan to soak, one ear tuned to the outside. Was someone sneaking around the house? If so, surely she must be the cause. Who would want to hurt Lillian? When the kettle whistled, she made their tea, and they sat in silence, awaiting Wyatt's return.

A few minutes later he came inside and set the lantern down. “Nothing to worry about, Aunt Lil. I didn’t see a soul.”

Ada offered him some tea, but he declined. “It’s getting late, and I’m taking the morning train to Nashville. I’m trying to convince the governor to push through the appropriations bill for the new college. I’d like to get that timber shipped before fall.” He patted Lil’s mottled hand. “Promise me you won’t be afraid tonight.”

Lillian squared her shoulders. “I know how to shoot a gun. If he comes back, I won’t think twice about blowing him clear to kingdom come.”

Ada followed him onto the porch. He closed the door and lowered his voice. “I don’t want to alarm you, but there are fresh footprints in the garden.”

“So she did see someone.” Ada swallowed. “Could it have been Klansmen wanting to scare me away?”

“Maybe. But I can’t think of what you’ve done to rile them up.”

“Perhaps the fact of my being here is enough. Perhaps I should leave before Lillian comes to harm.”

He shook his head. “Most likely it was a hobo off the train or some drifter looking for a handout. We get a lot of them in town during the summer. Anyone bent on actual harm wouldn’t have run away once he saw how frail Lillian is.” He paused. “I’ll speak to the sheriff tomorrow. In the meantime, I know it's hotter than blue blazes, but I want you to close the first-floor windows tonight and keep the doors locked. Just in case."

"All right. I'll put Lillian upstairs in your old room."

"I wish I could stick around to keep an eye on the place, but the governor is expecting me."

"We'll be fine." She wasn't at all sure this was true. But she didn't want to burden him when he had such an important meeting coming up, and she didn't want him to think she couldn't handle whatever situation arose.

"I'll ask Sage to come by tomorrow to check on you. Barring any delays, I'll be back the day after tomorrow." He touched her cheek, a questioning look in his eyes. Her heart stumbled inside her chest as he turned and headed for his horse.

After he rode away, Ada went inside. Lillian had fallen asleep at the table, her tea untouched. Ada moved quietly, washing the dishes and laying kindling in the stove for tomorrow. She closed the windows, locked the doors, then gently shook Lillian awake.

"Wyatt thinks you should sleep in his old room tonight. I'll help you up the stairs."

"But all my things are down here! What about my sewing? And my Bible?"

"You've done enough sewing for one night. I'll bring your Bible up, though. What would you like me to read tonight?"

Lillian opened her mouth as if to protest again, then closed it. "Psalms. If you don't mind."

Ada took Lillian's arm and they slowly made their way upstairs. She opened the door to Wyatt's room.

Lillian sniffed. "It smells like sawdust in here." She frowned. "And Wyatt's old boots."

Ada smiled to herself. *Yes, it smells like him. Wonderful.* The memory of their moment on the river, the feel of his hand when he touched the back of her neck sent goosebumps skittering across her skin.

She helped Lillian into the bed, opened the window, went down to fetch the Bible, then settled down to read.

"God is our refuge and our strength, a very present help in trouble. Therefore will not we fear, though the earth be removed, and though the mountains be carried into the midst of the sea . . . Be still, and know that I am God."

Lillian's eyes drooped. Ada set the Bible aside, but Lillian stirred and opened one eye. "One more? Psalm twenty-seven, perhaps?"

Ada turned the thin pages. "The Lord is my light and my salvation; whom shall I fear? The Lord is the strength of my life; of whom shall I be afraid?"

"Not ghosts."

"No. Not ghosts."

Ada set the Bible on the night table and turned down the wick on the lantern. Crossing the narrow hall to her own room, she quickly got ready for bed. Though she was exhausted from a long day of working in the heat, sleep wouldn't come.

She looked out her open window at the twinkling mass of summer stars, her mind replaying the night's troubling events. Was her presence here in Hickory Ridge putting her—and Lillian—in danger?

The last leg of Wyatt's return trip—from Knoxville to Hickory Ridge—seemed interminable. The train was crowded with harried mothers and crying children and half-drunk salesmen arguing politics. Wyatt rubbed his tired eyes, stretched one leg into the aisle. Despite his success with the governor, all he could think about was those few moments alone on the river with Ada.

The look in her clear gray eyes had told him what he'd wanted to know but had been afraid to ask: that her tender feelings matched his own. That and her quickened breath and the way she'd trembled at his touch.

The question now was, what did he intend to do about it?

Hats by Ada. He studied the small ad prominently displayed on page two of the *Gazette* in his lap. When he'd first seen it yesterday morning on the outbound train, he'd felt a familiar jolt of anger and a deep sense of diappointment. How could he trust her with his affections if he couldn't trust her to keep her word on something so simple ascanceling an ad? But as the train chugged toward the capital, he'd calmed down and tried to see things from her point of view.

She tried so hard to keep up appearances. Her shoes were always shined, her few dresses clean and brushed, but all the shining and brushing in the world couldn't hide the fact that the heels of her shoes were rundown and her skirts were threadbare and peppered with holes. He wasn't much of a fashion expert, but he'd seen enough well-dressed ladies in the capital to realize Ada's clothes were out of date. Nowadays, ladies wore some kind of little pillow thing at the back of the skirt, an armload of extra cloth that served no useful purpose as far as he could tell, and the top part—the bodice?—had more little bows and buttons and such.

Her hats were old too. Last Sunday she'd decorated the brim of the one she was wearing with a scrap of shiny ribbon, but underneath, it was still the same old worn-out hat. Obviously, she was saving every penny, forgoing even the most basic of necessities in order to establish her business.

He had to admire her grit. It couldn't be easy making a life on her own. He hated that she was being less than truthful with him. On the other hand, what choice had he given her? In the same circumstances, he'd do whatever it took to survive, regardless of his personal feelings.

The train lurched, sending the box on the seat

beside him sliding onto the floor. He felt a stab of guilt. After his meeting with the governor, he'd stopped off at Waterfield and Walker, the biggest hat store in Nashville, and treated himself to a brand-new Stetson. Now, thinking of Ada and of how little she had, he wasn't sure he wanted to wear it. Maybe he'd save it for a special occasion.

The whistle sounded as the train slowed for the last sharp curve before the Hickory Ridge station. Around him, other passengers gathered their belongings. He folded the newspaper and tucked it into his leather pouch, still thinking about Ada. He could give her a raise. She certainly deserved one. But he could well imagine her reaction to anything that smacked of charity. Just look at how she'd come undone when he'd bought that copy of Mr. Thackeray's novel.

He wished now he had given her a different kind of present. Something small she could carry in her pocket as a reminder, that despite what she might think, he really was on her side.

Seventeen

Ada grasped Wyatt's shoulder as he lifted her out of the rig and set her on her feet. He touched the brim of his hat and picked up his leather pouch. "I'll meet you back here when your errands are done."

"Thank you."

It was a Friday in late September. Ada had ridden into town with Wyatt, fighting the hard fist of anxiety forming in her stomach. During Homecoming Sunday at church last week, Carrie Daly had announced that, at long last, she was hanging up her widow's weeds. She said Pastor Dennis's sermon had reminded her of just how precious life was and that it wasn't hers to waste. She intended to buy a new dress at Norah's and rejoin the world.

Caught up in Carrie's happiness, Ada had reiterated her offer to make a hat for her as a kind of coming out present. Then Bea Goldston, of all people, had chimed in with an order of her own. And now in the bottom of Ada's reticule was a letter from the mayor's wife, requesting a new hat.

Torn between elation that her business was catching on and dread at further displeasing Wyatt, Ada understood her own mother's dilemma more than ever. Having a talent she was forced to hide, getting good news and having no one to share it with, must have made Elizabeth's life lonelier than Ada had guessed.

She watched Wyatt push open the door to the bank and head inside. Her thoughts returned to their evening walk on the river. Something momentous had seemed about to happen between them. But weeks had passed since then, and he hadn't mentioned it. Maybe she'd only imagined his feelings for her. Maybe he'd been caught up in the beauty of the evening and now had second thoughts. And she certainly hadn't the courage to bring it up.

It's probably better just to let things be. In her position, could she really afford to be waylaid by sentiment?

She gathered her bag and parasol and headed down the road toward the park. Mayor Scott and his wife, Molly, lived in the last house on the road, a low, redbrick structure shaded by a columned porch. Ada pushed open the gate and rang the bell.

A tall, broad-shouldered woman with iron-gray hair and eyes to match peered out. "Yes?"

"I'm Ada Wentworth." Ada held out the letter she'd received the week before. "You asked me to call on my next trip to town. About your hat."

"My . . . oh! Yes! Hats by Ada! Well, come on in. Sit a spell."

Ada went in. The woman grabbed her hand and pumped it. "Pleased to meetcha! I'm Molly Scott. The mayor is down at the town hall doing whatever it is they do down there."

She led Ada into a small sitting room furnished with a settee and a wing-backed chair upholstered in needlepoint. "Can I getcha anything? I made coffee this morning, but it's prob'ly gone to sludge by now. I can start a fresh pot if you're a mind to wait on it."

"No, thank you." Ada couldn't help smiling

at the woman's enthusiasm. "I have quite a few errands to run this morning. Perhaps we should get right down to business."

"Whatever you say." Mrs. Scott retrieved a magazine from the table beside the chair and handed it to Ada. "Page thirty-seven."

Ada flipped to a picture of a large hat with a fat pigeon perched on the wide brim. Two long pheasant feathers were tucked into the hatband. She stifled a laugh. It might be the latest thing, but it was hideous. "This is what you have in mind?"

"Exactly. I've already got the bird. My husband killed it accidentally, but he stuffed it for me on purpose. It's on the back porch if you want to take a look."

"That won't be necessary." Ada studied the picture. "This hat is made of felt. Is that the fabric you want?"

"You'd know better'n me. I reckon it'll have to be sturdy to support the weight of the bird."

Ada took out her notebook and pencil. "What color?"

"Brown. Same as the picture. And I want them pheasant feathers too. They add just the right touch, don'tcha think?"

"They're certainly dramatic." Ada made more notes. "I wonder if you're open to another suggestion."

"You mean a different hat?"

"Yes. In Boston last spring, I saw a lovely veiled

hat with a satin brim that might be just the thing." Quickly, she sketched the hat and handed it to Molly.

"That's a handsome hat, all right, and I do appreciate the suggestion, but I've got my heart set on that bird. The mayor's right proud of it. It'd break his heart clean in two if I changed my mind now." She glanced at the photograph of the mayor that graced the fireplace mantel. "He's had a hard time of it lately—needs some cheering up."

"Oh?" Ada took out her tape measure.

Molly dropped heavily into her chair. "Coupla men on the town council want to clear out the coloreds down in Two Creeks. They say the black folks are hamperin' the town's ability to grow. The truth is, they want that good bottomland for themselves."

"But surely they can't just come in and take it, can they? What about property rights?"

Molly looked confused. "Most all the folks in Two Creeks are sharecroppers. They don't have any say in what happens to land that don't belong to them."

"But if they're thrown off their farms, where would they go?"

"That's exactly the problem now, ain't it? There's enough poor folks in these parts without throwin' a buncha the blacks off the land. Folks coming into Hickory Ridge on the train think what a prosperous little town we got goin' here. And thanks to Wyatt Caldwell and his mill, we're doin' better'n most. But you go ten miles out of town and it's a whole different kettle of fish. They's people out there, black and white, just barely holdin' on."

Molly shook her head. "Me and the other women in my church circle do what we can, but it's never enough. I just don't see how it's goin' to help our town to clear out Two Creeks. My Hiram don't understand it neither. That's what's been weighin' heavy on his heart—and that's why I got to get that hat. He likes for me to look nice. Seein' me in that there bird hat will take his mind off ever'thing else."

"No doubt," Ada said. "Hold still while I measure your head."

She jotted Molly's hat size into her notebook. "That's all I need for now."

"You don't want my stuffed bird?"

"Not just yet. I'll come back for it when I'm ready to trim the hat."

"How much do I owe you?"

"Two dollars now. Two when I deliver the finished hat."

Molly whistled. "That's a lot of money, but it don't matter. Can't put a price on my man's happiness." She took the money from a green vase on the mantel. "When do you reckon you'll be finished?"

"Perhaps by the middle of October." Ada tucked the money into her bag. "You're in luck because I just received a shipment of supplies from Boston. I have a hat block in your size, so I won't have to send away for anything before getting started."

They went to the door.

"Charlie Blevins down at the mill, he's real good with his hands," Molly said. "He could make all the hat blocks you need. Save you the trouble of ordering 'em from back east."

"I'll keep that in mind."

Ada waved to Molly and retraced her steps, stopping first at the bank to open an account, then to the *Gazette*, where Patsy Greer greeted her with an open grin and handshake only slightly less powerful than Molly's. Patsy plopped down behind the desk and picked up her spectacles. "What can I do for you? You need a bigger ad?"

"Actually, I've come to cancel it." Ada set her parasol on the floor and perched on the chair opposite Patsy's.

Patsy frowned. "I thought you liked it."

"Oh, I do! It was exactly what I wanted. It's just that"—she swallowed, willing the words to come—"my duties at Mrs. Willis's are taking more time than I anticipated, and I can't take on any more hat orders right now."

"That's too bad. At church last Sunday, when Mrs. Scott was going on and on about her plans to buy a new hat, several more ladies said they wanted new hats too."

"Maybe later on." Ada laid a bill on the counter. "I believe this settles my account."

"Sure. Just let me know when you want to start

running it again." Patsy stood. "Did you happen to see the story we ran on the Founders Day incident?"

"I'm afraid not."

"Hold on. I've got an extra around here someplace." Patsy rummaged in the file cabinet and extracted a paper.

"Here you are."

Ada read the headline, printed in large, bold type. "Quick Action Averts Double Drowning on Founders Day. Caldwell, Whiting Save Boys from Certain Death in Raging River." She looked up. "Very dramatic."

"Dad thought it was a little too dramatic, but it's drama that sells papers."

Ada scanned the rest of the page, skimming stories about farm prices, the upcoming market days, and changes in the Hickory Ridge railway schedule. A small story at the bottom of the page caught her eye. "Why I Love Founders Day, by James Boleyn, Age 10."

"You're letting children write for the paper now?"

Patsy grinned. "That was Bea Goldston's idea. She thought the students might work harder at their lessons if they knew they might be published. Last spring she assigned this essay, and I picked the best one to run in the Founders Day issue. Bea isn't the most pleasant woman in town, but give her some credit—this was a brilliant idea." She bumped the file cabinet drawer closed with her hip. "I'm thinking of making it a regular feature when school opens again. It'll give the students something to work for, and help sell papers too. Mrs. Boleyn bought ten copies of this issue to send to all their kin."

She peered at Ada. "I haven't known you very long, but I'm a pretty good judge of what people are thinking. And right now, I'd say you've got a new idea running around in your head."

Ada nodded. "There's a child at the orphanage who's part colored and—"

"I know the one you mean. I saw you with her at Founders Day."

"She's very bright but barred from the school. Mrs. Lowell teaches her a bit, I think, but Sophie doesn't have the same chances as the others. She loves telling stories. I'm wondering if you would—"

"Publish one of hers?" Patsy considered this. "I don't see why not. If it meets my standards."

"Thank you, Patsy. That would be wonderful for her."

Patsy peered over her spectacles. "She'll have to do the work, mind you. I can't play favorites. Betsy Terwilliger is already up in arms because I didn't pick her granddaughter's essay."

"Of course she'll do the work." Ada handed the paper back. "Now, I must go. Thank you for your help."

She left the *Gazette* and continued down the street to Norah's Fine Frocks to find Carrie Daly waiting for her. Today Carrie wore a simple gingham dress with a ruffled hem and a green felt spoon bonnet. Both had clearly seen better days, but the soft colors made Carrie look ten years younger.

"Oh, Ada, there you are!" She led Ada to a display by the window. "I thought I'd missed you."

"I had some business at the newspaper office." Ada dropped her bag onto a little settee and studied the dress on the mannequin in the window. "Is this the one you have in mind?"

Norah bustled in from her storeroom in the back and stopped dead still. Ada turned away and pretended to study a pink embroidered shawl in the window. Even though she was the one who had been wronged that day at the picnic, she felt embarrassed and awkward, and sorry for her angry retort.

Norah busied herself behind the counter, rearranging a display of gloves and parasols. Finally she caught Ada's eye. "I owe you an apology, I reckon, for what I said on Founders Day. About Yankees. I didn't mean it—not about you personally. You're not a liar or a thief. I got caught up in the conversation and it slipped out."

Ada nodded. "I'm sorry, too, for what I said."

Norah's face turned red. "Well. So. I've got to unpack some new merchandise in the back. Carrie, give a holler if you need anything. And remember, I can make a dress to order if you can't find anything you like."

"Thank you, Norah." Carrie took a pale blue dress from the open clothes press beside the door.

"I love this one, Ada. But Bea says I'm getting too long in the tooth for such frilly things. What do you think?"

"I think you should ignore Bea and get whatever makes you happy. This one looks fine to me. And I know just the hat to go with it."

Quickly, she sketched a leghorn toque covered in filmy netting, with double streamers off the back. "I can trim it in the same color blue as the dress if you like."

"It's beautiful! How much?"

"My offer still stands, Carrie. I want to do this for you. No charge."

"It's sweet of you, but Bea says you're practically destitute. Not to be nosy or anything, but can you afford to be so generous?"

She couldn't. Not by a long shot. But a promise was a promise, and her pride was at stake. "It'll be my contribution to your new beginning."

"Well, if you're sure." Carrie smoothed the folds of the new dress, her eyes glowing.

"I'm sure." Ada patted her friend's arm. "Only please don't let it get around town that I'm giving away hats. One day I'll have to make a living from them."

Carrie pressed a finger to her lips. "I won't say a word! And thank you, Ada. I don't know what else to say."

Ada left Carrie to try on the dress and headed outside. The clock at the railway station read half past twelve when she spotted Wyatt emerging from the telegraph office. She waved and waited for him outside the mercantile. A whistle blew as a train chugged into the station.

"Train's half an hour late today," he observed, stepping up beside her. "You must have had a busy morning. I looked for you earlier, but you seemed to have disappeared. I wondered whether you'd struck out for home again on your own."

She shook her head. She was wiser now and, besides, her old shoes didn't have another seven miles in them. "I opened an account at the bank and met Carrie Daly at the dress shop." She held his gaze. "And I canceled my ad in the *Gazette*."

Despite her regret at losing her only means of advertising, she felt the weight of her long-festering guilt lifting from her shoulders. But there was more to tell him before she would feel truly free. She took a deep breath as if bracing for a plunge into icy water. "I need this job, but I care too much about your good opinion to lie to you."

Briefly she described the orders she'd taken in rapid succession from Carrie, Bea, and Molly Scott. He listened, his arms crossed, his expression unreadable.

"I didn't expect so many orders so soon," she finished. "Everything has happened all at once."

"Looks that way all right." He tossed his packages into the rig.

She hurried on. "That night on the river I was

going to tell you that I hadn't yet canceled my ad, but we were interrupted when Lillian—"

His expression softened. At last he smiled. "I've been regretting that interruption ever since."

Relief and happiness welled up inside her. "You aren't angry with me?"

"I'm not thrilled about it, and I still think you're biting off more than you can chew, but I'm willing to give it a try, see how it goes."

"Thank you. You have no idea what this means to me."

He nodded. "I'm hungry. How about some fried chicken?"

"If it's all right with you, I'd like to stop at the mercantile first."

"Fine. I'll check with Nate at the bookshop. Sage had a good idea about that knotty pine. Nate's going to take a lot of it off my hands. I'll meet you at Hattie's in . . . half an hour?"

He loped across the street, dodging a buckboard. A skinny yellow dog trotted over to the post office and curled into a ball in the shade, eyeing Ada as she passed. She entered the mercantile, hoping that Jasper Pruitt's clerk would be there to assist her, but it was the storekeeper himself who looked up from his work when the bell over his door jingled.

She nodded to him and headed to the back where the fabrics and sewing notions were kept. She gathered spools of thread, some ribbons, and a card of pearl buttons, happier than she had felt since her arrival. She couldn't believe Wyatt had given his blessing to her enterprise. What had caused him to change his mind?

She needed more felt for Molly's hat and reluctantly summoned Jasper to cut it from the heavy bolt of fabric on a shelf above her head. He spat a stream of tobacco juice into the spittoon beside the door and lumbered toward the back, shears in hand.

"How much you need?"

"One yard, please."

He lifted the bolt, laid it on the cutting table, and proceeded to lop off a portion.

"Excuse me, Mr. Pruitt." She rummaged in her bag. "I have a tape measure. I'll just—"

"Are you accusing me of cheatin' you, Yankee girl?" He squinted at her. Tobacco juice trickled from the corner of his mouth into his thick beard.

"Of course not! I'd think you'd want to measure too."

"Been doing this since I was a boy. I know what a yard looks like."

"Fine. I won't argue with you." She dropped her tape measure into her bag.

"What a relief. You Yankees think you know everything. You don't know nothin'." His hard, black gaze bore into her. "Especially about how things are down here. I'd watch myself if I were you."

"I have no earthly idea what you're talking about."

"I saw you on Founders Day." His shears made a snicking sound as they slid through the fabric. "Running around with that girl from Miz Lowell's."

Ada bristled. "It's no concern of yours."

He folded the cloth and returned the bolt to the shelf. "See, Yankee, that's where you're dead wrong. When strangers come to our town and start tryin' to change the natural order of things, I make it my business."

"The natural order of things?"

"Whites have their place and blacks have theirs. Long as ever'body knows which is which, things progress the way they're supposed to."

She glared at him. "Oh, with whites in charge and the blacks at their mercy. Isn't that what you mean, Mr. Pruitt?"

She gathered the cloth and sewing notions, quickly found soap, a bottle of rosewater, and a tin of celluloid hairpins, and took them to the counter.

Jasper Pruitt spat another stream of foul-smelling tobacco juice. "You owe me three dollars, and . . . lessee, eighty-six cents. Cash."

Her stomach churned with anger, but she kept her expression pleasant. She handed him the money, took up her purchases, and hurried toward the front of the store.

"And good day to you too," she muttered as the door slammed shut behind her.

Eighteen

"Ada, come sit by me." Carrie patted the empty chair next to her.

Ada took her place across from Lillian, Bea, and Mariah and dug her thimble and needles from her bag. Lillian was already busy, sorting through squares of calico and denim. The ladies were making quilts for a boy and his sister who had been orphaned when their parents' mule team spooked, sending their buckboard into the river. Outside the open window, a couple of noisy jays flitted among leaves just beginning to color. A bushy-tailed squirrel danced along the high branches, scolding the jays.

Ada smiled at his antics. Today, despite her constant worries about money, she was suffused with a rare sense of well-being. She had hats to make. And working on the quilts, making something beautiful and useful out of what had been worn out and discarded, gave her a feeling of accomplishment.

The women quickly finished piecing the quilt top. They attached it to the quilting frame and then began sewing it to the backing, their needles moving rhythmically through the colorful cloth. "Bea," Carrie began, "do tell! What is the new headmaster like? Do the children like him?"

"He's all right. He wants to impress the children, the older boys especially, with his authority. But his credentials are first-rate." Bea reached into her basket for another spool of thread. "We're offering Latin this term, and we're planning a course in higher mathematics next year."

"And our church Christmas pageant?" Mariah drew her needle through the fabric. "Will he help with that?"

Bea laughed. "Hardly! He thinks pageants are a woman's domain—beneath the attention of a distinguished Virginia scholar such as himself."

"At least he agreed to teach all the children today, so you could come here," Lillian said. "That says something for his character."

"I suppose." Bea huffed. "But I must say, Ethan Webster has quite a high opinion of himself."

Mariah rolled her eyes. Ada smiled at her across the quilt frame.

"I suppose Mr. Webster must attend the church in town," Carrie said. "I haven't seen him here."

"I wouldn't know." Bea threaded her needle. "I'm tired of talking about him." She glanced at Ada. "I'd much rather talk about our hats."

"Me too," Mariah said. "What about it, Ada?"

"Yours is almost finished, Mariah. I can bring it next week if you like."

"I can't wait!" Mariah stood and went to the cupboard, where she pulled out glasses and filled them with apple cider.

"What about *my* hat?" Bea's expression clearly indicated she thought hers was more important. "You haven't even taken my measurements yet."

Ada suppressed a sigh. She set down her glass, pulled out her tape measure, and jotted down Bea's measurement in her sketchbook. They were discussing Bea's preferences when Lillian plopped her empty glass onto the table. "*Some* people in this room have forgotten why we're here. There are two little children whose feet are going to freeze if we don't get these quilts done. I, for one, do not want that on my conscience."

"Coming, Lillian." Bea murmured to Ada, "We can talk about my hat later, but I want it as soon as possible."

The ladies worked until midafternoon. At last they removed the quilt from its frame, packed up their work, and went out to their rigs. Bea turned for town; Mariah climbed onto the Whitings' buckboard and headed for the mill. Ada helped Lillian into their rig and clicked her tongue. "Get up, Smoky."

The horse, accustomed at last to her voice, tossed his head and plodded onto the road. Ada urged the horse homeward.

When they pulled up to Lillian's barn, Ada watered Smoky, then left him in the barn with a bag of oats and a promise that Wyatt would arrive soon to remove his harness. Returning to the house, she removed her hat and tied an apron over her dress.

She had promised Wyatt a pot of Louisiana gumbo, the one dish she'd learned to perfection from her mother's New Orleans cousins.

While Lillian rested, Ada made the roux and added the okra and seasonings, and set the pot on the stove to simmer. She started a pot of rice and set a pan of cornbread in the oven to bake.

The mantel clock chimed. Ada glanced up. Wyatt wouldn't arrive for another hour, and Lillian had fallen asleep. There was time to start work on Carrie's hat. She spread her supplies on the table, lit the lamp, and pinned the pattern to the fabric, smoothing the thin paper with her fingers.

The familiar smell of the spicy gumbo and the feel of the new cloth beneath her fingers was a comfort. So often she felt exhausted from the drudgery of endless chores and Lillian's constant needs, and terrified that despite all her brave plans, she would fail at self-sufficiency. But tonight, sitting in the fragrant kitchen beneath the warm glow of the lamp, she felt calmer, almost at peace.

When the clocked chimed the three-quarter hour, Ada put away her work, stirred the rice into her gumbo mixture, and took the bread from the oven. Then she went to wake Lillian.

The bed was empty.

Ada checked the parlor and the rooms upstairs. Was Lillian hiding again? She peered beneath beds and into dark corners, calling out to the older woman. Lillian had vanished.

Though it was not yet completely dark, Ada grabbed the lantern and ran toward the river, her mind racing ahead of her feet. Had someone—a Klansman maybe—taken Lillian? Was she lying hurt somewhere on the dark path?

Every nerve in her body leapt and shuddered. Wyatt was right. Looking after Lillian demanded all her care and attention. Now Lillian was lost, or worse, and Ada had only herself to blame.

"Lillian?" She lifted the lamp and swung it in a wide arc. "Lillian Willis! Where are you?"

She heard a rustling in the underbrush, and her whole body went taut. At river's edge, not thirty feet away, a raccoon stood calmly washing its dinner. Ada rushed on, her hem catching on bushes and bits of exposed tree roots. The wind skirled up, sending a few fallen leaves into her path. Her heart jerked against her ribs. How long should she look for Lillian alone before going for help? And who would help her until Wyatt arrived? Oh mercy, he would never forgive her.

She heard a noise on the path behind her and whirled around. "Lillian?"

"Of course it's me."

Ada went limp. She searched the older woman for signs of injury. But Lillian, her hair mussed and her face streaked with dirt, grinned as if she'd just won a prize at the county fair.

Ada burst into tears.

"What's the matter with you?" Lillian demanded.

"I'm the one who should be upset. I'm the one who is treated like a jailbird in her own home."

"I . . . I thought something terrible had happened!" Ada wiped her tears on her sleeve. "Whatever possessed you to up and leave like that?"

"This is my home and my land." Lillian brushed dirt off her sleeve. "I reckon I can come and go as I please."

"Not without telling me! You scared me half to death."

"I don't care!" Lillian's expression was downright mutinous. "Those people down at the county hoosegow have more freedom than I do. I felt like getting out on my own for a while, that's all."

Ada's heart wrenched. For the past few weeks, she had devoted every spare moment to her hatmaking, neglecting Lillian in the process. Why hadn't she paid more attention to the older woman's needs? She searched her mind for some way to make amends.

"I'm sorry you've felt so confined," she said. "But I have an idea. Why don't we plan a picnic?"

The older woman brightened. "A picnic? You mean you and me?"

"Why not?" Ada found herself actually warming to the idea. "The weather is nicer now, and it might be fun to spend some time on the river. I saw some poles in the barn. We could try our hands at fishing."

Lillian's fine white brows went up. "And just which one of us is going to bait the hooks?"

Ada smiled. Trust Lillian to point out the practicalities of any venture.

"Just as I suspected." Lillian folded her arms across her chest. "Not that I blame you. I'm not much for handling worms myself."

Ada grinned and offered Lillian her arm. "In that case, maybe we'll just pack a picnic." She picked up the lantern. Lillian took her arm and they started up the path to the house.

"I suppose I owe you an apology, girl." Lillian pushed aside a low-hanging tree branch. "I'm sorry for giving you such a hard time when you first came here. And for being so cantankerous. I don't intend to make so much trouble for you."

"It's all right." Ada slowed her steps as they approached a thick root in the path. "But please don't disappear like this ever again. I was terrified. I didn't know what to do or where to go for help."

Lillian gave Ada's arm a reassuring squeeze. "When there's no other name to call, you can call on the Lord. He's the One who is always listening. Even in the darkness."

"I'll try to remember that."

Lillian nodded. "And I'll try to watch my tongue. Sometimes my mouth gets ahead of my brain."

Ada thought of Norah Dudley's blurted comment about Yankees and her own sharp reply. "That happens to all of us, I reckon."

Lillian burst out laughing. "Did you hear yourself just now? We might make a Southern girl out of you yet."

She tightened her grip on Ada's arm and they climbed the small hill toward the house. At last, they reached the kitchen door. Lillian paused to catch her breath. "You might be half Yankee, Ada Wentworth, but you're a good woman."

Ada's eyes filled. "So are you, Lillian Willis."

She opened the door and helped Lillian inside.

The older woman shuffled to her wheelchair and plopped down, obviously exhausted from the long walk. "I reckon you're just about the best friend I've got, this side of heaven."

"Yes," Ada said softly. "I reckon I am."

Wyatt tossed his hat onto the hook behind the door, toed off his boots, and heaved a weary sigh. What a day!

The steam generator had quit again, and it had taken him and Sage most of the day to fix it. Without enough work to do, Charlie Blevins and a couple of the other sawyers grew bored and quarrelsome, and Wyatt finally sent the three of them home to cool off. Then a wheel on one of the delivery wagons broke, and Josiah Dawson declared it beyond repair.

What a relief when the workday finally ended and he could ride Cherokee out to Aunt Lillian's for supper. To his delight, Ada had made gumbo.

It wasn't exactly the way he'd remembered it from his visits to New Orleans, but it was close enough—thick with okra and tomatoes and fragrant with spices and fresh fish. Ada had baked a peach pie for dessert, and she served it with plenty of fresh coffee.

Lillian looked tired but freshly scrubbed, and Wyatt was pleased to see that she and Ada seemed to be involved in some sort of mysterious female conspiracy. He couldn't help noticing the way they grinned at each other all during supper.

He was sorry now that he'd waited so long to give Ada his blessing for her hat venture. It had been good for both her and Lillian, though he couldn't help worrying that Ada would grow weary of all the burdens of running a business. He wished he could spare her the headaches he knew were coming, but there was little he could do about that.

What bothered him now was the town hall meeting he'd attended after dinner. Jasper Pruitt and a couple of his friends had shown up again, demanding that something be done about rousting the colored families out of Two Creeks.

"I tell you, Sheriff, they're stealing me blind. I can't turn my back on 'em for a single minute." Jasper pounded on the table so hard the mayor's wooden gavel jumped.

"Have you actually seen them taking anything?" Sheriff Eli McCracken never seemed to take Jasper too seriously—a mistake, in Wyatt's opinion. When a man's livelihood was threatened, there was no telling how far he might go to protect it.

"No," Jasper said. "Because I make 'em stay out back and give me their orders though the door. But I can't be everywhere at once, and all I know is, the last time I took inventory I was short on canned goods and flour. It's the coloreds sneaking in and taking things when my back is turned. You've got to do something, Sheriff."

"I can't arrest them for being black, Jasper." McCracken had pulled out a bag of tobacco and filled his pipe. "I've got more worrisome things on my mind these days."

Now Wyatt padded over to the stove in his stocking feet and poured himself a cup of coffee. He didn't want to alarm Lillian and Ada, but lately he'd been worried too. He couldn't forget the face in Lillian's window, that set of footprints in her garden. But without more to go on, what could he do about it?

He pushed open the door and sat down in his rocking chair, propping his crossed ankles on the porch rail. He looked out over the darkened road and sipped his coffee, watching as, one by one, the lights in the distant farmhouses went out. A whip-poor-will called. From the little creek behind the house came the deep rumble of frogs and the soft burbling of water flowing over stones. Normally such peaceful sounds took the edge off even the most frustrating of days, but now a deep concern for Ada and for the town crowded his mind.

The talk around the town hall was that some of the Klan were planning to take matters into their own hands and force the sharecroppers out of Two Creeks. As long as that land was up for grabs, the potential for violence was very real. And as long as the Klan were prosecuting their sick agenda, intimidating the coloreds among them, maybe they'd decide to rid Hickory Ridge of its resident Yankee do-gooder as well. But how to warn Ada, without causing her undue worry, was a problem. She was a stubborn little thing. She wouldn't take kindly to being told what she could or could not do.

Nineteen

"Oh, Ada! It's exquisite. I absolutely adore it!" Mariah peered at her reflection in the hand mirror she'd brought to the quilting circle. Her fingers brushed the velvet brim of her saucy toque and lingered on the silky rust and gold flower adorning the crown. "This flower is the perfect finishing touch. I've never seen anything quite like it."

"My mother bought it in Paris when I was a girl." Ada smiled, relieved that her first customer seemed satisfied with her purchase, and that the style she had chosen complemented Mariah's rosy complexion and lively brown eyes. "She found it in a little antique shop on the Left Bank. Supposedly it once adorned the hat of a French countess."

Mariah laughed. "I may not be a real countess, but this hat makes me feel like one."

Lillian took out her needles and thimbles. "If the fashion show is over, may we please get to work? We're shorthanded today, in case you haven't noticed, and I promised Mrs. Lowell we'd have these quilts to her by tomorrow." She peered at the others. "Don't make the orphans suffer because you're besotted with a hat."

The ladies settled at the quilt frame and began work.

"Where is Carrie today, anyway?" Mariah asked. "I saw her after church last Sunday, and she didn't say a word about not coming today."

"Henry isn't well," Mariah reported. "He hasn't been at the mill all week. No doubt Carrie is looking after him."

"He's probably just lovesick." Bea reached for her scissors. "I heard that he's over the moon about Mary Stanhope ever since she baked that pecan pie for his birthday. They say she left the telegraph office door standing wide open in the middle of the day to deliver it."

Lillian peered at Mariah over the top of her spectacles. "What's ailing Henry Bell?"

"I have no idea. Dr. Spencer drove out there yesterday morning to check on him." Mariah's hands stilled. "I'm surprised the doctor could even think straight after what happened on Monday night."

"What happened?" Bea asked. "I've been so busy at school, getting ready for the next board meeting, that I haven't heard any news all week."

"You haven't heard? While Dr. Spencer was in town last Sunday night, looking after a patient, a woman from Two Creeks rode up to the Spencers' place. Mrs. Spencer said the poor woman was half crazy with fear because her daughter was having a baby and it wasn't coming out the right way."

Lillian nodded. "Breech birth. My husband attended a few such deliveries during his career. Mariah, please hand me that last blue square."

Mariah handed it over. "Anyway, Mrs. Spencer went down there to see if she could help. And then, Monday night, somebody burned a cross in their yard and slaughtered all their chickens. And their chicken coop burned clear to the ground."

The women gasped.

"Is Eugenie all right?" Lillian asked. "They didn't harm her?"

"She's all right," Mariah said. "Terrified, of course. Sage said the Spencers might leave Hickory Ridge."

Fear and anger jolted through Ada. How could Mariah and the others take this news so calmly? How could anyone feel safe with such criminals running about? "I hope the Spencers reported this crime to the sheriff."

"I'm sure they did, but what good will it do?" Mariah's dark eyes flashed. "There's no proof of who did it. There never is. I wish that, just once, the Klan would get caught. That might make them think twice before they go around terrorizing people who are only trying to do some good around here."

"Well, it's too bad for the Spencers," Bea said, "but that's what happens when people don't follow the rules."

"I hope this isn't a foretaste of what's to come in Hickory Ridge," Mariah went on. "Sage said there was a long discussion about Two Creeks at the mayor's meeting last week. There's been some talk about moving the coloreds out of there."

Lillian picked up her scissors. "My lands, where on earth would they move them to? Leave 'em be, is what I say. They're not bothering anybody."

"Except the people who want that land for themselves." Ada picked up another quilt block. "Lillian is right. Two Creeks should be left in peace."

"For someone who's been here for such a short time, you sure have a lot of opinions," Bea said. "Maybe you should leave the running of Hickory Ridge to those of us who know what's what." She drew her needle through the cloth and snipped a few loose threads. "That bottomland could be put to greater production without the sharecroppers. Two Creeks is a den of iniquity anyway, with all that drunkenness and gambling and whatnot going on. Those people are a blight on the town, if you want to know the truth of it."

An uneasy silence fell across the room. Finally, to break the growing tension, Mariah told a story about Robbie that made them all laugh.

"He's one of the smartest boys I've ever known," Ada said, relieved to have something else to talk about. "I like having him around. But we haven't seen much of him lately."

"School keeps him busy." Mariah lowered her voice. "Too many long assignments."

Bea snorted. "I heard that."

They went back to work. An hour later, Mariah folded the finished quilt.

"If you don't mind, Mariah, I'd like to go with you to the orphanage." Ada gathered her things. "I want to speak to Mrs. Lowell."

"You're welcome to come along. I'd love the company."

"Ada?" Lillian frowned and tugged at Ada's sleeve. "Have you forgotten that you drove us here?"

"Of course not. You can come with us. I won't be long."

"I don't want to muddle your plans, but I'm tired today. My head has been aching for the past two days."

"Then we need to get you home." Ada smiled at the older woman. "Never mind, Mariah. I'll see Mrs. Lowell another time."

"I can deliver a message if you like." Mariah gathered her mirror and her quilting bag, and they all went outside.

"No message." Since Founders Day, Ada had thought about Sophie almost every day. Despite today's news about the Spencers, she meant to speak to Mrs. Lowell about the girl's sketchy education and about Ada's own hope that one of Sophie's stories might find its way to the *Gazette*. But that wasn't a conversation she was willing to delegate.

"Well, I have a message," Lillian declared.

"Fire away." Mariah tossed her bag and the quilt into her rig.

"The pastor thinks that we should involve the children from the orphanage in our Christmas pageant this year. I happen to agree with him."

"Well, I don't!" Bea snapped. "I've always been in charge of the pageant, and we've never had the orphans take part before."

"Why not?" Ada asked. "I realize I'm only an outsider, but I am curious."

"For one thing, it complicates the practice schedule." Bea pulled on her gloves. "Either I must take my students down the road to Mrs. Lowell's, or she must bring the orphans to me. It disrupts both our routines."

"And we can't let what's best for the children interfere with convenience," Ada said. "It seems to me that Christmas is the perfect time to let those children feel, if only for a little while, that they have some place to belong."

"Well said, Ada!" Mariah beamed at her.

"Bea," Lillian said, "what if you let the orphans sing a few carols either before or after the pageant? That way, Mrs. Lowell could conduct their practices without disturbing your schedule. Mariah is an accomplished pianist. I'm sure she wouldn't mind serving as their accompanist."

"What a splendid idea." Mariah climbed into her rig. "Good-bye, all. I'll see you at the harvest festival. I'll be the one in the fabulous hat!"

Lillian waved as Mariah's rig bumped down the road. "Then it's settled."

"I don't know, Lillian." Bea piled her things into her rig. "I'll think about—"

"I'll tell Pastor Dennis that it's all arranged."

"But I haven't decided for sure!"

"The pastor will be so pleased!" Lillian nodded a dismissal to the schoolteacher. "Come along, Ada."

They left Bea standing in the churchyard, staring after them. When they passed the mill, Wyatt was nowhere to be seen, but Josiah Dawson was bending over a broken wagon wheel in the side yard. He seemed completely absorbed in his work, an intense look on his face, the muscles in his arms straining the fabric of his sweat-stained work shirt.

Ada felt a stab of sympathy for him. Today's news of the events at the Spencers' place had left her with a creeping uneasiness at the bottom of her heart. With the Klansmen determined to stir up trouble, were the Dawsons safe?

Was she?

Twenty

"A penny for your thoughts." Lillian sat at the kitchen table watching Ada clear away a basketful of apple cores and an empty sugar sack. Apple butter simmered in the oven, filling the kitchen with the warm smells of cinnamon and anise. It was very early on harvest-festival Saturday; the sun was just rising over the rim of the mountains, suffusing the kitchen with fiery light.

Ada bent to stir the apple butter. "I've been thinking about Mother ever since I trimmed Mariah's hat with her Paris rose."

"I declare, I never have seen a woman as happy as Mariah over a hat. Your parents would be proud."

"Mother would." Ada took up the broom and swept the floor clean. "Father never acknowledged any of my accomplishments."

"Sometimes men aren't very good at saying what they feel." Lillian sipped her tea.

"Oh, he was sufficiently vocal. He was just indifferent to whatever I did—or that's the way it seemed." Ada emptied the dust bin and propped the broom in the corner.

"That must have been very hard for you."

Ada shrugged. "I finally stopped telling him anything. Now I wish I'd tried harder to understand him."

"You were very young and grieving for your mother. No sense fretting over what might have been." Lillian shuffled to the stove and peered inside. "Apple butter's done."

While the apple butter cooled, Ada changed her dress and pinned on her only other hat, a dark brown straw trimmed in brown velvet. It was so old and ratty it was downright depressing, but there was nothing she could do about it. She returned to the kitchen to spoon the apple butter into jars, then set the warm jars in a basket and helped Lillian with her hat.

Wyatt drove them to town. All of Hickory Ridge had turned out for the celebration. While their mothers laughed and chatted, children ran pell-mell through the park, playing hide-and-seek or rolling balls across the brown grass. Men brought out banjoes and fiddles, and strains of "Barbara Allen" and "My Old Kentucky Home" filled the brisk October air.

Everyone was talking about the great fire that had just consumed a huge portion of Chicago, spreading from shanties to the opulent mansions on Huron Avenue, destroying everything in its path and leaving behind thousands of displaced residents and many thousands of burned-out buildings. It was a wonder, Patsy Greer said, that so few people had perished. Ada nodded. Her heart ached for the families of those who hadn't been so lucky. But now was not the time to think of it.

Wyatt helped Ada and Lillian carry the jars of apple butter to a long table beneath the trees. He smiled at her, looking more handsome than ever in a new blue shirt that brought out the color of his eyes. "I love apple butter," he said. "Can I have a taste?"

Ada laughed. "Right now?"

"Sure, why not?" He picked up a jar and then lifted the towel covering a basket. "All I need now is some of Carrie Daly's cinnamon bread. Hers is better than the bakery's."

"Stop that!" Lillian swatted his arm. "Don't you have anything better to do than harass an old woman?"

"Yes ma'am, I surely do. I promised the sheriff I'd help him and Doc Spencer organize a horse-shoe tournament."

Lillian flapped one hand. "Get on with it, then."

He tipped his hat and sent Ada a smile that warmed her all the way to her toes. "I'll see you ladies at noon."

She watched him until he disappeared into the crowd.

"Let's go look at the exhibits." Lillian took Ada's arm. "I want to see the needlework."

They strolled about the park, admiring everything from wooden toys to woven baskets and embroidery. More tables had been set up to accommodate the mountains of food the townspeople had prepared. Mariah arrived with a raisin pie and a bowl of pumpkin custard. She set them down and twirled around, grinning, showing off her new hat.

Molly Scott, the mayor's wife, brought a basket of soft molasses tea cakes. "Try one," she urged Ada, after admiring Mariah's hat and inquiring about her own. "They're my specialty. I make 'em with sody and goose fat."

Ada bit into the sweet cake. "It's delicious."

Molly grinned and hurried off to join her friends. Ada, Lillian, and Mariah headed for the needlework exhibit. Despite the news from Chicago, everyone seemed in a festive mood. Even Jasper Pruitt tipped his hat to Ada as he passed.

Lillian bought a lace collar and an embroidered shawl. Ada admired a pair of delicate lace gloves, but they were one more extravagance she couldn't afford. Reluctantly, she set them aside.

Lillian turned to speak to one of her church friends just as Carrie Daly arrived in her new blue dress and matching hat. Several loaves of bread filled the basket on her arm. "Oh, Ada," Mariah exclaimed. "Carrie's hat is gorgeous! She looks like an illustration in a magazine."

Ada smiled, pleased at the compliment. "I like it too."

"You should bring some hats for sale here next year. Nothing too elaborate, but some simple designs that would appeal to everyone."

"Perhaps I will. If I have the time. I—"

A sudden commotion drew their attention. Mrs. Lowell had arrived with the children from the orphanage. They were scrubbed and tidied, and noisy with anticipation. Ada looked for Sophie and spied her bringing up the rear of the line.

"It's all right, Ada," Lillian said, taking up the conversation again. "I won't stand in your way much longer." She held up her hand when Ada protested. "I know the Lord, and he knows me, and frankly, I'm looking forward to our conversation. I've got a few questions for him."

Mariah laughed. "Lillian Willis, you're the only person I know who would dare question the Lord face-to-face."

A bell clanged, calling them to the noon meal. They joined the long lines that stretched all the way across the park. Wyatt made his way to where Ada and Lillian stood, waiting to fill their plates. He smiled down at Ada. "Having a good time?"

"I am. Miss Hattie brought more fried chicken." She indicated the restaurant owner, who was unloading a basket of food nearby. "I wonder what her secret is."

"It's no secret," Lillian said. "It's just chicken coated in flour and salt and pepper, dredged in buttermilk, and fried in hot grease. I've been making it that way since I was knee-high to a flea." She looked up at Wyatt. "I never knew you liked Hattie's chicken better than mine."

A smile tugged at the corner of his mouth. "I like them both the same. Hattie's tastes different, though."

"Chicken is chicken. Hold my bag, please. I can't manage it and fill my plate at the same time."

Wyatt slipped his aunt's drawstring bag over his arm and burst out laughing.

"Very charming," Ada said. "It matches your shirt beautifully."

He grinned and jiggled the bag. "This thing is heavy. What does Lil carry in here anyway?"

Ada laughed. "I have no idea."

"I missed you this week," he murmured. "Save me a dance tonight?"

"I will."

They found places to sit on a hay bale near a group that included the Whitings and the Spencers. From beneath her hat brim, Ada studied the doctor's wife. Eugenie Spencer's face was open and friendly, showing no evidence of the terrifying incident with the Klan. Ada buttered a piece of bread and chewed thoughtfully. *What a hideous bunch of ruffians!* It didn't make sense to punish someone for trying to alleviate the suffering of another. Hadn't Christ commanded his followers to heal the sick? And weren't all people, regardless of their color, equal in his sight?

Mrs. Spencer said something that made Sage Whiting laugh. She looked up and caught Ada's eye. Ada nodded and returned her gaze, feeling suddenly shy in the presence of such a brave woman. Ada couldn't imagine ever venturing into Two Creeks. Where had Mrs. Spencer found such courage? She wondered whether the mother and baby had survived the difficult birth, but she couldn't bring herself to ask.

Across the way Nate Chastain pulled out a book and began reading aloud to the children from the orphanage. Ada couldn't hear his words, but the children were clearly enthralled with the story; bursts of laughter punctuated his reading. Carrie Daly looked on, her eyes shining. Maybe the rumors were right—that Nate had something to do with Carrie's decision to come out of mourning.

When Nate finished reading, the children ran off to play, leaving Sophie alone. Ada's heart seized. She set aside her empty plate and stood. "Would you excuse me?"

"Of course," Mariah said. "I'm going to sit right here until the dance begins."

Ada crossed the meadow to where Sophie sat drawing pictures in the dirt with a stick. The little girl's eyes lit up when Ada knelt on the ground next to her.

"Hello, Sophie. Do you remember me?"

Sophie nodded. "You're Robbie's friend."

"That's right. I'm glad to see you."

"I still got my blue ribbon. I put it in my treasure chest, under my bed."

"I had a treasure chest, too, when I was your age." Ada made herself comfortable on the grass. A light breeze stirred her hair. The late afternoon sun warmed her face. "I lived by the sea then. I collected shells and bits of sea glass and driftwood. Once I found a piece of wood that was shaped like a cat."

"Mrs. Lowell got a cat. Her name is Lucy. She sleeps with me sometimes. I tell her stories."

"I've been thinking about your stories. Do you ever write them down?"

"I'm no good at writing. Mrs. Lowell says I'm too slow. And too messy. She says my writin' look like a old hen been scratchin' in the dirt."

"That's only because you need more practice."

"Maybe. But sometimes the stories in my head go faster than my fingers."

"I know what you mean." Ada paused. "What was the story Mr. Chastain read just now?"

"I don't remember. I was thinking about my princess story." Sophie fell onto her back in the thick grass and spread out her arms and legs like spokes in a wheel.

"I love princess stories! Would you tell it to me?"

Behind them, the musicians began warming up. Some of the farmers had packed up and were starting for home; animals had to be fed and cows milked even on harvest-festival day. A line of buckboards and wagons moved slowly toward the road. Sophie cupped her hands to her face and looked up at the clouds. “It’s too long.”

“Maybe just a bit of it then?”

Sophie sighed and closed her eyes. “Onct they was a princess, lived all the way in Africa. One day a ship came and the princess was kidnapped. They took her to a big white house on a island. All around was a big ocean the color of a robin’s egg. The sand was white as sugar.”

Ada sat motionless. The child’s voice was mesmerizing.

“They was a big storm. The house fell into the ocean. The princess floated to a strange new place and she lived there until she died.”

“Is that the end of the story?” Ada asked.

“The man in the white house?” Sophie, a born storyteller if there ever was one, paused for dramatic effect. She sat up, her green eyes flashing. “No one heard of him again. But people say he still looking for her.”

She got to her feet and brushed the dust from her dress, breaking the spell. “That’s all I know. I been knowin’ that story since my baby days.”

Ada reached up and caught the child’s thin hand in her own. “It’s a beautiful story. Would you write it down, just the way you’ve told it to me? I’m coming soon to see Mrs. Lowell. Perhaps you could give it to me then.”

Sophie frowned. “Why do you care ’bout some dumb old story ain’t even true?”

"It's a secret. Can you trust me, for a little while?"

"Maybe. I don't know. Can I go now?"

"Of course," Ada said, stung by the rejection.

Sophie ran across the grass, calling out to a slightly younger boy and girl. They waited for her to catch up, and Ada breathed a sigh. Perhaps these two, like Robbie, would accept the beautiful little outcast.

"Ada?" Carrie waved her over. "Hurry! The dance is about to start." She looped her arm through Ada's. "Have I told you how much I adore my hat?"

Ada smiled. "A time or two. I'm glad you're pleased."

They joined the others from their quilting circle. The women chatted quietly as the air cooled and the sun slid behind the mountains. Presently a crescent moon rose in the indigo sky, glimmering through the branches of the hickory trees. Ada followed the others to the temporary dance pavilion, where fiddlers and banjo players tuned their instruments.

A bushy-bearded man in a plaid shirt walked to the side of the dance floor. "First dance is the Wild Goose Chase," he announced. "Gents, claim your partners, and here we go."

Nate Chastain appeared and swept Carrie onto the dance floor. Mariah and Sage joined six other couples as the dance began. Ada stood alone, watching the colorful swirl of the women's dresses as they whirled and bowed to their partners. Onlookers drew nearer, clapping, laughing, and whistling as the dancers moved faster and faster.

A familiar laugh drew Ada's attention. She looked up. *Heavenly days!* Wyatt was crossing the meadow with Bea Goldston on his arm. Dressed in a bright blue skirt, white bodice, and straw hat, Bea clung to him like a barnacle to a ship, chattering away as they sauntered through the crowd.

A wave of sadness moved through Ada. Tonight she felt as if the whole world was made up of couples. She was alone and, if she were completely honest with herself, jealous of Wyatt's attention to the schoolteacher. She had no claim on him, but that fact didn't stop the ache of tears in her throat.

When they neared the dance floor, Wyatt nodded to Bea and turned to one of his men. Bea wormed her way through the crowd and stopped to speak to Ethan Webster, whom Ada had met in town. The new headmaster was short and rotund, with a shiny bald pate and a neatly trimmed beard that made him look like everyone's favorite uncle. In a black vest and long frock coat, he radiated an air of supreme confidence. From everything Ada had heard, the schoolchildren of Hickory Ridge could do worse than Mr. Webster.

Bea waved to Mr. Webster and continued her march toward Ada. "I saw you with that colored child," she said without preamble. "Didn't you learn anything from what happened at the Spencers?"

"She needs a friend. Except for Robbie Whiting, the other children ignore her. And Sophie is receiving only the barest of educations."

"If it weren't for Mrs. Lowell, she'd be sleeping in a shack down in Two Creeks, taking in washing like Libby Dawson. Or worse. The Dawson children aren't getting an education either, but you never hear them complain." Bea lowered her voice. "A word to the wise, Ada. People have noticed the interest you've taken in that girl. It might not be the best thing for your new business."

Ada crossed her arms. "Women in Hickory Ridge won't buy hats from me because I help a defenseless child? I don't believe they could be so narrow-minded, or so coldhearted either."

The first dance ended to laughter and applause.

"Ladies in the center!" the caller shouted. Ada glanced over Bea's shoulder. The Whitings clasped hands and led off the dance, the flower on Mariah's new hat bobbing in the breeze.

"They're not coldhearted," Bea said. "Who do you think fills up their stockings at Christmas? Sends over medicines when they're sick? The difference is that most people know where to draw the line." Her dark eyes flashed. "I'm trying to do you a favor here, Ada. You'd better learn where that line is before you get into trouble."

She whirled away, her ruffled hem swishing on the grass.

Wyatt headed toward Ada as the last notes of the reel died away. He looked at her with a smile in his eyes and the world righted itself again.

"Rumor has it that the next dance is a waltz." He offered his arm. "How about it?"

He led her onto the dance floor and swept her into his arms, his hand resting lightly at the small of her back. The music began. Ada relaxed in his arms and gave herself over to the music and the warmth of his body next to hers. He smelled wonderfully of soap and wood shavings.

He danced the way he ran his mill, with complete confidence and a gleam in his eye. He smiled into her eyes and hummed the song under his breath. It was the first moment of true bliss she'd known in years—something she had never expected to experience again.

All too soon the waltz ended, and Wyatt released her. The caller announced an old-fashioned Virginia reel.

"Mind if we sit this one out?"

"I don't mind."

He took her hand and led her away from the crowd. They skirted the gazebo and walked along the path toward the river, listening to the shouts and laughter of the dancers as the music sped up.

Wyatt stopped and turned to her in the darkness. "That night on the river, I never got to finish what I wanted to say to you."

Her heart thudded. It was hard to breathe. She

was only dimly aware of the scrape and thump of boots on the wooden dance floor behind them and the fiddle notes filling the air. "I'm listening now."

He tipped her face toward his. His lips claimed hers in a warm kiss that was both confident and tender. *Oh mercy.* Ada felt as if she might float away. She leaned into the circle of his arms, her head against his chest. Was it her imagination, or was his heart racing as rapidly as hers?

"I've wanted to do that since the day I first saw you," he murmured, his breath soft against her hair. "You looked so small and scared, and you were trying hard to look brave."

"I didn't know it showed." Without thinking, she stepped back and squared her shoulders.

"It's all right to need people, Ada," he said softly. "It's all right to want them in your life."

She thought about her parents, about Aunt Kate and Edward, and she was nearly overcome with the old bitter sorrow. She'd needed all of them, wanted all of them. And one by one they had been plucked from her life like weeds from a garden.

"Wyatt, I—"

"You may not know it or want to admit it, but you need me," Wyatt whispered. "As much as I need you. Come here."

He opened his arms. But she just stood there, shaken to her very core. Of course she wanted him. She needed everything his kiss promised—affection, companionship, somewhere to belong.

All of the things Edward had promised her.

She looked into Wyatt's shadowed face and all she saw was sincerity and hope. But then, she wasn't exactly the best judge of character. What if she gave her heart to Wyatt, only to have it broken again?

"Until you came to Hickory Ridge," Wyatt continued, "I didn't know why I was here, beyond looking after Lillian. But everything is different now. I realize the Lord in his wisdom brought me here to find what was missing in my life. You." He took both her hands in his. "Don't you see his work in all this?"

"I'm . . . not sure."

He nodded. "I can see why you'd hesitate, after I've given you such a hard time about your hat business. But I see that a lot more clearly now too. I finally realized why I was fighting you. I feared that once you became a success you wouldn't need me or Hickory Ridge any longer."

The bonfire flickered brightly in the darkness. Ada watched a shower of orange sparks spiral into the night sky. The lilting strains of another waltz floated on the air. What was he saying? That he'd decided not to go to Texas after all? Because of her?

He drew her closer and gently kissed her temple "Maybe I shouldn't have sprung all this on you at once, but I can't help it. I wanted you to know how I feel."

She looked up at him through a blur of tears.

"Help me out here, darlin'. Have I said too much?"

She shook her head, too overcome to speak. Hope, fear, and regret warred inside her. She laid one hand on his arm. "It's the most wonderful thing anyone has ever spoken to me. I don't know what to say."

"Say that I have your permission to court you properly." He grinned. "Or at least say you forgive me for being so stubborn."

"I've been stubborn too. And I do forgive you."

"Then you'll be my dear, beloved friend?"

She nodded and swallowed the knot of tears in her throat. "Always."

He lifted her hand and gently kissed it. "I'll do my best to be worthy of you. And maybe somday, if God so decides, we'll be more than friends."

She looked into his face, so open, so full of hope, and felt her heart crack open.

Mere friendship wouldn't be nearly enough to satisfy the deep longing she was beginning to feel for him. But if she let herself love him and need him, would he, like Edward before him, simply disappear?

Twenty-One

"I'm sure you mean well, Miss Wentworth, but what you're asking is impossible." Mrs. Lowell sat back in her chair and folded her hands on her desk.

"I don't understand." Ada watched the trees outside the orphanage bending in the late November wind. "I should think you'd want people to take an interest in the children. Otherwise how would any of them ever find permanent homes?"

Mrs. Lowell removed her spectacles and pinched the bridge of her nose. "Sophie is unadoptable."

"I'm not asking to adopt her, only for your permission to visit her on a regular basis, to help with her schoolwork. She's a bright child. Her potential should not be wasted." Ada let out an exasperated sigh. Why should this woman have sole control of Sophie's future? It wasn't fair. "In Massachusetts, a judge would decide what's best for—"

"This isn't Massachusetts." The director leaned forward in her chair. "Suppose I agreed. Suppose Sophie became the best-educated girl in the county. What could she do with all that learning? I should think that to be denied the chance to use her hard-won knowledge would only make her more unhappy."

Ada fought to control her temper. This woman

was as unfeeling and unmovable as stone. "Ignorance is bliss? Is that it?"

"Well, I didn't—"

"Sophie has an extraordinary way with words. Perhaps one day she'll become a writer. Perhaps she'll become a teacher and start a school for the children in Two Creeks."

"Not likely. From what I hear, the men down at the town hall are still jawing over that land." Mrs. Lowell leaned across her desk. "Miss Wentworth, I appreciate your desire to help Sophie. But some folks are getting up a head of steam over this Two Creeks business, especially after that incident at the Spencers'. This is not the time to do anything that would call more attention to the divide between us. I'm denying your request not only because I'm not sure it's best for Sophie, but also to protect our town from further strife."

"Surely you don't think the entire town cares whether or not I tutor one small child."

"Hickory Ridge is not so large that what one person does has no effect upon others."

"But you allow the other girls to go to school!"

"A waste of time, in my opinion. But the school board insisted." The director leaned back in her chair. "I can see the purpose of it for the boys. They must be educated enough to assume their rightful roles in our community. The girls, however, require no such training."

Ada gaped at her. She could not imagine a life

without the comfort of books, a life even more devoid of opportunity than her own. "How then do you propose that they get on in the world?"

"Natural feminine instinct will be their guide, as it always has been." Mrs. Lowell rose. "You'll excuse me now. I must see to the children."

Ada grabbed her shawl, pulled on her gloves, and picked up the hatbox containing Molly Scott's hat. "I can find my way out."

On the front porch, she met Bea Goldston coming in, a sheaf of papers tucked under one arm.

"Ada." Bea offered a curt nod. "This is a surprise. What brings you here?"

"I had some business with Mrs. Lowell."

"Oh, of course. About that half-colored child."

Ada brushed past her. "Excuse me. I have a hat to deliver."

"Speaking of hats, when are you going to make mine? I would like to have it for the Christmas pageant next month. Seeing as how I'll be up on the stage, directing, and all eyes will be on me."

"We can talk after church on Sunday if you like. I don't have time just now."

"Oh, I'm so sorry to have detained you. I didn't realize what a busy woman you are."

"All right." Ada set down Molly's hat and fished her pencil and notebook out of her bag. "What type of hat would you like? A toque, a cloche, a boater? Or perhaps a jocket hat. I'm sure I can find a rooster feather for it somewhere."

Wind whistled around the corner. Bea drew her cloak more tightly about her shoulders. "I want one like the one you made for Carrie Daly, only with more netting and a much bigger flower. White, if you have it. Oh! And some feathers and seed pearls too."

Ada scribbled. "A confectioner's cake, then, to be worn on the head."

Bea ignored that. "I'm sure it will be lovely. And now, I must deliver this sheet music to Mrs. Lowell. The children should have begun their practice weeks ago, but what goes on here is out of my hands." She opened the door and swept inside.

Ada picked up the hat and headed for the mayor's house. But today, hats were the furthest thing from her mind. Despite all the talk about the fire at the Spencers' and the growing unrest over the land in Two Creeks, she wasn't ready to give up on her plan to help the little girl with the preternatural storytelling skills.

She'd talk it out with Wyatt over lunch. He would know how to proceed without causing more trouble.

A wagon creaked down the road with one of Wyatt's mill hands at the reins. Ada stepped aside as he drove past, the harness clanking. He tipped his hat. She nodded and continued along the road to the mayor's house.

Molly Scott answered her door almost before Ada could knock. "Get yourself on in here, girl, before you freeze to death."

Ada came inside and took off her wrap. "It isn't that bad. In Boston we'd call this a warm day."

Molly cackled. "In Tennessee, forty degrees is considered pretty chilly—until you get up in the hills, that is. I got some mulled cider on the stove, if you're interested."

"That sounds good." Ada removed her cloak and gloves.

Molly filled two cups and motioned Ada into a chair. "Have a seat."

Ada sat and tasted the warm, cinnamon-laced cider. "This is good. Just the thing for a chilly day."

"It's my secret blend of spices." Molly took a sip from her cup. "My grandma Andrews from way over in McNairy County gave it to me the day I married the mayor."

Ada set her cup down and opened the hatbox. "I've brought your hat. All I need to do now is attach the bird to the brim."

Molly's broad, friendly face lit up. "I'll go get it." She hurried out of the room and soon returned with the stuffed pigeon. The feathers had faded to a dull brown, but the bird's tiny black eyes shone. Only a missing foot marred its perfection.

"I brought the pheasant feathers too," Molly said. "Thanks to my Hiram. He tracked that bird for two days before he caught him."

Ada took a needle from her sewing kit. With a few deft stitches she attached the bird to the ribbon and the ribbon to the hat, then tucked the two long feathers into the back and secured them. She knotted the thread, trimmed it neatly with her scissors, and handed the finished hat to Molly. "Here you are, Mrs. Scott. I hope you're pleased."

Molly went to the mirror and tried it on. "It looks even better than the one in that fancy magazine. I can't wait for my husband to get home. He'll be right proud!"

"I'm delighted." Ada rose and gathered her things.

"I'll get your money." Molly handed Ada two dollars and walked her to the door. "I hope you ain't walking all the way back to Lillian's place."

"I came into town with Mr. Caldwell. He's taking me home."

"That's good, because Hiram says some of the Klan have been actin' up again."

Ada nodded. "I heard about what they did to the Spencers. They seem to be beyond the reach of the law."

Molly shook her head. "You can't outlaw pure old meanness. When folks feel threatened, they get scared, and when they get scared, it brings out their bad side. Ever' so often, they put on their ghosty garb and ride around just to remind folks they're still here, law or no law." Her bright eyes bored into Ada's own. "They think they've got themselves a big old secret organization, but half the town knows who they are. Folks just pretend not to. It's safer that way."

Ada thought of Jasper Pruitt. If she were a

gambler, she'd bet her last dollar that the irascible store owner was involved.

"All this foolishness about Two Creeks has got their dander up." Molly went on. "Anyway, better be extra careful on the road for a while."

"I will." Ada waved to Molly, went through the gate, and returned to town. She was disappointed with the way her talk with Mrs. Lowell had turned out, and Molly's reminder about the Klan had put another damper on her spirits. She passed the bakery and inhaled the yeasty smell of fresh bread. For all its problems she was beginning to like Hickory Ridge. The mountains, the peaceful river, and the thriving town with its rows of shops appealed to her. She'd made friends. And there was Wyatt, her dearest friend of all. One day he would leave Hickory Ridge, and so would she. But she didn't want to think about that. For now, this little town in the foothills had become her home.

More delicious smells greeted her as she entered Miss Hattie's and looked around for Wyatt. He rose and motioned her to his table near the window. "I went ahead and ordered chicken and hot biscuits. I hope that's all right."

Ada draped her cloak over the back of her chair. "As you always say, nobody makes better chicken than Hattie."

"I assume the mayor's wife liked her new hat." Wyatt buttered a biscuit and took a bite. Ada smiled. She'd never known a man who so enjoyed his meals. It was one of the reasons she looked forward to the nights when he came to Lillian's for supper.

"Mrs. Scott was pleased. Her hat looks better than I expected, but I hope I'm not called upon to attach more dead animals to hats anytime soon."

"Doggone it," Wyatt said, above the clank of silver and the squeak of the door as patrons came and went, "I was hoping you'd sew that rabbit I shot last week to the brim of my new Stetson."

She laughed. "I understand Stetson is a well-respected company where you come from. I doubt they'd appreciate such embellishment."

He grinned. "Any more hat orders?"

"Only Bea's. These days everyone seems to be thinking of nothing but the Christmas pageant."

"It's quite a production around here, all right." He munched a bit of crust from the drumstick he was working on. "This year, with Mrs. Lowell's children taking part, it'll be bigger than ever. One of my customers from Knoxville is thinking about bringing his family out on the train just to see it."

"Don't tell Bea. She'll want to charge admission."

A smile played at the corners of his mouth. "I wouldn't put it past her. Maybe it isn't such a bad idea, though. Mrs. Lowell is always strapped for money."

"Speaking of Mrs. Lowell, my talk with her this morning was most unsatisfactory." Ada buttered her own biscuit and took a bite. "She refuses to allow me to visit Sophie. She thinks that an education will only make the girl more unhappy. But I simply cannot abide the thought of wasting that child's life." She stirred more cream into her coffee. "I realize that Sophie's opportunities are limited here, but she won't always be ten years old, and she won't always live here—or at least she doesn't have to. With a proper education, she can go somewhere else and make a life for herself. You'd think Mrs. Lowell would see my point, but she refuses to take the long view."

"This is very important to you, isn't it?"

"Yes, as important as anything I've ever done. Of course, Mrs. Lowell brought up Two Creeks as one reason for her refusal. But deep down, she doesn't think Sophie, or any female for that matter, deserves an education." She finished her coffee and set her cup down. "It makes me mad enough to spit nails!"

He nodded, his expression grave. "I can see that. But Mrs. Lowell has a point about Sophie, especially right now. I think it's admirable, your wanting to help the girl out, but maybe you should wait until some of this talk about Two Creeks dies down."

She frowned. Was Wyatt going to fight her on this too? "It isn't as if I'll be going down to the colored settlement. I just want to visit Sophie at the orphanage, maybe take her out to Lillian's once in a while. I don't see why anyone would care. Libby Dawson comes to the house every week and no one says a word against it."

"That's different. Her family works for me." He wiped the chicken grease off his fingers and motioned to Hattie for the check. "I just don't want you to put yourself into a dangerous situation."

"But it's the right thing to do. If Mrs. Spencer can be brave enough to go down to Two Creeks in the middle of the night by herself, surely I can muster the courage to visit Sophie in broad daylight."

He reached into his pocket for his money clip. "Let's not argue about it today. I need to get you home and then check on things at the mill. Charlie Blevins is back on the job, and I don't want him to overdo it."

Ada wasn't ready to let the conversation go; she wanted it resolved right now. But one look at the firm set of Wyatt's mouth told her this wasn't the time to pursue it. They went outside into the brisk air, and she drew her shawl about her shoulders. "Charlie's the one who cut his arm a few weeks back?"

Wyatt nodded. "I told him not to try to split that green hickory with an ax, but he didn't listen."

They went out to the rig. He helped Ada in and placed the empty hatbox at her feet. Then he climbed in on the other side and they turned for home.

"I almost forgot," he said as the horse clopped along. "I brought you a surprise."

"Another one?" She felt the same delight she'd known as a child when her mother brought her a doll or a new book. But even those gifts were not as special as these small unexpected tokens from Wyatt.

He reached inside his coat pocket and handed her a small paper bag.

Ada opened it. "Sarsaparilla candy! I love this!"

"I know."

She grinned and held out the bag to him. "Want one?"

He popped a piece into his mouth. For a few minutes they rode along without speaking, enjoying the sugary treat. Ada watched him handling the rig, her heart overflowing with affection for him. Since the night of the harvest festival, he'd come often to Lillian's for supper, bearing some small gift for her. Last week he'd shown up with three perfect red apples. The week before, he arrived with a handful of late-season flowers plucked from his garden. And now . . . she sighed. Sarsaparilla.

"Mariah said you may be getting another timber contract soon." She set the bag inside the empty hatbox at her feet.

"It's a possibility. I've got some good Eastern red cedar I'm trying to sell to the pencil factory over in North Carolina. Red cedar is too soft for furniture and such, but it's the best there is for making pencils."

As he described the art and science of pencil making, Ada buried her hands in the folds of her cloak and breathed a contented sigh. She loved listening to Wyatt talk about his mill. It seemed there was nothing he didn't know about timber, its characteristics and its uses. When he talked about the best way to strip bark from a tree, the hard work of getting logs down the mountain, or the satisfaction he got out of planing a rough log until it was a thing of beauty, she couldn't help but draw parallels to her hatmaking and the pleasure it brought to her and to the ladies of Hickory Ridge. She smiled to herself. Maybe it was a strange kind of connection, but it was one that increased her feelings for him.

They rounded the last bend. Wyatt drove into the yard and helped Ada down. She retrieved her bag and her hatbox. "Thank you for the fried chicken. And the candy too."

"You're welcome." He planted a quick kiss on her temple. "Always a pleasure spending time with you."

Libby Dawson came out onto the porch and closed the door behind her. Wyatt paid her and she started home.

"I should get back to the mill," Wyatt said.

"Will you be back for supper?"

"Afraid not. Too much paperwork."

She tried to hide her disappointment. She wasn't looking forward to a long evening without him.

He took both her hands. "I need to check on some timber up on the ridge. Want to ride up there with me?"

"When?"

"Saturday afternoon, if the weather holds." He scanned the overcast sky. "We'll see. Looks like we're in for some rain."

He climbed into the rig and drove away. Inside, Ada found Lillian still sleeping, her face slack, one hand lying palm up on her Bible. Ada added another small log to the fire and took Lillian's Bible to the parlor. Lately she'd found herself turning to it for comfort. Though she still had many questions—why her mother had to die young, why her father interfered with her engagement, why Edward hadn't defied him for her sake—the words of the psalmist and the prophets brought her the beginnings of peace. She changed her dress and headed down to the kitchen. There was time for tea before starting dinner. She set the kettle on to boil, curled into her chair, and opened the Bible.

A slight noise and a movement at the window startled her. She hurried to the back door and looked out. "Robbie? Is that you?"

Something rustled in the bushes beside the barn, and then she saw a flash of white moving toward the trees. She shoved down a rise of panic, hiked her skirt, and took off across the yard. "You! Stop!"

She reached the edge of the woods and cocked her ear, listening. But all was silent. She hurried back to the house, fear like a cold needle in her veins. There was no longer any doubt. Someone, most probably a Klansman, was keeping an eye on her and Lillian.

On the back step, right below the kitchen door, she spied a single sheet of paper folded in half and weighted with a stone. Trembling and out of breath, she took the note inside and opened it. The words spilled across the page at an angle, as if the writer had been in a great hurry.

A Wentworth stop yure medling with the culerds or yul be sorry. You have been worned!

Twenty-Two

Leaving Cherokee tethered in his usual spot outside the bank, Wyatt jogged across the street and headed to the sheriff's office. Located across from the Hickory Ridge Inn, the building had weathered to a dirty gray. It sported a single dusty window overlooking the street and, inexplicably, a bear-shaped weather vane that always pointed south.

Wyatt cast a wary eye at the leaden sky. Two days of cold, hard rain had precluded his trip up to the ridge with Ada. Now the rain had slackened to a gray mist and the weather had turned unusually cold for so early in December. Maybe it would snow.

The chill wind tore at his coat as he mounted the rickety steps, pushed open the door, and stuck his head in. "Sheriff?"

Eli McCracken set aside his newspaper and motioned him inside. "I was just about to send word to the mill. I need to talk to you."

“Same here.” Wyatt took off his hat, eased himself into the cane-backed chair opposite Eli’s desk, and scanned the row of wanted posters lining the wall. Last year he’d been stunned to see the face of one of his sawyers from North Carolina staring back at him. The man was wanted in three states for bank robbery and attempted murder. Now Wyatt made a point of checking Eli’s rogue’s gallery from time to time.

“You first.” Eli rose stiffly and headed to the stove in the corner to refill his cup. “Want some coffee?”

“No thanks.”

“What’s on your mind?”

Wyatt withdrew a wrinkled sheet of paper from his pocket and slid it across the desk. “Somebody left this on Aunt Lillian’s back porch the night before last. She and Ada are terrified.”

Eli plopped down in his chair and scanned the note. “Did Miss Wentworth see who left it?”

“No. She gave chase, but whoever it was had too much of a head start.”

“Could be just a prank.”

“I don’t think so.” Wyatt described the earlier incident in which Lillian had seen a “ghost.” “I’ve begun to suspect the Klan may be involved.”

“I don’t blame you for being concerned,” Eli said, “but with nothing more to go on . . .”

“I realize there’s not much you can do. But I’d appreciate it if you’d keep your eyes and ears open. People who do things like this often brag about it."

Eli nodded and sipped his coffee.

"Maybe you could ride out there and check around, help keep an eye on the place. I try to get out there every day or two, but I can't be there all the time."

"I'll do what I can, but it's a long way out there."

Wyatt watched rain misting the window. "That's what worries me."

"You could move Ada and Lillian into town, let them stay at the inn for a few days."

"I thought about it. I thought about moving them to my place too, but I don't have room. Besides, I don't want to alarm them. And I sure don't want whoever is doing this to think they can intimidate us. It will only make them bolder."

"Maybe." Eli set his cup down. "This Two Creeks business is making the whole town jumpy. It's too bad someone with good sense can't buy up the whole kit and caboodle and put the issue to rest."

"I tried to buy it five years ago, but I never could find out who the actual owner is. It's tied up in some kind of trust with a fancy lawyer in Nashville. All I got from him was a string of excuses."

"Maybe you could try again if you're still interested. A lot can change in five years." Eli cleared his throat, opened his desk drawer, and took out a set of keys. "I've got somebody locked up who's been asking for you."

Wyatt frowned. "Is one of my men in trouble?"

"Come on."

Eli led the way through a door at the back of the office to a dank room containing a couple of chairs and two cells. One was empty. In the other sat Jasper Pruitt's clerk. He was perched on the edge of the thin, bare mattress holding his head in his hands. He didn't look up when Wyatt and Eli entered.

"Powell?" Eli said. "I've brought Mr. Caldwell, like you asked."

The young man finally raised his tear-stained face and nodded.

"I'm going to let you out. You can sit right there"—Eli indicated a chair—"and say your piece to Mr. Caldwell." His hand rested ever so briefly on the revolver strapped to his hip. "You aren't going to try anything stupid, right?"

Powell shook his head.

"All right then." Eli let him out and waited till he and Wyatt were seated. "You've got ten minutes. I'll be in the office."

He left them alone.

Wyatt stretched out his legs and crossed his ankles. "What's this all about, boy? How come Eli McCracken's got you locked up?"

"I got caught stealing."

"From the mercantile?"

"Yeah." The boy's voice cracked. "I would have got away with it too, but Miss Greer was working late at the *Gazette* and saw me taking my wagon around back. She snuck over there to investigate and saw me puttin' stuff in the wagon. She ran and told the sheriff, and here I am."

"I see. But what's that got to do with me?"

"Sheriff McCracken don't care why a person does something. He only cares about the law."

"That's his job."

"Yeah, but I thought you might listen to my reasons and help explain it to him." Powell dropped his gaze. "I seen how you saved those two boys from drowning. And Jacob Hargrove said you gave him a job after his ma died. Seems like you got a good heart, and well . . . I thought maybe you'd understand why I did what I did."

"I'm listening."

"It's Mr. Pruitt and the way he treats the colored folks. When a black woman comes to the back door wanting to buy a slab of bacon, he sells her some that's about to go bad. And if she asks for a pound, he shaves a quarter pound off and charges her full price. It's the same whether they're buying nails or cheese or kerosene. They always get shortchanged."

Wyatt nodded. Outside, rain dripped off the eaves.

"Anyway, since the talk started up about moving the coloreds off that land, they're afraid to come into town. Scared they might be rounded up and not allowed to go back to Two Creeks."

"How do you know all this, son?"

Powell compressed his lips and shook his head. "Can't tell you that, Mr. Caldwell. Don't want to get anybody in trouble." His eyes filled with tears. "I couldn't let 'em starve, could I? So I've been loadin' up my wagon ever' so often and leaving food down in Two Creeks."

"How long has this been going on?"

The boy shrugged. "Couple of months, I reckon. Mr. Pruitt blames the coloreds for stealing from him. But it wasn't them, it was me." He jumped up and began to pace. "In the Bible, doesn't it say to feed the hungry? I know it's wrong to steal, but I couldn't figure out any other way."

He flopped into his chair. "I was trying to do something good, but I made a mess of it. The sheriff won't listen. I was hopin' you might see my side of it."

"You're right about feeding the hungry," Wyatt said. "But the Bible also tells us that when we've wronged someone, we're to make amends."

"But Mr. Pruitt is wrong too! When he overcharges people, isn't that stealing?"

"In my book, yes. But that doesn't change the fact that you took his merchandise and—"

"I have to pay it back. I know that. But Mr. Pruitt says I can't never come back into his store. Without a job I can't pay anything back. I was hoping—"

"Wyatt?" Eli opened the door. "Is everything all right in here?"

"We're just finishing up." Wyatt rose and clapped

the boy on the shoulder. "I'll see what I can do."

"Come on, Powell." Eli ushered the boy back into his cell, and he and Wyatt returned to the office.

"Well?" The sheriff poured himself a third cup of coffee. "What do you think?"

"I don't know, Eli. I guess I'm thinking that the Lord moves in mysterious ways."

"Huh?" Eli moved to the window and scanned the street.

"That boy back there just may have bought us more time. Now that Jasper can't blame the coloreds for stealing, he doesn't have as strong an argument for wanting to displace them."

"Maybe. But he isn't the only one who wants them gone. He's just the most vocal." Eli turned from the window and pinned Wyatt with a worried gaze. "We need a solution to this mess before it splits Hickory Ridge wide open."

Wyatt nodded and picked up his hat.

"I'll ride out to your aunt's place this afternoon," Eli said, "and take a look around."

"I'd appreciate it. I'll see you."

Wyatt left the office and headed back to where Cherokee stood patiently in the cold rain. On the long ride back to the mill, he turned the problems over in his mind.

The situation with the Powell boy was easy. Wyatt would offer him a job at the mill and see to it that Jasper Pruitt was repaid for his losses. But thinking about Ada and Lillian and how to keep them safe, about how to resolve the problem of Two Creeks, about Ada's desire to visit the mixed-blood girl at the orphanage left him with a chill that he couldn't blame on the weather.

Twenty-Three

The afternoon of the Christmas pageant came down cloudy and cold, with a rare hint of snow in the air. Ada, Lillian, and Mariah gathered early at the church to prepare for the evening's program. Carrie was at home making a huge vat of cranberry punch. Bea, who was still occupied at school, sent Jacob Hargrove over to help the women secure extra lanterns to the walls and attach swags of fresh greenery above the windows and doors. While the boy busied himself with hammer and nails, Mariah set baskets filled with holly along the edge of the temporary stage the pastor had erected.Lillian placed candles near the spot where Mary and Joseph, played by Jacob and Sabrina, would stand.

Lillian waved Jacob off his ladder and led him to the center of the stage. "You be careful tonight and don't stand too close to these candles. We don't want you and Sabrina going up in flames."

"I will." He gave them a sheepish grin. "We came over here last night and practiced our lines. I don't want to forget anything and mess up the pageant."

He looked up at Mariah. "Where do you want this mistletoe, Mrs. Whiting?"

"Traditionally it goes above the door, but why don't you let me keep it for now."

Jacob handed her the clump of green with its tiny white berries. "Is it true that if you kiss a girl under the mistletoe, she'll marry you?"

"Why, Jacob Hargrove! Don't tell me you're thinking of proposing!"

The tips of his ears turned bright red, and he ducked his head. "No ma'am. Not right now anyway. But I was thinking about proposing a pro posal . . . sort of a promise of one for later on, I mean. After school and such." He looked out the window. "School's prob'ly let out by now. I have to go get my little sister."

"We'll see you tonight," Ada said. "Thank you for helping."

Jacob buttoned himself into his coat. "Miss Ada?"

He took a small pelt from his pocket. "Caught this mink last week. I thought you might could use it for one of your hats."

Ada ran her hands over the soft fur. "This is beautiful. You must let me pay you for it."

"No ma'am. It's a gift." His face reddened again. "I got to go."

Mariah smiled as he loped across the churchyard. "He's so in love he can't see straight, poor boy." She draped a red paper chain across the front pew and sat down. "I remember being in love at that age. His name was Albie Fitzgerald, and he was the milkman's son. Such beautiful eyes." She pretended to swoon and the women laughed. "We were old enough to be in love, and too young to do anything about it."

"Well, we'd better do something about finishing these decorations if we want to be ready by tonight." Lillian consulted the watch that hung around her neck. "It's after four o'clock already."

The women completed their preparations and retired to their quilting room, which was now stuffed to overflowing with costumes, a carved life-sized Christ child, and a table for holding refreshments. Earlier in the week, Patsy Greer had printed programs listing the names of all the children in the pageant, as well as all of those from the orphanage who would be singing beforehand. On the cover was a picture of a single glowing candle and the words "A Blessed Christmas in Hickory Ridge."

"These are pretty." Mariah picked up a program and opened it. "There's Robbie's name. For a while, I was worried he would balk at portraying a shepherd. He took one look at the costume I was making and announced that he wasn't wearing a dress." She frowned. "This is odd. Patsy forgot to put in Sophie's last name. She's the only child without one."

Ada glanced at the program, dismayed. "She

didn't forget. Mrs. Lowell said they've never known her last name."

"I don't see what can be done about it at this hour," Lillian said. "It is a shame that the child will be singled out, but it's too late to reprint them."

Ada rummaged through her bag. "I have some pencils in here somewhere."

"Ada, what are you doing?" Mariah asked. "You can't mark out the other children's names! Their parents will be furious!"

"I'm not erasing their names. I'm giving Sophie one."

She handed each woman a pencil and a stack of programs. "Write the name Robillard beside Sophie's name." She spelled it out for them. "Make it match Patsy's printing as nearly as you can."

The women bent over their task, and half an hour later the programs were done and stacked neatly on the table.

Mariah rose and looked out the window. "I can't believe it! It's starting to snow." Her brown eyes shone. "I can't remember the last time it snowed for Christmas in Hickory Ridge."

Watching the falling snow collect on the winter-brown grass, Ada felt an unexpected jab of homesickness.

"Are you all right?" Mariah put her arm around Ada's shoulder.

"I was remembering the winters of my childhood. Before my mother got sick, we used to bundle into our cloaks and robes and take the sleigh out for evening rides. Once I counted a hundred candles burning in the windows of the houses on our street. It was like being inside a painting."

"Pastor's here," Lillian announced, turning from the window. "And here comes Bea and her bunch."

Half an hour later the church was filled to overflowing. Freshly cut pine boughs scented the air. Banks of candles bathed the church in soft, flickering light. Tables sagged beneath trays of baked goods and bowls of cranberry punch. The children taking part in the pageant rustled and wiggled and finally arranged themselves at the front of the church, their faces glowing with excitement. Mariah sat at the piano, her music at the ready. The orphans filed in, shiny-faced and solemn. From her seat in the third pew, Ada caught Sophie's eye and winked. Sophie winked back.

Ada tried to relax and enjoy the festivities, but she couldn't help worrying. The sheriff had ridden out to the house several times in the past two weeks, but he was no closer to finding out who had left the threatening note. Ada had taken extra care to lock the doors at night. For a few nights, she'd left a lantern burning in the kitchen all the way to morning.

Not surprisingly, once Lillian recovered from her initial fright, she had turned defiant, insisting that Ada not give up on her plan to help Sophie. "If you do," she insisted, "you've let evil win."

Bea, in a pale ivory bustled dress that complemented her elaborate new hat, strode to center stage and welcomed everyone to the pageant. She nodded to Mariah, who struck a single note. The children from the orphanage hummed it in near-perfect harmony, and the music began. Ada hummed the songs under her breath and turned her head, seeking Wyatt. Earlier that day, he'd driven her and Lillian to the church and then left for town to complete some last-minute errands. Now he sat across the aisle with Dr. Spencer, his dear face so serious and attentive that he might have been listening to a world-famous choir. That he showed such regard for a ragtag group of homeless children only increased her affection for him.

There was so much that she admired about him. For one thing, Wyatt was a peacemaker. He'd spent the past two weeks calming Jasper Pruitt's anger, talking with the townsfolk, looking for a compromise that would allow everyone in Hickory Ridge to live in harmony. His efforts seemed to be working, at least temporarily; on her most recent visits to town, she'd heard much less talk about Two Creeks and more about Christmas and everyone's hopes for the new year.

And to her surprise, Wyatt had not tried to further dissuade her from seeing Sophie. But it was clear that someone was out to stop her.

The notes of the last carol faded. The orphans,

their sweet faces bright with triumph, filed from the stage and sat in a row along one wall. A little girl, her hair done up in elaborate ringlets for the occasion, stepped forward, opened her Bible, and began to read. "And it came to pass in those days, that there went out a decree from Caesar Augustus that all the world should be taxed."

Ada felt a weight on her shoulder. Lillian had fallen asleep. In recent weeks she seemed to sleep more and more, for longer periods of time. It worried Ada. On one of her visits to town, she'd made a point of speaking to the doctor about it, but he hadn't seemed concerned. "She's just old. Let her rest all she wants. Encourage her to eat, to take a turn in the garden when it isn't too cold. That's all you can do."

Lillian began snoring. To quiet her, Ada put her arm around the older woman and drew her close. Wyatt caught Ada's eye and smiled so tenderly that it brought tears to her eyes. How drastically she'd changed. Six months ago she couldn't wait to earn enough money to leave. Now she feared that her time in Hickory Ridge might end long before she was ready to say good-bye.

Jacob and Sabrina, dressed as Mary and Joseph, took their places on the stage. Sabrina cradled the carved Christ child and rocked him softly in her arms. Jacob, his hair slicked back, his face shining in the candlelight, placed an arm protectively around her shoulders. The children in their angel costumes stepped to the front of the stage and sang "Glory to God in the highest, and on earth peace, good will toward men."

Pastor Dennis motioned the worshippers to their feet. Mariah moved back to the piano and struck a chord, and the church filled with the sweet harmony of "Silent Night." When the last note faded, he stretched out his arms palms up. "Lord, show us the way to live in your grace among all our brothers and sisters, and may the peace of this season be with us all today and forever. Amen."

"Amen!" The congregation rose and began greeting one another. Children rushed to the refreshments table. Bea stood at the front of the church, preening in her new hat and accepting congratulations for another outstanding program. Mrs. Lowell lined up her children and led them in an orderly fashion past the refreshments table.

Lillian woke and looked around. "My lands, Ada. Did I miss the whole thing?"

Ada smiled. "You were tired from our decorating, and I hadn't the heart to wake you."

"Oh, what a crashing bore I am! Where's that nephew of mine?"

"Just there." Ada inclined her head toward the door. "Talking with Sage and the doctor."

"Excuse me, will you? I have a bone to pick with him."

Lillian looped her bag over her arm and wove her unsteady way through the crush of people.

"Ada?" Bea, with her entourage in tow, towered over her. A formidable figure, but at least she was smiling. She pirouetted. "How do I look?"

Ada hid a smile. Bea wasn't after an honest opinion; she wanted to be sure her audience was paying attention. "Very dramatic. It suits you."

"Oh, I think so too! It turned out even better than I hoped." Bea patted her hat. "I must admit, Hickory Ridge has a true artist in its midst."

"Thank you." Ada felt a rush of relief. The schoolteacher seemed sincere; perhaps the two of them had at last reached an understanding.

"I have but one request." Bea leaned close and whispered, "Don't make another one like it. My uniqueness is my hallmark."

"You're certainly right about that."

Then, to Ada's further astonishment, Jasper Pruitt pushed his way though the crowd. "Miss Wentworth? Could I have a word with you?"

"What is it, Mr. Pruitt?"

"In private, ma'am? I mean, I know I've got no right, after some of the things I've said to you, but I'm hopin' you'll overlook that."

"Well, well," Bea said. "If this doesn't beat all."

"This ain't none of your business, Bea Goldston," Jasper said. "Go on back to the schoolhouse. Wash your chalkboard or sharpen some pencils or something. Leave us be."

"I was just leaving anyway," Bea said, "to show Wyatt Caldwell my new hat."

"Miss Wentworth," Jasper began as Bea whirled away. "I was rude to you when you first come here, and I'm sorry for it. I don't know what gets into me sometimes. Thinking about the Yankees and what they done to us down here just riles me up. But it wasn't none of it your doings. I shouldn'ta took it out on you."

"I accept your apology, Mr. Pruitt." Over Jasper's shoulder, she saw Mrs. Lowell gathering the children, helping them into their coats. Sophie stood alone, a copy of the program in her hands. "Please excuse me."

"I need a hat." Jasper placed one meaty hand on her arm. The stub of his severed finger twitched.

Ada looked at him, puzzled. "The men's haberdashery on Main Street has a nice selection. I believe Mr. Caldwell buys his hats there."

"No ma'am. I mean a lady's hat. Not for me," he added hastily. "It's for Jeanne. My wife."

Ada hadn't realized he was married. "I see."

"We lost a little baby a few months back," Jasper went on. "A girl, born dead. My Jeanne took it real hard, and she's still grievin'. I've been trying to cheer her up, take her for walks, bring her little trinkets from the store, but it don't do a bit of good. Tonight I noticed her starin' at all the fancy hats the ladies are wearin', especially Bea Goldston's, and I figure a new hat might be just the thing to bring her out of her misery."

"I can't speak from personal experience, Mr.

Pruitt, but I can't imagine anything that would compensate a mother for the loss of her child."

"No ma'am. I know that. I just don't like seein' her with such a bad case of the mullygrubs is all."

The church door opened as people began leaving. Snow swirled onto the floor. Somewhere outside, a child laughed. A harness jingled.

"This being the season for miracles and all," Jasper continued, "I hoped—"

"I'll do it." Despite his earlier treatment of her, and her near certainty that he belonged to the Klan, something in the man's voice and the defeated stoop of his shoulders touched her heart. "I'll make a hat for your wife. Something similar to Bea's, but not an exact copy."

"You will? That's real fine! And if you need credit at the store, for anything at all, just ask."

"Mr. Pruitt—"

"Yes ma'am?"

She searched for words. "You mustn't be disappointed if the hat doesn't have the desired effect. Time will soften the pain of your loss,but a mother's grief will not be assuaged this side of heaven." She gathered her shawl and bag. "Please ask your wife to call on me, and we'll get started."

"But . . ." He ducked his head. "I was . . . kinda hopin' it could be a surprise."

"But I don't know her hat size."

Jasper scanned the room. "That's her, talking to the preacher. I'd say she's about average."

"All right. Average it is. A hat like Miss Goldston's costs six dollars."

Jasper whistled softly. "Six dollars? Bea must have a secret gold mine somewheres."

"I wouldn't know about that. I'll deliver the hat to the mercantile when it's finished."

"Thank you, kindly. I appreciate it." He hurried off to join his wife.

Ada gazed after him for a minute, then went to find Sophie. She found the girl talking with Wyatt.

He looked up, his eyes gleaming. "Miss Ada? May I present Miss Sophie Robillard."

Ada dropped a mock curtsy. "Miss Robillard. So delighted to make your acquaintance. How do you do?"

Sophie giggled. "I'm not Miss Robillard. I'm just plain ordinary Sophie."

"There's nothing ordinary about you, my dear," Ada said. Sophie looked pleased.

"I thought it was time you had a last name," Ada told her. "Everyone else has one. Why not you?"

"I got one," Sophie said. "Nobody knows what it is, though."

"Well, this one was my mother's. I'm lending it to you until we find yours. How will that be?"

"All right, I guess." Sophie licked the piece of hard candy in her hand. "Mrs. Lowell said you can visit me. If you still want to."

"She did? Of *course* I want to." Ada looked at

Wyatt. “You had something to do with this, didn’t you?”

Wyatt grinned. “Must have been the Christmas spirit that got to her.”

Just then Lillian appeared, holding a cup of punch. “This is good. Have you tried it yet, Ada?”

“Not yet.”

“You coming to see me tomorrow?” Sophie tugged on Ada’s skirt. “I got a new story.”

“Not tomorrow, but in a few days.”

Mrs. Lowell clapped her hands. “All right, children. Hurry up. Time to go.”

“I’m going too, Wyatt,” Lillian said. “The Whitings will drive me.”

“I don’t want you at the house alone, Aunt Lil.”

“Sage and Mariah will stay with me. I’ve already asked them.” She winked at Ada. “You two stay and enjoy yourselves. I don’t mind a bit.”

“Well, if you’re sure. I had planned a surprise for Ada.”

“I love surprises!” Sophie grabbed Wyatt’s hand and smiled up at him. Ada laughed. *What a little flirt.*

“Sophie!” Mrs. Lowell called. “Come here this instant, or I’ll leave you to walk back in the dark by yourself.”

Sophie let go of Wyatt’s hand and ran to join the others. Sage emerged from the crowd. “There you are, Lillian. Are you ready?”

“I’m ready.” She handed him her cup and

pulled her gloves from her bag. “Goodnight, Wyatt. Goodnight, Ada.”

Wyatt kissed his aunt’s cheek. “Happy Christmas, Aunt Lil.”

“You too, son.”

“I’ll see you tomorrow for Christmas dinner. I’ll bring my famous raisin pie.” He smiled down at Ada. “Other than steak and beans, it’s the only thing I ever learned to make.”

Lillian snorted. “Better bring a hacksaw too.”

Wyatt laughed and took Ada’s arm. “Let’s say goodnight to the preacher and get out of here.”

Twenty-Four

Ada slipped her hand through the crook of Wyatt’s arm, and they joined others leaving the church. Outside she looked around for Wyatt’s rig and spotted Smoky harnessed to an ornately-carved sleigh. Painted in dark blue and bright gold, it gleamed like a jewel against the silvered snow.

With a cry of utter delight, she let go of his arm, ran to the sleigh, and climbed in. “I haven’t been for a sleigh ride in years. And I’ve never seen one as beautiful as this!”

Wyatt wrapped his muffler around his neck, pulled on his gloves, and climbed aboard. “I built it myself. After the war I needed something to do to clear my head. But I haven't had much chance to use it. This is the most snow we've seen in these parts for a long while."

He handed Ada a thick woolen lap robe and flicked the reins. The sleigh glided through the deep snow. They crossed the road and drove along a narrow trail that led upward through the dark trees.

"We never got our chance to ride up to the top of Hickory Ridge," Wyatt said. "How about it?"

She nodded and snuggled beneath the robe. As the sleigh ascended, Ada looked down at the snow-covered road below. A line of wagons, buckboards, and rigs, some with flickering lantern lights to guide their way, fanned across the valley toward home. Muffled in snow, the sounds of creaking wagons and jingling harnesses came to her softly, like music. The gently falling flakes drifted onto her cheeks and lashes and settled onto the robe warming her feet. Wyatt smiled down at her and clasped her gloved hand in his. Ada released a contented sigh. In this moment, all the world seemed beautiful and enchanted.

They passed through the tree line and continued on. At the top of the ridge, Wyatt halted the sleigh. Above them, a few stars glimmered through the snow clouds. Ada inhaled the cold, damp air. Up here she felt as if all her cares had vanished and the world was a more benevolent place.

Wyatt wrapped his arm around her and pointed

to the dark expanse of thick timber below. "All this belongs to my company—except for the bottomland in Two Creeks."

"I don't want to think about Two Creeks tonight."

He nodded. "At least Jasper has calmed down, now that the Powell boy is paying for the stolen goods."

"It was kind of you to give the boy a job."

"The sheriff had him locked up. I had to do something. Jasper sure wasn't in the mood to give him another chance."

"Mr. Pruitt is such a contradiction." Ada brushed away the snowflakes gathering in the folds of her robe. "He's so harsh and unforgiving toward others, but tonight he was quite tenderhearted when he told me about his wife."

"I wondered what you two were discussing."

Smoky stomped and snorted. Wyatt calmed him with a quiet word.

"He wants a hat for her. He thinks it will overcome her sadness at losing a child. I told him not to expect a miracle." She shrugged. "A hat is just a hat."

"I'm not so sure about that." Wyatt grinned. "Bea Goldston seemed like a different woman tonight. And look at how a hat has transformed Carrie Daly. I barely recognize her these days."

"I think perhaps Mr. Chastain deserves the credit for that."

"Perhaps." He smiled and snapped the reins,

and they continued along the narrow trail at the top of the ridge. At last Wyatt stopped again and pointed down the far side of the ridge. A narrow half- moon of a lake glowed silver in the reflected moonlight. "When I first came here, I built myself a little cabin down there."

Ada peered into the darkness. "I'd be afraid of getting lost."

"After the war, I wanted to get lost. All I could think about was death and useless suffering. How men begged for morphine when there wasn't any. Thousands of amputated arms and legs piled up in the yard like firewood." He took a ragged breath. "It's burned into me like a brand on a yearling. I won't forget it as long as I live."

Ada shuddered, unable to imagine such horror. She hated the war for what it had done to so fine a man. She watched his breath clouding the air. At last he said, "Hickory Ridge is surely one of the prettiest places on earth."

She brushed snow off his sleeve. "But you're not completely happy here."

"I can't get Texas out of my head. There's no denying the appeal of this place, but there's still a part of me that longs for wide-open spaces. A place where cattle can roam and a man can see farther than he can ride in an entire day. When I was a boy, staying the summer with Aunt Lil, I loved every day of it, especially when Billy Rondo was here, but by summer's end I couldn't wait to go home. I still feel that way." He looked down at her. "Maybe you can't understand that."

"I do understand. My mother married my father at eighteen and moved with him to Boston. But for all of her life, New Orleans called her back. Her dying wish was to be buried in the Saint Louis cemetery beside my grandparents."

"Then she's at peace."

"I hope so. I hated having my mother buried so far away. I missed having a place to bring flowers. But Father always said that we're bound forever to the place where we're born. He said there's an invisible thread that keeps us connected to it and longing for it, no matter how far away we go."

"I think he was right about that." Wyatt squeezed her hand. "What about you? Do you long for Boston?"

She thought for a second, then nodded. "It's funny. When I traveled abroad with Aunt Kate, I felt worldly and grown up, seeing so many exotic places. I told myself I could live happily in Venice or London or Barcelona. When we got home, I realized how much I'd missed it."

The wind sent a fresh shower of snow swirling into the sleigh. Ada snuggled more deeply into the folds of the robe. "But everything is different now. Father left so many debts that even the auction couldn't settle them all. Several of our friends lost a great deal of money investing in his schemes. The week before I came here, two of my closest friends snubbed me on the street—as if Father's failings were my own."

She sighed. "Even if I went back there now, it wouldn't be the same. I do miss the sight of Boston harbor, though. And spending time at the shore." She smiled up at him. "I guess it's the ocean that's calling me back."

"Hm," he said. "That might prove problematic."

She sent him a puzzled look.

He turned to face her in the snow-dusted sleigh. "Since the harvest festival, we've spent a lot of time together. And it has been wonderful. The best part of every day." He smiled. "Or at least it has been for me."

"For me too." The tenderness on his shadowed face made her heart race. Oh mercy, where was this conversation headed?

"I know your heart better than anyone," he said, his voice husky with feeling. "And I think you know mine."

"Yes." She thought of his honesty, his selfless decency, his bone-deep goodness. Mariah was right; there was not a kinder man in all of Tennessee.

"And, well . . . the truth is . . . I can't stop thinking that I want to spend even more time with you."

Tears crowded her throat. Never had anyone, even Edward, opened his heart to her this way. It was humbling . . . and frightening.

"Every day I find myself counting the hours until

I can close the mill and hightail it out to Lillian's for supper with you. I hate saying goodnight when the evening is done. I keep wishing that we never had to part, and I—"

"Wyatt." It was hard to breathe. In her heart of hearts, she felt the same way, and yet the thought of taking another step toward a life together filled her with trepidation. If only he would leave things the way they were . . .

"You mustn't say such things. I feel—"

"My darling girl. Please. Let me finish." He brushed snowflakes from her cheeks. He took her face in both his hands and gently kissed her lips. Everything—the dark trees, the pristine snow, the snippet of frozen lake far below—dissolved into a haze of perfect bliss.

"Ada," he whispered. "Marry me. Come to Texas with me. Let me take you home."

She drew away to look at him and felt her tears freezing on her face.

"You do love me."

"Yes." She loved him now, and she would love him forever, even after they had gone their separate ways. "But Wyatt, I—"

"I'm not talking about striking the tent and heading for Texas tomorrow. It all depends upon how long Aunt Lil needs us. I'll have to make arrangements for someone to take over the mill. And it's true there is no ocean in Texas." He grinned. "Well, there's the Gulf of Mexico, but it's a long way from the ranch land I intend to buy."

Ada thought about their initial clash of wills that had slowly evolved into mutual respect and understanding. They'd become a team, looking out for Lillian's welfare. They had argued and laughed with one another, and forgiven one another. Maybe this was the real thing, the kind of love that could overcome all her misgivings.

But how could she be sure? And if she made a mistake, the cost would be even greater.

"You don't have to answer tonight," he said. "I realize that when a woman marries, she starts out on a journey to the unknown. I don't mind if you take some time to think about whether you want to make the trip. Just don't turn me down flat. A man's got to have some hope, even if it's misplaced."

The snow had stopped. Ada watched the moon, high and bright, slide from behind the clouds, and the distant hills looming dark against the starlit sky.

"I will think about it," she finally said. "You are the finest man I know, and I only want what is best for both of us."

Wyatt planted a warm kiss on her forehead. "So do I, dearest friend. So do I."

Twenty-Five

Sophie slipped her hand into Ada's. "Where we goin' anyway?"

"To the mercantile, to deliver a hat to Mr. Pruitt."

Sophie stopped so suddenly that two farm wives, rushing along the sidewalk toward the bakery, almost collided with them. "I can't go in there!"

"I know. I'll only be a moment. I promise."

They stopped beneath the overhang outside the barbershop. With her free hand, Ada drew her woolen cloak more tightly about her shoulders. The January morning was frigid; their breath clouded the air. "Don't move," she told Sophie. "I'll be back soon."

Ada hurried past Nate Chastain's bookshop, the dentist's office, and the bank. The banker had just arrived and was unlocking the door with a key suspended on a long chain. He nodded as she passed. "Ma'am."

"Good morning, Mr. Gilman."

She continued past Norah's Fine Frocks to the mercantile and opened the door. Jasper Pruitt was standing on a ladder, running a feather duster over the rows of canned goods lining the upper shelves. Dust motes swirled in the thin winter light filtering through the grimy windows.

Jasper looked down at her. "Miss Wentworth."

"Mr. Pruitt. I've brought your hat." Ada opened the muslin pillowcase she had used as a dust cover on the way into town and set the hat on the counter. As he'd requested, this one was the same style as Bea's, but crafted in royal-blue velvet and trimmed with seed pearls and a double row of satin ribbon that ended in a neat bow.

He climbed down. "That's real pretty. I'm obliged to you."

Ada nodded, eager to collect her money and return to Sophie. "I'm glad you approve. I believe we agreed on a price of six dollars."

He whistled. "Sure seems like a lot for such a little bit of cloth and a scrap of ribbon."

"I use only the best materials, and they're costly. And you're forgetting the labor involved."

He ran one chubby finger gingerly over the delicate seed pearls. "I reckon maybe it wasn't easy at that—sewing on all them little doodads and such."

Opening his cash box, he counted out the bills. "Did I see you driving into town alone?"

"I had business at the orphanage."

"Wyatt Caldwell's letting you run around all over the county all by yourself?"

"I don't need his permission, Mr. Pruitt. But yes, he taught me to hitch the horse and rig so that I may come into town when necessary." She folded the pillowcase into a small, neat square and tucked it and her money into her drawstring bag.

Jasper closed his cash box and regarded her

solemnly. "With all the talk going on around here, you ain't afraid?"

She lifted her chin. "I must go. I hope Mrs. Pruitt likes her hat."

He tucked his cash box under the counter and aimed a stream of tobacco juice at the spittoon. "I'd be careful if I was you, hanging around that little darky from Miz Lowell's."

"I'm aware of your opinion." Ada headed for the door. "Good day, Mr. Pruitt."

"You think you're doing good, but you ain't!" he called after her. "You're just stirring up trouble, is all."

Ada hurried along the street toward Sophie. When she passed the dress shop, Norah Dudley opened the door and stuck her head out. "I saw you go by a few minutes ago. I was hoping to have a word with you."

Ada looked toward the barbershop where Sophie stood shivering in the cold.

"I won't take but a minute," Norah said.

With another glance at Sophie, Ada stepped inside.

"I'll come right to the point." Norah leaned against a glass case displaying her wares. "I'm thinking of selling my business and moving to Alabama. My only sister was widowed last year, and she's been after me ever since to come live with her. I've decided it's time."

"I see."

"And to tell you the truth, business has slacked

off lately. Times are getting hard. There's not much call these days for bespoke dresses and such." She sighed. "Even my ready-made dresses aren't selling as well as they did last year."

Ada fought a wave of apprehension. If Mrs. Dudley was having trouble selling something so basic as dresses, what hope was there for the success of a hat shop? So far, Ada had collected only twenty dollars for all the hats she'd made, and there was still her account with Horace Biddle to settle. By the time she paid for her supplies, there would be very little profit left. Establishing a business was fraught with more perils than she had imagined.

"On the other hand," Norah went on, "I can't stick my head out the door without seeing someone wearing an Ada Wentworth hat. So I'm offering you the chance to buy me out, inventory and all. I figure you'll eventually sell the dresses, and then you can convert the place solely to a hat shop."

"Well, I . . . I'm astonished. And grateful you thought of me, but I simply don't have the money."

"Wyatt Caldwell would lend it to you in a heartbeat. Anybody with one eye and half sense can see how that man feels about you." Norah paused. "At least think about it. I'm not planning to advertise the place for sale until winter's over. You've got some time to consider your options."

"I will. But now I really must be off."

"Bundle up. It's colder'n a well digger's grave out there."

• • •

Wyatt shuffled the messy stack of papers on his desk. Where in the Sam Hill had he put the letter from that Nashville lawyer? Could it really have been five years since he'd tried to buy Two Creeks? It seemed like only yesterday that he'd finally given up on the notion. Maybe it was worth another try.

He looked through several more stacks of canceled invoices, old telegrams, expired contracts, and the occasional letter from his father. Wyatt grinned to himself as he picked up the last one. Jake Caldwell was doing his level best to make his only son homesick. His letters were full of descriptions of glorious Texas sunsets, the birth of new stock, the rise in cattle prices, and the fancy new hotel going up in Fort Worth. *"Texas is booming, boy, and you're missing the whole shooting match. Get yourself on home as soon as you can."*

Through his office window he spotted Sage Whiting and Charlie Blevins tinkering with the steam generator again. He'd have to replace it soon, and he wasn't looking forward to the expense or the long wait for it to arrive from the manufacturer in Cincinnati.

And that wasn't the only aggravation, not by a long shot. The Powell boy had missed work twice in the last week, claiming his mother was too sick to be left alone. Maybe she was, but the boy needed to honor his obligation to Jasper—and to Wyatt. He was paying a good wage; the boy needed to earn it. He meant to have a talk with the former store clerk the next time he showed up.

Abandoning his search for the missing letter, Wyatt grabbed his coat and gloves and ducked outside to check on the generator. When had this mill become more of a burden than a pleasure? Had he always been this homesick for Texas, or was this sudden restlessness the result of his proposal to Ada?

An image of her lovely face, glistening with tears in the moonlight, rose in his mind. He wasn't sure what kind of response he'd expected. All through the fall, he'd felt her growing attraction to him. Now he saw it in her eyes, heard it in the tenderness in her voice. He didn't doubt the depth of her feelings. But she was skittish as a colt, still holding back, unable to love him as fiercely as he loved her.

Since Christmas Eve, he'd turned the situation over and over in his mind, trying to understand her hesitation. As far as he was concerned, the whole thing was pig simple. They loved each other; what more was there? He rounded the corner just as Sage gave a triumphant shout. The generator hummed to life.

Maybe it had been too much of a shock for her, imagining herself on a dusty ranch a thousand miles from the only life she'd ever known. Maybe he'd jumped the gun and proposed before she was ready. But he believed a man should go after what he wanted.

And Lord help him, he wanted Ada.

Twenty-Six

Ada found Sophie huddled against the building, her nose tucked into her cloak for warmth. The little girl stamped her feet against the cold. "Finally! My toes done nearly froze into a icicle."

"I'm sorry. I didn't intend to be gone so long."

"You said you'd be back *soon*. You was gone a *hour*."

"Well, I'm here now, and I have a surprise for you."

"Good surprise or bad surprise?"

"A good one, of course. Remember last week, when we talked about typewriting machines? I thought you might like to see one."

Sophie's extraordinary green eyes widened. "Somebody in Hickory Ridge gots one?"

"Has one. Yes, indeed—Miss Greer, at the newspaper office. Let's go."

They hurried to the *Gazette* office. Patsy was standing with her back to the door, her head buried inside a filing cabinet. "Take a seat," she called without turning around. "I'll be there directly."

"Take your time," Ada said.

Patsy turned around, a sheaf of papers in each hand. "Ada!"

"Good morning, Miss Greer," Ada said. "I've brought my friend Sophie to visit you. She's a very good storyteller who just might need a typewriting machine one day. I thought we might take a look at yours."

"Sure thing. Let me take these papers to Dad and I'll be right back." She disappeared through a swinging door leading to the back of the building.

Sophie sniffed. "What's that smell?"

"That's the hot lead they use to set the type and the ink that's used to print up the newspaper."

"Smells good," Sophie said. "Smells like a adventure!"

Patsy returned and led them into her office. She whisked the dustcover off the typewriting machine and motioned Sophie into her chair. The child sat down and twirled around. "This chair is like a merry-go-round."

Patsy laughed and rolled a sheet of paper into the machine. She showed Sophie how to strike the keys that imprinted the paper hidden behind the tall carriage.

The child was entranced. "Can I make my name?"

"Sure. You can make anything you want."

Sophie studied the keyboard. "*Q, w, e, r, t* . . . these letters all messed up." She looked up at Patsy and frowned. "How come it don't go like regular ABCs?"

"I'm not sure, to tell you the truth. But once you get the hang of it, you can write really fast. Look, here's the *S*."

"This machine magic! I see the *O!*" Sophie punched the key and grinned up at Ada.

Ada smiled, enjoying Sophie's wonderment as the child completed typing her name. Patsy rolled the paper out and handed it to Sophie. "See? There's your name, perfect as can be. No mistakes."

"Can I type my other name?"

"Another time." Ada gathered her cloak and bag. "We must go."

Sophie nodded. "I guess it would take all day to spell Robillard."

Ada drew on her gloves. "Thanks, Patsy. This means a lot to me."

"I enjoyed it. Someday Hickory Ridge will need another newspaper woman. Maybe Sophie will take my place."

They left the office, Sophie still clutching her sheet of paper. "Where we going now?"

"To my house. Or rather, to Mrs. Willis's."

Sophie trotted alongside Ada. "I never been to nobody's house before. I been living at Mrs. Lowell's since my baby time. Is it a long ways to Miz Willis's?"

"Not too far."

"And you're sure enough going to show me how to make hats?"

Ada smiled down at her. "I sure enough am. And we're going to work on your reading and writing too."

Sophie wrinkled her nose. "I made up a new

story 'bout the princess from Africa. But I ain't—I mean I *haven't* written it down nowhere. It's in my head, is all."

When they reached the bakery, Ada said, "If you can wait one more minute, I'll buy us a sticky bun."

Sophie grinned. "I can wait."

Ada went inside and quickly purchased three buns. Returning to the rig, she handed the bag to Sophie and climbed in.

"There's Miss Goldston!" Sophie said. "From the school."

At the sound of her name, Bea turned, her gray woolen cloak sweeping a wide arc on the sidewalk. "Why, Ada Wentworth—and dear little Sophie. What a surprise!"

"Hello, Bea." Ada gathered the reins. "You must excuse us. I promised Lillian we'd be back by noon."

"Of course. Don't let me keep you." Bea smiled at them, but Ada heard the barb beneath the sweetness.

Ada snapped the reins and Smoky started for home. Sophie kept up a steady stream of questions as they drove past the telegraph office and the Verandah Hotel.

"Where's the trains going?" The girl craned her neck to watch a train that was just leaving.

"Oh, everywhere—Nashville, Chicago, Memphis, Saint Louis. These days one can go across the entire country by train."

"Africa?"

Ada smiled. "I'm afraid not. You'd need to book passage on a ship to go that far."

"There's the church!" Sophie said when they passed. "Where we sang the Christmas carols." She craned her neck as they passed the mill. "That's where your sweetheart lives."

"What do you know about sweethearts?" Ada smiled down at her.

"Mrs. Lowell told Mrs. Whiting that Mr. Caldwell is sweet on you. She said that's why he gave her a big pile of money for the orphan house. Are you sweet on him too?"

"You know what, Sophie? I'm all out of answers just now. Why don't we play a game? See how many kinds of birds you can spot before we get home."

With Sophie busily counting blue jays and cardinals, Ada's thoughts turned to Wyatt. Since his proposal on Christmas Eve, he'd continued coming to supper at Lillian's each night, staying long into the evening to talk with her in the firelit parlor. To her immense relief, he hadn't pressed her for an answer. Instead, he'd let her get to know him better, leading her through his life as if turning the pages of a book. He talked even more about Texas and his vision for his ranch, about his life growing up with a mother who was often too ill to care for him. About a lonely boyhood relieved by long summers with Lillian in Hickory Ridge.

And about his father, Jake Caldwell, a larger-than-life rancher who couldn't wait for his only son to come home.

Despite her uncertainties, Ada found herself counting the hours each day until he appeared, smelling wonderfully of new wood and soap, his hair still damp with comb tracks, his extraordinary blue eyes full of love and hope. She smiled to herself. Wyatt was all the more appealing because he was so self-deprecating and unaware of his good looks. His kindness knew no bounds. Despite his concern about the town's reaction to her and Sophie, his gift to the orphanage was the reason behind the letter that arrived just after the New Year. Mrs. Lowell had given permission for Sophie to spend one day a week with Ada, learning millinery skills and studying her lessons.

A wave of love and gratitude washed over her. Maybe she should throw caution to the winds. Cast aside her fears and self-doubts. Say yes and trust Wyatt with her future, even if she couldn't quite imagine herself on a vast ranch in the middle of Texas.

She guided Smoky around a rut in the road. What would she do all day while Wyatt was off doing . . . whatever it was that ranchers did? Branding, she supposed, and rounding up strays. Of course there would be a house to tend and someday, perhaps, children to look after. Would she find friends her own age there, friends as kind and true as Mariah and Carrie? Wyatt had told her their nearest neighbors might be miles and miles away.

Maybe she could fill her days making hats, but who would buy them? From what she'd gathered, everyone wore either Stetsons or sturdy bonnets to ward off the broiling Texas sun. Seed pearls and fancy ribbons surely would have little place among thorny brush and longhorn cattle. And hadn't she heard there were still Indian wars going on in Texas?

She juggled the reins and drew her cloak more securely around her shoulders. Life in such a foreign place would be challenging, but no more so than living aboard ship with Edward would have been. She swallowed the bitterness rising in her throat. Clearly he'd forgotten his promise to her. But what good would it do to dwell on the past?

"Seven!" Sophie said. "That's how many kinds of birds I counted. I'm tired. How much further are we gonna ride?"

"Just around the next bend. If you look through that stand of trees over there, you can see the house."

Ada drove the rig into the yard. She left Smoky tethered for the moment while they took the bag of sticky buns inside. Libby Dawson was sitting in the kitchen watching Lillian take a pan of biscuits out of the oven. She looked up and grinned shyly at Sophie. Sophie wiggled her fingers in a little wave.

"There you are, Ada." Lillian set the pan on the table. "And this must be Sophie."

Ada made the introductions and was gratified when Sophie bobbed her head and said, "Pleased to make your acquaintance."

"Likewise." Lillian eyed the child and handed her a stack of plates. "As long as you're here, Sophie, you might as well be useful. Set these on the table and then get the silverware out of that drawer."

Sophie scurried about setting the table, seeming right at home. Lillian stirred a pot of stew bubbling on the stove. Ada paid Libby Dawson and thanked her for coming. "Can you stay again next week when you come to deliver the laundry?"

"I reckon, long as the mule don't freeze to death. Daddy says he can't remember the last time it was this cold."

"It's a bone chiller all right," Lillian said. "Try to stay warm on the way home, Libby."

"Yes'm." Libby sniffed. "Them biscuits sure do smell good. That stew does too."

"Then you can stay and have some!" Sophie said. "Can't she, Miss Ada?"

"Libby has work to do." Lillian flapped her hands at Libby. "Run on now, girl. Don't forget that bundle of linens by the stairway."

With one last look at the golden-brown biscuits, Libby turned to go.

"Wait!" Ada couldn't bear to send the girl into

the cold on an empty stomach. She ladled some stew into a jar and handed it to Libby along with a couple of warm biscuits wrapped in a napkin.

"Much obliged, Miss." Libby lifted the bundle of laundry with one hand and balanced her food in the other.

Ada opened the front door for her just as Charlie Blevins lifted his hand to knock. The burly sawyer watched Libby hoist the laundry onto her wagon before opening the container of warm stew and drinking it down. "It's bad business to feed them Two Creeks folks," he muttered. "They'll start expecting it, and the first thing you know you'll be feeding the whole lot of them."

Ada folded her arms across her chest. "Why don't you let me worry about that? What was it you wanted?"

"Mr. Caldwell sent me to tell you he can't come for supper tonight. He's got a meeting in town."

"I see. Please thank him for letting us know."

"It's some high mucky-mucks from Chicago or somewheres. Leastways, that's what he told Mr. Whiting."

Just then Sophie appeared at the door. "Miss Ada? Your biscuits gettin' cold."

"I'll be right there, Sophie."

Charlie Blevins frowned. "How many Negroes you got in there?"

"None of your business." Ada closed the door.

Twenty-Seven

"Well, Ada, that's it for today." Carrie swept the floor and cast a wary eye toward the potbellied stove in the corner. "I sure wish the reverend would get that thing to working properly so we could work here without freezing to death. With Henry at the mill all day, it gets lonely at the farm. I miss our circle when it's too cold to meet."

"You can always go into town and visit with Mr. Chastain," Mariah teased. "His bookshop is quite cozy."

Ada laughed and poked her friend's arm. "Leave her alone. You were young and in love once."

"Who says I'm in love?" Carrie blushed and picked up her sewing basket.

"You don't have to say anything." Mariah looked around for her sewing basket. "The look on your face gives you away. It's the same look on Ada's face anytime anyone mentions Wyatt Caldwell."

The women stilled and gazed fondly at Ada. "We'll be making another bridal quilt any day now," Mariah predicted.

Lillian, who had been napping close to the stove with her cloak pulled over her, yawned and rose stiffly. "Ada, get my basket and let's get on home. It'll be dark soon."

Ada glanced out the window. Long shadows

dappled the church and spilled across the thawing ground. Though much of the divisive talk about Two Creeks had abated since Christmas, she'd noticed an undercurrent of caution among some of the shop owners in town. They were more guarded in their conversations now. A few had begun bolting their doors, even during business hours.

Ain't you afraid? She hadn't wanted to give Jasper Pruitt the satisfaction of a reply. But the truth was, she didn't feel completely safe on the road after dark, even with Lillian beside her. She picked up her things and Lillian's, and the women went outside. With quick good-byes all around, they climbed into their rigs and started home.

Lillian, who usually had plenty to say after an afternoon with their friends, seemed subdued. Ada tucked a blanket around the older woman. "Are you warm enough?" she asked, climbing in beside her. Lillian nodded and drew the blanket more tightly around her shoulders.

"Did you enjoy the circle today?" Ada flicked the reins and they pulled out of the churchyard. "It was good seeing everyone, wasn't it?"

"I suppose."

They traveled in silence for some minutes. Ada glanced at her companion. The older woman had gone mute as stone. Ada reached across to tuck a corner of the blanket into place. After spending most of the afternoon in the under-heated church, maybe Lillian was simply too cold and uncomfortable for conversation.

"We'll be home soon," Ada promised. "And I'll make hot cocoa. Would you like that?"

Lillian nodded and Ada got the distinct impression that the older woman was displeased with her, though she couldn't imagine why. At last, when the house came into view, Ada could stand it no longer. "Lillian, have I done something to offend you?"

"What?"

"Are you cross with me?"

After another long pause, Lillian said, "Only if you intend to disappoint Wyatt."

"Disappoint him?"

"Don't be coy, Ada. My eyesight isn't what it used to be, but I can see the way that boy looks at you. I can hear the two of you in my front parlor every night, cooing like a pair of doves." Lillian shook her head. "Lawsa, he's smitten. And as fond as I am of you, I'm not sure Wyatt knows his own mind, falling for a Yankee girl."

Ada smiled. "I've fallen for him too."

"But?"

Ada watched Smoky's head bobbing up and down as he clopped into the yard. "We haven't really known each other that long. We need to be certain of our feelings."

Lillian waved one gloved hand. "Oh, piffle! I knew I was going to marry Pete Caldwell the first day I laid eyes on him. He knew it too."

Ada brought the rig to a halt beside the barn. She could feel Lillian's intense gaze boring into her. Clearly, Lillian now had more to say.

"Forgive my mawkishness, Ada. I'm an old woman. But here's what I know. When God opens a door, you have to take his hand and walk through it. Even when you have doubts."

"Yes, but—"

"Life is so much shorter than we think. I don't understand this dithering and excuse-making." Lillian grasped Ada's arm. "Either you love my nephew or you don't. Which is it?"

"With all due respect, it isn't that simple. I—"

Without waiting for Ada's help, Lillian threw off the blanket and stepped from the rig. "Fine. Have it your . . . oh!" A startled look crossed her face. She opened her mouth, but no sound came out. Then she bent double and toppled onto the muddy ground.

"Lillian!" Ada ran to kneel beside her. "Lillian, what happened? Did you lose your footing? Are you all right?"

Lillian's mouth moved, but she couldn't speak. Her skin had turned pale and clammy. Her eyes were open, but she seemed frozen, unable to see or hear.

"Oh! Oh, Lord! Please help her!"

Ada's heart pounded as she considered her options. She could put Lillian in the rig and head for town, but the long trip over the rutted road might make her worse. She could leave Lillian home alone and try to find Wyatt, but it would take at least an hour to reach the mill and return. She didn't dare leave Lillian that long. And what if Wyatt was off scouting timber, or in town making a delivery?

That left Two Creeks. She'd find Libby Dawson and send her to fetch Wyatt. Her decision made, Ada crouched behind Lillian and grasped the old woman's arms. She half dragged, half carried Lillian across the yard and into the house, keeping up a constant stream of talk to calm her rattled nerves.

"Lillian, something terrible has happened to you, but don't worry." Ada settled Lillian on her bed and removed the older woman's cloak and shoes. "I'm going to send for Wyatt, and he'll bring the doctor. You'll be fine. But you mustn't try to get out of bed while I'm gone. Do you understand?"

A trickle of spittle leaked from the corner of Lillian's mouth. "Unnnh."

Moving quickly, Ada covered Lillian with blankets from the cedar chest in the corner and rekindled the fire in the fireplace. "There. You'll be warm, and Wyatt will come, and Dr. Spencer too, and they will know what to do."

With one last look at Lillian, Ada ran for the rig and urged Smoky toward the Two Creeks turnoff. The rig rocked along the narrow path that snaked through the dense forest. She guided the horse around a bend, and the road opened up to reveal a row of tin-roofed shanties clustered beside a creek.

Few of the houses had actual windows; the openings were boarded up against the cold, covered with scraps of tin and ragged blankets nailed to the frames. Smoke twisted from chimneys, sending the smells of wood smoke and boiling cabbage into the air. Children ran barefoot along the hard-packed dirt yards, chasing a few scraggly chickens, seemingly oblivious to the cold and the coming darkness. Behind the houses lay the fields, fallow now in the dead of winter.

Despite her worry and panic, Ada felt her eyes welling with tears at the desolate sight. How could Mr. Pruitt, or anyone, justify taking away what little these people had?

A young boy of perhaps twelve or thirteen stepped into the road. Ada halted the rig. "You *lost,* Miss," he said. "You done took a wrong turn offa the road back there." He looked genuinely frightened. "You got to get outta here."

"I need help! I've come for Libby Dawson. Could you tell me which house is hers?"

He jerked a thumb. "Las' one on the lef'. But she ain't here. Saw her leavin' out with her daddy 'fore sunup this mornin'. They ain't come back yet."

Ada felt tears building in her throat. What if it was too late, and Lillian was already dead? "But I need her!"

"Can't help that. If she ain't here, she ain't here."

Ada sized him up. "Then you will have to do."

"Ma'am?"

"What's your name?"

"Ulysses, ma'am."

"Ulysses, do you know Mr. Caldwell? At the lumber mill?"

"Ever'body been knowin' who he is."

"My name is Ada Wentworth. I need to you to go to the mill and find him. Tell him his aunt is very sick and that he needs to bring Dr. Spencer to the house right away. Can you remember that?"

"Yes'm, I reckon. But how am I 'sposed to get there?"

"You haven't a horse or a mule? A wagon?"

"No ma'am. Not since las' fall."

"Then you'll come with me. I'll take you as far as the crossroad, but you'll have to walk from there. And you must hurry."

He crossed his skinny arms. "I don't want no trouble."

"Listen to me. I don't blame you for being afraid, I'm afraid too. But there will be more trouble if Mr. Caldwell's aunt dies because you wouldn't help me. Now stop arguing and get in!"

Ulysses complied. Ada turned the rig and drove as fast as she dared over the rough path to the main road, where a horse and rig passed them going the opposite way. Two men she didn't know turned to stare. She felt a wave of uneasiness but pushed it away. Getting help for Lillian was more important than anybody's rules about what was or wasn't proper.

"All right, Ulysses," Ada said when they reached the crossroad. "What message are you to deliver to Mr. Caldwell? Tell me word for word."

"Mr. Caldwell, your auntie sick," the boy recited. "Miss Ada say bring the doctor to the house right quick."

"Yes, that's right. If you can't find Mr. Caldwell, I want you to find his foreman, Mr. Whiting, and tell him. Anyone at the mill can tell you who he is." Ada handed him a coin. "Now run, Ulysses. Run as fast as you can!"

The boy sprinted down the road. Ada left Smoky in the yard and ran inside.

Lillian lay still, her breathing shallow but even. The fire still crackled in the grate. The clock in the parlor ticked into the silence. Too numb to think, Ada moved mechanically, lighting the lamps, building a fire in the cookstove, setting the kettle on to boil. When the tea was ready, she poured a cup and took it into Lillian's room to keep watch. Not knowing what else to do, and unnerved by the silence, she opened Lillian's Bible and read aloud. "The Lord is my light and my salvation; whom shall I fear? . . ."

The familiar psalm and the sound of her own voice calmed her and kept at bay the nagging worry that her sharp words to Lillian were somehow to blame for the older woman's condition.

Tears sprang to her eyes. She should have been kinder. She should have been more patient. After all, she and Lillian wanted the same thing: Wyatt's happiness.

Darkness had fallen. Through the window, she saw Smoky standing patiently in the yard. He needed to be freed of his harness, watered, and fed, but she lacked the energy, and she was afraid to leave Lillian again. Wyatt would never forgive her if Lillian died alone.

At last, she heard hoofbeats along the road and then Wyatt's familiar tread on the porch. He rushed inside.

"Ada." He gathered her into his arms. She sagged against him.

"Where's the doctor?" she asked when he released her.

"Right behind me. He'll be here shortly. What happened?"

Ada told him. "One minute she was fine, and the next . . ." Her voice trailed off, and her eyes welled.

Wyatt bent over the bed. "Aunt Lil," he murmured. "It's me. Can you hear me, darlin'?"

Lillian's eyes fluttered, but no words came. He drew up a chair and sat beside her, holding her hand. Ada heard the doctor's rig outside, and she hurried to let him in.

Dr. Spencer bent over the bed, his thin face serious in the flickering firelight. "Has she spoken at all since this happened?"

"No." Ada clenched her hands. "Nothing."

He nodded. "I saw a number of cases like this during my training in Philadelphia. Most likely it's a venous congestion of the brain. That would account for the sudden onset of her symptoms and her loss of speech."

"What can you do?" Wyatt asked. "Does she need an operation? Medicines? Whatever she needs, I'll take—"

"Wyatt." The doctor returned his stethoscope to his medical bag and snapped it shut. "I'm not going to lie to you. In cases like this, where there has been little movement and no speech for several hours, the prognosis is not good—especially in one so old and frail. I think—"

"What about a specialist?"

The doctor shook his head. "If it will make you feel better, I can summon one of my colleagues from Knoxville for another opinion. But frankly, by the time he gets here—"

"It'll be too late."

"It's hard to say. I've seen cases such as this where the patient lingers for many days. Others go in a matter of hours." He clasped Wyatt's shoulder. "If there's any other family who would want to see her before she goes, now would be the time to send word."

"There's no one. I'm all she has left."

Dr. Spencer picked up his bag. "People tend to forget their own needs at times like this." His voice was gentle. "It won't do Lillian any good for the two of you to go hungry. I'll send word to the Whitings. They'll want to help."

Wyatt drew his chair closer to the bed and grasped his aunt's frail hand. Ada followed the doctor to the door. "Please. Isn't there anything we can do for her?"

He patted her shoulder. "Pray, my dear. Just pray."

Twenty-Eight

Ada woke with a start, her heart jerking in her chest. The fiery nightmare had returned, haunting her sleep. The images of roiling smoke and blistering flames were as vivid and familiar as ever, but mixed into the horrifying dream was an image of Edward as she'd last seen him, resplendent in his uniform, laughing at some joke her father had told at dinner the night her world had shattered. And somehow she was in the dream too, alone in the cold. She sat up, waiting for her pulse to slow, and massaged the knot at the small of her back. Lillian's parlor settee was no place to sleep, but she'd been too worried and too exhausted last night to climb the stairs to her room.

She rose and opened the curtains. Outside, frost glittered on the brown grass. A thin winter sun rose over the mountain. She shivered. The fire had burned low in the grate. She knelt beside the hearth, added some kindling, and, with the bellows, coaxed a flame to life.

Wyatt, disheveled and bleary-eyed from a long night of keeping watch at Lillian's bedside, shuffled down the hall. Her heart twisted at the sight of him. *Dear Lord, please give me the right words to say to him. And please take care of Lillian.*

Ada stood. "Is she—"

He shook his head. "I think her breathing is slowing down. I wish the doctor would get here."

A sound drew her attention to the window. Ignoring the headache building behind her gritty eyes, she pushed her tangled hair off her face and opened the door.

"Ada." Mariah's brown eyes welled. She set her food basket on the table in the hallway and enveloped Ada in a strong embrace. "Ennis Spencer told us what happened yesterday. You must have been frightened out of your wits."

Ada felt her tears coming back. "It was so sudden. One minute we were talking, and the next . . ." She wiped her eyes and smoothed her hair. "Oh, I must look a fright."

"Well, you've had an awful time of it." Mariah turned and took both of Wyatt's hands. "This is terrible."

Wyatt nodded and swallowed hard. Ada's heart went out to him. Lillian had been like a mother to him; her passing would leave a huge hole in his life. She wished she could take his grief upon herself.

"I brought breakfast." Mariah picked up her basket. "I'll get everything ready."

"I'm not hungry," Ada and Wyatt said as one.

"You have to eat," Mariah said firmly. She headed for the kitchen just as the doctor returned.

He shrugged out of his coat and hung it on the rack in the entry hall. "Any change?"

"She's the same." Wyatt ran his hand over his stubbled face. "I tried talking to her this morning, but—"

"I'll take a look."

Ada and Wyatt followed Dr. Spencer into Lillian's room. Ada was stunned at how greatly Lillian had changed overnight. Her skin was slack and papery, her eyes shrunken into their sockets. Each shallow breath was accompanied by a faint wheeze. Ada's stomach clenched. She remembered that terrible sound. The death rattle, her mother's doctor had called it. There was surely no hope now for Lillian's recovery.

The doctor bent over the bed to examine Lillian.

"How long?" Wyatt asked, his voice rough with tears.

"A matter of hours, I should think." Dr. Spencer straightened and put away his stethoscope. "Is there anything I can do for you?"

"I'd be obliged if you'd stop by the mill. Tell Sage I'm closing down until after the funeral. And find Charlie Blevins. He's the best coffin maker around. Tell him to use some of that good oak we milled out last week."

"I'll take care of it. Shall I send the minister out here?"

"Lillian would like that. Tell him we'll have the service here at the house. The stove at the church isn't working properly." He massaged the back of his neck. "You'd best send word to the undertaker too."

The doctor nodded. "I wish I could stay, but I've a couple of very sick children who need attending and a mother with a baby due any minute."

"We'll be fine." Wyatt shook the doctor's hand. "I appreciate everything you've done."

They saw him out and went into the kitchen, where Mariah had set out breakfast—warm bread with strawberry preserves and fresh butter, a platter of bacon and eggs, a pot of strong coffee. Ada found herself suddenly famished. When had she last eaten? It seemed a lifetime ago.

The three of them ate in a heavy silence broken only by the clink of silverware on their plates and the soft chiming of the parlor clock. When the meal was finished, Mariah quickly washed and dried the dishes, retrieved her basket, and pulled on her cloak.

"I'll be back in the morning," she murmured to Ada. "There's nothing you can do for her now. Look after Wyatt."

When Mariah's buggy disappeared around the bend, Wyatt slumped onto the settee. "Go on up to your bed and get some sleep," he said gently. "You're exhausted."

"So are you. I'll wait with you."

"You're not obligated."

"I want to stay with you." Her eyes filled. "And with her."

They returned to Lillian's room. Wyatt replenished the logs in the fireplace. The fire flared, and the logs popped, sending up a gray plume of fragrant wood smoke. The birds awoke and chattered in the trees. Feeble sunlight pushed through the drawn curtains.

"She was quite fond of you," Wyatt said quietly.

Ada managed a weak smile. "I was fond of her as well. I'm sorry I vexed her more than I meant to."

He smiled. "So did I. But Aunt Lil could be difficult. Judgmental. Demanding. And stubborn to a fault."

"I wasn't certain how she'd react to my bringing Sophie here, but she seemed to enjoy having her around."

"She always had a soft spot in her heart for those in distress. I think that's one reason she took to you. She might not have always acted like it, but she knew how heavy your burdens were." His voice cracked. "I'm going to miss her."

"Oh, so will I!" She looked up. "Wyatt, could we pray for her?"

He gazed back at her. "I think that's exactly what we should do." They joined hands across the bed.

"Lord," Wyatt began, "you gave me this good woman, Lillian Caldwell Willis, at a time in my life when I needed her most, and now I reckon you're wanting her back. We thank you for her long life, for what she's meant to us and to our town. We ask you to remember her virtues, forgive her sins, and welcome her into your loving presence."

A soft sigh escaped Lillian's parched lips. Ada bent to kiss the older woman's cool, dry forehead and wondered about death. Did Lillian somehow know that the end had come? Was she afraid? Relieved? Expectant? Ada didn't try to stop her tears.

Outside, a cardinal took up its morning song. It seemed that minutes passed before Lillian took another shallow breath.

"The Lord is my shepherd," Wyatt began.

Ada joined him. "I shall not want . . ."

Lillian's breath grew fainter. Tears slid down Ada's face as she and Wyatt recited the ancient words.

"Yea, though I walk—"

Lillian's eyelids fluttered. Wyatt bent to kiss her cheek, and her expression grew peaceful. She released a final breath.

Wyatt and Ada stood for a long minute in the awful silence. Then Wyatt gently drew the covers over Lillian's head. "I wish the preacher had arrived in time."

Ada wiped her eyes. “Your prayer was lovely. Pastor Dennis could have done no better.”

She stood beside Lillian’s bed, wondering what came next. When her mother died, she’d been banished to her room while Elizabeth’s body was prepared for burial. What was expected of her now?

“Ada,” Wyatt said quietly, “you should rest now. The pastor will be coming soon, and I expect the undertaker will be along this afternoon too.”

“I *am* tired,” she admitted. “But what about you?”

“I’d like to be alone for a little bit—take a walk around the place while I wait for the undertaker. Go on up now. I’ll wake you in a while.”

Ada went up to her room and crawled into bed without bothering to undress. Now that the crisis was over, she was bone-tired and soul-weary. She slept without dreaming until Wyatt came upstairs to wake her.

He had combed his hair, but a two-day growth of beard still shadowed his cheeks. “The undertaker has come and gone,” he said, his voice raspy with fatigue and grief. “The Spencers are downstairs with Mariah and Sage. Pastor Dennis is here to talk about the service. I could use your help with deciding what to do. I’m not much good with ceremonies.”

“Of course. I’ll be right there.”

She donned the dove-gray dress she’d worn on her first Sunday in Hickory Ridge, saving her best one for tomorrow's service. She washed her face, pinned her hair, and pinched some color into her cheeks.

Downstairs, a fire popped and hissed in the grate. Beneath the window sat a wooden coffin stand. Someone had draped the hallway mirror in black and placed a black wreath on the front door. The doctor's wife bustled about, helping Mariah serve tea.

"Miss Wentworth?" Pastor Dennis set aside an empty cup. "Wyatt says you're to help choose the songs and readings for tomorrow."

Ada sat down and accepted a cup of tea from Mrs. Spencer. "She liked Psalms and Proverbs and Ecclesiastes. Whatever you choose, Pastor Dennis, will be fine."

"Very well. What about hymns?"

"'My Shepherd Will Supply My Need.' It was her favorite."

"Mine too." He licked the tip of a pencil and scribbled on a piece of paper. "What else?"

"'Abide with Me,' I think. She used to hum it when she walked in her garden."

The pastor scanned his notes as if checking a grocery list. "I suppose that's all I need. Much obliged for your help." He shook hands with Wyatt, bundled into his black frock coat, and picked up his hat. "I'll see myself out."

Late that evening, when everyone else had gone, Wyatt lit the lamps. He and Ada foraged in the kitchen, preparing a cold supper that they ate before the fire.

"I walked in her garden this afternoon," he said. "I could almost hear her fussing at me for trampling on her Louisiana iris. When I was a boy, she'd tell me not to take a shortcut through the garden, and I'd always forget and step on one plant or another. One time she switched me good for ruining a primrose bush." He smiled. "Of course, she had to catch me first. I took off for the river, thinking I could outrun her, but she cut through the trees and caught up with me just before I got to Billy Rondo's place. She walloped the tar out of me—not so much for ruining the bush, but for running from her. I guess I deserved it."

Ada laughed, then sobered. "I'm sorry. I shouldn't be laughing at a time like this."

"Don't apologize. Aunt Lil wouldn't mind your enjoying a laugh at my expense." He took a sip of his coffee. "She used to tell me I was too big for my britches. Nothing pleased her more than taking me down at notch or two from time to time."

They sat quietly for a long time. The fire collapsed on itself with a soft sigh. At last Wyatt rose. "I should go home, but I hate leaving you here alone. Will you be all right?"

She stood too. "I'll be fine."

"I'll be back early tomorrow to help prepare for the service. I want to be here when Aunt Lil comes home for the last time."

He looked so tired, so weighted with grief, that Ada's eyes filled again. "I'll have breakfast ready. I'd like to do whatever I can to make things easier for you."

"The whole day will be easier if I'm with you." He kissed her forehead. "Goodnight, Ada."

She walked him to the door. When he had gone, she extinguished the lamps in the parlor and went up to bed. But despite her weariness, sleep proved elusive.

Now that Lillian was gone, Ada no longer had a job or a place to call home. And she was scared. All her life she'd been a planner. She hated not knowing what would happen tomorrow and the day after.

The winter wind seeped into the old house. She drew her covers more tightly about her and tried to think. She had no doubt that Wyatt would honor his promise to let her stay on here until she could make other arrangements, but what possibilities were open to her? Should she move to that run-down ladies' hotel in town and try to support herself making hats? Look for another opportunity as lady's companion? Or should she leave Hickory Ridge for a larger town with more opportunities?

After all, she'd never meant to stay here forever. But that was before she loved Wyatt.

She punched her pillow and listened to the windowpanes rattling in the wind. Wyatt was still waiting for an answer to his proposal. All she had to do was overcome her fears and say yes to him, and her worries about her future would be over.

But she couldn't do that to him. It would be wrong to use marriage as an escape from her difficulties. Wyatt deserved better than that.

The events of the day finally caught up with her. Hot tears leaked from her eyes and trickled into her ears. She lay in the heavy darkness, listening to the screech of a bare branch raking against the window pane.

What was wrong with her that she couldn't give Wyatt her heart?

Twenty-Nine

Ada's heart lurched at the sight of Wyatt arriving at sunup in his somber mourning clothes. He looked pale but rested as he tethered his rig in the yard and crossed the yard to the porch.

Unable to sleep for more than a few hours, she'd risen at four to light the lamps, stoke the fires, and prepare his breakfast. The gesture, small as it was, had somehow made her own grief easier to bear.

He hung his hat on the rack in the parlor and smiled tenderly. "Didn't you sleep at all?"

"Some. Too much on my mind."

He nodded. "After I left here last night, I worked in the office for a while. Those fellows from Chicago who were here awhile back had a thousand questions about the mill. I sorted through them last night until I finally got tired."

She touched his arm. "Come on to the kitchen. Everything's ready."

Wyatt held her chair, and they sat down to their meal. Consumed with worry and grief, Ada felt as if she were muffled in cotton, all her emotions muted. She ate without tasting anything, only dimly aware of the rattle of branches of the trees lining the road and the twittering of winter birds in the bushes beside the kitchen door.

Wyatt finished a second helping of ham and fried potatoes and poured more coffee for both of them. "That was good. The fried ham hit the spot."

She smiled. "Lillian would have said it was too salty."

"I reckon when a person is as old as she was, complaining about things is one of the few pleasures that's left." He stirred sugar into his coffee and helped himself to another biscuit. "Although now that I think about it, Aunt Lil complained a lot in her younger years too. She was already past forty when I was born. It couldn't have been easy for her keeping up with me, but she gave it her all. I tried to do the same for her."

"I don't know many men who would have done what you've done."

"I'm not looking for accolades. Just stating a fact." He rose and looked out the window. "Here comes the undertaker."

Ada stacked their dishes in the dishpan and untied her apron, then she and Wyatt went out to meet Lillian's coffin.

The sight of it filled her with new sorrow. Until this moment, she hadn't allowed herself to absorb the finality of Lillian's death or the true depth of her feelings for the older woman. Serving Lillian in her last months of life had been a daunting responsibility and a sacred trust. Each memory of the good moments they'd shared seemed precious. She wished now that there had been more of them. For a moment, her knees went weak, and the winter landscape spun before her eyes, but Wyatt held tightly to her hand and whispered, "Steady, love."

Harlan Wentworth, a short, balding man in a black suit and frock coat, jumped from his wagon and released the ropes holding Lillian's coffin in place. "It's colder'n a witch's—uh, wagon tire this morning," he amended when he saw Ada. "We're lucky the ground is partially thawed. I checked with the gravedigger when I came past the church awhile ago. Ever'thing should be ready for the burying by the time the service is done."

He blew on his hands to warm them and squinted at Wyatt. "You reckon you can give me a hand getting your loved one into the house? Normally I have my boy to help me, but he's down with a bad case of the runs. Begging your pardon, ma'am."

Wyatt helped lift Lillian's coffin. Ada couldn't help noticing that Charlie Blevins had done a masterful job of it; the golden oak planks were sanded so smooth that they gleamed in the morning light. The men carried it in through the hall and placed it on the stand in the parlor.

"I've got to get back to town, but I'll be back this afternoon to transport the deceased to the graveyard," the undertaker said. "I assume you'll want to get the burying done before dark."

Wyatt nodded, ushering him out the front door. "It was Aunt Lil's wish that everything be done quickly. She never was one for drawing things out."

"Well, looks like the mourners are arriving." The undertaker pointed to a buckboard rounding the bend. "I'll be on my way."

He climbed into his wagon. Mariah and Sage drove into the yard, their horse snorting and stamping in the cold. Robbie, looking sober and grownup in a dark blue suit, sat behind his mother. No sooner had Ada greeted them than the Spencers arrived, followed by Carrie Daly and her brother, Henry Bell. Patsy Greer and Norah Dudley arrived together in Patsy's rig. Soon the parlor overflowed with mourners who greeted Wyatt warmly, murmuring words of comfort and regret.

Ada, standing quietly to the side, looked up when Bea Goldston appeared in the doorway, looking more severe than ever in her black dress and bonnet. She pushed through the crowd toward Wyatt and burst into tears. "Oh, you dear man!"

She clung to him and sobbed. “And poor Lillian. This is a situation not to be borne!”

“That’s the truth,” Mariah muttered, coming to stand beside Ada. “What a spectacle! Bea should be ashamed of herself.”

Wyatt peeled her off him and managed a tired smile. “Thank you, Bea. But you mustn’t be so distraught. Death is always with us. And Aunt Lil was quite prepared to meet her maker.”

“But I never got a chance to say good . . . good-bye.”

“That’s why we have wakes, isn’t it?” Mariah took Bea firmly by the arm and drew her toward the kitchen. “Help me serve tea. It’ll make you feel better if you have something constructive to do.”

“Of course I want to be helpful, but I don’t want to leave Wyatt.” She sniffed. “He’s all alone now.”

Mariah caught Ada’s eye and suppressed a smile. “I’m sure he can bear up. Come along, now; we’ve lots of people to serve.”

Ada passed among the mourners serving tea and platters of food, feeling that somehow she’d been marked for sorrow. It had been less than a year since she’d buried her father and Aunt Kate, and now she was saying good-bye again. She glanced at the closed coffin beneath the window, and her tears threatened once more. She’d grown comfortable in Lillian’s company—well, as comfortable as one could hope for with Lillian—and she had come to rely upon the older woman's counsel. Who would advise her now?

Pastor Dennis arrived on a blast of frigid air, his face red with cold. He sought out Wyatt and shook his hand. "So sorry to be late. I had to stop by the church to pick up the songbooks, and it took longer than I planned." He gathered the mourners and handed out the hymnals.

After the singing and the readings from Psalms, Pastor Dennis opened his Bible and read from Paul's first letter to the believers at Corinth: "And now abideth faith, hope, and charity, these three; but the greatest of these is charity." He spoke briefly about Lillian's life and then said gently, "Let us pray."

Ada bowed her head. Next to her, Wyatt clasped her hand and wept silently. The sight of his tears broke her heart. Silent sobs wracked her body as the prayer went on. Mariah squeezed Ada's shoulder. "We can't be sad for her," she murmured. "Only for ourselves at having to say good-bye."

And then at last it was over. One by one, the mourners said their farewells and departed.

"Now, Wyatt, dear, if you need anything, anything at all, you let me know." Bea donned her black lace gloves and picked up her cloak. "I'll come right over."

"I'm sure she will," Mariah murmured to Ada. "My lands, I never saw such an obvious ploy for attention. It's unseemly at any time, but especially now."

"I appreciate the offer, Bea," Wyatt said, "but

Ada will be staying on here for a while, looking after things for me." He smiled at Ada. "Between the two of us, we'll manage."

"Oh, that's right! How silly of me." Bea spun away and glared at Ada. "I forgot that Saint Ada is taking care of everything in Hickory Ridge—Wyatt, Lillian, the mulatto orphan girl, the quilting circle, our millinery needs. It seems we need not want for anything so long as she's around."

She yanked the door open, nearly dislodging the mourning wreath, and stomped onto the porch.

Ada clenched her fists. She had had enough. She followed Bea outside.

"What do you want?" Bea spat.

"Ever since I got here, I've put up with your insinuations and your outspoken disapproval, but enough is enough." Ada felt her anger rising, hanging like a dagger between them. "I don't expect that you and I will ever be friends, but I do expect you to keep a civil tongue in your head."

"Or what?" Bea lifted her chin. "You'll tell Wyatt on me?"

"This has nothing to do with Wyatt."

Bea laughed. "You little fool. This has everything to do with Wyatt. Things were just fine between us until you arrived. Now he won't give me the time of day."

"I'm sure that isn't true."

"It is true! And it isn't just Wyatt. Half the town is mooning over the wonderful, perfect Ada

Wentworth. My lands, even Jasper Pruitt is singing your praises!"

"What would you have me do?"

"Go back to Boston. Go anywhere you wish. Only stop interfering with me and my town."

Bea strode to her rig and drove away, slapping the reins much more than was warranted.

Ada turned to go inside just as the undertaker returned, stopping his wagon beneath the bare winter trees. Wyatt and the Whitings came out onto the porch. Sage clasped his boss's shoulder. "How about you wait here and let me give the undertaker a hand with the coffin."

Wyatt closed his eyes and pinched the bridge of his nose. "I'm worn out. I'd appreciate it." He and Ada waited with Mariah and Robbie while Lillian's coffin was loaded onto the wagon and secured and the coffin stand was stowed.

"We'll come with you to the graveyard if you like," Sage offered.

Wyatt nodded. "Thank you, I'd appreciate it."

Sage handed Mariah into their rig, uncertainty showing on his drawn face. "Wyatt . . . I hate to ask at a time like this, but the men were wondering whether to show up for work tomorrow, being that it's Saturday."

"A half day won't make a big difference this time of year. If you and Henry could take a couple of men up the Palmer trail and get that load of logs down to the mill, that'd save us some time come Monday."

“I’ll take care of it.” Sage touched the brim of his hat. “I’m real sorry about Miz Lillian.”

“Me too.” Robbie reached out to give Wyatt’s shoulder an awkward pat. “I liked her a whole lot.”

Wyatt nodded. “Thank you, Robbie. That means a great deal to me, coming from you.”

Mariah leaned forward in the rig. “Ada, I’ll see you at the cemetery, and we’ll talk more next week at the quilting circle, all right?”

“I don’t know.” How could they go on without Lillian to keep them on track and to keep Bea in line? “It seems much too soon to go on as if nothing has happened.”

Mariah tucked a woolen blanket around her knees. “I feel that way too. But Lillian was the practical sort.”

“She’s right,” Wyatt said. “Aunt Lil would be furious if she thought we were using her passing as an excuse for not getting on with things. I’ll come for you on Wednesday and drive you to the church if you like.”

Ada touched his sleeve. “I don’t want to trouble you. You’ll be busy catching up at the mill. I’ll hitch Smoky and drive myself.”

Wyatt stepped off his porch and headed along the path to the mill, where the saws had been whining since sunup. The sound comforted him. He’d been behind schedule since Lillian’s funeral last Friday, but now they were finally catching up.

The weather helped. It had been cold but dry, good for making up lost time.

He scanned the busy mill yard. In the clearing near the lumber sheds, Henry Bell was directing the unloading of the last of the logs harvested along the Palmer trail. At the opposite end, three wagons were hitched and loaded. Charlie Blevins was standing near the steam generator, talking to the very person Wyatt wanted to see.

"Powell!" Wyatt motioned to Jasper Pruitt's former clerk and watched as the boy shuffled across the yard, his expression sullen, his lank hair falling into his eyes.

Wyatt led him into the office and shut the door. "Where were you last week?"

"I was here!"

Wyatt crossed his arms and waited.

"I was going to come in, but I just couldn't make it."

"That's the third time in less than a month. Don't you want this job, son?"

The boy looked up. "You're not my pa."

"And it's a good thing for you that I'm not." Wyatt plopped down in his chair and spun around to face the boy. "When I acted like you are, my pa came after me with an ironweed switch. Straightened me up right quick. Now, you've either got a good excuse for not showing up, or you haven't. Which is it?"

The boy sat sullenly for a minute, then burst out,

"I hate this job! At least at Mr. Pruitt's I got to stay inside when it was cold, and I didn't get splinters in my hands. Lumbering is hard. It's no fun at all."

Wyatt grinned despite himself. "That's why they call it work."

"I wish I could go back to the mercantile, but Mr. Pruitt won't give me another chance."

Wyatt shook his head. "Once you betray a person's trust, it's awful hard to get it back. Maybe if you stick it out here, pay him back, show him you can own up to your mistakes, he'll take you back later on."

Powell shrugged and gnawed on a cuticle. "No, he won't. He hates me for trying to help the coloreds." He looked up. "I'm just not a lumberman, that's all."

"You asked for my help," Wyatt reminded him. "And here's the problem. When you agree to work for me, and then don't show up, it puts a hardship on my other men."

He glanced up and saw the sheriff riding into the yard. A sense of foreboding seized him; he couldn't remember the last time McCracken had ridden out here. He stood and placed a hand on the young man's shoulder. "The next time you decide to take a day off without notice, don't bother coming back at all. You understand?"

"I guess."

"Then go on out and help Blevins finish splitting out those logs." Wyatt picked up an extra pair of heavy gloves and tossed them to the boy. "Use these. They'll cut down on splinters."

Powell made a beeline for the door and almost knocked McCracken off his feet.

The sheriff watched him cross the yard. "Holy hash, Wyatt, what did you to say to that boy?"

"Shape up or ship out." Wyatt studied the sheriff's craggy face for clues as to what had prompted this visit.

McCracken peeled off his overcoat and drew up a chair. "Got any coffee? It's colder than a banker's heart out there this morning."

Wyatt poured two cups from the black enamel pot and handed one to the sheriff. "What brings you out this way?"

McCracken sipped his coffee. "Wanted to extend my condolences. And I need to talk to Charlie Blevins."

"What's he done?" Wyatt dropped into his chair and pushed aside a stack of papers.

"I've been looking into that fire out at the Spencers'."

"You think he's behind it?"

"Could be." McCracken took another sip of coffee. "I heard he got hurt awhile back."

Wyatt nodded. "He cut his arm splitting kindling. His ax slipped. At least that's what he told me when he showed up after three days." He looked out the window, seeking Blevins, but neither the sawyer nor the Powell boy were in sight.

"You happen to recall exactly when that was?"

Wyatt drained his cup and grimaced. The coffee had turned bitter. He set his cup aside. "Not exactly. Sometime back in the fall."

"When Blevins came back to work, did you ever see his wound?"

"No, he kept his arm bandaged for a long time. And he wears long-sleeved shirts. We all do."

"Is he around?"

"Let's go find him." Wyatt led the way out of his office, his heart pumping hard in his chest. If Blevins was behind the recent troubles in the area—especially the attempts to scare Ada—Wyatt meant to see he was brought to justice. He heard a shout as Henry motioned to the teamsters, and three loads of milled timber headed for the railway station. Behind them, the steam generator hissed and thrummed. Sawdust hung like powder in the air.

They found Blevins working in the planing shed, a pile of fresh shavings curling about his feet.

"Charlie?" Wyatt motioned him over and saw a flicker of fear in the sawyer's eyes before he set down his plane and pulled off his glove. "H'lo, Sheriff." Blevins nodded to Eli.

"Charlie." Eli towered over the sawyer. "I want to talk to you."

"Wha-what about?"

"Let's go back to the office." The sheriff motioned to Blevins, and the three of them went back inside. Blevins leaned against the door and crossed his arms.

"I've been investigating that Klan fire out at the Spencers' last fall," McCracken began.

Wyatt watched the color drain from Charlie's face. "I don't know nothing about that," Charlie said.

"Would you mind showin' me that cut on your arm?" Eli moved toward the sawyer. "I understand the wound was pretty deep."

"Yeah, but it's healed up real good. Ain't nothing to see."

"Just the same." With surprising quickness, McCracken grabbed Charlie's arm and pulled his sleeve up to his elbow. Wyatt stared at the underside of Charlie's left arm. The skin was bright pink, stretched tight, and ropy with scars.

"That's no ax wound," the sheriff said. "You've burned yourself. And badly."

"That don't mean I had anything to with what happened at the Spencers'."

Wyatt rounded on him. "Then why lie to me about what happened to your arm, Charlie?"

"I was embarrassed. Me and a coupla the boys had a little too much to drink one night. I stumbled and fell into the fire in the grate. I know you don't like it when we drink too much, Mr. Caldwell. I didn't want to get fired."

"And you were nowhere near the Spencers' place when the Klan torched their yard?" McCracken asked.

"No!"

The sheriff bore down on his quarry. "Have you ever been out to Lillian Willis's place?"

"Once. Mr. Caldwell sent me out there to tell 'em he couldn't come to supper one night. But that's the only time. I swear it."

McCracken nodded. "When you were out there that day, did you walk around, look in the windows, check out the barn?"

"No! I rode in, went up on the porch, knocked on the door. That Yankee woman from Boston came to the door. I told her what Mr. Caldwell said to tell 'er, and I rode right back out."

"You're sure about that."

"Yeah."

McCracken reached into his pocket and produced a small penknife. "Then can you explain to me why I found this in the woods at the back of Mrs. Willis's property? I believe it's yours. It's got your initials engraved on it."

"It's mine. I lost it. A long time ago."

"Uh-huh." McCracken eyed Blevins and turned the knife over and over in his hands.

Wyatt kept his eyes on Charlie. The silence spooled out. He could almost smell the fear on the younger man.

"You can't prove nothing!" Charlie spat. "It's my word against yours. I ain't gonna stand here and listen to any more of this." He pulled his sleeves down and buttoned the cuffs. "I'm going back to work."

"No, you're not." Wyatt fought to control his rage. He'd spent enough time among all kinds of men to know when they were lying. And Charlie Blevins was lying.

He opened his office safe and took out a couple of bills. "Here's your pay. Clear off my property. Don't come back."

Avoiding Wyatt's gaze, Blevins wadded the bills and shoved them into his pocket.

McCracken held the door open for Blevins. "I'm going to be watching your every move. Sooner or later, the truth will out. And when it does, I'm going to be on you like a hen on a June bug."

Wyatt went outside and watched until Blevins had saddled his horse and disappeared down the road toward town. McCracken shrugged into his coat. "I'd bet my last dime that he's guilty as sin. But he's right. Unless I can get somebody to swear he took part at the Spencers' and left that note, all I've got are my suspicions."

"And the knife."

"Which he claims to have lost." McCracken clasped Wyatt's shoulder. "He'd be a fool to try anything now. All the same, if I were Ada Wentworth, I'd lay low until Blevins has a chance to cool off."

Thirty

Ada led Smoky from the barn and into the February cold. She set her sewing box and a stack of Lillian's quilt blocks into the rig, tucked her blanket around her knees, and set off for the church.

It had felt strange worshipping on Sunday without Lillian asleep beside her, and stranger still to see the mound of bare dirt at the far end of the graveyard—a stark reminder of Wyatt's loss, and hers.

The gravestone he had ordered from Knoxville wouldn't arrive for another month. In the meantime, he'd placed a simple wooden cross at the head of Lillian's grave. In the absence of flowers, Ada had added a wreath of holly, the shiny red berries injecting a hopeful note into the gray winter landscape.

Ada planned to fetch Sophie from Mrs. Lowell's after today's quilting circle. She was eager to continue the girl's lessons and to teach Sophie more about making hats. And Wyatt was coming for supper. Ada looked forward to the evening. She hadn't seen Wyatt since Sunday. The mill was going full blast to make up for lost time and to fulfill an order that had arrived by telegraph on Saturday.

She approached the road to Two Creeks. Smoky

shied and came to a halt, his ears twitching, his withers quivering.

"Smoky, get up!" Ada clicked her tongue and rattled the reins. The horse whinnied and stepped sideways in the road.

"Get *up,* you bag of bones! What's the matter with you?"

Then she saw movement in the trees, a sudden glimpse of white and then nothing. A shiver of fear passed through her. *It was nothing. A trick of the light.*

Another moment of uneasy silence, and then horses' hooves pounded the ground behind her. A bloodcurdling scream echoed through the trees. Smoky let out a shrill whinny and reared in his traces, pulling the rig sideways into the trees. Ada hauled in the reins with all her might, but Smoky raced on, the wheels cracking as he lurched blindly through the tangled undergrowth.

Rough hands grabbed Ada from behind and yanked her from the rig. Facedown on the cold, hard ground, she couldn't breathe. She writhed and fought to turn herself over, but her attacker was much stronger and heavier. She heard the fabric of her dress rip before she was lifted and slammed into the ground again. All the air rushed from her lungs.

She fought back with all her strength. "Get off me!" Somehow she broke free and crawled away, raising herself onto her elbows. She felt a trickle of blood on her forehead and struggled to see through an eye that was rapidly swelling shut. "What do you want?"

Three riders on horseback appeared from the trees, silent as ghosts. Surrounded, Ada twisted and stared up at their white masks and robes. A wave of terror moved through her. "Who are you?"

Their silence was more terrifying than any words would have been. She tried to rise to her feet, but a savage kick to her ribs knocked her flat again.

"Shut up! Stop prattling, or I'll kill you!" The voice was muffled, but the meaning was clear as glass. Cold apprehension crawled along her spine. She looked up at the white figure looming over her. Through the ragged holes in the mask she saw dark eyes burning with hatred.

Another kick, and blinding white pain shot through her head. Panic jolted through her. Purple spots showered behind her eyes. But she was determined not to die. With her last bit of strength, Ada pushed to her feet and lurched away, but her attacker grabbed her arm.

Panicked, Ada swung an elbow and connected with her attacker's face. A bright circle of blood bloomed on the white mask. Ada grabbed the mask and yanked it free. A cold shudder seized her. "Bea Goldston!"

Bea wiped her bloody nose on the sleeve of her robe. "Surprised, Saint Ada?"

Ada took a shallow breath. Pain shot through her ribs.

"You were warned to stay out of Two Creeks, but there you were, riding around with that Negro boy like he was the king of Siam."

Then Ada remembered the rig that had passed hers at the crossroads that day. At the time, she'd been too terrified for Lillian to worry about appearances. "What was I to do, let Lillian die?"

"I told you to *shut* your face! The old crone died anyway, didn't she?" Bea shoved Ada against the trunk of a tree and forced her to sit on the ground. One of the silent riders tossed her a rope, dismounted, and grabbed Ada's arms. Ada kicked and clawed at them, trying to roll away, but she was injured and outnumbered. She tasted blood and salt in her mouth. Every breath felt like a knife in her chest.

"And then there's the matter of dear little Sophie." The rope squeaked when Bea and her accomplice knotted it.

Bound tightly to the tree, Ada felt her hands going numb. Sharp pains shot through her shoulder. She tried to wrench free, but the rope held fast. "She's . . . just a child!"

"She's got black blood in her veins."

"You're a teacher!" Ada fought for breath. "Charged with influencing young minds. The school board will not look kindly upon any of this."

Bea smirked. "And I suppose you intend to tell

them. You're always sticking your nose into things that don't concern you."

"This isn't about Sophie or Two Creeks. You've hated me from the first. This is nothing more than an excuse to punish me for coming here."

Bea gave the rope a final tug and got to her feet. She and the other one caught their horses and swung into their saddles. "Have a nice afternoon, Saint Ada. Maybe one of your little friends from Two Creeks will rescue you. But I wouldn't count on it. They know what's good for them."

"Bea, this is insane! It's criminal! You've made your point. You can't leave me here!"

"I *am* leaving you here." Bea wiped her bloody nose again. "But don't worry. Somebody will come along. Eventually."

The four left, melting into the dark trees as silently as they had come.

"Help!" Ada yelled. "Please. Somebody help me!" She screamed and cried until her throat felt raw and she was reduced to frantic moans in her throat. After a while, the cold began to seep in. Sometime later, a warm stream of urine saturated her clothes and assailed her nostrils. She slumped against the tree, its rough bark pressing into the sodden fabric of her dress.

She tried to recall the verses she'd read so often to Lillian, to concentrate on something to bring her comfort and hope, but her battered mind was a blank. As the long afternoon wore on, her thoughts drifted to her parents, to Edward, to the past few months in Hickory Ridge.

And to Lillian. What was it she said that night? *"When there's no other name to call, Ada, call on him."*

Ada turned her face to the brooding sky and closed her eyes. *Dear Lord, I know I don't deserve it, but I'm in a pickle here. I could use your help.*

Wind rushed through the bare trees. *Be still and know that I am God.*

Be still. How many times had she read those words to Lillian in the evenings? *Be still.* Her pulse slowed as her mind righted itself. By now Mariah and Carrie would be wondering where she was. Perhaps Libby Dawson or someone else from Two Creeks would find her here. Wyatt would leave the mill by five, six at the latest.

She hoped that Smoky had gone home. Wyatt would surely know something was wrong once he found the horse and the broken rig. All she had to do was to stay calm and wait for rescue. But suppose nobody came? Suppose Wyatt were delayed and she was left to face the darkness?

"Call on him."

Lord, help me stay strong. Help me . . .

She shifted her weight, trying to relieve the pressure on her shoulders and hands. Her sore ribs ached. The light waned and cast long shadows on the deserted path, and night birds settled in the trees. Something brown and furry—a rat?—

scuttled across her feet and into the underbrush.

Ada couldn't stop shivering in her ruined clothes. Pinpricks of light darted in the spaces behind her eyes. She blinked and tried to stay calm. *Don't faint. Wait for Wyatt.* But everything dissolved into a hot, black swirl. Images bloomed and faded behind her closed eyes.

"Ada! Ada Wentworth!" Someone was shaking her. Ada struggled to open her eyes. It wasn't a dream. He was real. How long had she been out, oblivious to her surroundings?

But as quickly as her hope flared, it died.

"Mr. Pruitt," she rasped. "I suppose you've come to finish the job."

The storekeeper blinked. "I'm not sure I follow you."

Already he was studying the knotted rope that held her fast and reaching into his pocket for his knife.

"The Klan," Ada said. "Bea Goldston and the rest."

He began sawing through the thick rope. "I don't know anything about them."

"They wore masks and white robes," Ada said. "Bea was the only one who said a word."

"Most likely it was a bunch of her loyal subjects out to give you a good scare." He yanked on the rope, and her hands came free. "Can you walk?"

"I think so." She struggled to her feet, mortified by the acrid stench of her soiled skirts. Her head swam. Her knees buckled.

He steadied her. "Never mind. My wagon's just there, on the road." Though she was desperate to get out of the woods, Ada hesitated, paralyzed with fear and mistrust. Was Jasper Pruitt telling the truth, or had he been one of the silent horsemen? What if this rescue was part of an elaborate ruse meant to lead her into worse danger?

"Thank you, Mr. Pruitt. I'm all right now. I can walk home."

"Listen," Jasper said. "I've already apologized for the things I said to you when you first come here. It's true that I don't think whites and blacks should be mixing together. And I still think you oughta stay away from that mutt of a girl over at Mrs. Lowell's. But I ain't no Klansman, and I never would hurt you, no matter how bad I disagree with you. Now come on. Let's get out of here."

Tears rolled down her face. She wanted someone, anyone, to tell her she would be all right. "How . . . how did you find me?"

"Saw your horse running across the road. Your rig is tore up pretty bad. I figured something spooked him and he throwed you out, so I took a look around. I never expected to find you tied up to no tree." He shook his head. "No ma'am, I surely did not."

Jasper Pruitt scooped her into his arms and carried her to his wagon. He removed a small box lying on the seat and set it behind them. "You rest easy, Miss. I'll get you to Mr. Caldwell's as fast as I can."

Ada sagged against the storekeeper's shoulder. Jasper clicked his tongue to the horses, and the wagon jostled over the road. "Funny how life works out sometimes, ain't it? Here I was, on my way out to your place to deliver a cake from my missus, to thank you for the hat."

"Not necessary," she managed. "You paid a fair price for it."

"Cost me a pretty penny, that's for sure, but you can't put a price on what that hat has done for my Jeanne. Not that it made the pain of losing our baby go away. Don't reckon there's no cure for that. But now . . . she seems stronger, is all." He glanced at Ada. "Never woulda thought a hat had such magical powers. But then, I don't pretend to understand womenfolk."

Ada massaged her rope-burned wrists and pressed her fingers to her temples. Never had she felt so afraid and so utterly defeated. It was clear to her now that staying on in Hickory Ridge was impossible. Tomorrow, when she was not so exhausted, she would sit down and figure out her next move. She swayed on the hard wagon seat.

"Hold on," Jasper said, "we're almost to the mill."

Minutes later he halted the wagon in the yard and jumped down. "Stay here. I'll get Mr. Caldwell."

He disappeared inside and emerged moments

later with Wyatt at his heels. Ada burst into fresh tears that grew into uncontrollable sobs. Wyatt's arms went around her and she leaned against his rough jacket, clinging to him, to safety. He smoothed her tangled curls and kissed the corner of her swollen and bloodied lip. "You're all right, my love. You're safe."

He lifted her as if she were made of air and carried her across the mill yard, up the hill, and into his house. He tugged off her shoes and tucked her under the covers, soiled clothes and all. "Don't move. I'll be right back."

Lantern light flickered against the rough-hewn walls. The room smelled of coffee and new wood. Ada sank into the soft featherbed and closed her eyes, listening to Wyatt's voice in the other room and then to the jingle of the harness as the storekeeper drove away.

Wyatt returned, his expression dark as pitch. "This was Bea's doing?"

"She berated me again for spending time with Sophie. She was outraged that I went to Two Creeks to get help for Lillian." Ada brushed away fresh tears.

He sat on the edge of the bed. "Are you all right? The others didn't do anything to you . . . they didn't . . . ?"

"No, it was only Bea. One of the others helped her tie me up. The rest just sat and watched." Ada rubbed her arm and flexed her fingers. "I knew she wanted me out of Hickory Ridge, but I never thought she'd go this far."

"You're safe now. I've sent for Dr. Spencer." He smoothed her hair off her face. "His wife will bring you some new duds. These are beyond rescue."

In the kitchen a kettle whistled. "I've made tea," Wyatt said, "and I'm heating water so you can have a bath. I'll be right back."

After he left, Ada's gaze drifted once more around the spacious room. The firelight illuminated a handsome cherry dresser and a matching table next to the four-poster bed. In the corner sat a rocking chair draped with a wrinkled work shirt. An untidy stack of books and magazines spilled onto the floor. On one wall was a pair of silver spurs and a framed photograph. Wyatt's battered Stetson hung on a hook behind the door. Except for the lace curtains framing the wide windows, it was a masculine room in every detail.

Wyatt returned and handed her a towel, a cake of soap, and a clean nightshirt. "It isn't the latest fashion, but it'll keep you warm until the Spencers get here." He set a steaming cup of tea on the table beside the bed. "The tub's all ready in the kitchen. I'll wait outside to give you some privacy."

Ada made her way down the short hallway. The air in the kitchen was warm and thick with fragrant steam. She undressed and sank into the deep metal tub. The warm, soapy water felt like silk on her skin. Lassitude moved like warm honey through her veins. She immersed herself completely again and again, washing away every physical trace of the afternoon's ordeal.

When the water cooled, she dried off, donned Wyatt's nightshirt, and returned to the bedroom. She drank her tea and lay back on the soft pillow. Sleep billowed like mountain fog behind her closed eyes. Images flitted and faded—wild-eyed Smoky tearing through the trees, the silent horsemen in the woods. Jasper Pruitt bending over her in the gathering gloom. Wyatt's dear face, his strong arms holding her close.

Tears leaked from her eyes and trickled into her ears, waking her. She thanked God for his mercy, for Wyatt's goodness and his strength, before sleep claimed her again. The next thing she knew, Wyatt was bending over her, telling her the Spencers had arrived.

The doctor's wife bustled about in the background while her husband examined Ada's scrapes and bruises. "I don't think anything is broken, though you have some nasty lacerations and contusions." He handed her a small jar of salve. "You'll be sore for a while, but after a couple of days' rest you should be fine."

"Thank you for coming."

He nodded. "I'm sorry that this happened. I hope you won't judge all of Hickory Ridge by the actions of a few mean-spirited ruffians." He snapped his bag shut. "When they set that fire at our place last fall, I was ready to leave, but I'm glad now that we decided to stay. I hope you will too."

"I'm not sure I *can* stay." Ada slumped against the mahogany headboard. "Bea Goldston is intent on getting rid of me."

"All the more reason to stay." He grinned. "You can't—"

"Ennis?" Mrs. Spencer interrupted. "Are you through with the examination?" She placed a soft bundle on the foot of the bed.

"Just finishing up." The doctor picked up his bag and nodded to Ada. "I'll leave you ladies alone."

When the door closed behind him, his wife perched on the edge of the bed. "I heard Ennis say that you'll be fine. You were lucky."

Ada shifted on her pillow. "Yes. But I don't think I can ever feel safe here again."

"Wyatt is beyond furious," Mrs. Spencer said. "He'll get this sorted out—you'll see." She indicated the bundle on the bed. "Norah sent these over—new underthings, new dress, new stockings."

Ada opened the package. The shop owner had sent the dress Ada had recently admired in her window—a deep green silk with a ruffled bodice and a small bustle at the back. She set it aside and ran her fingers over a soft cotton chemise and a pair of fine silk stockings. Norah had even included a new nightdress made of the finest lawn.

Ada sighed. It had been years since she'd worn anything so fine. But the cost of the dress alone would put a serious dent in her small nest egg at a time when she needed to save every last cent. She'd ask Mariah to ride out to Lillian's and bring her old clothes. "These are lovely, and I thank you for bringing them out here. But I can't afford them."

"Norah said to tell you they're a gift."

"But I barely know her!"

"She and Lillian were friends for years. And I think Norah still feels guilty for that awful thing she said about Northerners at the Founders Day celebration."

"Heavenly days! Does the whole town know about that?"

Mrs. Spencer shrugged. "Hickory Ridge is a small town. People talk."

The doctor knocked on the door and stuck his head in. "Eugenie, we should go. It's getting late."

Mrs. Spencer patted Ada's hand. "Get some rest."

"I will. I'm grateful to you and your husband. Please tell Norah I'll be in to thank her as soon as I can."

The doctor's wife rose and slipped into her coat. "You're one of us now, dear. We take care of our own."

Wyatt left his horse tethered outside the bank and walked over to the schoolhouse. He'd had a sleepless night, owing partially to the fact that he'd bunked in his office so Ada could have his bed, but mostly to the rage that roiled his gut.

Certainly he'd known that Bea Goldston had set her cap for him—just look at that embarrassing outburst during Lillian's wake—but he hadn't encouraged her in the least. Beyond the usual social pleasantries, he'd hardly spoken to her more than half a dozen times, yet somehow she'd decided that he was hers. He intended to thoroughly disabuse her of that notion, among others.

Anger coiled inside him like a rattler when he thought of what might have happened to Ada. He loved her with a fierceness that stunned him. He loved everything about her—the way she pinned on her hat, the delicious sound of her unexpected laughter. Her bravery and her vulnerability and even, to his surprise, the slight trace of Boston that sometimes crept into her speech. And now that he loved her, he knew he could never be completely happy, even on his ranch, without her.

He reached the schoolhouse just as classes were dismissed for the day. Standing by the flagpole, he watched the children running pell-mell into the bright February sunshine, coats and scarves flying, their joyous shouts rising into the wind. Robbie Whiting emerged with a couple of other boys. It seemed to Wyatt that the boy had grown at least six inches since last summer. He was quieter now and seemed to have outgrown the serious case of hero worship that Wyatt had found both flattering and embarrassing.

Robbie spotted Wyatt and jogged over to the flagpole. “Hey, Mr. Wyatt.”

“Robbie.” Wyatt moved to clasp the boy’s shoulder, but Robbie stuck out his hand and shook Wyatt’s firmly. “I prefer Rob now, sir. If you don’t mind.”

“Rob it is. How’s school this term?”

“Oh, you know. School is school. Mr. Webster gave me the highest mark in the class for debate. He says I’m a good talker and I could be a lawyer some day. Maybe even a senator or something.”

Wyatt smiled. “He may be onto something there.”

One of the other boys called to him, and Robbie waved. “I gotta go. I’ll see ya.” He ran off to join his friends.

The schoolhouse door opened again, and Bea and Ethan Webster stepped out onto the porch. The sight of her sent a fresh wave of anger through him.

The schoolmaster hurried across the yard to his buggy, his frock coat flapping in the wind, and drove away. Wyatt waited until Webster’s rig was out of sight, then he crossed the schoolyard.

Bea looked up, and he noticed with some satisfaction that her nose was bruised. “Wyatt! What a lovely surprise.”

“Go inside, Bea.” He kicked open the door. “After you.”

"What's this about?"

"Two guesses."

He followed her into the schoolhouse. She dropped her books onto her desk. "If this is about that little practical joke from yesterday—"

"There was nothing practical about it."

"We didn't hurt her." Bea grabbed a rag and wiped the chalkboard clean.

"She's got a cut on her forehead, a swollen lip, her ribs are bruised, her wrists are rope-burned. Not to mention the terror of being bound to a tree and left alone in the dead of winter."

"I knew you'd find her eventually." Bea's voice cracked. She tossed the rag onto her desk. "You've got quite a cozy little love nest, haven't you, now that Lillian is gone."

Wyatt moved closer until Bea dropped her gaze. "I want you out of Hickory Ridge."

"What?" She laughed. "This is my home, Wyatt. And no one, not even you, is powerful enough to make me leave."

"You're right. I don't have any legal authority. But Sheriff McCracken does. And Judge Blackburn."

"McCracken! All he does is go around trying to pin things on innocent people. Charlie Blevins said—" She stopped, clearly worried that she'd said too much.

"What about Charlie?"

"Nothing!"

"Was he part of your little practical joke yesterday?"

Bea glared at him. "You shouldn't have fired him, Wyatt."

"That has nothing to do with getting you out of Hickory Ridge."

Her hands stilled. "What are you suggesting?"

"It's pretty simple, actually. You're to plead some dire family emergency, pack up your things, and buy a ticket on Friday's morning train. Otherwise, we'll bring charges against you."

"But that's impossible! What about the children? I can't abandon them in the middle of the term. The school board will not allow it."

"They'll find a replacement. Mrs. Lowell is accustomed to dealing with children. Or maybe Carrie Daly can take over."

"Carrie Daly? That little mealymouth? Those boys will have her in tears inside half an hour."

"Maybe." He pretended to think. "Ada is well educated, and she's traveled extensively. The board might be pleased to have someone of her background assume your duties."

"Ada Wentworth? In *my* school?" Bea sputtered. "I will not have it, Wyatt. I simply won't."

He leaned against the desk, arms and ankles crossed, and waited.

"Besides," Bea went on, "she doesn't have the courage to bring charges against me. She's too much of a *lady* to stand up in court and admit she elbowed me in the nose like some common street thug. What would her customers *think?*"

"If she doesn't bring charges, I will."

"On what grounds? That I frightened your poor little Yankee paramour?"

"I'm still her employer. By injuring her, you've deprived me of her ability to look after my house. And then there's the damage to my property. Poor old Smoky tore my rig to bits trying to get out of the woods. It's too far gone to repair. I'll have to buy a new one."

Bea sank onto her chair.

"So let's review." Wyatt spoke calmly, though he was seething inside. "Just off the top of my head, there's injury to Ada's person, menacing, destruction of personal property, and violation of the state law prohibiting Klan activity." He paused. "I can probably think of a few more."

"I told you—I only meant to scare her. I'm not associated with the Klan."

"You wore a robe and a mask, terrorized a defenseless woman, and made threats based upon her conduct with the coloreds. Sounds like the Klan to me." He headed for the door. "I'll see you at the station on Friday."

"Wyatt! Please wait. There's something I haven't told you."

"I doubt that anything you have to say will interest me unless you're willing to implicate Charlie Blevins in all this. Sheriff McCracken is just waiting to get his hands on him. But go ahead. Make it quick."

"The land in Two Creeks—it's mine."

He turned, his hand resting on the doorknob. She sent him a triumphant little smile. "Finally, I have your undivided attention."

"Go on."

"It belonged to Sumner Redmond, one of my mother's . . . friends. When I was born, he deeded it to her—a consolation prize for not leaving his family to marry her. The price of her silence. When she died, it passed to me."

He raised his eyebrows. "Your name isn't on any of the documents my lawyers uncovered."

"Redmond insisted on that, to keep safe the secret of his affair with my mother. His lawyers handled everything." Her voice broke. "I hate every blasted acre of it."

"I would have bought it five years ago."

Her face flamed pink. "I know. But I was saving it as a . . . a present for you. For when we married."

"What?"

"I thought that one day, you and I . . . but then Saint Ada arrived, and I knew I didn't stand a chance."

"And you thought that if you terrorized her into leaving—with Charlie's help, I suspect—I'd fall into your arms?" He shook his head. "Even if she hadn't come here, things between you and me never would have worked out that way. You may as well sell that land to my buyers. You'll turn a profit, they'll deed it to the sharecroppers down there, and we'll keep the peace in the town you claim to care so much about."

Her dark eyes flashed. "I do care! Hickory Ridge is all I've got."

"Well then?"

"Why did she have to come here and ruin everything?"

He drew a long breath. "Come Friday morning, I expect to see you on that train."

She crossed her arms. "I'll be back. This is my town. And not even you can keep me away forever."

"You don't have to stay away forever. Only until Ada and I have gone to Texas."

"So the rumors are true. You *do* intend to marry that whey-faced Yankee."

"If she'll have me." He opened the schoolhouse door, letting in a blast of frigid air. "Friday, Bea. And don't forget to wear your new Ada Wentworth hat."

She hurled a book that narrowly missed his head.

Thirty-One

Ada stepped off the porch and into the thin April sunshine. Rain had fallen in the night, and the cool spring air was sweet with the scent of new growth. The trees along the road were budding, and the dogwoods were already in bloom. In the garden, patches of wild violets and pale, creamy daffodils peeked from beneath the stones lining the path. May would see the flowering of irises and wood hyacinths and lily of the valley, followed in June by hollyhocks and Lillian's prized roses.

Helping Wyatt sort through his aunt's things, Ada had discovered Lillian's gardening journal. Written in a faint, spidery hand, it chronicled the blooming of the various plants with notes about cuttings and new plantings and the various species she had cultivated with such care.

"Keep it," Wyatt had said when she found it. "Aunt Lil would want you to have it."

She crossed the cobbled path to the rose garden. There were signs of new growth here too. Wyatt had planned to transplant a rosebush to Lillian's grave, but now it would have to wait. According to Lillian's journal, that was a job best accomplished in late winter, before the bush began to put on new canes. With all that had happened after Lillian's death, there hadn't been time.

Ada bent to brush dirt from a daffodil. Above her, a robin darted among the branches of the magnolia tree, building a nest. Building a future.

Ada's eyes filled. Even here, surrounded by so much beauty and promise, her heart was as heavily burdened as ever. Her injuries had long since healed, but Bea Goldston's brutal attack had left her feeling more discouraged and fearful than ever. On her infrequent visits to town, she found herself searching every face, wondering who had accompanied Bea into the woods that day.

Like everyone else in Hickory Ridge, Ada had been stunned at Bea's sudden departure. A dear cousin in North Carolina had taken seriously ill, or so it was said. Then, near the end of March, Charlie Blevins had been arrested for setting the fire at the Spencers'. True to the Klan's code, he'd stead-fastly refused to implicate anyone else. According to Sheriff McCracken, Blevins continued to deny any involvement in Ada's ordeal, but since his arrest there had been no more intruders at Lillian's place and no more incidents on the road.

That doesn't mean there won't be.

Ada absently brushed a few ants off the fresh new rose leaves and bent to pull a weed, but her mind kept circling around to her dilemma. Soon she would have to give Wyatt an answer to his proposal. Just last week he'd gone to another meeting in Chicago, moving ahead with his plans to sell the mill and buy his ranch. It wouldn't be fair to keep him waiting forever.

Ada didn't doubt his devotion to her. The problem was her own inability to let go of all that had happened to her, to put her life in another's hands. Since the attack, especially, she couldn't help seeing herself as damaged goods—like a torn bonnet long past mending. She wanted to let go of bitterness and blame, but her raw feelings lodged like stones in her heart.

She didn't like the person she had become—older, sadder, but not much wiser. How could she promise herself to Wyatt when she felt this way?

The sound of hoofbeats on the road pulled her away from her dark thoughts. It was Saturday, a half day at the mill, and Wyatt had suggested a picnic by the river. Gathering her skirts, she hurried out to the road to meet him.

He reined in Cherokee and slid from the saddle. "Morning, darlin'."

"Good morning." Tamping down her misgivings, she smiled up at him. Just for today, she'd concentrate on being happy, on enjoying the day with Wyatt. She waved one hand toward the garden. "It's starting to bloom."

"Aunt Lil would be pleased. She always said that flowers were proof God hadn't yet given up on his creation."

They went inside. While Ada poured lemonade into a jar, Wyatt loaded a basket with bread and cheese, dried apples, and a small crock of butter.

"It's a good day to go up to the waterfall," he said. "I've wanted you to see it since that first Sunday at church."

She had an instant mental picture of Wyatt sunbathing on the rock in the middle of the stream. That had been the beginning of everything. "I remember."

"Seems like a long time ago." He smiled into her eyes. "So much has changed since then."

Ada wrapped the jar in a towel and set it carefully inside the basket. "The quilting circle certainly has changed. Without Lillian, we seem to have lost our enthusiasm for it. Bea's gone. Carrie hardly ever comes anymore. But I suppose I can't really blame her." She took a couple of napkins from the shelf and tucked them into the basket. "She lost so many years wrapped in mourning. She must feel as if she's starting life all over again."

"I kind of feel that way myself. Since you, my love, I feel like I've got a second chance too."

"I know," she said, her voice soft. She turned away and added a few more things to the basket. "But there was nothing wrong with your old life. Everyone looks up to you. And the mill is the biggest success in town."

"Success doesn't make up for loneliness. Life is always better shared with somebody you love."

"Libby Dawson said almost the same thing just last week." She handed him the basket.

"She did?"

"What she said was, 'It sure is a lonesome washing, Miss Ada, without a man's shirt in it.'"

Wyatt laughed. "Ready?"

She waited on the porch while he unsaddled Cherokee and led her to the pasture behind the house. He hitched Smoky to the new rig he'd bought, and they set out for the river.

"You haven't told me about your meeting in Chicago." Ada secured her hat and unfurled her parasol as Smoky trotted down the sun-dappled road. Sitting so close to Wyatt, knowing how he felt about her, stirred up so many emotions she'd rather not think about. Better to keep the conversation light.

"We're close to a deal. They agreed to let Sage stay on as foreman. The sticking point was Two Creeks. I want them to buy the land and deed it to the coloreds who have been sharecropping it all this time."

"Will they do that?"

"I think so, eventually. Since all the fires up north last fall, timber isn't as plentiful there. Prices are up. And Chicago is still rebuilding. Those investors want my mill so they can cash in on the increased demand. They won't get it unless they're willing to guarantee that the coloreds won't be thrown off the land."

"But I thought the current owner wouldn't sell."

"I believe that problem has been resolved." Briefly, he told her about his last conversation with Bea Goldston.

Ada stared up at him, stunned. "Bea owns Two Creeks?"

He grinned. "Finding that out was the shock of the ages. My lawyers are talking to hers. I think they'll work it out."

"For your sake I'm glad that she's willing to make a deal, but I don't understand why she'd do anything to benefit those sharecroppers. She's the one who said their presence was holding the town back."

He shrugged. "She loves Hickory Ridge more than she hates them. And if I know Bea, she's counting on coming back one day, a heroine for having made such a sacrifice." He shook his head. "She'll probably run for mayor."

"If anyone would try it, Bea would."

"In any case, Hickory Ridge doesn't need any more unrest. We had plenty of that when Brownlow was governor. It's time to move forward."

Ada watched Wyatt as he drove along, one hand resting loosely on his knee, the sunlight stippling his face. Though she'd tried to move forward, she still felt stuck in her own sad past. But Wyatt had learned to leave yesterday alone. With him, everything was always about the future.

"The papers say good cropland is renting for up

to six dollars an acre these days," she went on. "If Bea does sell that land, she can ask top dollar for it."

Wyatt grinned. "Why, Ada! If you ever get tired of making hats, you can be a land agent."

When they reached the church, Wyatt tethered Smoky in the yard. Ada crossed the churchyard and ran her fingers over Lillian's new marble headstone. The reality of Lillian's death assailed her all over again. She blinked back tears.

Wyatt stepped up beside her and put an arm around her waist. "Think she'd like it? It isn't too ostentatious? I couldn't decide between angels and flowers, so I got both."

Ada smiled. "Lillian wasn't exactly a shrinking violet. I'm sure she'd love it—especially the inscription." The familiar words from Lillian's favorite hymn were chiseled beneath her name: "My Shepherd Will Supply My Need."

Wyatt studied it for a moment and then turned away. "Let's go."

They unloaded the rig and headed along the path to the river, then followed an overgrown trail to the waterfall. Wyatt spread their blanket in a mossy clearing, and they sat down, their backs to the distant mountain. The first of the wildflowers were just blooming; the hillsides were carpeted with splashes of pink and blue and the shimmering white of the dogwoods. Water tumbled over gray boulders and splashed into the cold green river below, sending up a fine mist that glittered in the sunlight.

Opening their basket, Wyatt tore off a chunk of bread, buttered it, and handed it to Ada. She chewed with relish and licked a fleck of butter off her fingers. “I’m glad you brought me here. It’s so beautiful. Like a secret paradise.”

He nodded. “It’s been one of my favorite spots since I was a boy.”

She poured a glass of lemonade for each of them, then sat back, inhaling the clean spring air. “It sure is a fine day for a picnic.”

Wyatt brushed bread crumbs off his hands. “And a fine day to talk about our future.”

No. Not now. Not today. I’m not ready.

Ada set down her glass. She started to speak, but he stopped her with a kiss to her forehead, his breath warm on her skin. “Please, Ada. I’ve been thinking about this ever since I got back from Chicago, and I want to get it out.”

“All right.” She clasped her hands and waited.

“As soon as I can settle things here, I’m headed for Texas.”

Tears blurred her eyes. “I know.”

“A year ago I would have felt just fine about going back home alone, setting up in a little cabin on my own land. Fact is, I would have preferred it. Ranching is hard work—long hours, always something that needs doing. It didn’t seem right to ask someone to share that. But now I can’t imagine living anywhere without you." He tipped her face up and looked into her eyes. "For so much of my life I felt as if everything was matter of chance. Now I know better. We were put here to find each other. You know that as well as I do."

She looked into his beloved face, too overcome with love and dread to forestall the words she knew were coming next.

"I've been waiting for your answer since Christmas. I know you've had a lot on your mind, and maybe you still have doubts about living someplace where there are more cows than people. But I have to know." He brushed her lips with his. "My dearest friend, will you marry me?"

She brushed away the tears forming at the corners of her eyes. "You've been more patient with me than I deserve. And I would love more than anything to say yes."

"Well then?"

She couldn't meet his hopeful gaze. She looked past his shoulder to a patch of wildflowers nodding in the breeze.

"I don't understand." He took her hand. "What's bothering you, my love?"

"I can't—" She strove to discipline her voice, to take control of her emotions.

"If it's the hat business that's got you worried, I'll buy you a shop to rival Waterfield and Walker. Or I'll build you one. Fort Worth is growing so fast, there's sure to be plenty of ladies needing fancy hats." He laced his fingers through hers. "The most important thing is that we're together."

Ada finally found her voice. "That's the difference between you and me. You don't worry about the what-ifs. But I do. What if I disappointed you? What if you wake up one morning and realize that you don't love me after all?"

He shook his head. "That will never happen."

"It might. And then what? I couldn't bear it if you stopped loving me."

Wyatt gripped her shoulders. "Look at me."

She looked into his sea-blue eyes. All she saw reflected there was honesty. And love.

"I'm not Edward," he said, his expression fierce. "I won't leave. I love you."

"I know." It came out as a whisper.

He released her. "You think you're the only one taking a risk? What if you take one look at Texas and decide to get the next train back to Boston? What if you start resenting me for taking you to edge of earth? Don't you think it would kill me if you up and left?"

"Wyatt, please. It isn't only about—"

"Listen. Life is full of risks. But if you try to build a fence around all your fears, you'll shut out joy too."

She couldn't bear the raw emotions playing over his face. She scrambled to her feet and ran along the slippery trail, painful sobs catching in her throat.

Wyatt quickly overtook her and turned her around. "I thought your plan was always to leave Hickory Ridge. Now that I'm offering you that chance, you keep throwing out obstacles."

"That's what I'm trying to tell you. It isn't only about me and what I want. I have Sophie to consider."

That stopped him—for a second. "Sophie?"

"She's come so far. She reads as well as I do. Her handwriting is a hundred percent better. And she's talented with needle and thread. I can't abandon her now."

Wyatt cocked one hip and pushed his Stetson to the back of his head. "Mercy, darlin', but you drive a hard bargain. Just what do you have in mind? A boarding school back east, maybe?"

Ada plucked a sprig of wild blooms and held it to her nose. "I don't want to push her into some other cold institution. I've been thinking that when I decide my own future, I'll take her with me."

"You mean adopt her?"

"I don't know what the laws are down here. But it isn't as if Mrs. Lowell will go to any trouble to place her elsewhere."

Wyatt let out an exasperated sigh. "All right, then. We'll take her with us."

Ada studied him. "But you don't want to. Not really."

"Raising a child is a big responsibility."

She tossed the flower away. "But you've often

said you wanted sons and daughters. Just the other night you said—"

"That's different."

"Because Sophie is a mulatto." She felt a jolt of disappointment. She'd never thought Wyatt would hold Sophie's background against her. Maybe she'd been wrong about him after all.

"That isn't fair, Ada. You know me better than that. But I've always thought our children would be of our blood. Our love. Maybe that's selfish of me, but I won't lie to you about how I feel."

Ada looked up at him, tears shimmering in her eyes. Oh, what she wouldn't give to have everything be different!

"But look," he added. "I'm not saying I'm totally against the idea. I never thought of it before, that's all. I have to get used to it. We could—"

"Wyatt, I can't marry you." She blurted it out, so heartbroken she could barely form the words. "As much as I love you, and as hard as it is to say it, I . . . can't. And I won't keep you guessing, wondering whether I'll change my mind. It wouldn't be fair."

He went completely still. His blue eyes were so dark they appeared black. "I see."

Above the distant rush of the waterfall, a robin sang. They stood face-to-face, inches away, and a thousand miles apart.

"I'm so sorry," Ada whispered.

For several minutes he stared out at the greening mountains. Nothing moved. Insects ticked in the grasses beside the river. "What if I stay?"

She gaped at him. "What are you saying?"

"You heard me. What if I keep the mill? Forget about Texas. Adopt Sophie. What then?"

She was stunned. She'd never imagined such devotion even existed. "You love me that much? To give up everything you've ever wanted?"

"Yes, darlin'. May the saints help me, I do."

Fresh tears rolled down her face. "Oh, I *hate* this! And I hate that still I must say no. Not because I don't love you, but because I do!"

He frowned. "Come again?"

"From the first day we met, you've talked about that ranch. If I made you give it up, sooner or later you'd hate me for it."

"No, I wouldn't—"

"You would! Maybe you wouldn't want to, but you couldn't help it. You wouldn't be the same man if I forced you to stay." She felt as if her heart had actually shattered into a million little pieces. She put her face in her hands and sobbed.

His arms came around her. She clung to him and cried, weak with grief and regret. She hated that she was so full of mistrust and doubt. But she couldn't force herself to feel differently and she couldn't ask Wyatt to wait until she did.

Wyatt held her and let her cry until all her tears were spent. She leaned against him feeling numb and hollowed out. Finally she pulled away from him and dried her eyes. "I'll make arrangements to move out of Lillian's house. I've already stayed longer than I intended."

"There's no hurry. You know that."

"I do, and I'm grateful. But under the circumstances, I think it's best if I go."

They started back along the path.

"Where will you go?" he finally asked.

"The Verandah, I suppose. Until I can make more permanent arrangements. Norah Dudley offered me the chance to buy her shop. I'll speak to the banker next week."

"If you need a loan—"

She shook her head. "My father was terrible at taking his own advice, but he always said that before borrowing money from a friend, one should consider which is needed more. I'd much rather have you as a friend than a creditor."

They gathered their belongings and returned to the rig. Wyatt was silent on the drive home through the warm spring afternoon. Ada took in the set of his jaw, the planes of his tanned face, the way his strong hands handled the reins. She loved him. Loved the virtues of his heart—patience, compassion, kindness. She could live to be a hundred and never find another who would love her like Wyatt did. But she had made her choice. Perhaps one day he would see it was best for both of them.

He drove into the yard and stopped. Ada stepped out of the rig and reached behind him for the basket. She went inside while he tended to Smoky and led him into the barn. Through the kitchen window, she saw him leading Cherokee into the yard. The realization that she might never see him again sat like an anvil on her heart.

He came into the hallway, turning his Stetson in his hands. All the light seemed to have gone out of him. "I think I'll head back to Chicago in the morning, wait around for the papers to be signed. I'm not sure how long I'll be gone."

"All right." Her eyes went hot with fresh tears.

"Let me know when you're ready to go, and I'll send someone to help you move your things."

"I don't have much, but I'd appreciate that."

He nodded. "Good-bye, Ada."

Watching him mount Cherokee, she felt her heart slip its moorings, disconnecting her from the one person in the world who mattered most. She leaned against the door and sobbed.

Thirty-Two

The railway-station clock read ten o'clock precisely as Ada halted her rig outside the bank. Already, Hickory Ridge buzzed with activity. Travelers milled about outside Nate Chastain's bookshop, waiting for it to open, admiring India, who had curled into the sunny window for a nap. Patsy Greer arrived and waved to Ada as she unlocked the door to the *Gazette* office. Farm wives came and went from the bakery and the mercantile.

Ada tethered Smoky and entered the bank. The young man at the front desk looked up from his ledger. "Good morning. May I help you?"

"I'm Ada Wentworth. Mr. Gilman is expecting me."

"He's up the street at the barber's, getting a shave, but he'll be back shortly. Please follow me."

He rose and led Ada past the teller's cage to a small office in the back. He raised the window shade, letting in the morning sunlight, and motioned her into a chair. "Make yourself comfortable."

Ada smoothed the folds of her skirt and tried to calm her nerves. She'd spent all night going over her figures, hoping the banker would grant her the loan that was her last hope of remaining solvent. In the months since she'd been attacked on the road, she'd received only one more hat order. She wasn't certain whether it was a sign of the worsening economic times Norah Dudley had mentioned or whether potential customers were afraid to do business with her. She had banked the three months' pay Wyatt gave her after Lillian's death, but it wouldn't last forever. She would need more to tide her over until she could figure out what came next.

She looked around the banker's well-appointed office. A floral-patterned rug covered the wide plank floor. Framed hunting scenes hung on the wall behind a massive cherrywood desk. A table beneath the window held a small gold clock and a stack of leather-bound books. The room smelled faintly of tobacco and the same brand of hair tonic Edward had used.

She shook her head. It wouldn't do to think of Edward now.

The bell above the door emitted a faint chime. The banker strode into the room and greeted her with the same brisk efficiency as the bankers and lawyers who had overseen the dismantling of her family's estate.

"Miss Wentworth." The banker's voice was hearty. "Sorry to keep you waiting. My barber was a bit long-winded this morning." He sat down in his chair and smiled at her across the desk. "The whole town is talking about the sale of the mill and what it means for Two Creeks."

So. The deal was done. Ada swallowed the knot in her throat. She hadn't spoken to Wyatt in two weeks. It felt like a year.

Mr. Gilman reached into a drawer and brought out a leather folder. He cleared his throat. "Now, what can I do for you?"

"I—I want to take out a loan. To purchase the dress shop."

"I see."

"I intend to sell off Mrs. Dudley's inventory and convert the space to a hat shop."

He picked up a pen and opened the folder. "And how much of the purchase price will you need to borrow?"

"Actually, all of it. Or almost all of it, anyway. I've only been here a short time, you see, but I've filled quite a few orders already." She opened her bag and handed him the sheet she'd prepared detailing her expenses and income over the past months.

The banker glanced at it and set it aside. "I'm afraid you don't understand the enormity of what you'd be taking on, Miss Wentworth. The annual interest alone would amount to more than you've earned. In addition, there's the cost of supplies, advertising, taxes. Have you considered all that?"

She shook her head and clasped her hands so hard her knuckles turned white. He was turning her down.

"Do you have any collateral?" He pushed her paper back across the desk. "That is, anything of substantial value to secure the loan?"

"I know what collateral is. And no, I haven't any."

He shook his head. "That's too bad. My advice is to wait until you can show a larger profit. Perhaps in another year or two—"

"But how can I expand my business without a proper space and without enough money to buy supplies?"

He waved one hand dismissively. Clearly, he didn't care one whit whether or not she survived. "If we lent money to people in positions as precarious as yours, this bank would go under inside of a year. Perhaps there's a male relative, someone who'd be willing to be responsible for you?"

"No. There's no one." She rose, willing herself not to cry.

"I'm sorry I couldn't be more helpful." He got up to walk her out, and Ada saw a spot of shaving lather that had dried behind his ear. Somehow it made him seem a bit more human.

He opened the door. "I want to thank you for encouraging the Hargrove boy to make something of himself. My daughter is bound and determined to marry him someday. I'd hate to see her tied to someone who couldn't provide for her properly."

Ada pulled on her gloves. "There's more to a good match than money, Mr. Gilman."

He nodded. "I know. But Sabrina is my only daughter. I couldn't live with myself if I stood by and let her make a mistake." He smiled. "You know how fathers are about their little girls. We want them to have the best of everything."

As long as they get to decide what's best! She shook his hand and hurried from the bank before he could see the tears that threatened to destroy the last shred of her dignity. On the sidewalk, she paused to compose herself before heading to the mercantile. Lately she hadn't had much of an appetite or the energy to make meals only for herself. But yesterday she'd used the last of the tea and flour, and she was nearly out of oil for the lamps.

She retrieved her shopping basket from the rig and pushed open the door to the mercantile. Jasper Pruitt sat on a stool at the counter, adding up a column of figures. He looked up and nodded. "Anything I can help you find?"

She gave him her order. He slid off his stool and headed to the back. While he weighed out tea and flour, she picked up a tin of lard and a small round of cheese and took them to the counter.

Jasper returned and shook his head. "You don't want that cheese. It's about to go moldy. I've got some better in the back." He left and returned with a fresh round.

"Thank you. That's very kind."

"No trouble." He added up the total. "You want to put this on your tab?"

She shook her head and handed him a bill and a handful of coins. "Mr. Pruitt—"

"Jasper."

She smiled. "I never had the chance to thank you properly for coming to my aid on the road. I'm very grateful for your help."

He flushed. "That's all right. Anybody else woulda done the same."

"Perhaps. But I'm grateful nevertheless." She

headed for the door. Jasper lifted one hand in a little wave and went back to his work.

She drove home, unhitched Smoky, and turned him into the pasture. Then she put the kettle on for tea and set to work on a wedding hat for the mayor's niece. It was an elaborate confection of white netting and lace, just the sort of job she normally relished, but now the joy had gone out of everything.

She wondered about Wyatt. Was he still in Chicago after all this time or back at the mill? Maybe he'd already left for Texas and his new life. Did he think of her at all, or had he put her out of his mind?

She blinked away sudden tears. It didn't really matter. She had made her choice. She'd have to live with it.

She worked until it grew too dark to see and rose to light the lamp. Her stomach rumbled, reminding her that she hadn't eaten all day. As she headed toward the kitchen, a sound out on the road startled her. She looked out the window. Someone was in the yard.

Her mind raced. She wasn't expecting Sage or Robbie. Or Wyatt. Charlie Blevins was in jail. Was someone else stalking her, intending harm?

Footsteps sounded on the porch, and panic seized her. She grabbed the fireplace poker, ran to the door, and yanked it open. "Who's there?"

"Ada? Wait!"

Her heart jerked against her ribs. The poker slid from her hand and rolled across the porch. She peered into the gloom.

"Edward?"

Wyatt unlocked his door and carried his bags into the parlor. The air in the house was close and still after his two-week absence. He made a fire in the cookstove and put the coffeepot on to boil. While he waited, he threw open the windows to the evening breeze and sat in his rocking chair, watching twilight come on.

What was Ada doing right now? He could imagine her curled up on the settee in Lillian's silent house, reading a book by lamplight, or at the kitchen table working on a hat. Maybe she was rereading her travel journals and dreaming of happier times. He wondered if her heart felt as stone-cold and empty as his own.

He'd stayed in Chicago for as long as possible, hoping to put her out of his mind. But even as he huddled with a phalanx of lawyers, signing the papers for the sale of the mill, thoughts of her still haunted him. He tried to distract himself with the activities available in the city—dining with the new mill owners and their wives, touring the sections of the city that had been rebuilt after last October's disastrous fire, window-shopping, attending the theater. None of it brought him one iota of pleasure. Even the news that Bea Goldston had signed the papers finalizing the sale of Two Creeks had failed to cheer him.

Regret burned hot as a branding iron in his chest. Why had he fallen for Ada Wentworth in the first place? Because she made him feel alive and hopeful in a way he hadn't felt in a very long time. She was pretty as could be and whip smart and full of New England practicality. He couldn't imagine anyone who could suit him as well. He wasn't looking forward to a future without her.

He heard the coffeepot boiling over and hurried to take it off the stove. He poured a cup and walked around the house, deciding which things to take with him and which to leave behind. He wouldn't need much. He'd be bunking at his father's place while he negotiated the purchase of the old Caldwell acres—a surprise he was planning for Dad—and scouted for additional land. Now that Ada wasn't coming with him, he'd leave the pretty lace curtains and most of the furnishings behind.

He sorted through a stack of books. At the bottom of the pile was the copy of *Vanity Fair* that he'd bought for her last summer. What had he been thinking? Again, he wished he'd given her a different kind of gift, some small keepsake she could carry in her pocket as a constant reminder of his regard for her instead of a stuffy book that was not one of her favorites in the first place.

He sat down heavily and scraped a hand across his stubbled chin. He'd been certain that God's hand was in all of this, that God had arranged for him and Ada to find each other here in Hickory Ridge. Now he wasn't so sure. He had offered all that he had to give, and it hadn't been enough to overcome the deep inner wounds that held her back. So he'd had to let her go—from his life, if not from his heart.

He hadn't prayed for himself since the dark days of the war, but now he asked God to intervene. To heal Ada's heart, wash away her distrust, and show her what he knew to be true—that they belonged together.

Thirty-Three

"May I come in?"

Edward stood on her porch, his arms at his sides, looking nothing at all like the adventurous and confident ship's captain she had once adored. Now he seemed years older and thinner than she remembered.

"How did you find me?" Ada's voice shook. "What do you want?"

"I'll explain everything, but I'd really like to sit down. I walked all the way from the train station. I won't take much of your time."

She stood aside and showed him into the parlor. He sank into Lillian's favorite chair by the window and bent forward, his hands clasped loosely in his lap. Ada sat on the settee across from him and swallowed the bile rising in her throat. He had ignored her letters, leaving her to wonder why he'd sacrificed her happiness. Why had he come at all, when it was too late to salvage anything?

"I wrote to you last year," she began. "Twice. You never answered."

"I know. I'm sorry. I've been at sea almost continuously since . . . since the night I last saw you at your father's house. I arrived back in Boston only last month. That's when I found your letters waiting and learned Cornelius was dead. And your Aunt Kate." He shook his head. "I couldn't believe it. I'm sure it must have been a terrible shock."

"It was. But so was finding out that Father paid you to break our engagement."

"Is that what you think?" He shook his head. "That isn't exactly how it happened."

"Then what did happen, Edward?" She blinked away her tears. "You promised to tell me why. I waited and waited, thinking that if only I understood the reason, I could live with it. But—"

"That's why I've come."

"After all this time. How did you find me?"

"After I got your letters, I went to your house and discovered it had been sold. I contacted your father's lawyer, who told me about the auction, but he had no idea where you'd gone. Then he happened to mention Mr. Biddle, your mother's millinery supplier. It was a long shot, but it was all I had. Biddle told me he'd recently shipped an order to you, here in Hickory Ridge." He looked up and smiled. "It's quite a shock, finding you living in the backwoods of Tennessee. Whatever possessed you to come to a place like this?"

"I had no money. I needed a job. I found one here."

He looked around. "Is this your house? You live here alone? Or maybe you're married now?"

Suddenly she was very tired. "Why don't you say what you came to say?"

"You're right. I shouldn't be asking so many questions. It's only that I remember all our happy times together. All the plans we made for a life at sea." The color had come back into his cheeks. His eyes glittered with the old excitement she remembered. "We were going to travel the world, remember? Life was going to be our big adventure!"

"I remember." Now she recalled what it was about Edward that both vexed and excited her. He was bold, he was reckless. He believed he could have whatever he wanted, just because he wanted it. Where she was careful and measured, he was heedless and impulsive. And when he went too far, carried away by his enthusiasm, she'd always forgiven him.

But not this time. His actions had cost her too dearly.

"I know what you're thinking," Edward said.

"That I am a cad and a reprobate, not worthy of you."

"I wasn't—"

"It's all true." He rose and began to pace. "I don't deserve someone as fine as you. The truth is that even after I proposed and you accepted, I wasn't . . . faithful."

She was stunned. "You were seeing someone else?"

He nodded. "I'd known her a long time. She's a lot like me—fond of a good time, perhaps a little careless. I knew it was wrong to keep seeing her when I'd pledged myself to you, but somehow I couldn't close that door. Then one day she told me she was expecting a baby . . . and it was mine."

"Oh, Edward."

"It was a mess, all right. I offered to marry her, but marriage wasn't what she wanted."

"What then?" She braided her fingers together and waited.

"She wanted money—more money than I could have raised even if I'd sold my ship." Edward shook his head as if he still couldn't believe it. "I tried to reason with her, but she threatened to tell you, to go to the newspapers and expose the whole ugly story. I didn't want that to happen, and I couldn't think of what else to do. So I went to your father and confessed everything. He was furious, of course. For a moment, I thought he meant to kill me." His voice broke. "I wish he had. Death would have been preferable to walking around with this horrible guilt—knowing how much I've hurt you, that I'm the cause of your misfortune."

Ada didn't try to staunch the tears pouring down her face. His selfishness had destroyed both their lives.

"To spare your feelings, Cornelius agreed to lend me the money," Edward continued, "though truth be told, he had to scrape to get it. He said business was bad, but he'd find the money somewhere if I called off our engagement." He paused before the mantel, just as he had on that cold winter's night almost two years ago. "He made me promise to stay away from you. So I put out to sea."

Ada struggled to make sense of it all. She remembered her father's last futile business ventures, the ones that had seemed so foolish. He'd risked everything to protect her. And she had repaid him with anger, silence, and blame. A wave of shame and regret moved through her. She stared at Edward through a blur of tears.

"I can see in your eyes," Edward said quietly, "that I made the wrong choice. It's true that I've been at sea, but I should have spoken up sooner."

She nodded wordlessly. Edward had no idea what his silence, and her father's, had cost her.

"Then my ship hit a bad storm off the cape,

and I had to bring her in for repairs. That's when I got your letters and I knew it was time—past time, I guess—to honor my promise to tell you the whole truth."

He collapsed onto the chair again as if the confession had sapped all his strength. He looked up at her, the earlier sparkle in his eyes replaced with guilt and shame. "Now you know."

Outside, night birds fluttered in the trees. Finally Edward said, "You're probably wondering about the money. I wanted to pay Cornelius back, but one thing and another came up. Expenses and so forth." He blushed. "Babies aren't cheap. I had some bad luck, and . . . well, there isn't any."

"I'm not surprised." She studied him in the lamplight. How had she ever fancied herself in love with this man? Now she knew that all she'd felt was infatuation. Loving Wyatt had taught her the difference. But this knowledge had come too late.

She got to her feet. "I think you should go."

"All right." He stood. "I hurt you, and I'm sorry. I hope you can forgive me."

Could she? After his terrible betrayal and his lies? Did she want to?

Edward headed for the door. "That's all I came to say. I should get going. It's a long walk back to town."

"It's too late to walk all that way," she heard herself say. "You can sleep in the barn if you like."

He turned. “That’s kind of you, Ada. Much kinder than I deserve. But I’m too tired to argue.”

Leaving him in the parlor, she went down the hall and took a quilt from the shelf in Lillian’s room. She brought the quilt to her nose and breathed in the comforting scent of the lavender water Lillian had been so fond of. *Oh, Lillian. How I miss your wisdom.*

She handed Edward the quilt. “Just leave it on the porch in the morning. I don’t think I want to see your face ever again.”

He sighed. “I can’t blame you.”

She followed him outside and watched him cross the yard to the barn, her emotions a jumble of anger, sadness, and regret. She sat on the porch swing and looked up at the blanket of bright stars.

She felt nothing for Edward. But it was a relief to finally know the truth. And good intentions counted for something. She leaned back in the swing and set it in motion, listening to the rhythmic creak of the chains, letting her mind go blank. She thought of her father and was surprised by a rush of love and regret.

For all the pain his choices had inflicted, in the end, Cornelius Wentworth had sacrificed everything to protect her future and her heart. He had saved her from marriage to the wrong man.

But the trouble was that she’d sent the *right* man away. She’d hurt Wyatt terribly, and she couldn’t blame him for not wanting anything else to do with her. Her own fears and her lack of faith in Wyatt and God and in herself had cost her the love of her life. And those insecurities were because of the man who was at this moment sleeping in the barn.

Anger boiled up inside her once more. She closed her eyes. Edward had asked her forgiveness. But how could she absolve him of such a grievous wrong?

She stilled, not really expecting an answer, but needing one all the same.

When somebody needs your forgiveness, remember the One who has forgiven you. Forgive those who have wronged you. Let go of blame and bitterness and your heart will heal.

Oh, Lillian. I don't know whether I can completely forgive. At least all at once. But I can begin.

A dove rustled in the trees. A shooting star trailed across the sky.

Ada bowed her head and prayed.

Thirty-Four

"How come you're movin' to that ladies' hotel?" Sophie set down her scissors and looked up at Ada, her moss-green eyes serious.

"We've been over all that. This is Mr. Caldwell's house. Now that Miss Lillian has died, I'm not needed here."

"We still goin' to have readin' lessons and our stories?"

"Of course we are." Ada finished pinning the pleats on the crown of the hat she was making. "Now that I'll be living in town, perhaps I'll see you more often."

"I guess it's all right then. When are you movin' out?"

"Not for another week. The hotel is full until then." Ada set down her pincushion and smoothed Sophie's hair. "It's nothing for you to worry about."

Sophie's smile, swift and incandescent as lightning in a jar, went straight to Ada's heart. "I'm finished with this pattern. Can . . . *may* I go play?"

"For a little while. We'll have to get you back to Mrs. Lowell's soon."

Ada watched Sophie scamper through the garden. Despite the delight she took in the little girl, she felt a loss like death. Wyatt was very much alive, but no longer a part of her life.

At last week's quilting circle, Mariah had confirmed what the banker had told her. The sale of the mill and the land in Two Creeks was complete. Wyatt was moving on, heading to Texas to pursue his dreams without her. And though she'd urged him to do it, the news had filled her with such despair that she'd barely slept since.

She poured a cup of tea and watched Sophie climb the magnolia tree. How long would her money last before she'd need another position? Could she ever be content, living in other people's houses, looking after strangers? Despite Mr. Gilman's refusal to lend her any money, the idea of having her own business hadn't lost its appeal. But establishing her independence was proving much harder than she'd imagined.

The struggle had left her with a new appreciation of the challenges her father must have endured. Faced with a mountain of bills and shrinking profits, he'd been driven to ever more risky schemes. And he'd done it at least in part to spare her. The knowledge didn't take away the pain of her loss, but she was grateful to Edward for finally telling the truth.

"Miss Ada!" Sophie dropped from the tree and rushed inside. "Comp'ny's coming!"

Ada stepped onto the porch just as Sage Whiting drove into the yard.

"It's Robbie's daddy!" Sophie yelled.

"Yes, I can see that. Hello, Sage."

"Ada." He crossed the yard and stood on the porch as if uncertain of his next move.

"Come in," she said. "I've just made tea."

"I can't stay. I have to get back to the mill." He handed her a package wrapped in brown paper and tied with string. "Wyatt asked me to deliver this."

Tears sprang to her eyes. Her fingers fumbled with the string, but the knot held it fast.

"I can open it!" Sophie grabbed for the package. "Let me!"

"No, Sophie. I—"

But the little girl slipped the knot off the package and folded back the brown paper. "It's a book! Named *Va-ni-ty Fair*." She traced the title with her fingers. " 'A novel without a hero'—what does that mean?"

Ada burst into tears.

"What happened?" Bewildered, Sophie looked up at Sage.

He bent to the child. "Maybe you could play outside for a little while, let me talk to Miss Ada."

"But she's bawling her eyes out!"

"She'll be fine. I promise." He took an apple from his pocket and gestured toward his horse. "I was saving this for later, but maybe you could feed it to ol' Lightning. He's hungry after coming all the way out here."

"All right." Sophie grinned and ran out to the rig. Sage and Ada went inside.

Ada motioned him to a chair in the parlor and perched on the settee. "I didn't intend to make such a scene. This book reminded me of happier times." She opened it, caressing the pages, and a fat white envelope fell out. She handed it to Sage. "Wyatt must have forgotten this. Will you return it?"

"It's for you, Ada." He shook his head. "You've put that man through the wringer, and still he moons around like a lovesick puppy."

Ada broke the seal on the envelope and pulled out the contents. A single sheet of writing paper lay atop a thick stack of papers.

Ada,

Please accept this as a token of love and kind remembrance from your affectionate friend.

Always, Wyatt

"It's some kind of legal document." She scanned it, not quite believing her eyes. "It's the deed to this house." She looked up. "I don't understand."

"He let his house go with the sale of the mill, but he wanted you to have a place to call home."

Her tears started again. "I don't deserve it! I thought I was doing the right thing, but lately I've wondered whether I made the wrong choice."

Sage ran his hand through his sand-colored hair. "May I tell you something? From the day you got here, Mariah and I prayed that you and Wyatt would find each other, that you'd be open to God's dreams for you."

Ada wiped her eyes. She'd never before considered that God might have his own ideas about where she should end up—and with whom.

"God makes plans for each of us," Sage went on. "Better plans than we can ever make on our own. But you have to trust him. And other people. And yourself. Otherwise, you end up without the joy you're meant to have." He smiled gently. "Have a little faith, Ada. Take a chance on happiness."

The world shifted. Ada sat frozen, hardly daring to breathe as the possibilities washed over her.

All her life, she'd viewed each thing that happened as a separate event, unconnected to anything else. Now she saw that everything that had gone before, even those events that brought more questions than answers, had been leading her to this moment. When she most doubted, God had been there all along—preparing her, guiding her. But she'd let fear and mistrust rob her of the very thing she most wanted.

Could she take that step of faith? Claim her chance at happiness?

"You're saying I should go to Texas with Wyatt."

He nodded. "If you love him."

"Of *course* I love him—beyond all measure! But now it's too late. He hasn't spoken to me since the day I refused his proposal." She jumped up and began to pace. "Perhaps I should write him a note. No! I should go in person. Even if he no longer wants me, I should at least thank him for his generous gift. But what if—"

"Ada." Sage put out a hand to stop her pacing. "Enough. It's time to stop thinking and start doing. His train leaves in an hour."

"He's leaving today? Without saying good-bye?"

Sage nodded. "Here's a man who stared death in the face and never flinched. But I don't think he could have stood to look at you, knowing it was for the last time."

Fresh tears spilled down her face. He fished a handkerchief from his pocket and handed it over. "There's still time, if we hurry."

She ran her fingers over the heavy envelope, her thoughts racing. Suppose Wyatt wanted nothing more to do with her. Suppose his hurt went too deep. What if she'd lost him to hesitation, and true happiness had slipped away while she weighed out her choices?

"Ada?"

Sage was right. The time for deliberation was long past. Ada grabbed her spring hat, a new straw toque trimmed with bright-pink streamers. Sage called to Sophie, and they crowded into his rig.

"Where are we going?" Sophie, smelling of apples and sunshine, squeezed in next to Ada. "How come you're still crying?"

"I'll explain later." Ada kissed the top of Sophie's head.

"Get up, Lightning!" Sage rattled the reins, and the rig flew along the dusty road, past the road to Two Creeks and the lumberyard, and the church. They clattered into Hickory Ridge just as the train whistle screamed.

Sage drew up at the station. Passengers crowded the platform, seeing to their baggage and buying last-minute food and magazines from the peddlers. The engine huffed and hissed. Another whistle blew, and people hurried to board.

Ada tumbled from the rig, her heart near to bursting. Would Wyatt forgive her for her lack of faith in him, in God? *Give me another chance,* she prayed. *Give me a chance to get it right*. Her gaze darted along the platform, to the train cars and back. Perhaps she was too late, and he was already seated in the passenger car, a book open on his lap.

Then she saw him striding down the platform, a single bag in his hand, his duster draped over one arm. His new Stetson was pulled low over his eyes.

Her heart lurched. Watching him heading for the train, she felt as if her entire life had been compressed, as if everything had come down to this one moment.

"Wyatt!" She ran to meet him. "Wyatt! Please wait!"

A sudden gust of wind dislodged her hat and sent it tumbling down the platform. The long pink ribbons lifted, dancing wildly in the warm wind.

The movement caught his eye. He saw her then, and he stopped dead still, an incredulous smile spreading over his face. She waited, not daring to breathe, until Wyatt dropped everything and ran toward her, arms outstretched. The wind caught his hat too and sent it rolling along the platform until it came to rest beside hers.

He lifted her into his arms and spun her around. She laughed out loud, her face tipped to the bright summer sky. Wyatt set her on her feet and kissed her thoroughly, oblivious to the handful of passengers still milling about the platform. She wrapped her arms around him and kissed him back for all she was worth, pouring into it all of her love and gratitude and hope.

He smiled down at her. “You’re really here!”

“Yes.”

“No more doubts?”

“None.” She hooked her arm through his and smiled up at him through a blur of happy tears. “Buy me a ticket?”

“Just like that?”

“Mariah will send my things.” She grinned, imagining her friend’s shock at such impulsiveness. But she didn’t want to wait another second to start her future with Wyatt.

“It’s fine with me, darlin’, but our friends would never forgive us if we deprived them of a wedding . . . and the chance to say ‘I told you so.’ ”

She heaved a mock sigh. “I suppose you’re right. There’s no hope for it, then. I reckon we’ll have to hold a wedding.”

He wrapped one arm tightly around her waist. “You’re ready to be a rancher’s wife?”

"Just try to stop me."

He grinned. "No thank you. I've seen what happens when you make up your mind to do something."

He kissed her again, and the whistle blew. The train huffed and clattered slowly down the track, picking up speed as it steamed out of Hickory Ridge.

Epilogue

Special to the *Hickory Ridge Gazette*,
September 1873

Life on a Texas Ranch
by Sophie Robillard

At first it was too hot here in Texas. I didn't like it, but Mr. Wyatt said I'd get used to it, and mostly I have. We have a ranch named the Rocking C, after Mr. Caldwell. Our house has a wide porch, a kitchen with real running water, and a bathroom with a tub for taking baths. The trees are skinny and full of thorns. There is a windmill that creaks in the night and rattlesnakes that hide under the rocks. Behind the house is a creek. Mr. Wyatt and his daddy, Mr. Jake, take me fishing there from time to time, but so far the only thing we've caught is a cold.

It's a long way to my school, but I ride my own horse, which I have named Hickory. I guess you know why. I like the teacher, and here is the best part: she likes me back! Miss Ada says when I am older I will have to go away to finish my education, but I try not to think about that. Once you get a real home, you don't want to leave it for anything.

Mr. Wyatt spends a lot of time out riding with his cows and comes in at night smelling like dirt and cow pies, but Miss Ada just laughs and fixes him a bath, and after that we sit down to supper. We mostly have steak, but I try not to think about where that meat comes from. The first time I ate one of our cows I cried, which is why Miss Ada won't let me give them names. Not that I could think up two thousand names, which is how many longhorns there are, but she says if you give something a name you start to care about it. I know that's true, because she's the one who gave me my name, which is Robillard, and she cares about me greatly.

The first thing Mr. Wyatt did after we moved in was to build Miss Ada a studio for her hatmaking. It's a separate building next to the main house. It has a bunch of windows and shelves for all her ribbons and hat blocks and such and a special cabinet for drying felt hats. Ever since we moved from Hickory Ridge, we've been getting hat orders from just about everywhere—Alabama and Missouri and Colorado, places like that. We take them in to Fort Worth and ship them out and then pick up new orders from the post office.

Next spring it'll be mostly just me going into town, because by then the new baby will be here and Miss Ada, who is really Mrs. Caldwell, will be too busy. Mrs. Sage Whiting is coming down here then to see us, and maybe Robbie will come too. Miss Ada misses her friends. You could tell from the way they all cried at Miss Ada's wedding that day in Hickory Ridge what good friends they are. I think she and Mr. Wyatt miss Hickory Ridge. They talk about going back for a visit when the baby gets older. Maybe I will come too.

I have a good friend here. Her daddy works for Mr. Wyatt. Her name is Beth, and she lives in town. Sometimes I spend the afternoon at her house playing with her dolls and making music on the piano. Her mother gives us tea and cakes. It's a fine time, but I am always glad to see Mr. Wyatt's rig turning into the lane to take me home.

Until next time,
Sophie

Acknowledgments

I'm grateful to so many who helped bring this book into being.

A heartfelt thank-you to Leanna Ellis, my dearest friend of twenty years, who kept insisting that I write this book. I'm glad you didn't give up.

Thanks as well to Natasha Kern, my brilliant agent, for invaluable insights into the story and into the business end of publishing.

I'm grateful to the fabulous fiction team at Thomas Nelson. Allen Arnold, what an amazing gentleman you are. Ami McConnell, thank you for seeing the potential in this series. Natalie Hanneman, your editorial insights made this a much stronger book. Thank you. Eric Mullett, thank you for encouraging me to dream big and for your unbridled enthusiasm for all things Hickory Ridge. And Katie Bond, publicist extraordinaire, plus the entire Thomas Nelson sales team—all of you make publishing at Nelson a joy. Thank you. Anne Christian Buchanan, for your meticulous research and wise insights. Kudzu didn't get to Tennessee till 1900? Who knew?

To my readers, thank you for taking Ada and Wyatt and all of Hickory Ridge into your hearts. I love hearing from you through my website, www.dorothylovebooks.com, or by snail mail in care of Thomas Nelson (P.O. Box 141000, Nashville, TN 37214-1000, Attention Author Mail).

Finally and most especially, thank you to Ron, who jumped onto this roller coaster called a writer's life with me fifteen years ago and has never let go. I love you.

Reading Group Guide

1. At Nate's bookshop, Ada tells Wyatt that she'd rather have contentment than happiness. Which would you choose? Why?

2. Wyatt (referring to Thackeray) asks whether achieving one's desires increases happiness. What do you think?

3. Ada quotes her father as saying that an "invisible thread" connects us forever to our place of birth. Do you agree? Why or why not?

4. Upon her arrival in Hickory Ridge, Ada feels drawn against her will into the bonds of the community. What does community mean to you? Is there a downside to being part of a community?

5. Both Ada and Wyatt experience a distancing from God as a result of painful experiences. How did this affect their ability to grow as individuals and as a couple? How have you handled such experiences in your own life?

6. How does Lillian's advice to Ada help in her struggle to forgive Edward? Can you share

a time in your life when you were required to forgive someone? What spiritual teachings or scripture helped you to forgive?

7. Ada and Wyatt have very different ways of dealing with their pasts. How did their coping strategies affect them as individuals? As a couple?

8. Ada believed in God, yet she was unable to believe in a divine plan for her life. Have you ever had a similar experience? How did you handle it?

9. Ada is drawn to the idea of making her own way in the world, yet she fears that she may fail at it. Have you ever experienced a crisis of confidence? What was the outcome?

10. Ada's move to Hickory Ridge turns out to be a greater blessing than she ever could have imagined. Have you ever experienced a disaster that later turned into a blessing? What happened?

A Note from the Author

Dear Readers,

As women, we connect to each other first through our hearts. I hope that reading Ada's story of finding her faith, finding herself, and finding Wyatt has touched your heart as deeply as the writing of it touched mine.

In writing this book, I relied upon the contemporaneous diaries and journals of several nineteenth-century Southern women who lived through the War Between the States and its aftermath, numerous biographies of such women, and several general histories, especially *Tennesseans and Their History* by Paul H. Bergeron, Stephen V. Ash, and Jeanette Keith. These authors' careful research and thoughtful commentary were invaluable in helping me understand the people and their times.

Lumber mills were one of the few industries that prospered in the postbellum years. However, for purposes of the story, I made Wyatt's mill and the town of Hickory Ridge a bit more prosperous than most towns of the time actually were. I also bent the timeline just a fraction for the scene in which Sophie first sees a typewriter. Although quite a few prototypes of a "typewriting machine" appeared in the first half of the nineteenth century, a practical version was not commercially available until 1873. Otherwise I've tried to remain faithful to the historical record.

I hope you've enjoyed getting to know the people of Hickory Ridge and that you'll hop the train for another visit next year when Ada and Wyatt return to attend a wedding, and the widow Carrie Daly finds her life changing in more ways than she ever could have dreamed.

Blessings,
Dorothy

Center Point Publishing
600 Brooks Road • PO Box 1
Thorndike ME 04986-0001 USA

(207) 568-3717

US & Canada:
1 800 929-9108
www.centerpointlargeprint.com